DOUBLE EXPOSURE

DOUBLE EXPOSURE

E. Jay Hamblin

To Terry,
Beste wünsche
(Best wishes)
E. Jay Hamblin

iUniverse, Inc.
New York Lincoln Shanghai

DOUBLE EXPOSURE

iUniverse books may be ordered through booksellers or by contacting:

iUniverse
2021 Pine Lake Road, Suite 100
Lincoln, NE 68512
www.iuniverse.com
1-800-Authors (1-800-288-4677)

This is a work of fiction. All of the characters, names, incidents, organizations and dialogue in this novel are either the products of the author's imagination or are used fictitiously.

All characters in this book, except recognizable historical figures are fictitious, and any resemblance to persons living or dead is purely coincidental.

ISBN-13: 978-0-595-34905-0 (pbk)
ISBN-13: 978-0-595-79638-0 (cloth)
ISBN-13: 978-0-595-79621-2 (ebk)
ISBN-10: 0-595-34905-6 (pbk)
ISBN-10: 0-595-79638-9 (cloth)
ISBN-10: 0-595-79621-4 (ebk)

Printed in the United States of America

"Those who cannot remember history
are condemned to repeat it."

-Santayana-

Acknowledgements

The author's profound thanks to…

…my friend and editor, Margo Garber, whose professional expertise and infinite patience were invaluable. She made wonderful and timely suggestions. She blessed me with encouraging words through three years of toil until the last page was written. Thank you Margo. Words are inadequate in expressing my appreciation.

…Doctor Mulloy Hansen for the contribution of his valuable medical knowledge.

…Wolfgang Kelm whose knowledge of German history and customs were extremely helpful. He was a youth during Hitler's reign and provided insight into the language and mentality of those in power at that time.

…Helen Lund for her help with the German Language.

…Julienne and Allen Hardman for their patient and extremely helpful line editing.

…Allyson Ford for her brilliant and hopefully final editing.

…and last, but far from least, my wonderful wife Shirley Ann, for her patience and encouragement as she read the manuscript as each page was written.

PROLOGUE

An English farmer brought his cows in from the field for their morning milking while his wife busied herself with her household chores. The fog had started to lift early with the promise of a bright and sunny day. Days such as this help lift one's spirits a little. He breathed deeply, filling his lungs with the crisp morning air. The smell of manure and hay is a heady odor to a farmer. The war had been long and had brought great hardship and sorrow to this household and thousands like it all over England. Their youngest son had been killed at Gold Beach during the Normandy invasion. *He should be here to help with the farm,* he thought. Each new day was a reminder of how much he missed his son. His wife had never been the same, nor had he, since that dreadful day the message came from the war department notifying them of their son's death.

The farmer sighed and tried to focus on this daily ritual. Few tasks require more dependability than milking cows. It's a chore that cannot be put off and must be performed every day without fail. The cows eat, drink, and manufacture milk. The farmer drained the milk from the cow in the time-honored manner practiced for centuries. He squeezed the teats, one in each hand, grasping them at the top, just under the udder, with the thumb and forefinger pressed against the palm to make the initial squeeze. The teat swelled as the milk was forced downward. The other three fingers squeezed one after another from top to bottom in rapid succession shooting the milk out in a white stream with each stroke. This chore always brought him a measure of peace and calm. The warm milk splashed in the bucket with each downward pull, and steam rose into the cool air. The soft pungent smell of the milk filled his nostrils and he breathed it in with satisfaction. He dreamt of happier times and was as content at that moment as the cow, which patiently stood eating her breakfast of hay, relieved of the pressure on her bulging udder.

The wide door to the old barn where he kept his cows faced the English Channel, and he could look out over the water while he milked them. He had performed this task so many times his fingers and hands moved in a rhythmic pattern without thought. The muscles in his hands and arms were quite powerful from this exercise. He smiled as he remembered the surprised grimace on the face of a young government official that visited him in November of 1939 as they shook hands. It seemed like a century ago, but only a little over five years had passed since that day.

The man had come from London recruiting men who lived on the channel as members of the Coast Watcher Observers Corps. Their farm, just outside Eastbourne, was a likely landing place for a German invasion. Coast watchers were to report any suspicious boat or ship activity that might signal an invasion and also report enemy planes heading for targets in the interior.

He was very proud to be a part of Britain's great struggle. There was a time when many doubted their very survival. What had Churchill said about blood, sweat, tears and toil? Well, he and his wife had not shed any blood, but they certainly had shed their share of sweat, tears and toil. Their son had shed *his* blood and it was as if their own blood had left their bodies as well.

As his thoughts drifted, he became aware of a faint whining sound and recognized it as the sound of airplanes in the distance. He had become expert at identifying planes by their silhouette and could also tell, with surprising accuracy, the kind of planes that flew overhead even in the dark by the sound of their engines. He had seen and heard thousands of enemy planes come and go over the last four years, as well as Allied planes leaving and returning from missions over France and Germany. He had never felt threatened by enemy planes as they passed overhead. They had more serious targets than a little farm on the coast and Allied planes were a welcome sight.

The sound of the planes grew louder and he could tell they were fighters approaching. The war was now winding down and he had not seen a German plane for a long time. He could tell these were English or American. He strained to get a first glimpse of them and soon noticed their dim outline as they came within range. He watched them as they grew larger and larger and he could tell by their flight path they would pass directly over him. Almost without realizing it he stood up and walked outside of the barn to get a better view. The cow turned to look at the farmer as if to say, *Where are you going? You're not finished yet.*

As the planes passed overhead he counted 12 fighters; a mixture of P51s and Spitfires. But what astounded him was that in the middle of these fighters was a German four engine *Focke-Wulf Condor* 200 aircraft. *Where did this plane come from, where is it going, and why are those fighters escorting it?* These questions would remain a mystery. He would never know who was in that German plane. In fact, only a handful of men in the entire world would ever know. Nor would anyone except these few men know the dramatic events that preceded this mysterious plane appearing over England.

CHAPTER 1

▼

Friedrich and Freya Müller were products of the German upper class. Friedrich was an officer in the German Intelligence Service and was stationed in Berlin. Friedrich wouldn't be considered handsome by Hollywood's standards, but he had rugged good looks and women were attracted to him. His build was athletic, but he had little interest in sports. He was an intellectual, and more at home in a library than on a soccer field.

The war was not going well, and Friedrich feared for the nation's survival. He felt the Kaiser was a fool to have gotten Germany into such a mess. Friedrich's wife Freya worked as a volunteer at the hospital.

It was a time of great strain on both of them. They were worried about their situation with their first child on the way. They hadn't planned on having a baby until after the war was over, but babies are born during all kinds of conditions and circumstances. They are the renewal of life and their coming is as constant and regular as waves beating upon a shore.

Freya came from a very wealthy family. Her mother was Inge Canaris Von Kleist, whose brother, Wilhelm Canaris, became head of the *Abwehr,* the German Military Intelligent Organization, during the *Nazi* regime. Her father, Max Von Kleist, was an industrialist who built a large tool and die empire, with factories all over Germany.

The house in which she was reared was a very imposing one. It was situated in a high walled compound with a wrought-iron gated entrance. Gottfried Semper, a leading architect of his day, designed and built the house. It was a massive, two-story Gothic structure. Automobiles could drive up to the entry by way of a circular drive, and a flight of stairs led to a landing large enough to accommodate two dozen or more people. The overhang was supported by six Corinthian columns. The large double-entry doors were paneled with thick beveled, clear, amber and emerald green cut glass, which allowed the light from inside to glow through and hinted at the warmth awaiting their guests inside.

The cavernous entry hall was elegant. A huge crystal chandelier designed and manufactured in Belgium sparkled from the high ceiling. The floor was a checkerboard of black and white marble imported from Italy. A wide curving staircase ascended to a balcony, which overlooked the entry on one side and the living room on the other.

The rooms were filled with French furniture and Empire upholstery. The heavy drapes were made in France and were hand embroidered. Magnificent oil paintings, collected from all over the world, adorned the walls along with tapestries from India, Portugal and China. No expense had been spared in the design and furnishings of this home. Its opulence was a reflection of the status of this family in German Society. A large staff of servants met the family needs and extra staff was hired whenever social obligations required it.

Freya was very beautiful and well educated. She studied in France, Austria and at the Berlin University. She was articulate and poised. Because of her wealth, people might have thought she was self-centered and spoiled, but she was just the opposite. She was high spirited and very outgoing, made friends easily and was fun to be with.

Freya was considered to be the finest catch in all of Germany. Everyone thought she would marry a duke at least, but she fell in love with Friedrich, who was at that time an assistant professor of history at the university.

To fill a requirement for graduation, she enrolled in a class taught by Friedrich. He could hardly take his eyes off her, and it was hard for him to concentrate on his lectures. She was the most beautiful woman he had ever seen.

History was one of Freya's least interesting subjects and she was not doing very well in class. Friedrich offered to give her some personal tutoring. She accepted and that was the beginning of their romance.

He could hardly breathe when he was in her presence. He thought her long blond hair resembled the color of straw and smelled as fresh. Her eyes were large and pale blue and her furtive glances his way reminded him of a nervous deer. Her peach colored complexion was clear and flawless with a hint of blush on her cheeks.

Friedrich was as impressed with her mind as with her beauty. She was fluent in French, English, and Spanish and could carry on an intelligent conversation on almost any subject except history, in which she had very little interest.

They were married June 21, 1913. Freya was 24 and Friedrich was 27.

Freya was rolling bandages at the hospital when she began to feel a tightening in the lower region of her body. At first she did not know what was happening but finally realized she was experiencing the initial contractions that signaled her baby was on the way.

The contractions continued coming in a regular pattern and were more intense. *Well,* she thought, *I'm certainly in the right place to have a baby. Hospitals are the most popular place for this sort of thing.*

She stopped a nurse that came rushing into the room to get a supply of bandages.

"Excuse me. Can you help me? I'm having a baby."

The nurse looked down at her stomach and said, "I'm not blind. I can see that."

"No, you don't understand, I'm having the baby right now." This got a little more attention from the nurse and she questioned Freya about her contractions.

"What is your name please?"

"Freya Müller," she replied.

"*Frau* Müller, you are probably a long way away from having your baby. Just relax, I'm busy now." At that she rushed out of the room with the bandages.

Doktor Wilhelm Keppler came into the delivery room just moments before the head of the baby appeared. The *Doktor* had been attending one of the many wounded soldiers when the nurse rushed in and whispered to him, "The baby is coming."

He sighed and said, "All right, all right. I'm coming." He was bone weary. He had been on duty for eighteen hours and was virtually asleep on his feet. He was annoyed with the prospect of having to deliver a baby when so many wounded needed his attention.

"You are doing just fine, *Frau* Müller. The baby is on its way," *Doktor* Keppler explained.

Nurse Ilse Kelm knew exactly what Freya was going through. It was as if she were reliving her own nightmare less than a year ago when her baby was being delivered in this same room by this same *Doktor*.

"Just keep bearing down *Frau* Müller. Push really hard," nurse Kelm encouraged.

"I'm trying, but the pain is almost unbearable."

"The pain will soon be forgotten when you see your baby," a sympathetic *Doktor* replied.

"Have you ever had a baby, *Doktor*?" Freya asked. A smile creased the *Doktor's* wrinkled face, as he replied, "No, I'm afraid that's outside even my abilities."

"Then how do you know I'll forget the pain?"

"Because I've delivered hundreds of babies, many to mothers with multiple children. They wouldn't keep having additional children if the pain was an obstacle."

"That may be so, but I wish it would hurry. I don't know if I'll soon forget this pain and I'm anxious to know if it's a boy or a girl," an exhausted Freya said through clenched teeth.

"These things cannot be hurried. We'll just have to let nature take its course," the weary *Doktor* replied.

Freya let out a scream as she pushed with all her might. She wanted the pain to end. She didn't think she could stand it much longer. The baby's head was out now and the shoulders soon followed. The *Doktor* gently guided the little body until he was completely out of the birth canal.

In one smooth motion he held the baby by its feet and gave it a whack. Freya heard a lusty cry and smiled through the pain. Tears came to her eyes, not from pain now, but from the emotion she felt as she saw her baby for the first time. The *Doktor* glanced up at the clock, and then tied off the cord and cut it. The baby was now a separate, new human being.

Karl Müller had officially come into the world at 3:12 AM, September 11, 1917. *Doktor* Keppler asked Nurse Ilse Kelm to make a note of that fact. Germans were very meticulous and precise where records were concerned.

"No need to wonder any longer, *Frau* Müller. You have a fine baby boy." Freya smiled weakly, but her face was radiant as she looked down at her *Sohn*. It was a sublime moment. Never again would it be quite as exquisite as this first experience. Freya's body began to relax for the first time since the contractions began. Suddenly Freya cried out as she was gripped by another sharp pain.

"What is happening? I feel like I'm having the baby all over again." The contractions were continuing and she was alarmed.

"That's quite normal," *Doktor* Keppler explained. "You are having what is known as *after pains*."

"But it feels just like it did before." Nurse Ilse Kelm glanced at the *Doktor* and she saw him press his hands to Freya's stomach.

"Hmm…maybe we are not yet finished." The contractions continued and became more intense.

"*Frau* Müller, you may be having twins." Freya's head began to swim.

"Twins! No one told me I would be having twins!" A million thoughts ran through her mind. Oh, how she wished the pain would end. She was exhausted, but also exhilarated by the thought of two babies. *Won't Friedrich be surprised when he gets home? He should have been here with me. Why did he have to be in Munich at a time like this?*

Another powerful contraction began and the pain jarred her back to the reality of the task at hand. In just a few minutes the head appeared and the event of moments ago was repeated.

Again, the *Doktor* held the baby by its feet and gave this one a good whack. Nothing happened. He tried again. There was still no cry from the baby.

He laid the baby down and put his stethoscope to its tiny chest. A frown crossed his face. Nurse Kelm felt dizzy and thought she might faint. She had seen that look before on *Doktor* Keppler, and knew the horror that was about to erupt in that delivery room. The *Doktor* tied and cut the cord just as he had done with the first baby and handed him to Ilse. Ilse was in shock and she just stood there as if frozen to the floor.

"Nurse Kelm, are you all right?" Ilse was like a statue. Tears were blinding her. It was as if she were in a trance. The *Doktor* shook her by the shoulders, and she looked startled.

"The baby," he whispered and motioned toward the door with his head. She quickly wrapped the baby in a receiving blanket, picked it up and rushed out of the room. Freya watched this scene as if seeing it in slow motion.

"Where is she taking my baby?" she screamed. The *Doktor* took her hand and said softly, "I'm sorry, *Frau* Müller, but he is dead." A heart-rending scream shattered the quiet of the room. Freya began to sob uncontrollably. The *Doktor* whispered to nurse Kurtz and she handed him a syringe with a mild sedative. Freya didn't feel the needle enter her arm. She couldn't feel anything at that moment except a pain in her heart that made her oblivious to any physical pain.

As Ilse entered the hall she began to sob uncontrollably. It was as if she was reliving her own nightmare and she wanted to get the child to the morgue as quickly as possible. Her legs felt like rubber and the tears blurred her eyes as she stumbled along. Her first and only child had died just five days after it was born and she knew what *Frau* Müller was feeling.

She ran down the hall hugging the dead baby to her chest, pushed open the door to the stairs with her shoulder, and hurried down. In her haste she caught her foot on a step as she reached the first landing and slammed into the wall. The baby was pressed between her and the wall, and as they collided she heard air escape, followed by a cough and a cry. "*Mein Gott,*" she exclaimed. "He's alive." *Could it be possible? Frau Müller will be stunned.*

She pulled the blanket back from the baby's face. Wet mucous stained the blanket and a little was on his chin. She wiped it off with a corner of the blanket. Color had come into his face.

He really is alive. She put the baby over her shoulder and patted him on the back, speaking softly to calm him, as he was still crying. She started back up the stairs when a thought struck her. She hesitated…*I wonder…Do I dare?* "No!" She almost shouted. I shouldn't even think it. But she didn't move. The baby finally stopped crying and she felt his body relax in her arms.

Oh, the feeling. Is this what it's like to have and hold your own baby? I didn't even get to hold and cuddle my own child before he died.

The sensation was like none other she had ever experienced. She had held hundreds of infants in the nursery, but none felt like this because the others were not hers.

But this one is not mine either, she argued. *But he could be if I hurry. Frau Müller has one child. I have none. She thinks the child is dead. Don't I deserve as much happiness as she?*

Thoughts raced through her mind as she wrestled with this agonizing decision. It all seemed like a dream. It felt like she was outside her body watching this scene unfold.

She finally decided she couldn't let this chance go by. She rushed down the stairs, unlocked the door to the supply room and went in. There were towels, bedpans, bandages, sheets, and dozens of other items a hospital uses. She didn't realize it, but this was the same room in which Freya Müller had spent many hours wrapping bandages as a volunteer.

She grabbed a blanket and spread it on a table. She gently laid the baby on the blanket and wrapped it tightly around him. *His name will be Jacob,* she thought, *the name William and I chose for our baby who never lived. Oh how I wish William was alive. I miss him so much.* It was getting more difficult to remember what William looked like, and this frightened her.

The baby was wide awake. His arms and legs were moving in a jerky motion beneath the blanket and his eyes were blinking, trying to focus. He was so tiny and beautiful.

She could scarcely breathe from excitement and fear. She knew she had to hurry. They would be wondering what was taking her so long.

She tucked the baby between stacks of blankets and covered him with several more, being careful to leave an air space. If someone did come into the room they would not be able see him and if he cried the sound would be muffled.

As she turned to leave she heard a key turn in the lock. She gasped and grabbed a stack of sheets as the door opened. A nurse entered the room and saw the surprised look on Ilse's face.

"I'm sorry I startled you, Ilse. I didn't know anyone was in here."

"That's all right," she whispered.

"Why are you whispering Ilse?"

"My throat has been sore for several days," she lied. Ilse held her breath while the other nurse loaded a basket full of bandages and left. Sweat was running down her back. *What have I done?* She asked herself.

At that moment the baby began to cry. Ilse almost fainted thinking how close she had come to being found out.

Although the cry was muffled, if someone came into the room they would hear it. Her mind was racing again. *What should I do?* She knew the baby needed to be fed or he would continue to cry. She dropped the sheets back where she found them and grabbed a feeding bottle from the shelf. She raced back up the stairs to the kitchen and turned on the hot water tap so it would be steaming hot while she filled the bottle with milk. She held the bottle under the water until it was warm. It seemed like it took forever, but was only a few minutes.

What if someone else goes to the supply room before I get back? Trying not to think about it she raced back down the stairs, unlocked the door, and went inside. The baby was crying louder now. She uncovered him, picked him up, and jammed the nipple into his mouth. Now the only sound that could be heard was a sucking sound.

Ilse heaved a sigh of relief. Her nerves were raw, and she was near the breaking point. She relaxed a little as the baby enjoyed his first meal outside the womb. She was lost in the moment as she cuddled him against her breast while he drank the warm milk.

"That will make you sleep little boy."

She softly hummed a tune her mother sang to her when she was a child. *Is he really going to be mine? He will be if I'm able to get him home without being seen.*

"Hurry little *Sohn. Mutter* has to get back to her work," she whispered. The sucking finally stopped and a little milk ran down the corner of his mouth as he relaxed. He was sound asleep.

Quickly she laid him back in the hiding place and placed the bottle next to him. She covered him again with the blankets and raced back up the stairs. She was near exhaustion from the running and tension.

As she entered the hall, she slowed to a walk. She was breathing hard and needed to catch her breath. She wiped the sweat off her forehead with the back of her hand. As she entered the delivery room the *Doktor* and nurse Kurtz glanced up. They noticed her face was flushed and she looked frantic.

"I…I'm sorry I was so…"

"That's just fine," interrupted the *Doktor*. "We managed quite well. We're just about through here."

Doktor Keppler recalled that Ilse's husband had been killed in the war and was convinced the shock of his death contributed to the premature birth of her child. He had been the attending physician and there were complications. The baby lived only a few days and he remembered how shattered Ilse had been. He could understand how hard this experience must have been for her. *I don't know if I could have even come back into the delivery room,* he thought.

Frau Müller was asleep, her baby cradled in her arm.

"I'll have the death certificate prepared for your signature, *Doktor,* if you like. I know how tired you must be."

"Thank you nurse Kelm," he replied. "I would appreciate that. Why don't you do that now and nurse Kurtz can wheel *Frau* Müller to her room. You should have been relieved hours ago, so go home after that. I'm going to catch a little nap before the next batch of wounded swamps us."

Ilse went to the records office to give the information to the clerk about the birth of Karl Müller, and the death of his twin brother. The clerk was sound asleep. She awakened him and mildly scolded him for sleeping on duty. He apologized and took down the information as Ilse relayed it to him. She instructed him to have *Doktor* Keppler sign the certificate before he left. He yawned and promised he would.

Ilse now turned her full thoughts to the baby. She rushed to the supply room, holding her breath, hoping no one had been there since she left. She pulled the blankets away, fearful of what she might find. He was still there and asleep. Relief swept over her like a gentle ocean wave smoothing a sandy beach, and she relaxed a bit. He looked so peaceful.

She had been thinking about how she was going to get out of the hospital without anyone seeing her with the baby.

The biggest problem she faced, however, was how to explain the absence of the *dead* baby's body. She had formulated a plan in her mind, and now it was time to carry it out.

She picked up the nursing bottle and tucked it in her apron pocket, placed the blankets back over the baby and headed for the morgue. *Thank goodness old Fritz, who was in charge of the morgue, did not work during the night. He wasn't due to arrive for work until six o'clock. I would hate his job,* she thought, *but everyone has his place.*

When a death occurs during the night the corpse is left for Fritz to prepare the next day. A clipboard hung from the wall on which entries were to be made to identify bodies left during the night. The room reeked with the odor of antiseptics. Ilse shuddered at the thought of the dead that passed through this room, including her own child.

After making the initial entry, Ilse found a stringed tag and filled in the information. Name: *Müller.* Closest Relative: *Freya Müller.* Death Date: *September 11, 1917.* Cause of Death: *Still Born.* She signed the tag, made a loop about the size of an infant's ankle with the strings and tied a knot. She then took a pair of scissors from her apron pocket, cut the string and let it drop to the floor.

On the way back to the supply room she refilled the bottle and warmed it. It was now 3:45 AM, and still dark outside. *That is a blessing,* she thought.

Her bicycle, along with dozens of others, was kept in a locked shed behind the hospital. She moved the blankets back, and picked up the baby. Then took the bottle from her pocket and gently placed the nipple in the baby's mouth. He was asleep, but as soon as he felt the nipple he began to suck. She was anxious to leave the hospital, but knew if the baby had a full stomach, even if he awoke, he would be less likely to cry. Ilse was a little calmer now, but anxious to get home where they would be safe. The baby finally stopped sucking and was still asleep.

She made her way toward the back door, nervously looking up and down each corridor as she went. Suddenly she heard voices just around the corner of the intersecting corridor. She was by the door of a patient's room so she slipped in and closed the door just as a group of nurses came into view. They were headed in her direction and she held her breath.

Just then a patient called out, "Who's there?" Ilse didn't answer. "Who's there?" he shouted louder. Ilse decided she had to answer him or the nurses might hear him and investigate.

"I'm your night nurse," she whispered. "Keep your voice down or you'll wake the other patients."

"What do you want?" he whispered. Not knowing just what to say she blurted out the first thing that came to her mind.

"I've come to give you your enema…or…would you rather have your back rubbed, Herr Bloch?"

"*Mein Gott.* What a choice." I'll take the back rub, but I'm not *Herr* Bloch."

"Oh, I'm sorry I must be in the wrong room. Forgive me for disturbing you." Ilse could hear the voices fading in the distance. She opened the door and peeked out. The corridor was empty. She started to leave when the patient said, "Hey where are you going? What about my back rub?"

"Maybe later, I'm very busy now. Go back to sleep. *Gute Nacht.*"

Ilse finally made it to the back door. She opened it and stepped out into the cool night air. She took a deep breath and began to shiver. She wondered if it was from the cold or the nervous strain. She didn't care; she just wanted to get on her bicycle and leave.

She unlocked the shed door, and tenderly placed Jacob in the basket attached to the handlebar, pushed the bicycle out the door, took a quick look around, and not seeing anyone, she pedaled away.

Ilse rented a room from Emil and Lisa Jellinek who lived about two miles from the hospital. Emil and Lisa had three children: Eric, eight years old, Hanna, five years old and Otto, just two months old. Lisa was her best friend. She was a large *brüstige* woman in her early thirties, boisterous and humorous. Emil was quiet and more serious and one of the kindest and gentlest men Ilse had ever known. Emil and Lisa made an ideal pair. Their personalities complemented each other the same way opposites attract.

Emil worked in the Ministry of Public Records. Lisa ran the household and cared for the children.

They treated Ilse like one of the family and had been a great comfort to her since William was killed and her baby died. She didn't think she could have survived without them. Her parents died in the 1915 influenza epidemic. Her only brother was in the army, and was at the front. They were her only family now.

She quietly let herself into the house, and tiptoed up to her room. She closed the door, dropped into an old overstuffed chair, and put her feet up on the ottoman. It was chilly, and she pulled the lap robe over her and the baby, thinking, *I'll just sit here a few minutes until I can get my strength back.*

She peeled back the blanket and uncovered the baby's face. The moonlight filtering through the curtains provided just enough light to see him dimly. Nothing is more wondrous and miraculous than a newborn child, and this one certainly was a miracle. She smiled as she looked at him. For hours her body had been as tight as a coiled spring and now it began to unwind. She was completely drained.

As she sat there cradling this newborn child in her arms she thought about the enormity of what she had done and a new wave of guilt washed over her. The battle between guilt and rationalization raged in her mind. *But I gave this child life, didn't I?* She argued. *Well that's not exactly true. I was God's instrument and God gave him life. It's as if God has given this child to me to make up for the loss of my own, so he rightly belongs to me.*

Rationalization is a human weakness that has plagued mankind ever since God placed man on earth. Didn't Cain try to rationalize his guilt when God asked him, "Where is Abel thy brother? And Cain replied saying "I know not: Am I my brother's keeper."

If a guilty conscience is supposed to make sleep difficult, it didn't affect Ilse this night. Without even realizing it, she slipped into deep unconsciousness. Her body cried out for the kind of refreshment only sleep could provide.

Fritz Gort, punctual as ever, entered the morgue ready to begin his day's work. He wondered how many had died during the night. He picked the clipboard off the hook and saw only one entry: an infant.

"What a shame," he muttered. He reached for his rubberized apron and tied it behind his back. The log showed the body to be in compartment 22.

He slid the drawer out, but it was empty. Puzzled, he slid open all the drawers on either side, above and below number 22. There was still no infant and Fritz became very angry. He would have to open every drawer in the morgue until he found the child, and he silently cursed Nurse Kelm. He opened them all and found no infant.

Frustrated, he looked around the room in bewilderment. *This has never happened before.* Then he noticed the tag lying on the floor. He walked over and picked it up. The string had been cut. *Hmm...Müller,* he read, *that's the name on the sign in sheet.* It had obviously been tied to the infant's ankle. *Someone has removed it and taken the body. But why would anyone do that?* A number of things flashed through his mind, some of which made him shiver.

Possibly a medical student needed a cadaver. Yes, that could be the answer. If this was the case they were taking an enormous risk. They could be barred from ever becoming a Doktor if they were found out. This will have to be reported to Direktor Braun.

Doktor Joseph Braun, the Managing *Direktor* of the hospital, was a very stern and no nonsense man, and Fritz dreaded having to face him. He rehearsed what he would say all the way to his office. *It isn't my fault the body is missing, sir. It happened before I came on duty. Yes, all this is true,* he thought, *but someone has to be held responsible and the lower you are in any hierarchy the more likely you are to be the one to be censured. Blame, like water, rolls downhill, and whoever finds himself at the bottom is the one that receives a soaking.*

He took a deep breath and knocked on the *Direktor's* office door.

Fritz went back to the morgue a shaken man. The *Direktor* had screamed at him for five minutes. *What do you mean the body is missing? Where did it go? Who brought the body to the morgue? Where were you when this happened?* Finally in exasperation he muttered, "I'll be ruined if *Frau* Müller finds out. How can she not find out?" he shouted "We must somehow keep her from knowing, but how?"

After Fritz had been dismissed, *Doktor* Braun calmed down a bit. He was a shrewd man and a skilled administrator. *I'm not going to let someone else's incompetence jeopardize a reputation and career I've worked a lifetime to build.* He sat there thinking about the problem and the possible solution. He called his secretary in and asked, "What time does Nurse Kelm come on duty?"

"I'll have to check the duty roster, sir. It will only take me a few minutes."

"Find out! Have her report to me the minute she arrives."

Most dreams drift into our consciousness just before we awaken. Ilse was dreaming she was a little girl with her parents on a picnic and it began to rain. It was a deluge. They were completely drenched. They ran for cover, but as hard as they searched they couldn't find any. She was in a totally unfamiliar place.

As the dream faded she suddenly came wide awake. The baby was screaming at the top of his lungs. She realized she had slept in the overstuffed chair all night and was still in her clothes. She looked at the clock. It was 15 minutes to eleven. She had to be on duty at twelve. As she placed Jacob over her shoulder and patted him she realized he was sopping wet. Her lap had received a drenching as well.

Just then she heard someone knocking on her door and shout, "Who is that crying? Ilse, are you all right?" Ilse hadn't given much thought about how she was going to explain the baby to Lisa and Emil.

"Come in Lisa," she shouted over the baby's wailing. Lisa opened the door and with a quizzical look on her face asked, "Who is that?" All Ilse could think to say was, "This is Jacob, my new *Sohn.*"

"Well, mine took nine months to get here. How did you manage in just 24 hours?"

"It's a long story, Lisa, and I haven't got time to tell you now. I have to be at the hospital by noon, so I've got to hurry. Lisa, you are my closest and dearest friend. Will you trust me until I can explain when I have more time? I badly need your help in the meantime to care for the baby until I return from the hospital. No one must know about Jacob. No one," she repeated for emphasis.

Ilse arrived at the hospital five minutes late. She parked her bicycle in the shed and ran in the back door. *Doktor* Braun was very strict about punctuality and she was nervous about someone reporting her tardiness.

She rushed upstairs and checked in at her station. The supervising nurse gave her a stern look and said, "*Direktor* Braun wants you to report to him immediately." This shook Ilse. *How did he find out so quickly that I'm late?* Then, a much more foreboding thought crossed her mind: *the missing baby.* As she hurried to *Doktor* Braun's office she steeled herself for the inquisition.

Now try to stay calm. Just answer the questions simply. Don't elaborate or you might trip yourself up. She rehearsed in her mind the things she would have done last night if she had actually taken a dead infant to the morgue: *I took the dead infant to the morgue and deposited him in drawer 22. I signed the registry and filled in the required information. I did the same with the body tag. I attached the tag to the infant's right ankle, placed the body in the drawer, closed it and left.* It was as simple as that. It sounded simple, but she wasn't yet in front of *Doktor* Braun.

On the way back to her nursing station, a sense of relief flooded over Ilse. *Doktor* Braun had been very angry, but more out of frustration than at her. He kept repeating, "What am I going to do? What am I going to do? If *Frau* Müller and especially *Herr* Müller find out there will be…" The rest of the sentence drifted off into a whisper.

Ilse quickly said, "I have an idea that might provide a solution, *Doktor* Braun."

"What is it?" he asked pleadingly.

"All the details are not yet clear in my mind, but do I have your permission to implement it when they are?"

"How can I decide if I don't know what it is?"

"I can promise you it will not make things any worse than they now are, and may very well solve the problem."

"Are you sure you're not digging a deeper hole for us all to be buried in later?"

"I can promise you I am not."

"How are you today?" Ilse greeted *Frau* Müller cheerfully.

"I'm doing all right, considering."

"Yes, I understand. Losing a baby is a traumatic experience. Have you chosen a name for your surviving *Sohn* yet?"

"If it had been a girl, we had decided to name her Inge, after her grandmother, and if it was a boy, we would name him Karl."

"That's such a strong, manly name. Your new *Sohn*, Karl, is such a handsome boy. Have you considered how fortunate you are?"

"How can you say I'm fortunate? I don't consider losing one of my *Sohns* as being fortunate."

"Yes, I understand, but to keep it in perspective, you still have one *Sohn*. Some women never have any. May I tell you a story that might help make a difference in the way you feel about your loss, and provide you with a measure of peace of mind in the years to come?"

"Yes, of course. Please do," Freya replied.

"I know a woman who lost her only child. He was born premature and lived only five days. She and her husband had been married only two weeks when he left for the front. He was killed in the battle at Messines a month before the baby was born. When he died it devastated this woman. She was now all alone. She had neither husband nor child to remember him by. Her parents were dead and her brother was at the front where he could very likely be killed. She was totally alone now. After the child died she spent hours looking at him. She wanted to engrave his face into her memory so she would never forget what he looked like. That was a mistake she would regret for the rest of her life. Would you like to know why?"

"Yes I would. It seems to me that any mother would want to keep the memory of her child forever."

"Yes, but what kind of memory? If your other *Sohn* died how would you like to remember him?"

Freya shuddered at the thought, but replied, "I believe it would be the way he smiles and looks at me with those big inquisitive eyes."

"That's a very wise answer. Would you like to know what this other mother sees when she remembers her *Sohn?*"

"Yes, I would," Freya replied.

"She sees her baby void of life. His eyes are closed, and she knows they will never open again. He is as pale as milk and inanimate as stone. His features are like wax. She sees him like this in her nightmares almost every night. She wakes up soaked in sweat, and sleep after that is impossible. She wishes she had never seen him in death. Our eyes are like the lens of a camera and our mind is the film. The last time we see anything, it becomes the developed picture of what we last saw. The memory she now wishes she had of him is the last time she saw him alive. My suggestion to you is to look at your living *Sohn's* face and let that be the memory of your dead *Sohn.* After all, they are twins."

Lisa heard Ilse come in the front door. She could hardly wait to talk to her. It was late and everyone else was asleep.

While Ilse was at work, Lisa had diapered, clothed and fed Jacob. She had more milk in her breasts than Otto needed, so she breast fed both babies.

"Is that you Ilse?" Lisa called out.

"Yes it's me," a tired voice replied. As Ilse came into the room Lisa saw a somnambulistic figure moving very slowly.

"How is Jacob…and the other children?" she remembered to include.

"They are all just fine and sound asleep. You look terrible," Lisa said.

"I am a bit tired. Did Jacob give you any trouble?"

"No, not at all, He is a well behaved little boy as long as his stomach is full."

"I'm glad for that," Ilse said as she turned to leave.

"Hold on just a minute. I can tell you are really tired, but we need to talk." Ilse wanted to put off as long as possible the explanation for Jacob, but knew Lisa deserved some answers.

"We'll both sleep better if you clear up this mystery." Ilse took a deep breath, sat down and told Lisa the essentials of what transpired the previous day, but did not mention the name of *Frau* Müller.

"That is an amazing story, Ilse. For the first time in my life I'm at a loss for words."

"I have been terribly worried about what you would think of me when you knew the truth. I don't really know what to think of myself."

"It will take me some time to digest all of this," Lisa replied.

"I understand. I feel a great weight off my shoulders just having told someone. What do you really think I should do? I'm so tired right now I almost don't even care what happens to me."

"That's enough of that. Go to bed and you will feel better in the morning. Don't worry about Jacob. I'll keep him down here with me tonight and if he wakes up I'll feed him. You need some rest."

"*Frau* Müller, *Herr* Müller, may I again extend my deepest sympathies at the loss of your *Sohn?* The entire staff asked me to extend their condolences as well."

"Thank you, *Doktor* Keppler," replied Friedrich. "We appreciate your concern. Thank the staff again for us if you would."

"They have been marvelous Friedrich. They have taken such good care of Karl and me. Would you especially thank Nurse Kelm," Freya said. "She told me a story I will never forget."

"Certainly, she is a very fine and dedicated nurse."

"Yes, I realize that. Well, goodbye for now. I'm ready to go home. These last few days have been bittersweet ones."

"Yes, I understand," *Doktor* Keppler replied. "I hope all the rest of your days will be sweet ones."

After the Müller's left, Fritz reported to *Doktor* Braun. "*Herr* Müller instructed me to prepare the body for burial. He said he had ordered a coffin sent to the hospital for their *Sohn*. He then instructed me to seal the coffin lid so it could not be opened. He was very emphatic about that. He said he had ordered a *Leichenwagen* to pick up the coffin. Neither he nor his wife came to the morgue to view the body before they left."

You could see visual relief spread over the *Direktor's* face. He had dark bags under his bloodshot eyes, and looked like he hadn't slept for days.

"Thank you Fritz. The face of providence has smiled on us this day."

CHAPTER 2

▼

"On November 9, 1918, the presses of Berlin's largest newspaper, the *Berliner Zeitung am Mittag*, were suddenly stopped. The paper had received a phone call from the Imperial Chancellor, Prince Max of Baden, saying an announcement of great importance would soon be forthcoming. In just a few minutes the phone rang again and an almost hysterical voice exclaimed, His Majesty the Kaiser has abdicated!"[1]

As the newspapers hit the streets, newsboys were shouting, "The Kaiser abdicates! Ebert made Chancellor! Armistice imminent!"[2]

It had been only four years since Kaiser Wilhelm II reviewed his troops as they marched past the Brandenburg Gate on their way to war. Nationalistic fervor had been high on that day in 1914. Thus began one of the most brutal wars the world has ever known. 1,773,000 Germans would be killed. The total dead from all the countries that participated would be 8.5 million, and 4 million more would be wounded. Opposing troops fought in trenches, and the term *trench warfare* was coined.

The airplane and dirigibles were new instruments of war, and poison gas was used for the first time. The conditions under which men fought and died were horrible. There are no words that can properly conjure up the ghastly images of the mutilated and dead.

As German forces drove deep into France, the campaigns at Marne, Somme and Verdan took a terrible toll.

---

1. *Before the Deluge,* by Otto Friedrich
2. Ibid

Early in 1918, Hindenburg promised the Kaiser they would capture Paris by April 1st, but at a small town named Chateau-Thierry, the advancing German army was met by fresh American troops and the German advance was battled to a standstill.

British, French and American troops began a counter offensive, attacking the Hindenburg Line, and marching on to the Argonne as the German lines collapsed.

General Ludendorff did not have enough troops to stop the advance. In a rage the two commanders, General Ludendorff and Marshal Hindenburg, informed the Kaiser and his ministers "that the war is lost and recommended an armistice be signed immediately."[3]

"On October 3, 1918, the German government, through the good offices of the Swiss Minister in Washington, formally asked for an armistice based on President Wilson's celebrated *Fourteen Points*."[4] Thus negotiations began.

The Kaiser agreed to the formation of a new democratic coalition headed by Prince Max of Baden and Social Democratic opposition leader Friedrich Ebert. Ludendorff thought the armistice would provide a temporary halt in the fighting, while both sides reinforced their troops. But the Allies were demanding unconditional surrender.

Ludendorff let it be known that unconditional surrender was unacceptable to the military. An angry Prince Max demanded Ludendorff's resignation, and it was tendered.

By this time, the Kaiser, who had not actually abdicated, refused to give in. He angrily argued with his generals, who were trying to convince him the war was lost. Exhausted, he finally gave in and boarded a special train that took him into exile in Holland. Thus ended the *Hohenzollern* emperors.

Now began a series of tumultuous events that shook Germany to its foundation. It was difficult to tell who was in charge, and this uncertainty fomented riots, strikes, mutiny, revolution and intrigue from every political spectrum, with several different military or pseudo-military groups roaming the streets at will.

Political parties and their leaders began maneuvering to control Germany, using sophistry or force as the situation presented itself, pouncing on every opportunity like buzzards over carrion. Karl Liebknecht, an independent social-

---

3. Ibid
4. Ibid

ist, claimed he wanted to build a new order of the proletariat, called a general strike, and declared a free socialist government of Germany.

Karl Ebert aligned himself with the old officers' corps, gaining the support of the army. Ebert decreed an amnesty for political prisoners and complete freedom of speech, press and assembly.

With all this going on there still remained the necessity of formally ending the war.

It seemed unimaginable to the civilian leadership that their mighty army had so completely collapsed. Prince Max asked the High Command if a remobilization might have any hope of success. They said there was none, so Prince Max then appointed Matthias Erzberger, a civilian cabinet official, to head a three man German commission to negotiate an armistice.

Any thoughts the German leaders had that the Allies would negotiate were delusional. The Germans were given 72 hours to sign the unconditional surrender terms demanded, or the Allies would begin the invasion of Germany.

The terms were harsh and stunning. The Allies demanded the evacuation of all German forces behind the Rhine and the surrender of the fleet and all heavy armaments.

France was to get Alsace-Lorraine and would occupy all German territory west of the Rhine for fifteen years and then take possession of the rich coal mines of the Saar district, which would be governed by the League of Nations. Poland would get the important industrial region of Upper Silesia, most of Posen providence and West Prussia so as to establish a Polish corridor to the sea, thus cutting off East Prussia from the rest of Germany. Denmark and Belgium would slice off several border regions, and the League would take charge of Germany's African colonies.

Disarmament would apply to Germany only. Her military forces would be cut to 100,000 volunteers and her General Staff would be abolished. Since the army was to be purely for internal use, Germany would be forbidden to possess any warplanes, tanks, or armored cars.

The Weimar Republic would have to admit formally that it was responsible for "causing all the loss and damage to which the Allies have been subjected as a consequence of the war imposed upon them by the aggression of Germany."[5] A Reparations Commission would be established to assess the amount Germany must pay, which was estimated to be at least 120 billion dollars. And finally, Kai-

---

5. Ibid

ser Wilhelm and all other *war criminals* would have to be turned over for prosecution by the Allies.

A futile attempt was made to submit a German counter proposal, and the treaty was taken back to Berlin. Chancellor Scheidemann rejected it and resigned. "While Ebert searched for someone to take over the Chancellery he also had to ponder whether his generals would try to fight on, accept defeat or attempt a coup against him."[6]

Two days before the Allied deadline, Erzberger had engaged in private discussions with various Allied diplomats to see if they might agree to drop the galling clauses about war guilt and war criminals. After a violent debate the Reichstag voted to accept the treaty on the conditions Erzberger had sought. The Allies promptly rejected the proposal, replying that "the time for discussion is past,"[7] and warning that the Germans had only twenty-four hours left before the Allied invasion began.

After much discussion, threats of resignation, and hand wringing, the government sent the Allies its answer. Germany still viewed the treaty as an "unheard-of-injustice,"[8] but it was "yielding to overwhelming force,"[9] and it was "ready to sign."[10]

"The message reached Paris just an hour and one half before the new invasion was scheduled to start."[11]

And so, on November 11, 1918, with the signing of the armistice, the horrible carnage of World War I came to an end. The New York Times said, the "fighting stopped at 11:00 o'clock this morning. In a twinkling, four years of killing and massacre stopped as if God swept his omnipotent finger across the scene of world carnage and cried, enough!"[12]

In their desire to wreak retribution, revenge and humiliation on Germany, the Allies had unwittingly sown the seeds that would twenty years later plunge the world once again into a horrible conflagration. Few, if any, at that time were able to fathom what lie ahead. Politicians proclaimed that World War I was *the war to end all wars,* but history would prove that to be a hollow phrase.

---

6. Ibid
7. Ibid
8. Ibid
9. Ibid
10. Ibid
11. Ibid
12. Ibid

CHAPTER 3

▼

"Friedrich, I'm at my wit's end. About the only food to be found in the markets are turnips. We have eaten turnips cooked in every conceivable way Martha can think of until I can't stand to look at another one. The markets are out of almost everything. We have very little left of anything and I'm frightened. Karl will be seven years old next month. A growing boy needs more nourishment than we have been able to provide lately."

"I know dear, and I have some good news for a change. Your father just got back from Heidelberg, and he made a barter arrangement with a farmer there. Your father will provide him with spare parts for his farm machinery in exchange for food."

"Oh Friedrich," Freya said, as she broke down crying. "What a relief. Father has been so kind to us."

"Yes he has, and foresighted as well. When he transferred his gold to Switzerland before the war I wondered if that was a wise move. I'm glad I listened to him and sent our meager holdings along with his. That small amount seems huge now in light of the inflation that has ravaged Germany. Right now it doesn't help much with essentials, since they are so scarce, but gold, your father pointed out to me, gives us some wonderful opportunities. He is a very intelligent businessman. I wish I were as astute as he is when it comes to business, but I guess history professors just don't have a feel for it."

"He has always had the *Midas touch*," Freya replied.

"Did you know he has been buying up land, buildings, machinery and materials all over Germany?" Friedrich said.

"No, I didn't. But, as you know, women don't get involved in such things."

"Well, he has, and he encouraged me to look around for some opportunities, and I have. I noticed a large piece of property outside the city that is for sale. I believe we could buy it for a fraction of its worth. It's in a lovely neighborhood and closer to my work. Labor and materials are cheap now and we could start building as soon as we have plans drawn up."

"Do you think we really could Friedrich? What a thrilling prospect. I'm so excited I've even forgotten how hungry I am. When can we go look at the property?"

"Right away, if you'd like."

"Let's do. Speaking of the university, dear, how are things there?"

"They are about the same as usual. There are still shortages of everything, as well as students, but time will take care of that as well as everything else. We just need to hang on until things improve. History teaches us that the economic health of countries is cyclical. We are at the bottom of the cycle, but I see signs of it changing for the better. We are much more fortunate than most. I have a good position at the university, a beautiful wife, a handsome son, and enough to eat."

"You are always so reassuring and positive," Freya replied with a smile.

Ilse took Jacob by the hand as they walked through the zoo. The Berlin Zoo was one of the finest in the world. Their collection of animals and birds was equal to or better than any other zoo.

It was August 9, 1924, and they were celebrating Jacob's seventh birthday. This was not his real birthday, of course, but this was the date on the birth certificate of her dead child. Ilse had constantly worried that even though she had a birth certificate to use in place of Jacob's real one, she also knew her real son's death was recorded some place. She shared this fear with Lisa and Emil, and Emil had said, "Let me see what I can do." What he did, since he had access to the birth and death records where he worked, was to destroy the record of Ilse's own son's death. Everything now was illegally legal.

She reflected on her good fortune. She was still working at the hospital and had a comfortable home living with Lisa and Emil. Things were scarce and there was never enough to eat, but they were still alive. It was a beautiful warm day and more importantly, she had Jacob. She had been wracked with worry for a long time about being discovered, but as time passed this feeling subsided, along with much of the guilt she harbored.

Jacob interrupted her thoughts as he squealed in delight. He let go of his mother's hand and dashed to the monkey compound. The antics of the monkeys were a favorite with children, and Jacob was no exception.

"We would like to make an offer on the residential property that you are advertising on *Stusenstraße* near the university," Friedrich said to the real estate agent.

The agent's heart leaped. Not too many people were buying residential property these days. Commercial real estate was the more desired property sought by speculators.

"And what might that offer be?" asked the agent, trying to keep his voice calm.

"We are proposing an offer of ten percent of the asking price, and…"

"No, no, no, impossible!" interrupted the agent.

"In gold," Friedrich continued. The agent's jaw dropped. He looked stunned and could hardly catch his breath.

"In…in gold," he stammered.

"Yes, gold," Friedrich emphasized. "We are prepared to sign the papers now and give you a letter of credit drawn on our bank in Zurich where the gold is deposited. I demand an immediate answer, and this offer is not subject to negotiations. And by immediate, I mean before we leave this office."

The agent said, "I will need to contact the owner to see if he is willing to sell under those terms."

"*Natürlich,*" Friedrich replied.

"Please have a seat while I telephone him."

"Of course, go right ahead." The real estate agent went into an adjoining office and closed the door. Friedrich let out a sigh of relief.

"I believe this is one of the hardest things I have ever done," he said to Freya.

"It's going just the way Father said it would."

"Yes, but I can tell you this makes me very uncomfortable. I'll just continue teaching and leave business negotiation to your father in the future, thank you."

"You are doing wonderfully. Father will be so proud of you."

"That's right sir, *gold,*" the agent repeated. "Can you believe it? My advice is to accept this offer quickly…No, if you try to bargain with them they will walk away. They made that very clear."

The agent desperately did not want this sale to slip through his fingers. He was mentally figuring his commission as they talked.

"You *will* accept then?" He almost shouted. "I'll have them sign the papers immediately…Yes sir, and thank you, sir."

Friedrich hired Professor Heinrich Tessenow, a professor of architecture at the Institute of Technology in Berlin-Charlottenburg, to design their new home.

Professor Tessenow was a champion of simple craftsmanship in architecture. His buildings were more modern than the heavily ornamented German Baroque structures that were popular in the 19th century. They did not jar the senses like those of that period, but rather evoked emotions of a more tranquil nature. Once given a client's general desired particulars, his artistic temperament allowed no interference.

"There is one particular feature Frau Müller insists on having in our new home."

"And what is that?" Tessenow replied.

"The front doors are to be designed exactly like the ones in her parents' home where she was raised. Here is the address. I've called Herr Von Kleist informing him you will stop by to see them."

"I'll be delighted to do so," the Professor replied.

"*Herr* Brandt, I'd like to make an addition to the house before you start building. You will probably be too far along with the construction to be able to include it after Professor Tessenow returns from his summer field trip with his students."

"What is it you have in mind, *Herr* Müller?"

"I completely overlooked the fact that I wanted to include a wine cellar before approving the plans. I'd like you to build one."

Gerhard Brandt, the contractor, thought that one over for a few seconds before replying.

"I'm a little hesitant to include anything that is not in the plans Professor Tessenow gave me. You know how temperamental he is about changes without his approval."

"Yes, yes, I know, but he is gone for the summer and I don't want to hold up the project until he returns."

Brandt hesitated, but finally replied, "I'm sorry *Herr* Müller, but I don't dare…"

"For crying out loud, Brandt," Friedrich snapped, "This is my house. I should be able to have it built any way I want."

Friedrich was a little embarrassed by his outburst and said, "I'm sorry *Herr* Brandt. I guess I'm a little frustrated that I didn't get this settled before Tessenow left. I'll tell you what; you build me a wine cellar, and I'll provide you with a nice bonus. Tessenow does not even need to know about it. The cellar will be under ground and out of sight anyway. Do not revise the plans. Just leave them as they are. Tessenow will never know. This will be just between you and me."

The idea of a bonus swayed Brandt, and he finally said, "I'll do it, but Professor Tessenow must never know or he may never let me build another building for him."

"Fine. That's settled. You decide where it should go and just build it. Oh, by the way, I promised Karl, our son, he could use part of the cellar as a hideaway. You know how boys are. They want a secret place to go to escape from parents. They like to pretend they are all kinds of people, from pirates to secret agents. Could you install a toilet down there so he won't have to keep running upstairs?"

"I can do that, but it will require a pump in addition to the fixtures. It will add an additional expense."

"I understand. Just let me know what the cost will be."

Brandt laid the blue print for the ground floor out on a table to study it. *Let's see now, where can I put that wine cellar?* As he studied the plans, it struck him that there was no way to conceal a wine cellar, even though it would be under ground and out of sight, because the entrance to it would be visible. *Now that is a problem. I've gotten myself into a real pickle,* he thought. He found the ideal location, however. He noticed Professor Tessenow had included a fireplace in the library. The face of the fireplace was flush with the library wall and the back of the fireplace was flush with the inside of the wall of the room adjacent to it. This left a dead air space between the two rooms the size of the fireplace, which was just about the right size for a landing leading to stairs descending to the cellar below. *However, how does one get to the stairs without an entrance?*

"Lisa, I'm taking Jacob to the market with me. I hope I can find something besides turnips for a change. Is there anything you especially want if I can find it?"

"Yes, I'd like a big fat beef roast, potatoes, fresh vegetables for a nice salad...and...Oh, and all the ingredients for *Strudel.*"

"Funny! I'm not shopping in fairy-land, but in reality-land."

As Ilse was about to cross the street, she froze in horror. On the opposite corner was another woman holding a child by the hand. In the instant it took Ilse's brain to take it all in, it seemed like she was looking into a mirror. The only difference was she did not look like the woman, but the child was the exact reflection of Jacob. She jerked Jacob around and walked swiftly in the opposite direction.

"*Mutter you're* hurting my arm." Ilse released her grip a little, but kept a tight hold on Jacob so he could not turn around.

Had the woman recognized her? More importantly, had she seen Jacob? Ilse was almost paralyzed with fear, expecting a voice to yell at her to stop. She had an almost overpowering urge to turn around and look, but knew that would make Freya even more suspicious if she followed them.

"Is that you Ilse?" Lisa called out.

"Yes, it's me."

"You're back awfully early. What happened, no luck?" When Lisa saw the look on Ilse's face she said, "What's wrong, Ilse?"

"Jacob, run upstairs and change your clothes while I talk to Lisa."

"Can I go out and play then?"

"Yes that would be fine, but stay near the house." Ilse was still shaking as she began to tell Lisa what happened.

"I have never been so frightened in my life…well, maybe the day when Jacob was born might be comparable. I never thought in a million years that our paths would cross in a city this size."

"Whose paths?" Lisa asked.

"Jacob's real mother and his twin brother Karl. I've got to leave Berlin, Lisa. I've thought about it all the way home."

"Are you sure? Where would you go?"

"I don't know, but I must leave."

"*Guten Tag, Frau* Müller, *Herr* Müller."

"*Guten Tag, Herr* Brandt. It looks like you are making good progress."

"Yes, everything is moving along quite smoothly. With the extra help you authorized we are way ahead of schedule."

"Oh Friedrich, it's going to be a magnificent home when it's finished. I can hardly wait to move in."

"Professor Tessenow has returned and will be here tomorrow to inspect our work," Brandt said.

"Good, now show us where you put the wine cellar."

"*Herr* Müller, you presented me with a very difficult problem."

"Don't tell me you didn't build it!"

"Oh, but I did," Brandt said with a smile.

"My problem was how to build it without Professor Tessenow knowing I did so without his approval. Please walk through the rooms on this floor and see if you can find the entrance." Freya and Friedrich walked into every room without finding the door to the wine cellar.

"I do not see an entrance. Is it outside?" asked Friedrich.

"No, it's inside and on this floor. Remember, we agreed it must be built so Professor Tessenow would not know it existed. Let me show you." Brandt led them into the library. It was not completely finished, but it was plastered and enclosed. A fireplace was in place, as well as built in bookshelves.

"The entrance is in this room. Do you see it?" They looked around, and an irritated Friedrich said, "There is no entrance to a wine cellar in here."

"Ah, but there is. If the entrance was visible, Professor Tessenow would see it and there would be quite a fuss when he noticed the unauthorized change I made to his plans." Friedrich thought to himself, *that's right, what a Dummkopf I am. I never even thought about the fact that an entrance would be a dead giveaway.*

"Let me show you," Brandt said as he walked over to the wall on the side of the room where the fireplace had been installed. On either side of the fireplace were beautiful heavy walnut panels. In each was carved a forest scene of trees, shrubs, birds, squirrels and a magnificent stag. A border of rosettes framed the panels.

Brandt stood in front of the panel on the left side of the fireplace. Reaching up he slid one of the rosettes down slightly, and the third one just below it he slid up. Unless you knew, it was impossible to tell they were movable. He then pushed on the left side of the panel and it pivoted in the middle, swinging open to reveal a landing and stairs leading down to the cellar. Freya gasped with amazement.

"What a clever idea, Friedrich."

"It certainly is, but it was not mine. All the credit must go to *Herr* Brandt. It certainly is ingenious, and the workmanship is flawless. Tessenow will never know this is here." Brandt's chest seemed to swell just a little and he smiled.

"Not only will *he* not know it is here, but no one else will either if you don't want them to. It will keep your guests from wandering into the cellar and disturbing the wine."

Friedrich stepped through the opening onto the landing. He looked up, and saw there was a shaft alongside the chimney wall, with a ladder embedded in the bricks, all the way to the underside of the roof. Brandt seeing him look up, commented, "The shaft to the roof provides ventilation to the cellar so a person will not feel discomfort from lack of oxygen if the door is closed."

"You seemed to have thought of everything. I'm very pleased. You can count on a very sizable bonus for your work."

The beaming builder replied, "*Danke sehr,* Professor Müller."

"You're *willkommen, Herr* Brandt."

Ilse could not get out of her mind the experience of almost running into Freya and Karl. She had decided to leave Berlin, but where should she go?

I could move to any number of cities that have good hospitals, if I could secure a position there, she thought. *That will not be easy, as jobs are scarce. If I resign my position and just leave without a job assured someplace else, how long can we live on our meager savings? Also, another city in Germany does not guarantee someone will not see Jacob who knows the Müller family and think they are seeing Karl.* These and a hundred other thoughts were constantly racing through her mind, and she was becoming physically and mentally exhausted from the effort.

One sleepless night as she lay staring at the ceiling, she suddenly sat upright. A thought had come to her like a thunderbolt crashing in the storm of her mind and was as illuminating as a flash of lightening.

"America!" She whispered out loud. "Where did I put *Mutter's* letters from Aunt Margaret?" Quietly, so as not to awaken Jacob, she got up and opened the lid to an old trunk that had belonged to her parents. She moved her hand carefully through the treasured remembrances until she felt the packet of letters her mother had received from her sister in Milwaukee. It had been some time since she had seen those letters. After her mother's death she had read and re-read them, imagining she could still hear her mother's voice as she read them to the family. This link to her parents had given her great comfort after their deaths, and now they may be the source of life for Jacob and her.

CHAPTER 4

▼

Ilse had never been so sick in her entire life. If she could just stop the never ceasing undulation of the sea and stand on the steady surface of land once again, she would give everything she owned. She tried to lie as quiet as possible, hoping she would not vomit again. She had long since lost everything in her stomach but continued trying to throw up.

She couldn't keep anything down, and even the thought of food made her gag. She was so weak she didn't think she would ever be able to stand again.

A kindly woman, *Frau* van Luven from Amsterdam, had offered to watch Jacob until she felt better. Normally she would not have let a stranger take Jacob, but seasickness causes the brain to give way to reason, and she didn't care who had him or if she even lived. *Thank goodness Jacob isn't seasick,* she thought.

Ilse had written her aunt and uncle expressing her desire to immigrate to America and asked them if they would sponsor her and Jacob. Not only were they excited and happy to do so, they even sent money for the passage. Ilse could hardly believe their good fortune.

They had taken a train to Amsterdam, which was their port of embarkation, and as they crossed the border into the Netherlands, the realization that she may never see her homeland again pierced her heart like a dagger. She dabbed at her eyes as she thought of her wonderful friends, Lisa and Emil, to whom she owed so much. They were as sorrowful to see Ilse and Jacob leave as Ilse and Jacob were in leaving. Ilse would also miss her friends at the hospital, and the thought of not being able to visit her parents' graves with a handful of flowers occasionally hurt deeply.

Her brother had been reported missing in action and was presumed dead. There were no living family ties left in Germany, and she knew she had made the right decision. Her American relatives would now become her family.

After three days Ilse started to feel a little better. It felt good to be on deck and breathe the fresh ocean air. She had even been able to hold down a little soup and tea, and her strength was returning.

Jacob was having a wonderful time. He had seen whales spouting in the distance and porpoise swimming and racing alongside the ship. He loved to lean over the railing at the bow of the ship, while Ilse held onto him, and watch the flying fish scatter like a covey of flushed quail as they came out of the phosphorescent waves caused by the ship's bow knifing through the sea. They whipped their tails back and forth so fast it propelled them out of the water and launched them into the air. Their wing-like fins spread out and they glided through the air like birds, skimming just over the waves until finally plunging back into the sea. Every day was an adventure and Ilse had to keep a close eye on Jacob to be sure he didn't fall overboard.

After eight days they finally saw land. Excitement filled the air as passengers clambered to get a position at the railing that would provide them with the best view as they entered the harbor. They slowly cruised past the Statue of Liberty. Ilse had seen pictures of it, but to see it in person was awe-inspiring. She dabbed at her moistening eyes as she squeezed Jacob's hand.

"That lady holding the torch was a gift to the United States from France," Ilse said to Jacob.

"Who is the United States?" Jacob replied.

"It's another name for America."

"Oh," said Jacob. *There will be so much to learn,* Ilse thought.

"Look at all the big buildings, *Mutter,*" Jacob said.

"Yes, they are big, aren't they?"

Several tugs were scurrying to meet them. Ilse was standing next to a tall, aristocratic looking man with a well-trimmed mustache and goatee. She asked him what the little boats were doing. He looked down his nose at her and said, "Madam, I can tell you have never traveled by ship before. Those little boats, as you call them, are tugs. Don't be fooled by their size. They are very powerful and will guide this ship to the dock."

Ilse thought they looked insignificant alongside the ship and wasn't convinced anything that small could push this floating hotel. The tugs nestled themselves against the side of the ship and slowly nudged it toward the dock, much like herring nipping at the side of a whale.

Ilse marveled at their power. They reminded her of the train on which she traveled to Amsterdam. The train engine looked as insignificant to its task as the tugs did to theirs, but surprisingly to Ilse it was able to pull several dozen passenger cars strung out behind it. *There are so many things to see,* she thought.

They felt a small jar as the ship's bumpers squeezed into the dock. Ship personnel were scurrying to thread the thick ropes through the chocks and tie them off to secure the ship.

Margaret and Ernst Weisner, Ilse's aunt and uncle, were to meet them as they disembarked. Ilse was just a little girl the last time she had seen her aunt, and she wondered if she would recognize her. Margaret was three years younger than her mother. In the letter she received from Margaret, she said they would be waving a small white flag and to watch for it. There were hundreds of people on the dock and everyone seemed to be waving something.

Jacob yelled, "There they are" and pointed at the mass of humanity below them.

"Where?" Ilse asked.

"Right there." Ilse was searching frantically in the direction Jacob was pointing. Then she saw the flag waving back and forth in a wide arc. When she saw her aunt she caught her breath. She looked so much like her mother it made her cry.

"Why are you crying, *Mutter?*" Jacob asked.

"Because I'm so happy," Ilse replied. Jacob couldn't understand that. He only cried when he was unhappy.

Soon the stairs were lowered to the dock, and passengers began to disembark. As they stepped ashore, Ilse felt like a prisoner on his first day of release. She fell into the arms of her aunt and sobbed. She hadn't realized the tension she had been under and almost collapsed at the relief that spread over her. Germany was thousands of miles away and there would be no more worry about Jacob being recognized.

"Welcome to America," Margaret and Ernst said in unison.

"*Danke schön.* Excuse me I should say thank you. My English needs some practice."

"You will get plenty of that. We have a million questions, but they can wait until we get home." *Home, what a pleasant sound,* Ilse thought.

"So this is Jacob. What a handsome boy," Margaret said.

"Come here, Jacob, and let me shake your hand." Ernst said. Jacob clung to his mothers' leg and didn't move.

"He's a little bashful right now, but later you may wish he stayed that way."

"We will have plenty of time to get acquainted," Ernst replied, "but let's get you through customs first."

CHAPTER 5

▼

"Let me present you with the keys to your new home," Professor Tessenow said as he handed them to Friedrich. It's finally finished and I hope it brings your family much joy and satisfaction for many years to come."

"*Danke sehr,* Professor." They walked through the front entry doors that Freya had specifically requested.

"Aren't the doors beautiful, Friedrich? Every time I walk through them they will remind me of the home where I was raised."

"I'm happy they please you, *Frau* Müller. Let *Herr* Brandt and myself walk your family through the house and see what it looks like now that it is completely finished. If you see anything, any detail that needs attention, please point it out and *Herr* Brandt will attend to it."

"I'm so excited I can hardly wait to get moved in. Come along, Karl. Let's see what your room looks like."

They walked through room after room, making comments about this and that as they went. When they came to the library, Friedrich walked over and stood in front of the fireplace. Brandt became a little uneasy. Friedrich ran his fingers over the carved panel entrance to the wine cellar and said, "This is my favorite piece in the whole house." Brandt turned white and looked faint. Friedrich turned and gave Brandt a little wink as he walked away smiling. Brandt let out his breath slowly like air escaping from a tire and his complexion turned back to normal.

Friedrich hired Dorsch and Gobler, a leading interior design company, to decorate and furnish their home. He instructed them they were to work with *Frau* Müller and she would have final say on the choice of materials and furnishings. Friedrich did not want to be bothered with those details. The only specific instruction they received from him was to stay within the budget he gave them, which was very generous.

The Weisners, Ilse, and Jacob were seated comfortably in the dining car of the train waiting for their breakfast. Ever since boarding the train in New York Ilse could hardly stop watching the landscape passing before her eyes as the train rolled toward Milwaukee. It was to be a trip of 895 miles and would take the better part of two days. Ernst had purchased a sleeping compartment for her and Jacob, and they both had a good night's rest The swaying of the train rocked them to sleep, which was in stark contrast to the motion of the ship that had made Ilse so seasick.

As she lay in bed, Ilse reviewed in her mind the events that had brought her to America. She felt a tinge of homesickness, but the excitement of being in America, and the safety that provided, took the edge off that feeling. Her thoughts drifted off as sleep overcame her.

During the night the train passed from New York, through Pennsylvania, and was now in Ohio. Ilse marveled at the beauty of the countryside.

The porter interrupted her thoughts as he began serving breakfast. She was amazed at the amount of food the porter laid before them, and she ate like she hadn't eaten for a month. Jacob gobbled up his ham and eggs; like a seagull swallows a fish. Ilse apologized for his table manners and Margaret and Ernst just laughed. "I think you both need a little fattening up."

"Food is very scarce in Germany. I can't tell you how much we appreciate what you have done for us."

"You have got to stop thanking us. We are just thrilled to have you both here," Margaret said.

"Look *Mama*, there's the ocean."

"It looks big enough to be an ocean, Jacob, but that's Lake Michigan. Milwaukee is situated on its shore. My great-great grandfather, Edward Weisner, emigrated from Leipzig in 1830 and settled here. There was a large contingent of Germans as well as Irish, Scandinavians, Swiss, Bohemians, and Hollanders who came to Milwaukee in the early to mid 1800's. Of the general population, however, the Germans accounted for fifty percent of the total."

The train jolted slightly as it came to a stop. Steam from the idling engine escaped like the sigh of a huge beast as it rested after a laborious run.

The conductor passed through the cars announcing their arrival. They gathered up their personal belongings and moved to the door. As Ilse stepped down from the train and set foot in her new land her emotions were a mixture of anxiety, excitement and fear. Not the fear of discovery she felt in Germany, but the fear of the unknown. Everything was so strange to her.

Passengers were being greeted by friends and relatives and there was a babble of voices everywhere.

"Mr. Weisner, your car is waiting. Here, let me take your things."

"Thank you, Ralph," Ernst said. A porter was with Ralph and together they retrieved the luggage and stacked it on a cart.

A chauffeured car was the second indication Ilse had that the Weisners were wealthy. She suspected as much when they boarded the ship in Amsterdam and found out the tickets she received for the ship's passage were for first class accommodations.

Ralph and the porter loaded everything into a large Packard, and when everyone was settled in their seats, off they went.

"What is that odor, *Herr* Weisner?" Jacob asked.

"That comes from the breweries, Jacob. It was almost inevitable that Milwaukee would become famous for its beer, since Germans are so fond of it. A man named Reutliehberger established the first brewery in 1841, which eventually became known as the Pabst Brewery. Soon after that, other beer companies established their businesses here. The industry is so large and Milwaukee is so well known for its beer, that our Minor League baseball team is called the Milwaukee Brewers. You probably don't know very much about baseball, but it is America's favorite pastime."

"I've never played baseball," Jacob said. "In Germany we play *Fußball*."

"You and I will have to begin your American education by taking in a game at Borchert Field," smiled Ernst.

CHAPTER 6

▼

"Friedrich isn't it wonderful to finally have the house finished, furnished and decorated."

"Yes, I'm glad we're finally settled. I was getting tired of house plans, fabric swatches, carpet samples and all the other paraphernalia that has been cluttering our lives for over a year. It's nice to be able to concentrate on more important things."

"Such as?" Freya inquired.

"Such as my teaching and studies."

"I wish you would spend more time with Karl."

"I see him every day."

"I know dear, but just seeing him is not the same as doing something with him."

"I know. I'll try to make a point to take him someplace with me."

As Karl grew he became more difficult to handle. An only child runs the risk of being a spoiled child, and Karl was certainly spoiled. Friedrich didn't know how to relate to Karl the way a father would who does things with his son. Friedrich didn't like sports, camping or hiking, which were the activities Karl and his peers enjoyed most. Friedrich didn't seem to be interested in what he referred to as *boy things*. He spent his time, when he was not at home or in the classroom, perfecting his lectures and researching everything from the Napoleonic wars to Tibetan culture. Friedrich's lack of involvement with Karl turned Karl into a ripe candidate for Hitler's Youth Organization.

Actually, Karl had no choice. In 1936, the Hitler *Jugend* Law made membership in the Nazi Youth Organizations compulsory for boys and girls between the ages of ten and eighteen. All other youth organizations, such as the Boy Scouts, were banned.

In Germany, people that were devoted to hiking and the outdoors were known as *Wandervögel:* the birds of passage. Those youth, who were inspired by the love of the outdoors and repulsed by industrialization with its pollution, tended to be idealistic and anti-capitalist. It was this feeling the *Nazis* successfully captured and incorporated into their appeal. An organization called the *Jungvolk* was for very young boys, and boys fifteen to eighteen were known as *Hitler Jugend. Jungmadel was* for girls ten to fourteen and the *Bund Deutsche Mädel* for girls fifteen to eighteen.

These organizations were well suited for indoctrinating the youth with *Nazi* ideals. Their aim was to take adolescents out of their social class and turn them into good and obedient *Nazis* by the age of eighteen. It was a point of immense pride for a boy to wear the uniform and carry a dagger with *Blut und Ehre* (Blood and Honor) engraved on the blade.

Hitler's Youth were held up as examples for all youth to follow. Boys and girls of that age, no matter their origin or nationality, want to be part of the popular group. Karl, who was starved for acceptance from his peers, and by the lack of involvement with his father, threw all his energies into these activities.

At first, both Freya and Friedrich were supportive of his interest in these groups, but as time went by, Karl became more insolent and rebellious and his parents became alarmed.

Freya doted over Karl. She saw only what she perceived as his angelic qualities, and ignored his selfish, egotistical, and cruel side. Karl may have shown some angelic qualities as a baby, but as he grew older, he developed characteristics that most would consider devilish. A conversation with him was like climbing through barbed wire.

Because Karl was the Müller's only child, and because Freya was not able to have more children, she understandably became an overprotective mother. Losing his twin brother at birth made her paranoid about anything happening to him. Her relationship with Karl created a great deal of friction between her and Friedrich. She undermined Friedrich's attempts to discipline him. Karl's hatred of his father grew as he grew, and he became increasingly contemptible of Friedrich's authority. He was constantly looking for ways to hurt his father. When he was seventeen he found the perfect way.

The Müller's entertained quite often, and they were invited to many parties.

Their association was primarily with the university educational social groups. Albert Einstein, who postulated that light had mass and was therefore subject to gravity (which became known as the theory of relativity), was a contemporary of Friedrich's at the university.

In addition to the university crowd, their circle of friends included some of the most distinguished business and political leaders of the time. Freya's father saw to that.

Freya was the perfect hostess. Her reputation for providing the most delicious food and wine available was the envy of her guests. Friedrich was a very gregarious host; just the opposite of what a university professor is normally thought to be. He mixed well and was very knowledgeable about all kinds of subjects. Those who were acquainted with him sought him out for his lively conversation, and he became a magnet to strangers. The one subject he tried to steer clear of was politics, but politics was a hot subject in Germany in the 1920's and 1930's, and it was impossible not to get involved. Anger over the Versailles Treaty, reparations, inflation, unemployment and the fight for political control of Germany were the subjects of heated discussions. Friedrich was very vocal about his distaste for the National Socialist German Workers Party, and he thought Hitler was a dangerous man.

The post-war years of the new German republic were fraught with political crisis, sparked by the extreme left, who wanted a social revolution, and the extreme right, who had never accepted Germany's defeat and powerlessness.

The radical Communist Party was the center of the revolutionary movement and urban revolt of 1921 and 1923. There were several coup attempts, one of which was The *Putsch* of March 1920, led by Wilhelm Kapp, and another in Munich on November 8, 1923, led by Adolph Hitler's National Socialist Party, which became known as the beer-hall *Putsch.* Both were backed by armed militia and resulted in considerable bloodshed. The armed forces were finally forced to step in to ensure the political survival of the Republic.

The beginning of the NSDAP *(Nazi* Party) began in the province of Bavaria. During April 1920, the party changed its name to the National Socialist German Workers Party, and in July 1921, Hitler was elected its chairman.

In November of 1923, Hitler launched an armed coup in Munich, which failed, and the local police arrested him. He was sentenced to five years in prison, but only served nine months. During his imprisonment, he wrote *Mein Kampf,* (My Struggle) which became the Bible for the Party.

Hitler made use of the paramilitary group established by Herman Ehrhardt called the *Sturmabteilung* (SA). They were brown-uniformed, truncheon-wielding storm troopers. Hitler was not above using whatever force it took to gain his objectives. Inflation was brought under control in 1924, and between 1924 and 1928 there was relative calm. Then came a period of higher economic growth and expanded trade helped by the Allied powers.

In 1929, Germany successfully renegotiated the reparation issue and a promise to remove the remaining occupation forces. Just as the still weak German economy brightened, it experienced a catastrophe.

The stock market crash in the United States in October of 1929 had a disastrous rippling affect on the world economy, and it threw Germany as well as other nations into a deep depression.

Germanys' trade fell two-thirds, and the income of farmers and artisans was halved. By 1932, industrial production had fallen by almost half. Confidence in parliamentary government weakened and the anti-parliamentary left and right became powerful electoral forces.

By 1932, the population had become more radical, and it again produced political violence. The Communist Party doubled its parliamentary vote and fear of communism pushed the conservative populace to support Hitler's National Socialist Party. Hitler did not yet have a parliamentary majority; however, Franz von Papen, who was Chancellor from June to November 1932, recognized the need to swing the parliament to a more conservative bent because of the communists' increasing power. Von Papen helped broker an agreement between conservatives and nationalists, and on 30 January 1933, Hitler became Chancellor.

After trying to gain control of Germany through the illegal beer-hall Putsch in November, Hitler finally at last gained power by legal means. This opened the door for still another move. He called for another election and this time garnered 43.9% of the vote, but was still short of a majority. Then, on March 23rd, Hitler presented an Enabling Act to the *Reichstag,* which was designed to give him permanent emergency powers. By wooing the Centre party deputies, he gained sufficient votes to pass the bill, which finally freed him from the limitations of a parliamentary system, and he embarked on the construction of a dictatorship.

CHAPTER 7

▼

Jacob came home from school with a black eye. He and Ilse were still living with the Weisners. Ilse was alarmed and asked what happened. He said the kids at school were teasing him because he couldn't speak proper English.

"But you mustn't fight." Ilse said. "I think you speak very good English."

"I think what Jacob is referring to is that the children are teasing him because his English has a British accent," Margaret said.

"Oh…that's true. Germans learn English with a British accent, instead of an American accent,"

"Well I wouldn't worry about it Ilse, kids pick up languages as fast as dogs pick up fleas. Jacob will be Americanized before you know it."

"Well, Jacob, I understand you had a little boxing match at school today," Ernst said, "What does the other guy look like?"

"He has a black eye just like mine," Jacob said. "Mother told me I shouldn't fight."

"Well she's right, of course. Just don't forget to duck the next time." Ernst said as he gave Jacob a wink. Jacob walked away with a grin on his face.

"What would you like to do this weekend Jacob?" Ernst asked.

"I would very much like to watch the airplanes takeoff and land at the airport. I can see them flying around from the school yard during recess, but I would very much like to see them up close."

"So, you are interested in airplanes. All right that's what we'll do. We'll ask your mother and your Aunt Margaret if they will pack a lunch and after the airport visit we'll have a picnic." Jacob was beaming, and he ran to tell his mother about the plans.

Jacob could hardly concentrate at school he was so excited. At recess he spent his time watching the small planes in the distance, and could hardly wait for Saturday to come.

Time moves at a steady precise pace, in spite of exorable pleas. Time cannot be made to move faster or slower by our wishing, but it does seem longer or shorter depending on the circumstance. For Jacob, it seemed like time was standing still.

Saturday finally did come, however, and Jacob was up early and ready to go before anyone else. After breakfast they piled into the Packard and with Ernst driving, they took off for the Milwaukee County Airport.

It was a beautiful sunny day, with a few cumulus clouds in the distance. Their enormous puffy snow-white towers were in sharp contrast to the vivid blue sky.

"It looks like perfect flying weather, Jacob," Ernst said.

"How close to the airplanes can we get, Uncle Ernst?"

"I wouldn't be surprised if we were able to get quite close." They stopped in the airport parking lot and Jacob was the first one out of the car.

"Hold on, Jacob," his mother yelled. "Let your Uncle Ernst lead the way." They all got out of the car and Ernst took them to a gate that led directly to the field. A man in flying coveralls and a Milwaukee Brewers baseball hat greeted them as he opened the gate to let them in.

"Hi Ernst. Hi Margaret," the man said.

"Hi Eddie," they both replied.

"I'd like you to meet Margaret's niece, Ilse Kelm. This is Eddie Halder. He's the flying instructor here at the airport."

"Nice to meet you," Eddie said, "and who is this?" Eddie asked as he stuck his hand out to Jacob.

"This is Jacob," Ernst replied. Jacob shook Eddie's hand and stared up in awe.

"Jacob wants to get a close-up look at the airplanes," Ernst said with a wink.

"Well that can be arranged. How would you like to take that little plane over there up for a spin with me, Jacob?" Jacob could hardly believe his ears.

"You mean to fly," he replied.

"Yes siree, that's what I mean. That little plane is a two place, fore and aft seat Aeronca. It has a stick control, and is a very reliable little craft. Come on. Let's take her up and see what she can do. This is one fine day for flying." Jacob was thunderstruck. He looked up at his mother with pleading eyes and said, "Is it all right, Mother?" Ilse could hardly refuse, as she knew it would break his heart if she said no.

"Go ahead, but please be careful Mr. Halder."

"Please...no *Mr.* stuff. Just call me Eddie...and I'm always careful. If the plane goes down I hit the ground just like the passenger, so I'm always very careful." That didn't give Ilse much comfort, and she almost refused to let Jacob go, but Eddie and Jacob were already walking toward the plane.

"So, Jacob, you are interested in airplanes, is that right?"

"Yes sir. I sure am."

"Do you want to be a pilot some day?"

"Yes sir, I very much would like to learn to fly when I'm a little older."

"Well you're talking to the right guy. That's what I do for a living." Eddie placed Jacob in the front seat, buckled him in tight, placed a set of earphones on his head, and climbed in the back.

"When you want to communicate with me press the button on the mouthpiece. To listen, just release it. Got that?"

"Yes sir."

Another man emerged from the hangar and stood in front of the plane with one hand on the propeller. This man called out, "Switch on?" and Eddie replied, "Switch on." The man then said, "Contact," and Eddie replied, "Contact." With that the man swung his leg up and gave the prop a downward pull with great force and at the same time moved his leg back out of the way.

The engine caught and the propeller began to spin. The man reached down, grasped the ropes attached to the blocks in front of the wheels, and jerked them away. The plane was now ready to taxi. Eddie pushed the throttle forward slightly, and the plane began to move. He taxied the plane to just off the end of the runway and let the engine idle and warm up. He wagged the ailerons and rudder while he radioed permission for take-off.

"This is Aeronca 425 requesting take-off."

"Roger 425, wind south by southwest at 5 knots. Clear for take-off on runway 2, over."

"Roger, over and out." Having received clearance, Eddie pushed the throttle forward slightly and taxied the plane onto the runway.

"Jacob I'm going to give you your first lesson. See the pedals on the floor?"

"Yes sir."

"When you depress the left pedal the plane moves to the left. When you depress the right pedal the plane moves to the right. Pretty simple, huh?"

"Yes sir."

"All right. When you pull back on the stick the plane goes up, and when you push forward on the stick the plane goes down. Got that?"

"Yes sir."

"After we are in the air, if you push the stick to the left the plane turns left. If you push the stick to the right, the plane turns right. To make a proper turn it requires the use of both the pedal and the stick. When we get in the air I'll show you how we coordinate a turn."

Eddie was having as much fun as Jacob. He was thinking of the first time his father took him up and gave him these same instructions. He could still remember his excitement and knew exactly what Jacob was feeling.

The Aeronca is called a *tail dragger* because it has a small wheel under the tail. This feature allows the plane to sit at an angle to the ground, which makes it impossible to see the runway straight ahead while taxing or during the first several hundred feet or so on take-off. Once the plane reaches a certain speed the tail lifts up and becomes horizontal to the runway and the pilot can then see straight in front of him. Until that time comes the pilot watches the edge of either side of the runway and makes whatever correction is needed if the plane begins to drift to one side or the other.

"OK, here we go. Are you all set?"

"Yes sir."

"You're not scared are you?"

"No sir."

"I didn't think you looked like a *scardy cat*." Jacob had never been this excited, and expectant in his life. Even the voyage on the ship to America paled in comparison.

Eddie pushed the throttle forward and the plane began to roll. Faster and faster they went. Soon the tail came up and Jacob was looking straight down the runway. Everything was a blur when he looked down at the ground just outside the side window. Suddenly the plane jumped into the air and they were flying. It was an exhilarating feeling Jacob would never forget. As they began to climb Jacob looked down and everything became smaller and smaller.

Eddie made a left turn and flew back parallel to the runway and Jacob could see his mother and aunt and uncle waving at them. Eddie wagged the wings of the plane as they passed over them, turned east toward the lake and then turned north, paralleling the west shore of Lake Michigan.

Jacob could see boats on the lake, cars on the roads and people on the beach. They looked like ants. The farms off to the west, delineated by fences and roads were a patchwork of different shades of greens and browns, depending on the crops or plowed fallow fields. Jacob thought this must be what birds see as they fly through the air. Right there and then he vowed to himself that someday he would learn to fly.

His thoughts were interrupted as Eddie said. "How would you like to take the controls?"

"Do you really mean it?"

"Sure, why not? OK, put your right hand…are you right handed?"

"Yes sir."

"All right, take hold of the stick with your right hand. Have you got it?"

"Yes sir."

"OK, pull it back slowly…that's good. Can you feel the plane climb?"

"Yes sir."

"OK, push the stick forward slowly. Can you feel the plane start to descend?"

"Yes sir."

"OK, pull the stick back again until we are flying level…You're doing just fine. Watch the altimeter needle. Can you tell which instrument is the altimeter?"

"I'm not sure which one it is."

"It's the round instrument to your upper left, and it has the numbers 0,1,2,3,4, etc. It looks something like a clock."

"Yes I see it now," Jacob replied.

"Each number represents a thousand feet. If for instance, the needle is on the 3 we would be flying at an altitude of 3,000 feet. If the needle is half way between the 3 and the 4 we would be flying at an altitude of 3,500 feet."

"OK, can you reach the pedals?"

"Just barely, sir."

"All right, I'll give you a little help if you need it. We're going to make a slow left turn. Remember I told you to turn the plane left you push the stick to the left."

"Yes sir, I remember."

"All right, at the same time you push the stick to your left, depress the left pedal, and pull back slightly on the stick during the turn as the plane will have a tendency to lose altitude. Have you got that?"

"I think so," Jacob replied.

"Don't worry if it isn't perfect. If you get into trouble, I'll say *I have the controls,* and you are to take your hands and feet off the controls. OK here we go. Start your left turn by slowly pushing the stick to the left and at the same time depress the left pedal slightly. Execute the maneuver now."

Jacob pushed the stick to the left and pressed on the left pedal with his toe. The plane banked and turned to the left.

"Pull back a little more on the stick. The plane is losing altitude. That's good, just hold it right there. Now bring the stick back to the center position, which is the position it was in before you started the turn. Take your foot off the left pedal and depress the right pedal until the plane is flying level and straight."

As the plane leveled, Eddie neutralized the turn by giving it just enough left rudder to keep the plane from continuing its right turn.

"That was a great job, Jacob. You are going to be a great pilot someday." Eddie couldn't see his face, but Jacob was grinning from ear to ear.

"How would you like to do a loop?"

"What's that?" Jacob replied.

"We'll put the plane into a slight dive to pick up speed and then pull back on the stick and the plane will go straight up and over until we are upside down. The plane will continue making the loop until we are flying level and straight again. Do you feel up to it?"

"Yes sir. It sounds fun."

"OK, I want you to take the plane up to 5,000 feet. We want to have plenty of clearance above the ground when we come out of the loop. OK, take her up to 5,000 feet." Jacob pulled back on the stick and watched the altimeter needle until it was on the 5. He pushed the stick forward and leveled off at 5,000 feet.

"Great job. You're getting the hang of it. OK. Hang on, here we go." Eddie started the loop with a slight dive to gain speed. Back came the stick and up and over they went. At the top of the loop, Jacob felt himself hanging from his harness, as he was upside down, and then was pressed hard into his seat as the plane completed the loop and leveled off.

"How did you like that, Jacob?"

"It was great."

"It wasn't too much for you, then?"

"No not at all, can we do it again?"

"OK, but this time put your hand lightly on the stick so you can get the feel of it." They did another loop. Jacob was having the time of his life.

"OK, we're going to do another loop, but this time you fly the plane. I'll keep my hand lightly on the stick in case you need a little help." Jacob put the plane in a slight dive, pulled back on the stick with all his might until they completed the loop.

"That was great, Jacob, you're a natural born flyer. How would you like to do some more acrobatic maneuvers?"

"I'd like that," Jacob replied. Eddie proceeded to do an Immelman, a barrel roll, a High Yo-Yo and a Split S. Jacob was a little dizzy after all that, but he was elated.

"How was that, Jacob?"

"Super," Jacob replied.

"Well, that's enough for today. We'd better be getting back because your mom might be getting a little worried." They flew back to the field; Eddie made a perfect landing and taxied to the hangar. The man who spun the propeller told them his mother, aunt, and uncle were in the restaurant having a cup of coffee, so they headed that way. Ilse saw them first and was very much relieved to see they were back safe.

"Well, how did it go, Jacob? Did you enjoy the ride?" Ernst asked.

"It was super, Uncle Ernst," Jacob replied. "I flew the plane all by myself. We did loops and Yo-Yo's and all kinds of things. Eddie told me he would teach me to fly and land the plane and everything when I'm a little older."

"This kid was born to fly. He's got the feel and the temperament for it," Eddie said. "No doubt about it. He reminds me of myself at that age." Eddie felt an attachment to Jacob, but he was just more than a little interested in getting to know his mother a little better.

CHAPTER 8

▼

Between 1933 and 1939, Germany began to free itself from the restraining bonds imposed by the Versailles Treaty. Even before Hitler came to power, German foreign policy was directed toward regaining world status and parity with other nations and to rebuild the military.

Allied occupation of the Rhineland was withdrawn in 1930, and reparations were suspended in June of 1932; all this took place before Hitler came to power.

In October 1933, when Hitler did come to power, he took Germany out of the League of Nations, charging the other world powers with trying to keep Germany a second class nation. Hitler declared that no further reparations would be paid, and in so doing, he asserted Germany's economic independence.

Due to the worldwide economic slump, nations were more concerned with their own internal problems and less inclined or willing to enforce the Treaty.

The next step was to rebuild the military. Hitler used the Youth movement to not only indoctrinate them with *Nazi* principles, but to provide a forum for military training. Boys drilled with shovels instead of rifles, and glider clubs were established providing the first volunteers to fly Germany's forbidden aircraft. As these youth came of age to serve in the military, there were millions of men already familiar with military protocol and structure.

The armed forces began to develop aircraft, submarines, and tanks in secret collaboration projects with the Soviet Union, Sweden, the Netherlands and Spain. A new air force was established in secret; aircraft was camouflaged, dispersed, and housed in civil aviation facilities all over Germany.

On 16 March 1935, Hitler formally announced his intention to establish a 36 division, 700,000-man army and an air force of more than 200 squadrons. There was very little international protest.

Karl turned seventeen on September 11, 1934, making him eligible to begin actual flight training in the glider club to which he belonged. Ever since he saw his first glider in flight it had been his dream to be able to fly. He watched the older boys be towed to a thousand meters altitude, cut loose, and soar like a bird until they landed.

At the age of 15 he was enrolled in classroom instruction. They studied such things as the theory of flight, the evolution of the airplane, and the exploits of German World War I pilots. They actually helped in some phases of the construction of a glider and received hands on instruction in the function of the controls in a simulator. Karl was now ready to take to the air and learn how to actually fly.

He was so excited about the prospect of flying he could hardly sleep. He awoke after a restless night, and could hardly wait to get to the training field. He came down stairs and heard Martha, their cook, in the kitchen preparing breakfast for the family. He went in and poured himself a cup of coffee.

"I'll have a nice breakfast for you in a few minutes," Martha said.

"I haven't got time. I need to get to the airfield as soon as possible. Today I start my glider instruction."

"Oh, really." said Freya. Karl had not heard his mother come into the kitchen. "Why didn't you tell your father and me?"

"It's none of your business what I do outside the house."

"That's not a very congenial attitude. We are concerned about your outside activities, and flying sounds like a very dangerous one. I wouldn't want anything to happen to you."

"It's not dangerous. I'll have an instructor in the glider with me, and they are very well trained."

"Well, as usual, it sounds like you're not going to listen to your father or me."

"I listen until I'm sick of listening."

"Don't you mean you hear what we say but don't really listen or understand what we are saying?"

"You're right. I hear you, and I understand what you're trying to do. You're trying to control my life. It's my life and I'll do with it as I please." Freya was becoming increasingly fatigued by these arguments. She didn't want Karl to leave upset, so she succumbed to his protests.

"Won't you at least eat some breakfast? You'll need your strength if you are going up in a glider."

"Forget it. I don't have time." At that, he left the house. Just then Friedrich walked in.

"What's that all about?"

"Nothing dear, everything's fine."

"Where is Karl off to this early in the morning? Did he get breakfast?"

"No, he said he wasn't hungry. He starts his glider training today."

"What! Glider training! I didn't know he was taking glider training. It would have been nice to know that. I might have gone and watched."

"Really, you haven't seemed that interested in what he does." Friedrich just grunted and sat down to his breakfast.

Karl arrived at the grass airfield at 9:00 am. There were twelve boys to fly that day, and a few of the other boys were already there. At 9:30 the instructor called them together and said they would draw slips from one to twelve to determine their turn.

Karl drew number eleven. He was furious. "I should be number one. I had the best scores in preflight training," he said as the instructor walked over to the glider for a final inspection. Karl grabbed the boy that drew number one by the arm and swung him around. He hated this person. Their rivalry was the most intense of any in the class. Karl drew his *Blut und Ehre* dagger from its holster and put the tip of it under the boy's chin.

"Give me that slip. I should be number one."

"No, it's mine."

"Give it to me or I'll run this blade to your eyeballs." The other boys were aghast.

"You wouldn't dare." Karl raised the blade slightly and a trickle of blood rolled down his neck."

"All right, here, take it." Karl took the slip, dropped his to the ground, walked to the glider, and handed the slip to the instructor. The instructor told him to climb into the front seat. He then checked the towrope clamp on the nose of the glider and Karl's safety harness and climbed into the back seat.

The towing plane was already warming up. The instructor reviewed the controls with Karl and told him to lightly place his hands and feet on them. This would allow Karl to get a feel for them during take-off, but he was not to at any time exert pressure on the controls.

Another instructor held a green flag in his hand. When everyone was set, he raised the flag and quickly sliced it in a downward motion to signal the pilot of the towing aircraft to go.

It started to move forward very slowly, the towrope tightened, and the glider began to move. Gradually they picked up speed, and the glider shot into the air before the towing plane left the ground. The towing plane finally escaped the ground, and they were both in the air and climbing.

The feeling was one that cannot be described, but only experienced.

Slowly, they gained altitude as they flew higher and higher. At a thousand meters the instructor pulled the rope release lever, and they were free of the airplane. The airplane turned to return to the field to pick up the next glider, and as it receded in the distance they could no longer hear the engine. It was completely silent except for the wind rushing by the fuselage and wings. The instructor didn't say a word. It was as if he didn't want to spoil the mood. The sensation was indescribable, and Karl didn't want it to end. Finally the instructor said, "How does it feel to fly?"

"It's more wonderful than I ever imagined."

"I agree. It is special. I guess we better get down to business. I want you to take the controls. You will be flying the glider. Just remember your instruction in the simulator. It's the same up here. Take the controls now." Karl took the stick in his right hand and placed his feet on the pedals. "Now make a left turn and head back in the direction of the field. Easy does it. That's very good. Just continue making turns, both left and right, but work your way back to the field. Keep in mind we need to maintain enough altitude and air speed to make an approach and landing in the same direction from which we took off."

"Yes sir." Karl thought; *this is the life, to be able to command the flight of the glider by the slight movement of feet and hands.* It was a powerful feeling. He loved being in control.

"Did you feel that, Karl?" the instructor asked.

"Yes sir, it feels like the plane is rising."

"It is, as you can tell by your altimeter. We just hit a thermal updraft."

"What's that?" Karl asked.

"As the sun heats the ground it heats the air above it, and this air begins to rise. When the plane enters this rising air it rises with it. A good pilot can sometimes ride these updrafts for hours."

"That sounds fine to me."

"Yes, I understand, but there are others waiting to fly. Can you see the landing field up ahead?"

"Yes sir, I see it."

"We need to maintain enough altitude to pass the field about one half kilometer on the starboard side, go by the field about one quarter kilometer, make a left turn and decrease your altitude and head in for a landing. Watch the air speed indicator to be sure we are well above flying speed so we don't stall. I'll do the actual landing this time."

"Yes sir."

Karl made the turns as instructed and lined up the glider with the field. The instructor took the controls and made a perfect landing; sliding the glider smoothly onto the grassy field until it came to a stop. As they got out, the instructor told Karl he did a good job and would soon be flying by himself. Karl felt a pride of achievement he had not known up to that time.

When Friedrich returned home that evening, he summoned Karl to his study.

"Karl, I think we should talk."

"What do you want to talk to me about?"

"I'd like to talk to you about your attitude and your involvement with the National Socialist German Workers Party."

"The Party is the future of Germany. It will restore Germany to its rightful place in the world. It will build a strong Germany, and no one will be able to stop us."

"That's what the Kaiser thought. Look what happened to Germany, and to us."

"Hitler is different. He wants to build a pure Aryan Society, to rid ourselves of the Jews who suck the blood from our cultural and economic life. To move beyond the shallow thinking of your generation to a glorious Germany, where no one will dictate to us what our future will be."

"Son, history reminds us what our future might be. If we ignore history, we learn nothing. Hitler is a manipulator and a demagogue who plays upon people's prejudices and fears to further his own ambitions. He will lead Germany to its destruction if he ignores history."

Karl's anger rose to the boiling point. The frustration caused by his father's refusal to accept his point of view was intolerable. He angrily shouted, "We *are* making history, and no one can stop us. Some day we will rule the world."

"Is that so? Many have tried, but none have succeeded. Where is Fredrick the Great, Charlemagne, Genghis Kahn or Napoleon? Does Rome rule the world? Hitler will burst onto the scene like a meteor that flashes across the firmament for a moment and is then spent into oblivion."

"You'll see," Karl shouts. Livid, he stormed out of the house. *I'll teach you.* This thought exploded in his mind.

He was still seething when he walked into Gestapo headquarters. A receptionist asked, "May I help you?"

"Yes, I'd like to speak to someone about a person who is betraying our country."

"Wait right here, and I'll find someone to talk to you." Karl could hardly wait. He smiled slyly to himself. He could taste vengeance and it was sweet.

"Come this way." Karl was led down the hall and into an office.

"Sit down please. My name is Ernst Kaltenbrünner. What is your name, and what is this all about? You claim someone is betraying Germany?"

"My name is Karl Müller, and it's true. My own father is a traitor. He rails against the Regime. He teaches his students falsehoods about *Nazism* and berates me for my loyalty to the Party."

"What is your father's name?"

"Professor Friedrich Müller. He teaches at the university."

"Thank you for coming to us. You did the right thing. We will look into this matter."

CHAPTER 9

▼

In the summer of 1936, Hitler drafted a Memorandum called *The Four Year Plan*, which he announced at the Nuremberg Party rally in September. Its purpose, although Hitler did not say so, was to prepare Germany for war in the 1940's. There was never a clearly orchestrated plan. Hitler, who by nature worked in a disorderly fashion, never wanted to be tied down by established procedures. He preferred to be flexible and act on opportunities as they presented themselves.

In May 1938, Hitler saw one such opportunity and acted. He felt the time was ripe, and he set in motion a plan to wage a swift war against Czechoslovakia, so as to bring the Sudeten Germans under German rule.

Ribbbentrop, Hitler's Foreign Minister, convinced him that Britain and France were too isolationist to interfere. Hitler had his eye on the valuable economic resources this area could provide for the military build-up undergoing in Germany. As tension between Germany and Czechoslovakia grew, Britain and France sought to intervene in the conflict.

The British and French were not prepared to allow Hitler to gain control of the Balkans and further his ambition of building a new German Empire. Britain's Prime Minister, Neville Chamberlain, flew to the *Berghof,* Hitler's Bavarian Alpine retreat, to try and reason with him. Hitler flew into a rage, saying, "I shall settle this question one way or another." Chamberlain, trying to calm the Führer, suggested self determination for the Sudetens and Hitler seemed agreeable.

Chamberlain flew home to consult with his allies. He said Hitler could be trusted when he has given his word. Chamberlain flew back to Germany to tell

Hitler of the allies' acceptance and was stunned when Hitler told him, "I am exceedingly sorry, but self determination is no longer acceptable."

Chamberlain flew home frustrated. Germany was mobilizing and France was also, to some extent.

Mussolini proposed the issue be discussed at a Great Powers conference, and Hitler reluctantly agreed. This meeting took place at Munich on September 29, 1938. In attendance at this meeting were Hitler, Mussolini, Prime Minister Edouard Daladier of France and Chamberlain. Although the meeting was to decide the fate of Czechoslovakia, shamefully no one from that country was invited to attend. The agreement that was signed at this meeting gave Germany the Sudetenland so as to avert a war between the two countries. Chamberlain flew back to England, and as he stepped off the airplane, waved a copy of the treaty in the air and proclaimed a diplomatic victory that would guarantee *peace for our time*.

In England, Queen Mary, other government officials, church leaders, and the people in general gave enthusiastic approval, and greeted this news with celebration. A lone dissenting voice proved prophetic when Winston Churchill stalked out of Parliament saying, "The government had to choose between shame and war. They chose shame and will get war."

Six months later German forces invaded Czechoslovakia unopposed and partitioned it into a Protectorate of Bohemia and Moravia and an autonomous Slovakia. Chamberlain was haunted the rest of his life by the words he uttered to his colleagues and countrymen when he said, "When he (Hitler) had given his word, he could be trusted." Munich from that time forward has become the symbol of the folly of appeasement.

"We got everything we wanted just like that," snorted Göring as he snapped his finger. Hitler vowed he would never again give way to what he felt were hollow threats from Britain and France. The concessions that were made to him at Munich were seen as a green light to further expansion in the east.

Hitler next turned a greedy eye toward Poland and Hungary. When Poland refused to become a dependant state like Slovakia, Hitler ordered the High Command of the *Wehrmacht* to prepare for war. This fateful decision was the catalyst that started the world on the slippery slope toward World War II.

In March 1939, hoping to discourage Hitler from further expansion demands, Britain signed a unilateral guarantee of sovereignty with Poland, which France also reluctantly agreed to honor.

Hitler's generals were unanimously opposed to war with Poland. They did not think Germany was prepared for a war that would almost certainly bring England and France into the conflict. But egged on by Ribbentrop, who felt Britain and France were too weak to protest, Hitler ordered an invasion.

However, before invading Poland, Hitler, afraid of a confrontation with the USSR, had Ribbentrop fly to Moscow where he negotiated a comprehensive non-aggression pact with Stalin. This agreement was signed on 23 August 1939.

The incursion into Poland began on 1 September 1939. Two days later, to Hitler's consternation, England and France declared war on Germany.

In 1933, one of Hitler's goals had been an alliance with Britain against the USSR. In 1939, he achieved just the opposite.

The die had now been cast. German forces swept into Poland. *Stuka* dive bombers screamed overhead, and bombed Polish troops, whose forces were scattered and their defenses obliterated. The *Blitzkrieg* (lightening strike) techniques employed by Germany's Panzer division tanks moved so fast they outpaced their ground forces and were forced to hold up until the troops could catch up.

Russia then attacked Poland from the east so as to claim their share of the spoils agreed to by Hitler and Stalin.

On 27 September, after less than a month of fighting, Warsaw surrendered, and on 6 October, the last Polish ground troops surrendered.

Poland was then partitioned, as agreed to prior to the war, in the friendship treaty between Germany and the Soviet Union. The Soviet Union then began to pressure the Baltic States into pacts which enabled their ships to use Baltic ports. This gave them control over the waters of that region, and access to more ice-free harbors.

In the spring of 1940, Hitler turned his attention to the west. Germany attacked Denmark and Norway, and by June Hitler had swallowed these nations in one gulp. They were then occupied under German political and military control.

An assault on France began on 9 May 1940

Hitler set in motion his western offensive by invading Belgium, Luxembourg and Holland without a declaration of war. These countries are quickly over run and German armies continue attacking through the Ardennes. They simply ignored the French Maginot Line, thus avoiding the greatest pocket of resistance and drove toward Paris. Patton later said, *The Maginot line is a monument to man's stupidity.*

This campaign had taken only six weeks and Germany now controlled most of Europe. Marshal Petain of France and Hitler signed an armistice, at Hitler's insistence, in the very same rail car at Compiegne, where the Allies had forced Germany to sign the humiliating Versailles Treaty at the end of World War I. One can only imagine the irony of this event and Hitler's vindictive satisfaction this occasion afforded him.

America watched these events from afar. The country was wary of again getting caught up in a war in Europe. World War I, still fresh in people's memories, fostered an isolationist atmosphere. Roosevelt was constrained somewhat by this isolationist feeling because of the possible political consequence. Even so, he began to prepare the country for war.

On 31 May 1940, Roosevelt introduced the country to a massive armament program. This was his way of providing the Allies with the necessary war materials as well as making sure the country would be ready if America entered the war.

Then on 2 September 1940, he agreed to provide Great Britain with 50 older, but serviceable destroyers in return for bases in Bermuda, the West Indies and Newfoundland.

In spite of isolationist politician's outcry at Roosevelt's moves, he is elected on 5 November 1940, to an unprecedented third term.

On 2 December 1940, Roosevelt gave a radio address stating that America would be *The Arsenal of Democracy*, and by so doing, effectively announced a full-hearted support for the Allied cause.

In March 1941, Roosevelt assured Great Britain in a speech of *aid until victory*, and a Lend-Lease bill was passed in Washington, which demonstrated America's full support for the Allied war effort.

CHAPTER 10

▼

On 10 July, 1940, in clashes over the straights near Dover at what came to be known as *Hellfire Corner*, the RAF suffered one of their worst defeats. They lost 50 fighters. *Luftwaffe* raids on military targets in Southern England were designed to test RAF response and willingness to engage. The British did engage and the drain on both aircraft and pilots made clear these needs were becoming critical. Being short of pilots, Britain began a worldwide search for volunteers.

After a yearlong courtship, Eddie and Ilse were married on 2 February 1930. Contrary to the bitterness that often shapes a child's attitude toward a stepparent, Jacob was thrilled to have Eddie as his stepfather. Eddie loved Jacob as if he were his own flesh and blood, and he had thoroughly enjoyed teaching him to fly and working with him at the airport, where Jacob was now employed. Eddie felt his marriage to Ilse was one of the best things that had ever happened to him, and their marriage was a happy one. Ilse had been worried and anxious about Jacob's flying, but gave into the inevitable.

After Jacob's first flight with Eddie when he was seven years old, he began to work at the airport after school and during summer vacation in exchange for flying lessons, as they had agreed on earlier.

One day when Jacob was sixteen years old, he and Eddie were shooting take-offs and landings. After one particular landing Eddie told Jacob to pull over to the side of the runway.

Puzzled, Jacob did as Eddie instructed. Eddie got out of the plane and said, "OK, you're ready. Go ahead and take off. Fly around for a while, and I'll see you when you get back." Jacob's heart almost stopped beating.

"Are you sure?"

"I'm sure, but are you?"

"Yes, I'm ready."

He had known this time would come some day, and he had wondered how he would react. Excitement and fear competed for his emotions. He felt confident that he was ready, but he was still a little fearful.

He glanced over at Eddie as he walked away and pushed the throttle forward. The plane rushed down the runway. As the plane left the ground, a feeling came over him that cannot be described, only felt. It is unique to those who fly for the first time without their instructor. Never again would this feeling be duplicated. There would be other thrilling flying experiences, but nothing would ever feel exactly the same as the first time a person goes up in a plane without an instructor. It was an exhilaration that may be compared to the first time you kiss your sweetheart. The second kiss is great, but it cannot compare to the first. Jacob glanced back at the empty seat behind him, and the reality that no one was there to help him land the plane if he needed help slowly sank in. This caused a tightening in his stomach. He was on his own.

He flew around for about fifteen minutes and decided he couldn't put it off any longer; it was time to land. As he approached the runway his training took over and his reflexes were automatic. When he touched down and taxied back to the hangar he wondered why he had even been worried. "Nothing to it," he said to himself. Then he could hear Eddie's voice in his mind saying, *don't ever get too cocky. There are old pilots and there are bold pilots, but there are very few old bold pilots.*

In August of 1940, Jacob, who was now 23 years old, made a decision that would alter his life and those around him forever. Under the tutelage of Eddie Halder he had become a highly skilled aviator. Ilse wanted him to go to college, but he preferred to work at the airport with Eddie and fly. He now had his instructor's license and became a third generation instructor.

One day Jacob casually said to his step father, "Eddie, I've joined the RAF and will be leaving for England in two weeks."

"You what! Are you nuts? What made you do that?"

"I just feel like it's the right thing to do. It doesn't look like the United States has the will to enter the war. The British need pilots and Hitler has got to be stopped."

"And you think you can stop him?"

"Not all by myself, but I can help."

"Don't you know that the United States Neutrality Act prohibits foreign recruiting of individuals for service in the armed forces of a foreign government?"

"That was only true before the fall of France. Since then the United States has abandoned that part of the provision. Colonel Charles Sweeny, who is in charge of recruiting American volunteers, explained all of this to me. He said that even though there are certain restrictions still in place, the United States abandoned enforcement of a number of the provisions. He also said he had received unofficial encouragement from the United States government to recruit pilots, because it was believed that we would eventually be in the war and would need trained pilots. They are seeking to recruit 25 pilots and 25 reserve pilots, which will form *Eagle Squadron* number 71."

"I suppose you haven't told your mother about this yet, have you?"

"No, I wanted to talk to you first."

"I see. You want me to smooth the way."

"Not exactly, but I know mother will be against it."

"That's an understatement if I ever heard one."

"I do want your support, however, when we talk to her."

"What do you mean *we?*"

"Well, you know. You can help calm the waters."

"I don't know if either of us will survive this storm. I don't want you to do this myself, so I don't know if I'll be much help."

"My mind is made up, and no one can talk me out of it. I want to leave with both of your blessings."

"When are *we* going to give your mom the news?"

"I thought tonight at dinner time might be a good time."

"Wait until after dinner, so only my digestion will be affected."

"That was a great dinner, Mom. You are the best cook in the world." Ilse gave Jacob a look only a mother can give when sensing one of their children wants something.

"What is it Jacob? Why am I suddenly the best cook in the world?"

Jacob glanced over at Eddie, and seeing Eddie look down at his plate, took a deep breath and said, "Mom, I've got something to tell you." Ilse, who had started to clear the dishes from the table, sat back down in her seat and folded her hands on the table in front of her.

Looking directly into Jacob's eyes she said, "What is it, Jacob?" Jacob almost backed out as he looked at his mother. He knew it was going to hurt her and that was the last thing he ever wanted to do.

"You know how much I love to fly, Mom…and you know I'm old enough now to make my own decisions…and well,…I may sometime do something, with which you won't agree…and…"

"What is it Jacob? What is it that's so hard to say?"

"I've joined the RAF and will be leaving for England in two weeks," Jacob blurted out. Ilse gripped her hands so tightly her knuckles turned white. She was determined to stay outwardly calm.

"I see, and you made this decision all by yourself."

"Yes, I did."

"Eddie did you know about this?"

"I just learned about it this afternoon."

"And what did you tell Jacob when you learned about this thing?"

"I asked him if he had told you yet, and he said no."

"And do you approve?"

"Well, yes and no."

"It can't be both, Eddie."

"Well, I told him I was against it, but after thinking about it for awhile, I decided Jacob is old enough, and should be able to exercise his God-given right to make his own decisions. Both of us knew Jacob would have to move on in life at some point. It may not be what we want, but if Jacob thinks its right for him, we shouldn't interfere."

"Well, that's quite a mouthful, Eddie." Eddie looked a little sheepish, and didn't say any more.

"Do you realize you would be fighting and maybe killing your fellow country-men?"

"Mom, I'm an American now. We both are. Hitler is a thug and we had better take a stand against him, and the sooner the better."

"I understand how you feel, but America is not in the war."

"I know, but I believe we will be eventually."

"Can't you wait until that time comes, if it does?"

"No, I just feel like this is something I have to do." Ilse doesn't say anymore. She sensed it was hopeless. *Is this God's punishment for stealing Jacob?* She couldn't even share this tormenting thought with Eddie. She got up and continued to clear the table. Jacob got up at the same time, came around the table, and took his mother in his arms. Ilse couldn't hold it in any longer and began to quietly cry. Jacob's resolve almost dissolved, but he didn't say anything. He just held his mother.

As they waited in the Milwaukee railroad station, it was not lost on Ilse that fifteen years ago they stood in this same place with Margaret and Ernst Weisner, Ilse's aunt and uncle, upon their arrival from New York. *That was such a happy time,* Ilse thought. *Isn't it strange how we never know what lies ahead? It's probably a good thing we don't know. If I had known at that time what would be taking place now…*she shuddered a little, and Jacob, noticing said, "Are you cold mother?"

"No, I'm fine. Now remember to keep warm on the train. Be sure you eat properly so you will stay well. Write as often as possible."

"Mother you have told me these things a dozen times already. Don't worry I'll be just fine."

"Don't worry, he says. That's easy for him to say." Eddie just smiled, but didn't say anything. He was lost in his own thoughts. He would miss Jacob terribly. Their whole lives were about to change and the future was shrouded in uncertainty.

"All aboard." Those words pierced Ilse's heart like an icicle. There was finality in them. Would she ever see her son again? She grabbed Jacob and clung to him, not wanting to let him go. Jacob gave her a big hug and kiss, and then hugged Eddie. "Goodbye son and Godspeed," Eddie said.

"Not goodbye, just *so long*, and thanks for teaching me to fly." *Maybe that was not such a good thing I did,* Eddie thought.

CHAPTER 11

▼

French Premier Paul Reynaud made a call to Winston Churchill. Churchill picked up the receiver of his bedside phone and heard the French Premier say, "The battle is lost, France has been overrun and defeat is imminent."

Churchill was stunned. Certainly this couldn't be happening so soon. Reynaud informed him that the Germans had broken through near Seden, and were pouring through in great numbers with tanks and armored cars.

This put Britain in a very precarious position. As German troops overran France, the retreating English expeditionary force that had come to help save Europe from Hitler was driven to the sea.

Churchill, realizing the gravity of the situation, put out a call to the British people asking for those with any kind of seaworthy craft to sail across the English Channel to France and help pluck their beleaguered army from the beaches.

The response was overwhelming. The operation called "Dynamo" was launched on 26 May 1940. 1,200 Allied naval and civilian watercraft heroically succeeded in removing 338,000 British military personnel and 112,000 French forces from the city of Dunkirk, which is the northern most port in France, escaping what Churchill feared would be the greatest military disaster in British history.

With victory only moments away, Hitler ordered his Panzers to halt on the outskirts of Dunkirk. He was afraid his tanks would get bogged down in the marshy terrain. This decision turned out to be a blunder with monumental consequences and a reprieve for the English and French troops trapped between the German forces and the sea. Hitler let Göring talk him into letting the *Luftwaffe* deal with the retreating forces on the beaches. Hitler hadn't counted on the weather turning foul. Cloudy skies limited the *Luftwaffe's* ability to bomb and strafe the beaches and keep the British and French forces from escaping. The three day reprieve allowed Field Marshall John Gort to beef up his forces in the west as a blocking force and established a strong perimeter around the Channel port. For ten days this battle raged. Troops were attacked and ships were sunk, but in the end a disaster had been averted.

Another lesson Göring learned was that it was not going to be as easy as he thought to control the air war. It was the first time the *Luftwaffe* had encountered the Spitfire, and Göring grudgingly recognized them to be a formidable foe.

General Erhard Milch attended a meeting of the *Luftwaffe's* High Command called by Field Marshal Göring. Göring was in a jubilant mood. Euphoric over the capture of Holland, Belgium and Northern France and now with the expulsion of the English expeditionary force at Dunkirk, he felt the war was virtually over.

He knew there were already feelers out from certain French sources concerning terms for an armistice. He consulted Field Marshal Erhard Milch as to what he thought should be the next move. Milch reminded Göring that even though the expeditionary force had lost most of their equipment at Dunkirk the force was still intact. He advised an immediate transfer to the Channel coast of all available *Luftwaffe* forces, and the invasion of Great Britain without delay. He warned Göring that if the English were given three to four weeks to recoup, it would be too late.

Göring at first was cool to the idea, but he finally felt that Milch was right. The following day he presented this plan to Hitler as his own, calling it a blueprint for victory. The answer Hitler gave Göring mystified him. He told Göring the plan was a good one, and would probably succeed, but he did not think it was necessary. He thought England would soon come to the negotiating table. He said he was reluctant to destroy and humiliate England. He genuinely admired the British, their empire and their civilization. As Anglo-Saxons he felt they measured up to his standards of a master race.

Historian Peter Fleming commented on Hitler's ambivalence toward Britain by saying he alternately wanted them on his side and at his feet. Churchill had no such ambivalence. He knew that war was coming and in one of his famous speeches he said: *Let us therefore…so bear ourselves that if the British Empire and the Commonwealth last 1,000 years, men will say 'This was their finest hour.'*

Milch was outraged when he heard what Hitler had decided. However, unknown to Göring and Milch, Hitler had put out peace feelers to London through various neutral sources. Prime Minister Churchill let it be known that he might be interested if the British Empire was preserved as a counterforce to the German Empire so as to provide world equilibrium. The truth was that Churchill was buying time. The man who said, "We shall fight on the beaches, we shall fight on the landing grounds, we shall fight in the fields and in the streets, we shall fight in the hills; we shall never surrender," was not about to agree to appeasement and negotiations with Hitler.

Later, Hitler knew he had misjudged Churchill, and realized he was not going to come to the peace table. Through his evasiveness, Churchill had gained valuable time that England needed to build up her forces.

On 2 July 1940, Hitler decided upon an invasion of England and the operation was given the name *Seelöwe*. (Sea Lion). He felt the only chance for success would require the *Luftwaffe* to first neutralize the RAF and completely destroy British air defenses. He knew Germany would need air supremacy if the invasion was to succeed.

This threw the ball squarely in the lap of *Reichsmarschall* Hermann Göring. Göring was contemptuous of British aircraft and pilots and bragged about the superiority of German planes and their flyers. The crushing blows, with which the *Luftwaffe* was credited in their successful campaigns to date, gave him every right to feel confident.

Seelöwe was to be launched on 15 September 1940. Göring set the *Luftwaffe's* campaign to destroy British air defenses to begin 10 August 1940. The code name given this operation was *Eagles Day*. He promised to render helpless and vulnerable Britain's air defenses before the invasion date.

Germany proved to be over confident. Britain's air defenses were not as weak as Göring had predicted. Although the *Luftwaffe* had an estimated 4,500 first line aircraft to the RAF' 2,900, the protagonists that would decide the *Battle of Britain* were more closely matched in numbers of fighters.

To secure air superiority, Germany unleashed 2,670 planes of the *Luftwaffe* against 1,475 of the Royal Air Force. Churchill knew if they could hang on long enough to keep Germany from gaining air superiority they might be able to weather the storm.

In the month following the evacuation at Dunkirk, Britain built 446 Fighters, at least 100 more than Germany was turning out for the *Luftwaffe*. Also Britain had perfected the all-seeing radar and was far more advanced in this new technology than Germany.

Another tremendous advantage Britain had was that the fighting was on their home ground. When a German plane was shot down the pilot was either captured or killed and was lost to the *Luftwaffe*, whereas when a British pilot was shot down, if he survived, he could be recycled back into action; sometimes within hours. This was crucial since experienced pilots were in short supply on both sides.

The *Luftwaffe* began to concentrate their attacks on RAF airfields. These attacks cost the RAF their greatest casualties. In two weeks, 295 fighters were destroyed, and 171 damaged, but the most serious loss was the loss of 103 pilots killed or missing. Had this continued, England would have undoubtedly lost air supremacy and very likely the war.

As sometimes happens, unlikely events intervene, and the fates of nations are altered. In retaliation for a small raid on Berlin, Hitler, in a rage over his beloved Berlin being bombed, ordered the *Luftwaffe* to bomb London. This marked the turning point in the *Battle of Britain*.

The *Luftwaffe* turned away from the RAF airfield and toward the civilian population of London. British fighters no longer had to fight over their airfields and could concentrate on the great armadas of bombers making their way to London.

Because the *Luftwaffe* did not have long-range fighters, the Me 109's had to operate at the limit of their range and were only able to defend the bombers a few minutes on raids over London.

On 15 September 1940, the RAF attacked a vast formation of bombers. The loss of 60 German aircraft proved to Göring that air supremacy over England was as far away as ever.

The British people's perception of fighter pilots was that they were the saviors of England. Winston Churchill enhanced this feeling when he said, "Never in the field of human conflict was so much owed by so many to so few." These fighter pilots, and Hitler's decision out of anger to change tactics in the air war, proved to be his eventual undoing.

Jacob was only one of many pilots from all around the globe that responded to Britain's call for their services. In addition to pilots from the United States, they came from Belgium, France, Poland, Norway, South Africa, New Zealand, Czechoslovakia, Australia, The Netherlands, Canada, Russia, Yugoslavia, and Denmark. Most were experienced military pilots that had been displaced when their countries were overrun by Germany. Some of these men were so reckless in their thirst for revenge that they were shot down early in their RAF careers. Jacob would soon be flying alongside these men, but he needed to be trained first.

Jacob was on a British Military transport plane bound for England. It was carrying electronic supplies. He felt lucky to hitch a ride on this aircraft rather than make the arduous and dangerous passage on a ship as most RAF recruits were forced to do.

Before they took off, the senior pilot introduced himself as Flight Lieutenant Harold Smyth. Jacob shook his hand and said, "My name is Jacob Halder. It's nice to meet you." The co-pilot was already aboard the plane.

"I understand you have joined our jolly ranks."

"That's right I have."

"Well welcome aboard. We can use the help."

They climbed into the plane and were soon in the air. Jacob was in a jump seat behind the co-pilot. Out of curiosity, Jacob asked some questions about the instruments and controls. Lieutenant Smyth said to the co-pilot, "Why don't you stretch your legs and let the American take your seat?" He was only too glad to comply with that request. Jacob slipped into his seat, and Smyth gave him a quick run down on the planes instruments and controls. Jacob had flown many different types of aircraft and this one was pretty much like all the others.

Smyth said, "Look, old boy, would you mind taking the controls for a few hours? We only had three hours sleep before turning this crate around. Here are the charts. Take her up to 4,500 meters. Our way point is 058. Our destination is St. Johns, Newfoundland, where we will refuel. It is now 0500 Eastern Standard Time. We will pass Halifax, Nova Scotia, on our port side at approximately 0715 Wake me up in two and a half hours." With that, he slumped down in his seat and seemed to fall instantly asleep. The co-pilot, overhearing this conversation, laid down on the floor. Jacob soon heard snoring that competed with the hum of the engines.

Well, I joined the RAF to fly, but didn't know I would be doing so this soon. However, it felt good being at the controls of an airplane again.

It looks like we are right on course. That must be Halifax on the left. Jacob glanced at his watch and it read 0705. *Just a little early,* he thought. *We must have a little tail wind. That's good.* He glanced at his fuel gauge. The plane still had better than three quarters of its fuel left.

Jacob picked up the chart and did some mental calculations. It was a little less than 1,000 miles from New York to St. Johns. St. Johns to England was approximately 2,500 miles. That's a long haul. When Jacob first got on board he noticed the plane had auxiliary fuel tanks. *I can see why we will need extra fuel for that last leg, especially if we lose this tail wind.*

Jacob reached over and shook the pilot. He hated to wake him, but two and one half hours had passed. Lieutenant Smyth rubbed his face and shook his head to clear the cobwebs.

"That nap felt good, but it was too short."

"Too bad I had to wake you, but we should be only thirty minutes out of St. Johns."

Lieutenant Smyth looked back at his co-pilot, Pilot Officer Cobb, on the floor and yelled at him to wake up and get in the jump seat and buckled up. Cobb staggered to his feet, plopped into his seat and snapped the safety buckle. His head fell forward and he appeared to fall asleep again. They both chuckled and Lieutenant Smyth said, "Let him sleep. It's his turn next."

Smyth made a smooth landing at the St. Johns International Airport. The tower radioed them to follow the truck to the refueling area. A pickup truck with small green flags attached to the fenders and a sign on the tailgate that read, *FOLLOW ME* pulled up in front of them.

While the plane was being refueled they went into the airport café and had something to eat. By the time they were finished, the plane was refueled. Smyth signed the fuel ticket, and they all piled into the plane.

Jacob was in the jump seat now. As they were climbing to altitude, Lieutenant Smyth said, "That was the easy leg. It may get a little hairy when we get near home base. We just never know what will be operating in that sector."

As they neared England, Jacob was still in the jump seat but could see out the windshield, and off in the distance was the English coastline. Their destination was the air base at Westhampnett. Smyth said, "Everyone keep a sharp lookout for any air activity." Jacob's alertness intensified considerably.

Directly ahead at the same altitude, they all saw three planes in the distance coming directly at them. "Look, directly ahead...planes closing fast," Cobb said.

"I see them," Smyth replied.

In his headphones Jacob heard a static laced voice say, "Red Rover, Red Rover this is Bluebird 3, we are here to shepherd you home and tuck you in, over."

They all gave a sigh of relief.

"Blue Bird 3 this is Red Rover, lead the way, over."

"How was the crossing? Over"

"Just fine, but we're very low on fuel, over."

"Can you make it to base or do you want to try for an alternate field, over?"

"I believe we can make it if there are no detours, over and out."

Unknown to the escorting fighters, the Germans had launched a surprise attack from the direction of the North Sea. When they arrived at Westhampnett it was under attack.

As they approached the field, they could see the landing strips had been bombed and the craters made it impossible to land. Just as Smyth pulled up, Cobb yelled, "Look out!"

Dead ahead, coming straight at them was an Me 109. Jacob caught a glimpse of the tracers as Smyth violently veered the plane to avoid being hit. It was too late.

Everything next happened so fast it was like watching a movie whose frames were accelerated. Bullets crashed through the Plexiglas windshield and Jacob heard Smyth scream. Blood darkened his shirt at the shoulder. He looked at Cobb, who was slumped in his seat. He could tell he was dead. Blood was everywhere.

Jacob unbuckled his safety belt and lurched forward. He removed the harness from Cobb, dragged him out of his seat, lowered him to the floor, and took his place. Smyth was still fighting the controls with his left hand, as his right arm hung useless. Jacob yelled that he had the controls and Smyth let go. The plane was only a hundred feet off the ground. The right engine was in flames and dead. Jacob knew he had to get the plane down some place fast or the loss of air speed would cause them to crash. He was thankful the fuel tanks were almost empty. *One less danger,* he thought.

They were now directly over a grassy meadow and they hit the ground like a diver belly flopping into a swimming pool. The plane dug into the ground and slid forward leaving a long deep furrow, and finally came to rest. Jacob, who had not had time to buckle up, was thrown into the windshield and knocked out cold.

He awakened with a throbbing headache. He looked around and realized he was in a hospital. He felt his forehead and there was a knot the size of a golf ball under the bandage. Memory of what happened flooded over him and he wondered if Smyth was okay. He knew Cobb had to be dead. Several bullets had riddled his body and he was completely blood soaked. *I owe him my life,* Jacob thought. *He was right in front of me and shielded me from those bullets. If it hadn't been for him I would be dead.*

His thoughts were interrupted as a nurse walked into the room. "Oh, I see you finally decided to wake up. How are you feeling?"

"I'm all right, except for a headache."

"I can imagine. That was a nasty bump on your head. It took eight stitches to close the wound."

"Can you please tell me what happened to Lieutenant Harold Smyth?"

"He's just fine…that is…he did suffer a very bad injury to his shoulder, but he is coming along nicely. He's in the room next to this one, but is still asleep. His arm has been repaired and he's sleeping off the anesthesia.

"Could you tell me what happened to Pilot Officer Cobb?"

"I'm sorry, but he was killed."

"I figured as much."

"Everyone is saying you're a hero."

"Not really. My hero is Pilot Officer Cobb. You know, I don't even know his first name?"

"Charles, I believe. Such a shame…so young. This war is a bloody nuisance." *Bloody is right,* Jacob thought.

CHAPTER 12

▼

"Mr. Halder, my name is Colonel Geoffrey Millburn. Sorry about the reception at Westhampnett. I want to officially welcome you to England and tell you how pleased we are that you are joining our ranks."

"Thank you Colonel. I'm anxious to get started. They tell me I will be released in the morning."

"Good, I'll have a car sent around to pick you up. We are anxious to get started on your training. There are three other American flyers that will be training in your group. I have taken the liberty of having our quartermaster look over your clothing to determine your sizes. A new uniform will be here in the morning for you. We can't have a Pilot Officer in the RAF running around in civilian clothes."

"Thank you Colonel."

"You're welcome Pilot Officer Halder. I'll see you tomorrow."

Wow, a Pilot Officer in the RAF. The same rank held by that unfortunate Charles Cobb. I'm not sure what that rank means, but it's quite a change for this Milwaukee boy.

"Good morning gentlemen. My name is Group Captain David J. Green. May I introduce you to a Supermarine Spitfire Mk I? You will be assigned one of these aircraft after you have learned to fly her, and she will be your constant companion for the duration of the war. Treat her like you would treat your sweetheart, with tender loving care. This fine airplane has a top speed of 362 mph and is powered by a 1,175-hp Rolls-Royce Merlin engine. Its four recessed .303 caliber Browning machine guns and two Hispano 20-mm cannons give it quite a sting.

"Gunfire is guided by a reflector-type GD 5 gun sight. It has a tighter turning radius than any fighter in the world and its range is 350 miles. Its main competition, the German Me 109 has a top speed of 357 mph. It sports a pair of 7.9 mm machine guns and two 20mm cannon. It's a fine aircraft, but its greatest weakness is its range, which is only 410 miles."

"But, sir that's 60 miles better than the Spitfire," Jacob commented.

"That's right, Yank, but the *Messerschmitt's* principal function is to fly escort for their bombers. When you take into consideration the miles they have to cover getting to their target and the number of miles it takes to return to their base, it leaves them only a few minutes of combat time. If you can keep them busy long enough they will run out of fuel and crash before they reach their home base. Our planes rise to meet them after almost half their fuel has been expended. But let me tell you, a few minutes in combat with an Me 109 will seem like forever."

The instructor proceeded to describe and demonstrate every feature of the aircraft, such as the controls, gauges, brakes, landing gear, propeller, ignition, armament, and its handling and flying characteristics.

"All right gentlemen, that will be all for today. Tomorrow we will begin your ground instruction on tactics, radio transmission, and fighter command protocol, location of bases, and the surrounding terrain and so forth."

At the end of two weeks, they were visited by veteran flyers who had experienced combat. These pilots gave lectures on enemy tactics, planes, and pilots. At the end of the lecture, Jacob buttonholed one particular flyer who impressed him most, and pumped him with questions for another hour.

The instructor told them it would be several weeks before they would get into a plane. "The first plane you fly will be a two seat training aircraft," he told them. "The Spitfire is a single seat aircraft so before you fly that aircraft you will train with an instructor in an airplane that is similar in its handling characteristics, but not quite as *hot*."

At 0500, a fully dressed Group Captain Green woke them up with a clanging bell. They sleepily rolled out of bed, showered, shaved, dressed, and went to a breakfast of eggs, toast, marmalade and coffee. There was a lot of excited chatter in anticipation of their first day of flight training.

"This is what I have been waiting for," Jacob said.

"Me too," said fellow recruit John Sellers.

They spent a week flying the trainer with an instructor. They shot take-offs and landings, studied navigation and aerial tactics. At the end of the week they were informed they would begin their training in the Spitfire. Jacob could hardly believe that day was about to arrive. A certain amount of patriotism had influenced Jacob to volunteer to join the RAF, but the real motivation was the opportunity to fly the Spitfire.

Jacob lowered himself into the cockpit. "It was like pulling the aircraft on like a glove. It fit perfectly, was wonderfully compact, and the instruments and controls were easily accessible, which gave him a comfortable and reassuring feeling."[1] He strapped himself in and began his pre-start check. That completed, the Spitfire was now ready to start. He turned the ignition switches on, pressed the starter and boost coil buttons simultaneously, and the engine jumped to life. "The sound from the exhaust stacks and the vibration transformed to the seat of his pants communicated visceral power, almost a desire to go kill something. This creates an impatience to be turned loose for the hunt. He then raised and lowered the flaps. A flip of the parking brake catch releases the brake lever on the spade control grip and the airplane is taxiing with minimal power."[2] Jacob had an overwhelming desire to push the throttle forward and take off, but he was warned only to taxi on this day, so he did. Up and down the field he moved, gingerly getting the feel of the controls and the response of the plane.

After a day of this exercise, their instructor said to them, "Gentlemen, the day you have all been waiting for has arrived. You will take off; fly for one hour and then land. I will be in radio communication with you at all times. If you get in trouble or need any instruction, I'll be as close as your radio. Good luck and be careful. We can't spare any of you or the planes."

This time it was no longer a taxiing exercise. This was the real thing. As soon as his harness was secured, Jacob taxied to just short of the runway, the same way he had practiced so many times before. He could still hear the instructor's repeated warning. Any rapid throttle movement or too much power would nose the Spitfire over. The pre-flight check completed, his harness locked, and canopy open, he taxied onto the active runway and lined up for the take off. As the plane reached a speed of 80 to 90 knots, "liftoff goes almost unnoticed."[3] He raised the landing gear, closed the canopy, and gave it full power. "The earth fell away at a frightening rate"[4] Never had he been in such a powerful aircraft.

---

1. *Warbird History, SPITFIRE*, by Jeffrey L. Ethel and Steve Pace
2. Ibid
3. Ibid
4. Ibid

In the air there are no barriers such as fences or rivers. There are no turns in the highway to follow, or cities to meander through, or any of the other earthbound impediments that automobiles have to deal with. The freedom he felt was intoxicating.

Jacob put the plane through several barrel rolls, loops and other maneuvers they had practiced in the training plane. "This is really flying," he said to himself. He reflected back to the day he soloed, and thought, *what a long way I have come since that day.* He felt that if he could not fly his life would be useless.

He looked at his watch and realized the hour was almost up. Time seemed to fly as fast as the Spitfire. He didn't want the ride to end, but his orders were to limit the flight to one hour.

He began his pre-landing checklist. As he approached the runway, he made a 100-knot curving approach in order to keep the runway in sight as long as possible. Then he lowered the landing gear, opened the canopy, and at 85 knots touched down like a feather and taxied to a parking slot.

Jacob, along with the other trainees, was lined up at attention as Air Marshal Sir Sholto Douglas stood facing them.

"At ease, gentlemen. May I congratulate you on the completion of your flight training? You are now part of the greatest flying organization in the world, the Royal Air Force. Oh, I know the Germans may dispute that statement, but I know better. You are about to become engaged in a struggle so important, so historic that you will only realize its significance from the perspective of time. For the present, however, our task is clear. We must defeat the enemy in the sky or we will have to fight him on the beaches. That we must prevent at all cost. Good luck and God bless you."

That was short and to the point, Jacob thought. A chill ran down his spine as he suddenly realized the time had come to face reality. Up until now it had just been fun. Now it was about to become a deadly serious business. He had seen the statistics. He knew how many planes were lost and how many pilots were killed or wounded. He wondered if he would become one of those statistics.

It's too late now, he thought. He tried to brush those thoughts from his mind.

Jacob and John Sellers were admiring the new shoulder patches just sewn on their uniforms. On each patch was the American spread Eagle embroidered in white against a gray background. Over the top of the spread Eagle are the letters E. S. This patch identified them as members of the American Eagle Squadron. There was an *esprit de corps* among the American flyers and the patch seemed to solidify that feeling.

Jacob had just finished writing a letter to his mother and Eddie when John said, "How about a game of hearts."

"Sure. Go ahead and deal 'em."

Jacob was a little homesick but tried to put thoughts about home out of his mind. He was now in his new quarters in the base at Martlesham Heath. He was glad his best friend, John Sellers, was stationed with him. John was from Kansas City, Kansas. They both had similar backgrounds and a lot in common, which provided for an easy relationship.

The clanging of the alert alarm interrupted Jacob's thoughts. Pandemonium broke loose as men struggled into their parachute packs and raced to their planes where ground crews waited to help them aboard.

Jacob quickly performed the pre-flight checklist he had practiced hundreds of times, and soon his plane, along with all the other fighters at this base, were airborne. While climbing to the designated altitude, he heard the controller providing battle instructions.

"Thirty Jerry bombers and twenty escorts 50 kilometers from base at 5,000 meters, heading is 285. Good hunting."

At take-off, Jacob's heart was pounding. By the time he reached the proper altitude he had settled down a bit. He rehearsed in his mind everything he had read, heard, and learned about combat from veteran flyers, as well as the *Ten Rules for Air Fighting* that were posted on the barracks bulletin board. He had read them so many times he could recite them in his sleep. Even so, he began to review them:

"*1. Wait until you see the whites of their eyes. Fire short bursts of 1-2 seconds and only when your sights are definitely ON. 2. Whilst shooting think of nothing else; brace the whole of the body; have both hands on the stick; concentrate on your ring sight. 3. Always keep a sharp lookout. Keep your finger out. 4. Height gives you the advantage. 5. Always turn and face the attack. 6. Make your decisions promptly. It is better to act quickly even though your tactics are not the best. 7. Never fly straight and level for more than 30 seconds in the combat area. 8. When diving to attack always have a proportion of your formation above to act as top guard. 9. Initiative, aggression, air discipline and teamwork are words that mean something in Air Fighting. 10. Go in quickly. Punch hard and get out.*"[5]

---

5. *American Pilots in the RAF, The WWII Eagle Squadrons,* by Philip D. Caine

I can recite them, but can I perform them? I'll soon find out because here they come.

The Spitfires had the height advantage, so rule number 4 was in their favor. In the earphones, Jacob heard the Squadron leader say, "There are the bombers. Just like a flock of big fat geese. Let's see how many we can *cook*. Tally Ho."

Jacob winged over left and dove straight at the bombers. The last rule, number 10, came to mind. *Go in quickly. Punch hard and get out.*

A Junker 88 came into his sight and he saw tracers spitting at him. He squeezed off a two second burst, and as he pulled up he saw black smoke trailing behind the bomber as it turned over in its death throes.

Coming out of his dive Jacob glanced into the rear view mirror each Spitfire had attached to the top of the windshield outside the canopy. An Me 109 was turning toward him from above on his starboard side, coming up on his tail. *Where did he come from?*

Jacob instinctively began a *Break* maneuver. He throttled back to make a very tight turn. The German, diving from above, was approaching at such a high speed that he could not turn with the Spitfire, and he overshot him. Jacob continued the tight turn, gave his plane full throttle, and was now at the six o'clock position, directly behind the Me 109.

Jacob knew he had to shoot fast because of his deceleration and tight turn. If he missed, the enemy had the advantage. The Me 109 came into his reflective sight and he remembered rule number 2: *Whilst shooting think of nothing else; brace the whole body; have both hands on the stick and concentrate on your ring sight.* This was easier said than done. He had an overwhelming compulsion to keep glancing in the mirror to see if anyone was on *his* tail. That kind of distraction usually allowed the enemy to escape without a shot.

Jacob forced himself to concentrate, and he squeezed off several 1 and 2 second bursts as he struggled to keep the wildly maneuvering Me 109 in his sight. Suddenly a thin streak of black smoke, like a narrow ribbon, streamed out from behind the German plane, and he saw a parachute open as the pilot bailed out. Jacob was glad to see the parachute. He fought to win, not to kill. He knew some would die, but killing gave him no pleasure. He wondered if shooting down the German fighter had been more luck than skill, but he would take a *kill* any way he could get it.

In the distance he could see contrails weaving all over the sky as the battle continued. Jacob called Fighter Command Headquarters for instructions.

"This is Eagle 21 calling Fighter Command, over."

"This is Fighter Command, what is your situation, over."

"Enemy engaged. Two kills on camera. Bombers now approximately 60 kilometers from first encounter. They are still under attack. I can try to re-engage, but would be too low on fuel to return to Martlesham Heath. Need instructions."

"Two kills, splendid. Return to base and refuel so as to be ready to engage bombers when they return."

"Roger, over and out." He knew many of the bombers would get through to their target, but he also knew there would be one less Junker 88 and one less Me 109 to face on their return. He wondered if Sellers was OK. He was feeling pretty good with two *kills* to his credit. *Beginners luck,* he thought. *On the other hand…*

Jacob landed, and the ground crew was all over the Spitfire like a swarm of bees. They refueled the plane, replenished the ammo, and checked everything. There were no discernable hits. He went to his bunk to lie down. He couldn't believe how tired he was. The veterans told him about this post fight letdown. The rush of adrenalin and tension took a heavy toll on one's strength. He reviewed in his mind what had just taken place. During the battle, everything happened so fast that there was no time to be frightened. Now, on reflection, he realized there was real danger out there. He could still see the tracers coming at him from the Junker 88 and the Me 109 that sneaked up behind him gave him the shivers. *Those were real bullets coming at me.* That was a sobering thought.

The sound of fighters returning brought him out of his reverie and he got up and walked outside. Several pilots had congregated near one of the fighters and Jacob watched as their hand motions mimicked the aerial exploits of the battle just concluded.

Others were walking toward him, their helmets in their hands, talking about what they had just experienced. One was crying and being consoled by a flyer on either side of him. Jacob heard the tearful pilot say, "I followed him all the way down and kept screaming at him through the radio to get out, but he just dived straight in…it was horrible. He was my best friend." *Every flyer will have a tale to tell after today's action and we are not through yet,* Jacob thought.

The alarm sounded again and the rush was on. The adrenalin started flowing for the second time that day. Planes roared down the runway in two's and three's until they were all airborne.

Jacob and Sellers' planes were in the first wave. Fighter Command gave them bearing, speed and altitude for intercept.

Jacob felt the plane strain as he pushed it to its limits to get to the required altitude fast. He didn't want to be caught below the enemy. He and Sellers were in the lead, and they saw the enemy first.

"Bogies at one o'clock low," Sellers yelled. Jacob watched the Me 109's that had just arrived to escort the bombers home and climbed to intercept them. He accelerated and dove toward the enemy formation. Sellers fired at the nearest 109. Jacob overtook the same plane from below and fired a half-second burst from about 100 yards. It burst into flames. He then broke away to port and found himself in position for an attack on another Me 109 and gave him a burst. The plane pulled up and dived with smoke pouring out. He thought he saw a man bail out. The plane hit the ground. He saw another Me 109 below, dived on him. He followed him down to 300 meters where he gave him a one-second burst. The Me 109 never pulled out, and he hit the ground as Jacob pulled up.

Back at Martlesham Heath pilots were being debriefed. There was a noisy hum as everyone talked at once to the officers taking notes. Those hits that were on film were proof of a kill. A plane breaking up, exploding, or diving in flames were accepted as a kill. Also, a pilot seen bailing out, a plane crashing, or a crash itself was a confirmation.

Jacob was credited with five kills. A Junker 88 bomber and four Me 109 fighters were confirmed. One more and he will be designated an ace. His excitement over this achievement was dulled by the fact that Sellers didn't make it back. No one seemed to have seen him go down. Jacob hoped for the best, but feared the worst.

That night Jacob wrote to his mom and Eddie. "Not much going on over here. Everything is pretty quiet. Sure do miss you both. The chow is not the same as your home cooking, mom. The English weather is damp, damp, damp. Don't worry about me. It's dullsville over here. Love, Jacob."

When they received this letter, Ilse was overjoyed. "It sounds like he is not in combat. I'm glad for that," Ilse said.

"Yes, that's nice," Eddie replied, but he suspected this letter was for Ilse's benefit. He hid that day's newspaper so Ilse would not see the headlines in the Milwaukee Journal that read, *Three American Eagle Squadron pilots killed.* Eddie frantically read the names and was relieved Jacob's name was not among them.

CHAPTER 13

▼

"You say he got five kills on his first mission. That's unheard of."

"You're right, sir, but they were all confirmed."

"Where is he stationed?"

"At Martlesham Heath, sir."

"I'll tell you what. Send him out on convoy patrol for two weeks."

"But sir, we need pilots like him where he is now, especially with that kind of record."

"Yes I understand, but I have a hunch he needs a little taming. He might think he is indestructible and get careless, believing he can do that on every mission. No, he's much too valuable. Besides, the North Sea will be a challenge and sharpen his skills. By the way, what is his rank?"

"Flight Officer, sir."

"He just became Flight Lieutenant. See to it."

"Yes sir."

Jacob began his new assignment flying convoy patrol, escorting shipping on the North Sea and searching for targets of opportunity.

He was disappointed to be transferred. Patrol here was somewhat boring, but it was a mission in which the hazards were very real. Contact with the enemy was rare, but it did happen. His weather flying skills were tested to the maximum. Take-off and landings were often made in terrible weather conditions, and clouds over water blended into the gray sea and created a condition referred to by pilots as *vertigo*. It could be terrifying as well as fatal.

Jacob was drifting along at minimum speed, darting in and out of the low gray clouds scudding across the water. He was at an altitude of 800 meters circling just below the clouds. The weather was always treacherous on convoy patrol, and flying between a hostile sky and a deadly sea gave him an uneasiness that made his skin crawl.

"What was that?" Jacob said to himself. He thought he saw something out the corner of his eye at eleven o'clock low. *I'd better investigate. It might just be another flock of Cormorants. It will give me something to do besides just loafing along up here.* Jacob heeled over to port in a shallow dive and leveled off in the direction of whatever it was he saw. He is at 500 meters elevation.

Up ahead, to his surprise and satisfaction, he spotted a single *Dornier* 17 lumbering along. "Looking for ships in this area are you?" Jacob said. "Is *he* going to be in for a surprise? Whoops, maybe not." The *Dornier* had spotted the Spitfire and tracers slammed into the left wing. The plane felt sluggish, but Jacob was able to take evasive action by turning to starboard and disappearing into a cloud. The Spitfire was still able to maneuver, but not as well as before being hit. *Careful now, this water is cold, and I don't want a bath.*

Jacob was wary about entering the cloud on the *Dornier's* tail. *I don't want a mid-air collision. Now what would I do if I wanted to evade a Spitfire? I'd go through the cloud and turn back the direction I just came, if it were me.*

Jacob reduced his speed so as to turn as sharply as possible to port and retraced his flight path. This put him on a parallel track with the *Dornier* if he guessed right…and he had. The *Dornier* was in the clear about a 500 meters ahead and just off his port wing.

Jacob gave the Spitfire more throttle, turned port, and the *Dornier* was in his sight. It was a sitting duck. A one second burst and it was all over. Down it went into a gray, watery grave. Jacob felt a tinge of guilt at the slaughter. *They would have gladly finished me off if they had the chance,* he reasoned. He shook the feeling off and headed back toward his base. The wing cover was starting to unravel from the damage caused by the *Dornier,* and he was getting low on fuel. He reduced his speed to the minimum because the plane was bucking and becoming more difficult to control. He was still over water, completely enveloped in clouds, and losing altitude. *I sure don't want to join that Dornier in those icy waters. I wouldn't survive ten minutes.*

"This is Eagle 21 Emergency Homing, please!" Jacob radioed. A calm female voice responded: "Eagle 21, steer ten degrees magnetic for Coltishall." It was like an angel's voice from heaven. *Apparently I have been under radar surveillance ever since I had encountered the Dornier,* Jacob surmised.

Fighter Command vectored him down through the clouds in stair-steps as he watched his altimeter getting closer and closer to the sea level altitude of Colt-ishall. Then they suggested that he lower his wheels and flaps and suddenly, despite the awful visibility, just over his nose he saw the most gorgeous, most beautiful flare path in the world. All he had to do was reduce airspeed, ease back on the stick, land, and roll down the runway.

Finally his North Sea patrol was over and Jacob returned to Martlesham Heath. He was greeted by his buddies and was ecstatic to find out that Sellers had sur-vived the mission. He had been shot down, but he had bailed out and badly sprained his ankle when he hit the ground.

"Good to have you back, Lieutenant," Sellers said.

"It's good to be back. It's especially good to see you're OK."

"I lost a plane, and that makes me sick. They need them so badly."

"They need pilots worse. They can build another Spitfire, but they can't find another John Sellers overnight."

"Yeah, I guess so."

"They gave me a three day pass for a little R & R in London," Jacob said. "Do you think you can wheedle one out of the Commander?"

"Not a chance. They say I'm already on R and R."

"I don't know if I'll even go. I'm anxious for another shot *at Jerry*."

"Don't be a fool, go. You may not get another chance."

"Maybe you're right. It would be nice to get away for a few days rest."

"By the way, congratulations. You're the newest ace in the Squadron," Sellers said.

C H A P T E R   14

On 13 August 1940, Germany was about to launch 1,500 *Junker* 88 and *Dornier* bombers and 250 Me 109 and Me 100 fighters on raids in the east and southeast of England. Their purpose: destroy as many planes and airfields as possible. The Battle of Brittan was about to experience its greatest test.

Karl sat in a ready room along with other fighter pilots. In other ready rooms in this and nearby bases were additional pilots and crewmembers of *Luftwaffe* Bomber Group XXI. They were also being briefed on this mission. Karl had already flown his Me 109 on twenty missions and had shot down seven enemy aircraft, making him one of Germany's aces.

As soon as this force took off from their bases in France, English radar, designated CH for *Chain Home*, began to track them. In the plotting room, members of the Women's Auxiliary Air Force (WAAF), using long rods, moved blocks, each of which represented a German plane, across a giant chart of the area under radar surveillance. In addition to these reports, other reports were being telephoned in from members of the Coast Watching Observer Corps.

From a balcony in the plotting room, overlooking the chart was Air Chief Marshal Sir Hugh Dowding along with his air-controllers. From the time German planes were spotted, their movements were plotted on this chart.

As the WAAF's began to move the symbols across the chart, a battle disposition would be made. In deciding how to allocate his resources, Dowding had at his disposal another asset so secret that not even his subordinates knew of its existence. The British had in its possession a machine that enabled them to decipher the German code. This electro-mechanically operated computer enciphered radio transmissions. A group of British intellectuals, code name the *Baker Street*

Irregulars, had broken the German codes that were sent via this machine. The British code name for the machine, one of the most tightly held secrets during the war, was *Ultra.*

Even before German planes left the ground, radio intercepts were deciphered and available to Dowding. This gave him an enormous advantage in knowing in advance where the most effective places were to position his fighter planes.

"This is going to be a big one sir," said one of the controllers to Dowding.

"Right you are. Better alert the Prime Minister. He will want to be in on this one."

"Yes sir. Right away, sir."

In fifteen minutes Churchill was on the balcony alongside Dowding. They peered down at the chart as the WAAF's moved the blocks. German planes were moving closer to the English shore.

"Are we going to have enough fighters to engage this entire force?" Churchill asked Dowding."

"Just barely, sir. It remains to be seen how effective we are." Churchill was somewhat relieved, even though he was still very worried. Soon the German planes begin to divide and set off in different directions according to their bombing assignments.

Before the German planes lifted off in France, Dowding had a hint of their targets from radio intercepts that had been decoded by the *Ultra* machine, and he had tentatively decided on the positioning of his forces.

When the bombers split, orders went out to the different fighter groups and alarms sent pilots scrambling to their Spitfires and Hurricanes. Their task: knock down as many bombers as they could while avoiding being shot down by the escorting German fighters.

The largest air battle in history was about to begin. Even before the bombers crossed the English coast, British fighters dove at them out of the sun with guns blazing. The German fighters met them, and the dogfights began.

From this clash the sky became a painted, wildly swirling, criss-crossing pattern of vapor trails as opposing planes maneuvered to get a shot at the other. The vulnerable and unwary were quickly eliminated.

In this initial clash, three bombers burst into flames and went down. Black smoke and fire trailed behind them and as they hit the sea their bombs and gasoline tanks exploded into huge, red billowing flames.

Karl pressed his firing button as a Hurricane flashed in front of him, and smoke came from the plane. Karl then committed a cardinal combat sin. He watched, mesmerized, as his kill spiraled out of control and fell. He saw a parachute billow.

Suddenly tracers streaked passed him. He turned violently to his left, but it was too late. His plane was thrown into a spin as his left wing disintegrated. Karl slid the canopy back, unbuckled his harness, and as the swirling plane fell, he struggled to free himself from the cockpit. The centrifugal force threw him against the canopy brace, and his head was cut as he finally fell free. He waited until the last minute to open his chute to avoid being a sitting target for some RAF pilot that wanted to add him to his list of kills.

As he floated down he mentally kicked himself for his lapse of concentration. Blood was running down his face, and he wiped it off with the back of his gloved hand. He looked down to see where he was going to land. It struck him how beautiful and peaceful the English countryside looked. The fields were neat and tidy, with stands of trees here and there. Off about five kilometers was a stately old mansion.

His feet hit the ground, and to break the fall he rolled head over heels and came to a stop sitting up. There was a stiff breeze and the chute began to drag him. He dug his heels into the ground and struggled to undo the harness. He finally succeeded, and the chute floated away as it collapsed on the ground when there was no longer any resistance to hold it open. He stood up and was about to run to a clump of trees nearby and hide when he was startled by a voice behind him that said, "Hold it right there." Karl turned around and there sitting on a beautiful black mare was a mustached English gentleman of about seventy or so. He wore a tweed jacket, riding pants and boots and a sporty looking brimmed hat with a feather in the band. It struck Karl that he could have just stepped out of a magazine ad. The man was aiming a double barrel shotgun at him. A brace of quail hanging by a strip of leather from the back of the saddle discouraged Karl from reaching for his sidearm.

Karl was ordered to very carefully undo the buckle on his shoulder holster and let the holster and gun fall to the ground. This he did, moving very slowly so as not to alarm this imposing figure. He was then ordered to march toward that same mansion he had seen in the distance.

Karl was eventually picked up by a constable, put in a police wagon, taken to the local police station, and locked up. Karl was incensed. He was an officer in the mighty German *Luftwaffe* and a citizen of the greatest power on earth, and these country bumpkins were holding him prisoner in this puny cell.

He was not the only prisoner. Two other *Luftwaffe* flyers had been captured and he was put in the cell with them. One of the prisoners he knew well. He had trained with him. His name is Franz-Walter Vandieken.

"I see they caught you too, Karl, "Franz, said.

"Unfortunately, yes."

"Do you know how well the Group did on the mission?" Franz asked.

"Not really. I got one kill and then some English swine got lucky." Karl would never admit he made a mistake.

"At least we are alive," Franz replied.

"A lot of good that does us. We're useless now."

"I believe you're right. We may spend the rest of the war in prison."

Karl, trying to bolster Franz's spirit, replied with some bravado. "Don't despair. When England is invaded we will be set free and can continue the fight."

"I hope that happens. I don't think we are going to like it here."

Every German POW was interrogated to determine his loyalty to the *Nazi* regime. They were then graded by a color patch that was sewn on their uniform. A white patch meant the person in question had no particular loyalty and was indifferent to National Socialism. A gray patch meant that the prisoner, although not an ardent *Nazi*, had no strong feelings either way. A real hard-core *Nazi* wore a black patch. These prisoners were usually sent to a Scotland prison camp. Karl and Franz both wore such a patch.

"My name is Colonel Charles Ashburn. May I inquire what your name is?" Karl smiled and said, "You speak very good German for an Englishman."

"*Danke.* Do you speak English?"

"Yes I do; we are taught English in school," Karl replied in his best British accent.

"That's very good. You could pass as an Englishman."

"No thank you. I wouldn't want to be thought of as an English swine."

"I see. Well, do you mind telling this English swine your name?"

"My name is *Hauptsturmführer* Karl Müller; my military number is 264 32 677."

"*Hauptsturmführer* is a rank equivalent to the rank of Captain in our military. Isn't that right?"

"You're the expert in such things. But, yes that is correct."

"What is your Squadron number?" Karl did not answer that question.

"Are you being well treated?"

"I have no complaints."

"Good. Would you like a cigarette?"

"No, I don't smoke."

"Good for you. It's a filthy habit, but I can't seem to break it. Do you know where you are? You know, where you are being held?"

"Not specifically, but somewhere in Scotland, I understand."

"That's right. You're in Perth. May I inquire if you have any bothers or sisters?"

"Now that's a stupid question. What military value would that kind of information provide you?"

"None of course, I just wanted to get to know you a little better." Karl thought, *I'll string this fool along for a while. He thinks he is so superior.*

"No, I do not have any brothers or sisters."

"Then you are an only child?"

"If I don't have any brothers or sisters, it should be obvious, even to an Englishman, that I'm an only child."

"Parents both alive?"

"Yes, they were the last time I saw them."

"You were born in Berlin, weren't you?"

"Yes, but how did you know that?"

"As you probably know Berliners have a distinctive accent. Much like a New Yorker, who, even though they speak English, have a distinctive accent, and you are definitely a Berliner."

"I don't know anything about New York."

"You should visit that city sometime. It's an exciting place."

"Maybe I will in the not too distant future," Karl said with a smirk. "After we have conquered England maybe we will begin an offensive there."

"So you really think you can conquer England?"

"Yes and it won't be long now. My uncle told me the time…" Karl stopped in mid-sentence. He realized he was talking too much. *I have to admit the guy is good,* he thought.

"And who is your uncle?"

"Sorry, this conversation is over."

"*Guten Tag, Frau* Müller and *Herr* Müller. My name is *Obersturmführer* Gustav Schreck, may I come in please"

"Of course do come in. What is it *Herr Obersturmführer?*" Friedrich asked.

"I'm afraid I have some bad news for you. Maybe you should sit down."

Freya tightened and let out a pitiful moan. "Oh no. Is it about Karl?" Friedrich put his arm around her and led her to the sofa.

"Yes it is. The news is not all bad, however," Schreck replied trying to soften the blow.

"Your son's plane was shot down over England, and a parachute was seen as the plane was falling. There is no way of knowing if he survived, of course, but if he did he would now be a prisoner of war."

"Oh Friedrich, do you think he is all right?"

"It sounds very hopeful. If he was able to get out of the cockpit and jump and someone saw his chute open, I would think he survived."

"I hope they treat him well. Is there any chance he could be released?" Freya asked."

"No, that would be out of the question. But when we invade England all our people will be rescued and back ready to fight again. If we hear any more we will inform you immediately. I now must get back to my duties." *Obersturmführer* Schreck raised his arm, clicked his heels, and shouted, "*Heil* Hitler."

Friedrich, with very little enthusiasm, said, "*Heil* Hitler," but did not raise his arm. "We want to thank you for coming personally with this news, *Herr* Schreck," Friedrich said.

"It was my duty. *Gut Tag, Frau* Müller, *Herr* Müller."

Jacob was seated by himself in the Officers Club on Bellflower Street in London He had one hand wrapped around a glass of English beer sitting on the table in front of him. He wished the beer was cold, but the English preferred it warm. A pretty English girl with a sultry voice was singing, "When the deep purple falls, over sleepy garden walls and the stars begin to flicker in the sky…"

Wow, does that bring back memories. It was our Jr. Prom and I'm dancing cheek to cheek with the prettiest girl in school…"In the midst of a memory, you wander back to me, breathing my name with a sigh."…Jacob sighed to himself at the thought. *Yes, a memory of you wanders back to me. I wonder where you are tonight?*

He was completely lost in his thoughts. *Let's see, that was five years ago I believe. A lot has happened since that night.*

Colonel Charles Ashburn of British Military Intelligence MI6, was seated at the bar in the same Officer's Club. He was facing a huge mirror hanging on the wall behind the bar and could see everyone in the club by its reflection. He lifted his glass of Scotch to his lips, and his hand froze in mid air before he could even take a sip. He couldn't believe his eyes. Slowly he lowered his glass and whispered, "Bartender, do you have a firearm?"

"No sir, why do you ask?"

"Never mind, do you have any kind of a weapon?"

"No sir, there are no weapons allowed on the premise."

"How fast can you get the military police here?"

"Why the military police, sir? What do you want with them? Everything seems to be in order. It's very peaceful, sir."

"Now you listen to me very carefully. I'm only going to tell you this once. Pick up the telephone and put in a call for the military police."

"Yes sir. What should I tell them, sir?" Ashburn was about to explode, but he kept his voice low and as calm as he could, so as not to attract attention to himself.

"Tell them to get here as fast as they can, you bloody fool."

"Yes sir." With that the bartender walked to the end of the bar, picked up the telephone from a shelf under the bar and dialed.

He covered his mouth to keep from being overheard and whispered into the phone, "This is Corporal Harris at the Bellflower Officers Club on Marley Street. A colonel has just ordered me to phone you and ask you to send the military police by…He didn't say why. He is very agitated and very emphatic…No, there doesn't seem to be any trouble, but please hurry, he looks like he is about to have apoplexy.

"They said they would send someone over right away, sir"

"Thank you, Corporal. I very much appreciate that." Corporal Harris let out a soft breath of relief as he walked away.

Ashburn stared at Jacob in the mirror while he sipped his drink. *He looks so calm, just sitting there drinking a beer. How did he get away, and where did he get that RAF uniform, and what is he doing here?*

Ashburn stood in the foyer of the club by the door. He didn't take his eyes off Jacob. *Where are those bloody police? They would probably take their time even if Hitler was here having a beer.* Finally the door opened and two MP's sauntered in. "Well it's about time. What took you so long?"

"We were told there was no emergency. What can we do for you, sir?

"What you can do for me is to arrest that man sitting over there. The one in the RAF uniform."

"Which man is that, sir?"

"That man, just to your right, the one sitting alone with a beer in front of him." The sergeant thought Ashburn might have had a little too much to drink.

"And what would we be arresting him for, sir?"

"He's an escaped prisoner of war." The sergeant gave Ashburn a skeptical look and said, "Are you sure, sir? What would an escaped prisoner of war be doing here…and in an RAF uniform?"

"I don't know, but we can sort that out after we arrest him."

"Sir, this is a very unusual situation. If I arrest an RAF officer, and he is who he appears to be, I'm in very deep trouble."

"All right, I'm giving you a direct order to arrest that man. Your partner can be a witness to the fact that I ordered you to do so."

The sergeant took a deep breath, looked over at his partner and they began to walk toward Jacob. They stopped at his table, one on either side of him.

"Excuse me sir, but would you please stand up." Jacob looked up at one and then the other and asked, "What for? Who are you?"

"Never mind, just stand up." Jacob, puzzled, put his drink down and stood up. The sergeant patted him down for weapons and said, without much enthusiasm,

"You are under arrest, sir."

"I'm what?"

"You are under arrest sir," he said with a little more authority in his voice.

"What have I done? I've just been sitting here minding my own business, enjoying a beer listening to that lady sing. She's terrific. Why don't you sit down and have a drink on me." Jacob tried to make light of the situation, but the sergeant wasn't buying it. Ashburn was amazed at how cool he was.

A brigadier walked over to see what the disturbance was all about. "I say, what's happening here?" The sergeant looked at Ashburn, hoping he would answer the brigadier's question.

"Sir, I have ordered this man arrested." Ashburn replied. "He is an escaped prisoner of war."

The brigadier looked Jacob up and down and said, "Nonsense. Can't you see he's an American volunteer flying for the RAF. We should be treating him with respect, not arresting him."

"That's what he appears to be sir, but he is in fact a German prisoner of war."

"What is your name, son," the brigadier asked.

"Flight Lieutenant Jacob Halder, sir."

"See, Colonel. There you have it."

"I'm sorry sir, but this man is *Hauptsturmführer* Karl Müller, recently a pilot in the *Luftwaffe.*"

"How do you know that, Colonel?"

"Because, I was the interrogating officer after he was captured."

The brigadier put a finger to his lips and thought that one over. "Hmm…You're certain, Colonel?"

"Yes sir, I am."

"You'd better be, or I'll watch with pleasure at your court martial." Jacob was handcuffed and taken out to the Military Police car. On the way to the station, Ashburn asked Jacob in German,

"How did you manage it? Where did you get that uniform?"

Jacob replied in German, "I haven't the slightest idea what you are talking about, and as for the uniform it was issued to me by your government."

"Ah ha, you do speak German and your accent tells me you are from Berlin."

"Yes, I was born in Berlin."

"I knew it. You *are* Karl Müller. There is no need to pretend any longer."

"You're nuts, and you sure know how to spoil a three day pass."

"Back where I come from, they give you at least one phone call after being arrested," Jacob said.

"That's also true here. Who do you want to talk to, and I'll ring him up."

"I want to talk to Group Commander Jeffery Taylor at Martlesham Heath RAF base."

"That's a toll call."

"I'll be happy to pay for the call. Please hurry, will you?"

"Hello, Commander Taylor, is that you, sir?"

A sleepy voice replied, "Yes it is. Who is this?"

"This is Jacob Halder, sir."

"I thought you were in London."

"I am, sir, but I'm in a little bit of a jam."

"Got drunk and got into a fight, did you?"

"No sir, nothing like that, sir. It's a little confusing. They think I'm an escaped prisoner of war."

"A what?" The suddenly wide awake Commander exclaimed.

"They think I'm an escaped German prisoner of war, sir."

"Are you serious? I haven't got time for games."

"I'm serious sir, and they seem to be also."

"Where are you?"

"I'm in a military compound on Larkspur Street in London, sir"

"Let me talk to the commanding officer."

"There are no officers here right now, only a sergeant, sir"

"When will the commanding officer be there?

"Not until tomorrow morning, sir."

"All right, just sit tight, and I'll get up there as quickly as I can."

"I don't have much of a choice, and thank you sir. It's not very pleasant here."

Taylor flew to London and took a cab to the military compound. The corporal at the desk said, "May I help you sir?"

"Yes you can. I'm Group Commander Jeffery Taylor. I want to see Flight Lieutenant Jacob Halder, who is being held here."

"Who is he, sir?"

"He's one off my officers, you bloody fool."

"No need to get nasty, sir." The sergeant looked at the prisoner roster sheet and said, "I'm sorry sir, but we are not holding anyone here by that name."

"I received a telephone call from Flight Lieutenant Jacob Halder less than three hours ago from this very station. Who is in charge here?"

"Right now I am sir. Everyone of officer rank has left for the night."

"Well you had better get someone here *of officer rank* right away. I got a call from Flight Lieutenant Halder, saying he was being held here on some ridiculous charge of being an escaped prisoner of war."

"Oh, that one sir. You must mean *Hauptsturmführer* Karl Müller."

"I mean Jacob Halder, you bloody fool. Who is this Karl Müller?"

"He's the escaped German prisoner of war, sir."

"Let me talk to this so-called escaped prisoner of war."

"I can't do that without the permission of Captain Kilgrove, sir."

"And how can I get in touch with him."

"He comes on duty at 0800, sir, would you care to wait?"

Taylor looked at his watch, and irritatingly said, "I'll wait."

At promptly 0800, a uniformed officer of about sixty walked in the front door. Taylor got up from the chair he had been trying unsuccessfully to sleep in, and walked toward him.

"Are you Captain Kilgrove?"

"Yes sir, I am. What can I do for you, sir?"

"My name is Group Commander Jeffery Taylor. I'm the Commanding officer at Martlesham Heath RAF base. I got a call from your compound from one of my pilots saying he was being held there on some ridiculous charge of being an escaped prisoner of war. I want him released immediately."

"What is his name, sir?"

"Flight Lieutenant Jacob Halder. I already told that to the sergeant"

"We have no one here by that name, but we are holding a prisoner here on that charge. His name is Karl Müller."

"Let me talk to this so called Karl Müller, and we'll get this sorted out."

"I'm sorry Colonel, but no one is allowed to talk to that prisoner without the permission of Colonel Charles Ashburn of MI6." Taylor exploded.

"How do I get in touch with this Colonel Ashburn?"

"Come into my office sir, and I'll see if I can get him on the telephone for you."

"You'd better, and fast." Captain Kilgrove picked up the telephone, and dialed the number on the card Ashburn left him.

"It's ringing, sir." The seconds ticked by as Taylor nervously tapped his finger on the desk.

"It doesn't sound like...Oh, hello is Colonel Ashburn in please?...I see...not until then. I'm afraid this is an emergency. Can he be reached right away?...Yes it's urgent. Tell him it is in regards to *Hauptsturmführer* Karl Müller...My name is Captain Charles Kilgrove. He has my number." Kilgrove put his hand over the mouthpiece and whispered, "They're going to try and reach him." By now Taylor was pacing up and down the room like a caged tiger, and getting more irritable by the minute.

"Ah, there you are Colonel. I have Commander..." again he put his hand over the mouth piece and said, "What was your name again please sir."

With great effort to control his rising temper, said through clenched teeth, "My name is Colonel Jeffery Taylor!"

"Ah yes, a Colonel Jeffery Taylor is here inquiring about prisoner Karl Müller."

Taylor grabbed the phone from Kilgrove and yelled, "Look here, I've been given the run around all night, and I'm getting sick and tired of playing games. Why are you holding one of my pilots?...I don't know who this Karl Müller guy is, but the man I talked to on the telephone is Flight Lieutenant Jacob Halder, one of my pilots.

"No I have not seen him yet. I've been refused permission to see him on your orders...Yes, you better get down here fast. I want to see your face when I'm talking to you." With that Taylor slammed the phone down and said to Kilgrove, "I want to see Flight Lieutenant Halder right now."

"I'm sorry sir, but like I told you before, I cannot allow you to see the prisoner without Colonel Ashburn's permission."

Taylor could hardly contain himself, as he shouted, "Stop referring to him as a prisoner. He is in fact an American pilot who came to this country at great personal risk to fly with the RAF, and to be treated like this is a travesty. If you don't let me see him right away, I'll tear this place apart until I find him!"

Kilgrove caught the eye of his clerk and motioned with his head toward the door. The clerk got up, and in short order two husky military policemen came into the room followed by the clerk.

"Have a seat, Colonel; I'm sure we'll be able to sort this out when Colonel Ashburn arrives." Taylor eyed the policeman, and decided it might be better to cool down and just wait.

Ashburn had his car pick him up at the curb. The conversation with Taylor had put a dent in his confidence. *That has got to be Karl Müller. I'm sure of it; at least I'm quite sure of it. I couldn't have made a mistake.* Ashburn was giving himself a little pep talk before the confrontation with Taylor.

"Colonel Taylor, this is Colonel Ashburn," said Captain Kilgrove as he introduced the two men. Ashburn extended his hand, but Taylor just ignored it.

"I'd like to know why you had one of my men arrested."

"This man you claim is…what was the name?…Oh yes, I remember, Flight Lieutenant Jacob Halder. What makes you think that the man we have in custody is one of your officers?"

"Because I talked to him on the telephone several hours ago and I recognized his voice. We discussed things only he could have known."

"Hmm…That is interesting."

"What makes *you* think he is this Karl Müller to whom you keep referring?"

"My belief is based on the fact that I was the interrogating officer after his capture. He was shot down in a raid over North Weald."

"Why don't you just bring this man we are arguing about out here so we can get this settled once and for all?"

"Good idea. Bring in the prisoner, Captain Kilgrove," Ashburn instructed. While they were waiting for Jacob, Ashburn asked, "How long have you known the officer you have been referring to as Flight Lieutenant Jacob Halder, Colonel Taylor?"

Taylor opened his briefcase and took out a file. He thumbed through several pages and said, "Since June 3, 1940." Here is his personnel file. It contains everything to be known about this man. Every American RAF volunteer is vetted before they are accepted. Here, take the file. Read it from cover to cover if you can read. I understand you are an Intelligence officer. Why don't you use some now? If this doesn't convince you that you have made a major blunder then *Intelligence Officer* is a misnomer."

Ashburn, now somewhat shaken, took the file, opened it, and began to read. The more he read, the more disturbed he became. There was Jacob's picture, place and date of birth, names of his father and mother, and their address, where he went to school…everything. He just stared at the file. *What have I done?* His concentration was interrupted as Jacob was escorted into the room. Taylor rushed over and took his hand.

"Boy, it's sure good to see you, Colonel, sir."

"It's good to see you as well, Flight Lieutenant Halder," Taylor said with emphasis on his name and rank.

"I can't say I'm too happy to see you, Colonel Ashburn," Jacob said.

"Sit down, please. I'd like to ask you a few questions."

"Anything to get this straightened out." Jacob remained standing. "What do you want to know?"

"I see your mother's name is Kelm, but you go by the name of Halder."

"That's right, my father was killed in World War I, and my mother remarried. My stepfather's name is Eddie Halder. He adopted me after he married my mother, and I took his name."

"That's all in the file," Taylor snarled.

"I see." Ashburn flipped through a few more pages in the file, trying to buy a little time, wondering how he was going to extricate himself from this mess. The words of the brigadier come back to haunt him.

Finally he took a deep breath and said, "It appears I owe you a profound apology Lieutenant. You could be Karl Müller's twin, you look so much like him. I seem to have made a terrible mistake, an honest one mind you, and I am sincerely sorry."

There was an awkward silence and finally Jacob said, "Well, I guess nobody's perfect, Colonel. Apology accepted, but you sure screwed up my leave."

"I want to apologize to you also, Colonel Taylor, for dragging you all the way to London away from your duties." Taylor was not as mollified as Jacob and didn't reply.

"You haven't heard the last of this, Colonel. This is a major screw up. I've wasted enough time here, and I've got to get back to my base. Can you arrange a ride for me to my plane, Captain Kilgrove?"

"Let me take you, Colonel. I have a car outside waiting for me," Ashburn said. "Also Colonel, would it be possible for you to extend Lieutenant Halder's pass one more day to make up for the day he missed by my stupid blunder? I'd like to make it up to him by inviting him to my parent's estate near Coventry. We have horses to ride, quail to shoot and fish to catch. The food is excellent, and he can relax to his hearts content."

"I'll extend the pass, but where he spends his time is up to him."

"How does that sound to you, Lieutenant Halder?" Ashburn asked.

"It sounds pretty interesting. Maybe I'll take you up on it."

"Well, that's settled. Let's get Colonel Taylor back to his plane."

CHAPTER 15

▼

After dropping off Colonel Taylor, Ashburn said to Jacob, "Lieutenant, I need to stop by my office for a few minutes and then we can be on our way to Coventry."

"That's fine by me Colonel; I'm just along for the ride."

"Ah, here we are. This is where I spend a great deal of my time. Come on in, Lieutenant." They took a lift to the second floor. There were British Military personnel on the lift, in the halls, and in every office they passed, Jacob observed.

"This building houses most of the Military Intelligence personnel of MI6, except of course our field staff."

"Quite a layout," Jacob commented.

"Here's my office. It will only take a few minutes. I need to let my staff know where I'll be the next few days." As they walked in, a pretty woman in a tailored military uniform approached them and handed an envelope to Colonel Ashburn.

"Lieutenant, this is my secretary, Miss Jones. This, Miss Jones, is Flight Lieutenant Jacob Halder."

"I'm pleased to meet you Lieutenant."

"Likewise Miss Jones."

"Miss Jones would you get the Lieutenant a cup of tea while I pick up a few things from my desk."

"Certainly sir, come this way Lieutenant." Colonel Ashburn opened the door to his office and disappeared inside. He quickly tore open the envelope and read the telegram. "Concerning your inquiry one Karl Müller, military number 264 32 677, this prisoner still under detention this facility. Regards, Major David Milne."

Well, that's that. If I hadn't gone off half-cocked and checked with Milne in the first place, I wouldn't have made an ass of myself. I'll know better next time, if there is a next time. I hope that brigadier doesn't get wind of this.

"Are you ready, Lieutenant?"

"Yes sir."

"Miss Jones, I'll be at my parent's home until Saturday. You know how to get in touch with me if the need arises."

"Yes sir. Have a nice holiday." *Holiday! This is business,* Ashburn was about to say.

"It was nice making your acquaintance, Miss Jones, and thanks for the tea."

"You're welcome, Lieutenant. It was nice meeting you also."

Driving through London was not so easy these days. Many buildings along the way were in ruins from the constant bombing. They were sidetracked by detour after detour.

"It's terrible what is happening to this city. I feel a little guilty going on a holiday when I would be more useful in my Spitfire knocking off a few German bombers."

"I can understand your feelings, but you will be more effective when you get back by getting a little relaxation. It may even save your life. It must be a high-stress business you're in, and a little rest will sharpen your reflexes"

"I guess you're right, but it still bothers me, sir"

"Well, let's forget about the war for a few days. It will still be there when you get back to Martlesham Heath. You can forget the *sir* bit. I've never been impressed by rank."

"Thank you si…Whoops, it's a hard habit to break."

"So, you were born in Berlin. Do you remember very much about the city?"

"Some, but not a lot. I was only seven years old when we immigrated to America. We settled in Milwaukee, and lived with my great aunt and uncle until my mother remarried. Milwaukee is a great place in which to grow up. That's where I fell in love with flying. Eddie, my step dad, took me up soon after we arrived. He taught me how to fly, you know."

"No I didn't know. What else do you remember about Berlin?"

"I remember going to the zoo on my seventh birthday. I also remember the place where we lived and the family we rented a room from. Their names are Jellinek, Lisa and Emil Jellinek. They have three children. Mom wrote to them regularly until the war stopped any correspondence. Emil worked for the government…in the Division of Records, I believe." This bit of information sent Ashburn's interest soaring.

"Do you know if he still works there?"

"Not really. I believe he did the last we heard."

"About how old would he be now?"

"Golly, I'm not sure. He's probably 50 or so. I remember my mother saying she would be forever in their debt for what they did for her and me. I sure hope they're OK."

"*Sie sprechen die Deutsch Sprache sehr gut.*"

"You speak pretty good German yourself, but you do not have a Berlin accent."

"But you do."

"*Meine Mutter wollte die deutsche Sprache zwischen uns lebendig erhalten. Darum habend wir viel deutsch miteinander gesprochen*" (My mother wanted to keep the German language alive between us, so we spoke German to one another quite a lot).

"You speak it like a native Berliner."

"I am a native Berliner…or at least I was."

"How do you feel about shooting down Germans?"

"I try not to make it personal. It's a contest. A deadly one, mind you. I fight to win because if I lose I could lose a lot, like my life."

"But you take the risk anyway, knowing that any one mission may be your last?"

"When you are up there at the controls of the world's greatest airplane you feel indestructible. It never crosses my mind that I might get shot down…only that the other guy will lose."

"That's a great philosophy. I hope for you it is always the reality."

"Thank you, Colonel. You're not such a bad guy after all." They both laughed at that.

CHAPTER 16

▼

Upon hearing of the attack on Pearl Harbor, Churchill said, "What a horrible tragedy, but a fortunate one for us. The Americans will be in it now. Get Roosevelt on the telephone," he told his adjutant.

"Mr. President, my deepest sympathies for the loss of the brave men at Pearl Harbor as well as the loss of a significant part of your fleet."

"Thank you, Mr. Prime Minister. We can build new ships, but we cannot restore those gallant men to their loved ones. Japan will pay dearly for this dastardly deed. Every American is incensed by its perfidy."

"What will you do now?"

"In the morning, I'll address a joint session of Congress and declare war upon Japan. The whole might of this nation will avenge this loss."

"I'll look forward to your speech. Let's keep in touch as events unfold."

"That we will do, I promise you. Good evening and thank you for calling."

Jacob and Sellers listened intently as Roosevelt addressed the nation.

"Yesterday, December 7, 1941, a date that will live in infamy, the United States of America was suddenly and deliberately attacked by naval and air forces of the Empire of Japan..."

"It looks like we'll be in for a lot of changes around here. New command, different aircraft, different uniforms, you name it, everything is going to be different," Sellers said.

"You're probably right, but Roosevelt did not include Germany or any of the other Axis nations in his declaration of war; just Japan."

"True, but it's just a matter of time before the United States is at war with Germany. That's what we want and certainly that's what England needs."

On December 11, 1941, Hitler, to the surprise of the whole world, and to the consternation of his own General Staff, declared war on the United States and the United States responded with its own declaration of war against Germany and Italy. Congress then empowered its armed forces to operate anywhere in the world.

Upon hearing this news, Churchill's spirits soared. Addressing his staff Churchill said, "Hitler has just made the biggest blunder of his career. He must be mad. He just sealed his fate. There is much to be done, but we can take heart at this turn of events. The task will not be easy, but we *will* be victorious in the end."

A country that had been so divided over becoming embroiled in war in Europe was so incensed by the sneak attack on Pearl Harbor, and Germany's declaration of war, that overnight the American people were united in a way that seemed impossible just a few days before.

▼

CHAPTER 17

"We *must* take the risk, sir," Ashburn said.

"The risk may be too great," replied General Percival Shaw.

"The greater risk is not to try, sir."

"Maybe you're right. Now the Americans are in it, we will need to run this by them."

"Of course. Do I have your permission to approach them, general?"

"Go ahead. See if they agree or think you are bonkers."

"Thank you sir, I'll contact them immediately. This operation will be so sensitive that secrecy is paramount. May I suggest that only those at the very highest level be aware of its existence. It could backfire if there was a leak or if a mole discovered the operation."

"Who do you propose should be in the know?"

"Here is a list, sir."

"Well, you *have* thought this through." General Shaw read the list. It included himself; Ashburn; Churchill; General Allen Brooke, Chief of the Imperial Staff; Roosevelt; General George C. Marshall, Chairman of the American Joint Chiefs of Staff; William J. Donavan, head of the Office of Strategic Services (OSS); and Dwight D. Eisenhower.

"Is that all?"

"Yes sir."

"That's a pretty exclusive list. Who is going to train this man? Won't they need to know?"

"They will only know he is being trained for a mission, but will not know any of the particulars. Everyone at that level will be compartmentalized. No one will know what the others are doing."

"Does he have any training in this sort of thing?"

"No sir, he does not, but he is very smart and has many of the assets needed for the assignment. We can provide him with training by experts of every sort. It will be very intense so we can insert him at the earliest, but safest moment. A crash course you might say. Nothing will be spared in getting him ready. If it succeeds, and I think it will, we will have planted a dagger in the heart of the enemy."

"Which of the Americans will you contact first?"

"I'll start with Donavan. He of all of them should grasp the significance of the operation, and be able to convince Roosevelt of its importance. They don't call him *Wild Bill* for his bashfulness. It's right up his alley. If the Americans agree, it will be up to you, sir, to get Churchill on board."

"I can do that. Just let me know if the Americans agree. What if we make all this fuss and the boy isn't interested?"

"Just leave that to me. I'm a pretty good salesman."

Ashburn was on the next available military plane to Washington. All the way across the Atlantic, his mind was churning with ideas. He made notes about the ones that seemed feasible and discarded the others. He arrived exhausted, but excited. The British ambassador met him as he deplaned.

"Welcome to America, Colonel. How was the crossing?"

"Uneventful, thank goodness, but long."

"I'm glad you arrived safely. I've arranged an appointment early in the morning with Mr. Donavan."

"Thank you, sir. I'm looking forward to this meeting."

"What's it all about, Colonel?"

"Sorry sir. I'm not at liberty to say. It's very hush-hush."

"I see. There's a lot of that these days. If there is any thing I can do while you're here let me know."

"May I help you sir?"

"Yes, I have an appointment with Mr. Donavan."

"And your name, sir?"

"Colonel Charles Ashburn."

"Yes, Colonel. Mr. Donavan is expecting you. Right this way sir."

Ashburn was ushered into Donavan's office. He was struck by the simplicity of the furnishings. *Standard government issue, no doubt.* A small table with six chairs surrounding it was on one side of the room. Several file cabinets were standing against the wall on the opposite side. In the center of the room was a large desk and behind it a comfortable looking leather high back chair, in which Donavan was sitting. It seemed ostentatious alongside the other pieces.

The desk was uncluttered except for a pen set; a yellow legal writing pad, on which Donavan was writing; and three telephones. One was red the other two were black. He thought he knew to whom that red line was connected. He could only imagine the secrets that were inside the head of the man that was seated behind the desk.

As he entered, Donavan looked up, stopped writing, turned the pad over, and came around the desk to shake hands.

"Colonel Ashburn, welcome to Washington. I'm glad you came. I'm anxious to talk to you. I hope we can work more closely with British Intelligence now that we have entered the war. I have a lot of catching up to do, so prepare yourself for a million questions."

"I'll be happy to accommodate you the best I can, sir. I'm sure I'll be asking you just as many. It's in both our interests to coordinate our efforts."

"Yes, I agree. Ambassador Gailbraith said you had a proposal you wanted to discuss with me. Tell me about it."

"Thank you, sir. I'd be delighted."

Ashburn proceeded to relate the story about Jacob Halder and Karl Müller. Donavan listened intently, occasionally asking questions and making notes on the yellow pad on which he had been writing.

When Ashburn had finished, Donavan put his hands behind the back of his head, leaned back in his chair, and stared into space over the head of Ashburn. After a few seconds, Donavan leaned forward, looked Ashburn directly in the eye and said, "That's an amazing story. The possibilities are endless. My mouth is watering over the kind of information this could provide. What can I do to help?"

"First, as I mentioned, Jacob Halder is an American citizen. He was a volunteer with the RAF. Now that America is in the war I'm sure he and the other American RAF volunteers will be transferred to the United States Army Air Forces. So, we need American approval to approach him. He's an outstanding pilot; an Ace, as a matter of fact. It will take some pretty persuasive arguments to get him to accept this kind of an assignment. Not because he would be afraid, mind you. He's proved his bravery, but because he will have to give up flying, which he loves with a passion.

"Second, as you can realize, if this works he will be our most valuable agent in Germany. His mission must be kept a very closely guarded secret. Here is a list of people that we recommend should only know of its existence."

Ashburn handed Donavan the same list he had prepared for General Shaw. Donavan read it and handed it back.

"That's a pretty short list, but I think you're right to limit it to as few people as possible. We can't be too careful protecting this kind of an asset. The fewer people that know, the safer it will be."

"General Shaw will discuss this operation with Churchill the minute we have American approval. He's awaiting my call. If Prime Minister Churchill and President Roosevelt approve the plan everything will be put in motion. Would you talk to your President as soon as possible?"

"Absolutely, I only need pick up that telephone," *I was correct in my assessment of that red telephone,* Ashburn remembered.

"When and if we get approval from both sides, I suggest you and I brief those under our respective countries. Everyone should be cautioned that any reference to this operation be kept to only those on the list and no one else. Everything connected with it should be classified as TOP SECRET and any correspondence should be marked *For Eyes Only* of the recipient," Ashburn commented.

"Without question, that is vital," Donavan agreed.

"We need a code name for this operation," Ashburn said. "Do you have any in mind?"

"Not really," replied Donavan. "Do you?"

"Yes, I do. I'd like to call it *Serendipity.* The word, as you know, means making fortunate discoveries accidentally."

"That fits the situation perfectly. Operation *Serendipity* it is."

CHAPTER 18

▼

Colonel Charles Ashburn and General Percival Shaw presented themselves at the gate to the military prison in Perth. As the automobile stopped at the gate a guard stepped forward, and upon seeing General Shaw, saluted and asked, "May I help you sir."

"We are here to see Major David Milne," General Shaw replied.

"Do you have an appointment, sir?" the guard asked.

"No, we do not, but I believe the Major will see us."

"What are your names, sir?"

"We are General Percival Shaw and Colonel Charles Ashburn," General Shaw replied.

"Do you have identification, sir?" Both Shaw and Ashburn handed him their military identification cards. The sergeant looked at their photos and then at them. Satisfied that they were who they claimed to be, he said, "Just one moment, sir." He picked up the telephone, and told the person on the end of the line to inform Major Milne that two officers, a General Shaw and Colonel Ashburn, were requesting an audience with him. After a few seconds the sergeant was informed that an escort would meet them at the gate.

"May I compliment you on your security? Have you had any prisoner escape from this compound?" Ashburn asked.

"Not to my knowledge, sir. Most of them seem to be very satisfied with their situation here. The war is over for them and they're out of danger. They get three meals a day and a warm bed at night."

"Sounds almost good enough to join them," Ashburn commented. *Too bad we will have to spoil their no escape record,* he thought.

"An escort is on its way to lead you to Major Shaw's office, sir."

"Thank you, sergeant. By the way, four other members of our party are due to arrive here in a short while. Would you please direct them to Major Milne's office as well?"

"Yes sir. I'll do that if they have proper identification."

"I believe you will find everything in order."

In a few minutes a vehicle pulled up at the gate, and the driver motioned them to follow him. After a short distance the escorting vehicle stopped at a small building. As they got out of the car, Major Milne stepped forward and greeted them personally.

"Welcome General Shaw, sir. We don't often have a general visit us. And Colonel Ashburn it's nice to finally get to meet you personally. What can I do for you gentlemen?" Ashburn answered even though the question was not directed specifically to him.

"May we speak to you privately, Major?"

"Of course, please come inside." They entered a rather austere foyer. Several men were engaged in different activities. Major Milne led them through the room to an inner office where he invited them to sit down.

"Would you like some tea? This is about the time of day I take mine."

"Yes, thank you Major, that would be refreshing," General Shaw replied.

"And to what do I owe this visit?"

"You have a prisoner here we would like to interrogate," Ashburn replied.

"I see, and what is his name?"

"*Obersturmführer* Franz-Walter Vandieken."

"Ah yes. One of the pilots shot down by our RAF. He's in the officer's compound. I can have him brought over right away."

"Major, it's extremely important that he be summoned on some natural pretext. We do not want any other prisoner to know we have talked to him."

"Yes, of course Colonel. Let's see, we routinely have the prisoners report for periodic physical examinations. We could have him brought to the dispensary, which is housed in this building."

"Perfect, could you do that right away?"

"Yes, of course, sir."

"By the way, we are expecting four technicians that will be joining us momentarily. I asked the guard at the gate to have then directed here when they arrive. They are here to plant a microphone in Vandieken and Karl Müller's quarters. One technician will remain to monitor and record their conversation. Others will arrive periodically to relieve him. At least one technician will be on monitoring duty at all times. It will take about an hour to make the installation. When we are through with Vandieken, can you have Müller brought to the dispensary for a physical examination by the real doctor? The doctor must keep him there until the technicians are through with their work. Also it would be most convenient if all the prisoners were excused for yard exercise while the technicians are installing their equipment. One last thing, two of our men posing as German prisoners of war will arrive in approximately 30 minutes. They are very specialized German speaking British agents. We'd like to *plant* them here to keep an eye on Vandieken and Müller. Process them just as you would any other prisoner. They are to be housed as near as possible to Vandieken and Müller's quarters. You are to be the only person to know their true identities. There may be an occasion they need to get word to me quickly. They will complain of a toothache. Have them brought to the dispensary, take their message and call me immediately," Ashburn instructed.

"This all sounds pretty *cloak* and *daggerish*. It seems like I need some kind of authorization for all this."

"And you shall have it. Here, read this," General Shaw said as he handed Major Milne an envelope. The Major opened it and removed a single sheet of paper on which was the letterhead of the Royal Government. It read, *Major Milne: Please extend your fullest cooperation to General Percival Shaw and Colonel Charles Ashburn. Signed Winston Churchill, PM*. Major Milne cleared his throat.

"Huh hum, I rather think this is sufficient." The British are famous for their understatement.

Vandieken was escorted to the dispensary expecting to be examined by a doctor. Instead Ashburn and General Shaw greeted him. Ashburn invited him to sit down. Vandieken had an astonished look on his face and said in German, "Who are you? You are not the regular doctor."

Ashburn replied in German, "You're correct. This will not be a physical examination, but its outcome will have a great deal to do with your health,"

"What do you mean by that?"

"You will understand in a few minutes."

"Will you please speak in English so I know what's going on," said General Shaw.

"Yes, of course, General. Sorry, I wasn't thinking. You heard the general. We'll converse in English."

"I remember you, Colonel. I thought you looked familiar. You interrogated me after I was shot down."

"You have a very good memory. Are they treating you well here?"

"Yes, better than I expected."

"Good, we want that treatment to remain better than you expected. It can change dramatically, however, depending on the outcome of this little chat."

"What do you mean?"

"We'll get to that, just be patient. What we want is your cooperation."

"What kind of cooperation? I'm not a traitor, so if it involves anything that is harmful to the Reich, I will not cooperate with you in any way."

"It will not be harmful to your precious Reich," Ashburn lied. "All we want is to learn some details about Karl Müller. I understand you were acquainted with him before the war, and you know quite a lot about his life."

"Why do you want to know anything about Karl Müller?"

"Let's just say we are interested and would like your help."

"Why don't you ask Karl what you want to know? He knows more about himself than I do."

"We don't want Karl to know we are inquiring about him."

"I'm sorry. I will not help you."

"Oh, you will not, will you? I think you might cooperate after we are through with our little chat."

"What makes you think I'll help you? In fact, I'll inform Karl about your ridiculous request as soon as I see him."

"No you won't."

"What makes you think I won't?"

"Because you would not want your fellow prisoners to know that your mother is a Jew."

Franz went red in the face and shouted, "That is a lie! She is as German as I am!"

"Really, but you are only half German. The other half is Jewish."

"I don't believe you. My mother would have told me if she were a Jew."

"Not really. She and your father did not want you or anyone else to know she is a Jew. You see your father helped her have her name legally changed from Feinstein to Fiedler before they were married. I expect they have held their breath for quite some time hoping this information never sees the light of day."

"I don't believe any of this."

"Oh, but it is quite true. As you know, it's not very healthy to be a Jew in Germany these days or in this prison camp either."

"Where did you get this bogus information?"

"Let's just say we have our sources. I can just imagine the reaction around here when this information is leaked, as well as the reaction in Germany when we see to it that this information gets to the *Gestapo*."

"And how will they find out these lies here?"

"It will come about in a very natural way. A new prisoner will be transferred here who worked in the public records department in Berlin. He will recognize your name and recall seeing a record of your mother's name and lineage change. He will drop this information casually and you can imagine the reaction of your fellow prisoners. How long do you think you will last? One night? A week? I wouldn't give you more than a fortnight."

"No one will believe him. You can't frighten me. This is blackmail."

"And this is war, Franz. Our purpose is not to frighten you, but to help you…help you stay alive. Do you want to take the chance they won't believe this information?"

Franz was silent, deep in thought. He looked subdued. Finally he replied, "What is it you want me to do?"

"Now that's being more cooperative. From time to time we will give you a list of things we want to know about Müller. It must be very boring being a prisoner here. Pleasant conversation between old friends can help the time pass more quickly. It's fortunate you are quartered with Karl. Each of us is egotistical enough to enjoy talking about ourselves, and Karl has an over abundance of egotism." *That's true,* Franz thought to himself. *What can it hurt? It isn't like they are asking me to reveal military information. For some reason they just want to know about Karl. What is the harm in that,* he rationalized.

"I'll cooperate on one condition."

"And what condition is that?"

"Double our cigarette ration." Ashburn looked at General Shaw and he nodded.

"Agreed. By the way you are not to say anything to Müller about this conversation. If you do, we will know it as soon as it's out of your mouth. A microphone will be secreted in your quarters. We'll be able to hear every word you say. I realize you could tip Müller off in any number of places outside your quarters. The exercise yard would be a good place or the shower. You could even write him a note. But what you don't know is how we will have you watched. You will be under surveillance every minute, day and night. You won't be able to fart without our knowing it. If you betray us you'll be shot." Both Franz and General Shaw blanched upon hearing that statement.

"Here is a list of things we want to know for now. Memorize them and get us the information. Just ask Karl lots of questions about his life. Get him talking about himself and I'll bet you will hardly be able to get him to shut up. We'll be in contact from time to time with other questions." Franz read the list and handed it back to Ashburn.

"I believe this prisoner is in excellent health. Don't you agree, *doctor*?"

"Yes, and if he takes good care of himself, he will probably remain so." General Shaw replied.

As they left the compound, General Shaw said to Ashburn, "Colonel, we do not shoot prisoners who fail to cooperate with us."

"I know that, and you know that, but Franz does not know that."

CHAPTER 19

▼

At first light on 22 June 1941, Hitler unleashed a surprise attack on Soviet Russia. The code name for this operation was *Barbarossa*. The Soviets were caught completely off guard, even though they had received warnings of such an attack. The Russian Military attaché in Berlin had received an anonymous letter containing the details of the *Barbarossa* directive 21 issued a week earlier. Still Stalin refused to believe Hitler would break the friendship treaty they had signed when Poland was invaded, not because he trusted him, but because he did not believe Hitler was foolish enough to open a second front in the east.

Although the German onslaught was unexpected, Russia was in much higher military preparedness than Hitler thought. Newly appointed chief of the Soviet high command, Marshal Georgi Zhukov, implemented a defensive strategy on a plan developed during the 1930's. Instead of massing his forces near the border, he set up three successive lines of defense reaching more than 150 miles into the interior. He reasoned this would weaken the German offense at each defensive ring and the final defensive forces could then mount a successful counter-attack. However, even these preparations did little to slow the German juggernaut enough.

Hitler had several reasons for attacking the Soviet Union. First and foremost was his hatred of communism. He saw it as a clash between two different ideologies and he was determined to stamp out Bolshevism. Second, he believed that the defeat of the Soviet Union would be a *backdoor* defeat of England. He felt the collapse of Soviet Russia would cause England to give up the struggle. If there were no hope of Russian assistance it would lead to no assistance from the United States.

To avoid the accusation of an unjust war on Russia, Hitler ordered section L, which was the National Defense section of the Supreme Command, or *OKW*, to assemble information on all recent frontier violations and probing by the Russian Army and Air force, and back date them. In that way Hitler could use these violations as a legal excuse for the invasion.

Hitler waited thirty-six hours after the attack to move his Field Headquarters to East Prussia in the Forest of Gorlitz, a few miles east of Rastenburg. He named it *Wolfschanze* (Wolf's Lair). Established in this "HQ 1 area were to be found Hitler and his entourage from State, Party and *Wehrmacht*. The working area consisted of some wooden huts that served as conference rooms, mess, and administrative offices. In general, the inhabitants lived and worked in concrete bunkers which were above ground and contained two more small rooms. Newly constructed roads and tracks criss-crossed the entire area, which was sheltered by thick trees. Hitler's hut and bunker lay at the extreme northern end, all windows as usual facing north, since he disliked the sun."[1]

Prior to the invasion, as far back as 13 March 1941, Hitler began indoctrinating the High Command (*OKW*) with *Special Instructions,* which came to be known as the *Commissar Order.* This called for Soviet Commissars and officials not to be treated as prisoners of war, but "treated as criminals whether they belonged to the armed forces or to the civilian administration. When captured they were to be handed over to the Field Section of the *SD* (for elimination) or if this was not possible, shot on the spot by the troops. When fighting the Soviets, there was no place for soldierly chivalry or out of date notions of military comradeship. This was a struggle in which not only must the Red Army be beaten in the field but communism must be exterminated for all time."[2]

"The German invasion plan called for Field Marshal von Leeb's Army Group North to head for Leningrad; Field Marshal von Bock's Army Group *Centre* to move on Smolensk; Field Marshal von Rundstedt's Army Group South to advance on Kiev."[3] A drive to capture Moscow, the Russian Capital, was to take place only after the aforementioned objectives were obtained. Finland would attack from the north and Romanian troops attacked on 1 July. These armies

---

1. *Inside Hitler's Headquarters*, by Walter Warlimont
2. Ibid
3. Ibid

penetrated deep into Russian territory, which was so vast it seemed almost endless. By 4 July, Hitler believed that for all intents and purposes the Russians had lost the war. This feeling proved to be premature. As time went on there was substantial resistance by the Red Army. "Hitler now began increasingly to take command of operations into his own hands. He appointed himself Supreme Commander of the *Wehrmacht* and Commander-in-Chief of the Army."[4] He declared: "the Russians will not be beaten by large scale victories because they simply do not recognize that they have been beaten. They must therefore be smashed piecemeal by small tactical operations."[5]

4. Ibid
5. Ibid

CHAPTER 20

▼

On 28 September 1942, Eagle Squadron numbers 71, 72, 121 and 133 officially became attached to the United States Army Air Forces.

All the Eagle squadron members were assembled in line review on the parade ground in front of Air Marshall Sir W. Sholto Douglas, KCB, MC, DFC; Major General Carl Spaatz, DFC, DSC; Air Marshal Edwards, RCAF; and Brigadier General Hunter, DFC, DSC. The squadrons were brought to attention, and General Salute was played. The squadrons were then inspected, and Air Chief Marshall Sir Sholto Douglas delivered an address.

In part, he said, "We of Fighter Command deeply regret this parting for in the course of the last eighteen months, we have seen the stuff of which you are made and we could not ask for greater companionship with which to see this fight through to the finish. It is with deep personal regret that I today say *Goodbye* to you whom it has been my privilege to command. You joined us readily and of your own free will when our need was greatest. The U.S. Army Air Forces' gain is very much the RAF's loss."[1]

Thus one chapter closed and another opened. A number of difficult issues had to be addressed. How to deploy these former RAF Eagle Squadron members? What rank should be assigned to each member? What aircraft would they fly?

It was decided that rank and deployment would be made on the merits of each individual's record, leadership qualities, and experience. Since there were no acceptable U.S. Army Air Forces fighter planes yet in England, an aircraft

---

1. *American Pilots in the RAF,* by Phillip P. Caine

exchange package was agreed upon whereby the United States received 200 Spit-fires in exchange for 200 P-51's to be delivered at a later date.

In a week, Jacob received an envelope within which contained a directive informing him that,

1. The Secretary of War has directed the Theater Commander to inform you that the President of the United States has appointed and commissioned you a temporary Captain in the Army of the United States, effective October 23, 1942. This appointment may be vacated at any time by the President and, unless sooner terminated, is for the duration of the present emergency and six months thereafter. Your serial number is 00 103 973.

2. This letter should be retained by you as evidence of your appointment, as no Commissions will be issued during the period of the war. By command of LIEUTENANT GENERAL DWIGHT D. EISENHOWER, Adjutant General of Headquarters of the European Theater of Operations, US Army.

Jacob read the directive with a mixture of sadness and excitement. He did not realize how radically different his role in this war was about to change. It looked to him as though things would pretty much remain the same as before. He held the same rank and he would still be flying his beloved Spitfire. His salary would more than triple, which was a welcome perk, although he would have been willing to fly for just food and shelter.

"Hey, Jacob. Commander Hunter wants you to report to him immediately," Sellers yelled.

"What does he want?"

"I'll be darned if I know. He just said to get Halder over here pronto."

"OK, thanks." Jacob made his way immediately to the Commander's office. The adjutant asked Jacob to wait while he informed the Commander of his arrival. He disappeared into an office and almost immediately the door opened and Major Joseph B. Hunter motioned Jacob to come in. Jacob entered the office, saluted and said, "Captain Jacob Halder, reporting as ordered, sir."

With a somber look on his face, the Major said, "Come on in Captain." Jacob entered the office, wondering for what reason he had been summoned. He couldn't think of anything he had done wrong but was worried by the look on the Major's face. Very gently Major Hunter said, "At ease, Captain. Please take a seat." Suddenly a cold chill went through his entire body. A feeling that something might have happened to his mother or Eddie entered his mind like an uninvited guest.

Jacob couldn't wait for an explanation. He blurted out, "What is it Major, is something wrong?"

"No, not really Captain. It's just that I received a puzzling order for you to report to a Colonel Charles Ashburn at British MI6 Military Intelligence Headquarters in London. The order was signed by no less a person than Lieutenant General Dwight D. Eisenhower."

"How would General Eisenhower know who I am? Of course, I received my commission signed by him, but that was no doubt just a form letter that went out to all American RAF volunteers being reassigned to the U.S. Army Air Forces."

"Obviously, there must be some reason," Hunter replied.

"I do know Colonel Ashburn," Jacob replied. "I met him under some very peculiar circumstances. It was…"

"Hold it right there, Captain. The directive was very specific in its instructions. You and I are not to divulge this order to anyone or to speculate as to its reason to anyone, including myself. I won't lie to you. I'm more than a little curious, but I'm not about to ignore an order from Eisenhower. I've prepared a pass for you for an undetermined period of time. No doubt, I will receive follow up orders as required."

Commander Hunter provided an automobile and driver and Jacob was driven to London. They arrived at 1100 hours. During the entire trip Jacob speculated over what this could be all about. He tried to think of something that might give him a clue but discarded each thought that came to him until he was mentally exhausted.

"Here we are sir. This is the address you gave me. Enjoy your holiday."

"Thank you Sergeant. I appreciate the ride. Have a safe trip back to the base." The driver let Jacob off at the Officer's Club on Bellflower Street. He did not want the driver to know his real destination, as that would have kindled all kinds of speculation.

It felt a little weird standing in front of the Club where he had been arrested at the insistence of Colonel Charles Ashburn. He smiled as he thought about that incident. *Boy, a lot has happened since then.* When the car was out of sight, Jacob hailed a taxi and gave the cabbie the address of British MI6 Military Intelligence Headquarters.

"I have an appointment with Colonel Charles Ashburn." Jacob told the guard.

The guard thumbed through papers on his clipboard and said, "Yes sir, here it is. I'll have you escorted to his office." He motioned to a woman of about 50 in a military uniform and said, "Take this officer to room 252. He's here to see Colonel Ashburn."

"Yes sir. Right this way, sir." Jacob followed her to the lift. He could have found his way to Ashburn's office by himself, having been there before, but he obediently followed his guide.

His pulse picked up a little at the thought of seeing Miss Jones again. He had thought about her often since his last visit here, but didn't know if he would ever see her again. *I don't even know her first name,* he thought. He hoped she was still Ashburn's secretary.

He entered the outer office, and there she was, seated in front of a typewriter. She looked up at him and smiled, and Jacobs' heart beat a little faster. She got up and said, "It's nice to see you again, Captain Halder." *How did she know I was now a Captain? They seem to be very well informed around here.*

"It's also nice to see you again, Miss Jones. You are looking especially radiant today."

Miss Jones blushed just a little and replied, "Thank you Captain. Colonel Ashburn is expecting you. I'll let him know you are here." She knocked on Ashburn's door, opened it, and went in. Ashburn came out almost immediately and greeted Jacob with a handshake.

"Captain, it's really nice to see you again. Come on in, there is someone here who is anxious to meet you." As Jacob entered Ashburn's office, a man of about fifty dressed in a black pinstriped suit and red tie with white stripes got up and, with a big smile on his face, extended his hand to Jacob.

"My name is William J. Donavan. I have very much looked forward to meeting you." Jacob had a puzzled look on his face.

"What's this all about, sir?"

"Have a seat Captain and I'll explain. Jacob, Mr. Donavan is a fellow countryman of yours. He is head of the OSS."

"What is the OSS?"

"It stands for Office of Strategic Services," Donavan replied. "It's a relatively new organization. It's America's Intelligence Service. We are America's counterpart to the British SIS; or Special Intelligence Services."

"This is all very interesting, but what does all this have to do with me, and why am I here?"

"Yes, well this *is* a little different cup of tea. I can't blame you for wondering what this is all about," Ashburn replied.

"You can say that again."

"Well, where should we begin? First, let me ask you a question. If you could do something that would shorten the war and save thousands, maybe hundreds of thousands of lives, would you do it?" Jacob thought that one over. The obvious answer was yes, who wouldn't, but he wanted to know what they were asking.

"What do you mean by that, sir?" Jacob asked.

"Well, I'm sure you remember me making an ass of myself when I had you arrested."

"I'll never forget that, but what has that to do with all this?"

"Do you remember why I had you arrested?"

"Yes. You thought I was an escaped POW named Karl something or other."

"That's right. And why did I think you were Karl Müller?"

"You said I looked just like him. You asked me if I had a twin."

"Quite. Do you have a twin?"

"Not to my knowledge, sir. As far as I know I'm an only child."

"Let me show you a picture of Karl Müller." He handed Jacob a photograph. Jacob took it and stared at the image.

"Does he look familiar?" Jacob kept staring at the photograph. He was visibly shaken.

"He certainly looks a lot like me."

"He looks exactly like you. Wouldn't you agree?" Jacob took a deep breath and said, "Yes sir, I would have to agree, he looks like he could be me."

"You sure you don't have a twin?"

"Like I said, not to my knowledge. I was raised as an only child."

"Let me tell you who this Karl Müller is. We know he is a pilot in the *Luft-waffe*. His father, Friedrich Müller, is a professor of history at the University of Berlin. His mother's name is Freya. Freya's mother has a brother whose name is Wilhelm Canaris. Do you know who he is?"

"No, Colonel, I do not."

"He is head of the *Abwehr*. The *Abwehr* is Germany's Military Intelligence organization. Does all this suggest anything to you?" Jacob let all this information marinate in his mind. He was troubled by the thought of where this was heading.

"I'm not sure. What do you have in mind, Colonel?"

"OK, it's time to put all the cards on the table. No more beating around the bush, so to speak. What we are suggesting is that you become Karl Müller." Jacob was stunned. He tried to speak, but couldn't form the words. He finally found his voice and asked, "How do you propose I do that, and why?"

"The how is by learning everything there is to know about Karl Müller. You will be taught how to walk and talk like him. Even though your voices sound the same, everyone has a unique way of expressing themselves. You will need to learn how to duplicate his mannerisms, know all about his parents, his family life, his relatives and friends. There will be a great deal to learn, the list is almost endless, but I know you can do it"

"And the why?"

"Our plan is to substitute you for Karl Müller and insert you into Germany. Müller is in a prison camp in Perth. When you are fully briefed and prepared we will arrange for you to take his place, escape from the prison camp, and return to Germany."

…"And then what?"

"We're working on a plan to have you transferred from the *Luftwaffe* to the *Abwehr*. If it succeeds, and we think it will, we will have planted a dagger in the heart of the enemy." Ashburn remembered saying these same words to General Shaw.

"You're working on a plan! What if the plan doesn't work and I end up flying *Messerschmitts* shooting down Spitfires? This is crazy."

"The whole purpose of this operation is to put you in a position to provide us with vital military and political intelligence. Only the *Abwehr* can provide that. Trust us. A way will be found." Jacob remained silent; his mind a turmoil of doubt.

"How do you propose to get enough information about Müller for me to be able to impersonate him?"

"We have already started. We have sources in Germany and we have a German prisoner that rooms with Müller at the POW compound who is acting as an agent for us."

"How in the world did you get him to do that?"

"Actually, it wasn't that difficult. Do you remember mentioning the name of Emil Jellinek to me when we first met?"

"Sort of."

"One of our agents recruited him. He hates the *Nazis*. He has been a gold mine of information because of where he works. I don't believe we could pull this off without his help. I know this must sound fantastic to you, but it has been very carefully thought out, and it has a good chance of success."

"How good?" Jacob asked.

"I can't tell you what the odds might be. We've never done this before, but we believe you can do it."

"And if I fail, then what?"

"In war, there are no guarantees. What are the odds of you being shot down in aerial combat or a bomb falling on your barracks while you are asleep?" Jacob mulled that one over and replied,

"I don't know."

"The odds of success become greater depending on how well you perform at becoming Karl Müller. The better you are, the higher the odds. Experts will train you, and nothing will be left to chance. It will be grueling and demanding, but I know you're capable of pulling this off."

"I would like…,"

Ashburn interrupted Jacob saying, "Let me finish before you say anything. You need all the facts before we can expect you to make a decision. Once in Germany, you will be wearing a German military uniform. That means you are out of your normal American uniform and will be considered a spy if you're caught. If you are discovered, you will be executed." Ashburn waited to see what Jacob's reaction was to that. Jacob squirmed a little, but kept his composure.

"I realize how much you enjoy flying and it will be a sacrifice to give that up. Now comes the hardest part." Jacob couldn't think offhand of anything harder than what he had just heard.

"We have taken steps to make sure this operation is extremely hush-hush. Your safety depends on it. Only a handful of people, both American and British will know of its existence. The operation code name is *Serendipity*. Your parents will wonder why they are not hearing from you. They cannot know where you are or what you are doing. A slip of the tongue heard by the wrong people could compromise you. Milwaukee has a large German-American population. Some are sympathetic to Germany. Mr. Donavan has pointed out to me that Germany has informants in that city. Some they know, but they probably do not know them all. If your parents knew where you were or what you were doing, they may inadvertently say something that could cost you your life. How would they feel if that happened? Your parents must be kept completely in the dark about this," Ashburn concluded.

"How can you do that?"

"They will receive a visit from a United States Army Air Forces officer informing them that you have been killed in action," Donovan explained.

Jacob's mouth dropped opened, but he couldn't speak. Tears blurred his eyes. He could only imagine the pain that would cause his mother and Eddie.

"I know this will be difficult, maybe the hardest part of all," Donavan said. "If it wasn't necessary, we wouldn't ask it. When this is all over they will understand. If something happens to you in Germany that…," Donavan stumbled for the right words, "prevents you from coming back safely they will have already mourned your loss. If you return safely, and we expect you will, they will be over-joyed. Captain, I realize this is a lot to take in. What we are asking may seem overwhelming. The opportunity this presents is a rare one. It probably will never present itself again. The results it could bring about are staggering. You have most of the assets it requires. The others can be learned. You speak fluent German with a Berlin accent. You are somewhat familiar with Berlin. You will be able to blend right in. You are familiar with German society to a certain degree, and you are acquainted with the Jellinek's. We cannot order you to take this assignment. It's strictly voluntary. If you say no, you will return to your unit in Debden. We will not think any less of you. You have proved your courage in combat and we are proud to have you serving in the United States Army Air Forces. You have 48 hours to make a decision. After you decide, one way or the other, I must leave to go back to the United States."

Jacob just sat there for a few minutes in stunned silence. He couldn't think of anything more to say. They each shook Jacob's hand and escorted him to the door. He walked out in a daze.

"Well, what do you think?" Ashburn asked Donavan.

"It's hard to say. It's a toss up," Donavan replied.

"We better get started on a plan to have him transferred to the *Abwehr* or this whole thing is a waste of time. If we pull it off, however, the fox will be in the hen house." This suggested a code name for Jacob and *Fox* was officially agreed upon. After Jacob left Ashburn's office he saw Miss Jones looking at him. Jacob's demeanor was somber, and she had a concerned look on her face. On impulse, he said, "Miss Jones would you like to have dinner with me tonight?"

"I'm expected at my parent's home for dinner tonight, but I'm sure they would love to have an American Army Air Forces officer join us. Where are you staying and I'll pick you up?"

"I'm staying at the Officers Club at 14 Bellflower Street, but I feel like I'd be intruding."

"Nonsense, pack a bag for the weekend, and I'll call my parents and tell them to set another plate at the table. I'll pick you up at 1700 hours. See you then."

"That's very nice of you. By the way, I don't even know your first name."

"It's Janet, but my friends call me Jan."

"I like Janet better." She just smiled, and Jacob could have melted. The invitation perked Jacob's spirits up considerably after the somber meeting with Ashburn and Donavan. The prospect of spending the weekend with this beautiful woman made that harsh reality disappear like magic.

Jacob walked out in front of the Officers Club at 1700 hours, and with perfect timing, Janet drove up in a white Rolls Royce convertible, her honey blond hair flying.

"Hi Captain. Hop in."

"Nice car. I've never ridden in one of these before." *How she can afford a car like this on a military secretary's salary is beyond me,* Jacob thought.

As if she had read his mind, she said, "Thanks, I just love it. It's a gift from my parents."

"Wow, you must have some very nice parents."

"They *are* wonderful. I think you'll like them. It will take us about two hours to drive to my parents' place. They live in the country just north of Coventry. I hope you enjoy the drive as much as I do. It's nice to breathe some fresh air after being cooped up in an office all week. I'm a country girl at heart. Don't get me wrong, I love my job, but it's nice to get away for a weekend. Jacob loved the sound of her voice. It had been a long time since he had had a conversation with a girl.

"I hoard my petrol ration all month so I'll have enough to make the round trip. Do you like to drive?"

"I haven't driven a car in a long time, been too busy driving Spitfires."

"Would you like to drive?"

"No thanks, I'll leave that to you. I'd probably embarrass myself. Besides everyone here drives on the wrong side of the road and I might forget I'm in England." Janet just laughed. They drove in silence for a while, and Jacob's thought turned to his conversation with Ashburn and Donavan. *What a turn of events,* he thought. *Am I up to doing what they are asking,* he wondered? *This Müller guy, how come I look just like him? I've heard it said that everyone has a twin somewhere in the world. If that's true, how many people bump into them in the course of their life?*

"A farthing for your thoughts," Janet said.

"They're not worth that much."

"Let me be the judge of that. I have a hunch you were thinking about your meeting with Colonel Ashburn and Mr. Donavan."

"You must be a mind reader. I'd better be careful about what I think." Janet just laughed. *She laughs easily,* Jacob noticed, *and I love that. If she is a mind reader, I hope she knows I think she is something special.*

"I'm really not a mind reader, but I am curious about what Colonel Ashburn and that Mr. Donavan wanted with you."

"I wish I could tell you. I'd like to be able to discuss it with someone, but they asked me not to discuss it with anyone."

"I understand. Most of what goes on within those walls deals with secrets. I'm used to it. We only have a few more kilometers to go and we'll be there."

"The countryside *is* beautiful. I can see why you like it here."

"It rejuvenates my soul. It helps me survive another month in London."

"Tell me a little about your mother and father."

"Well, they're just normal parents. They worry about their daughter being all alone in the big city. Mother is a special friend. We talk about everything when we are together. Father is quite reserved. He was a member of the House of Lords for many years, but he's retired now. He received a knighthood in 1907. He was 50 years old at the time. He's 85 now."

"So, he is Sir Arthur Jones. Is he a duke or something?" Janet just laughed.

"No, he's only an earl."

"Oh, he's only an earl, huh? I believe I'm out of my class."

"Nonsense. Fighter pilots are in a class of their own. They are looked upon as the saviors of England."

"Here we are," Janet said as they turned into a gravel driveway. Up ahead was a huge country estate, a castle actually. Large, neatly trimmed Irish yews lined the driveway. Massive, stately trees were scattered throughout the immense lawn as far as the eye could see. Sheep were grazing on the grass.

"How do you like our lawnmowers?"

"Huh?"

"The sheep, they do a marvelous job keeping the lawn trimmed, as well as providing us with wonderful mutton dinners."

"Oh, I get it. I'm kind of dense." Janet pulled up in front of the stairs leading to the front door and stopped.

"Well, we made it. Come on, let's find Mum and Dad." Jacob got out and stood looking up at the mansion. He quickly looked down as out of the corner of his eye, he saw Janet smiling at him. He thought he must have looked like a hayseed from Iowa looking up at the Empire State building.

"Wow, do you live here? This is something else." They walked up the stairs and, as if by magic, the door opened and there stood a very old man in a butler's uniform.

"Welcome home, Miss Janet," he said.

"Thank you, Jarvis; it's good to be home." Jacob had the feeling he had stumbled onto a movie set. *A castle, a beautiful girl and a butler named Jarvis? Perfect casting,* he thought.

Enter stage left came Mum and Dad. Janet rushed to greet them and gave them a big hug and kiss. Again, it was perfect casting. *There was Lady Edith played by Ethel Barrymore and Sir Arthur Jones played by Sir Arthur Hardwick. Janet could be Joan Fontaine. No, more like Carol Lombard. And let's see. Who am I? David Niven possibly? No, too British. I've got it, Clark Gable.*

Jacob was jarred out of his fantasy when Janet said, "Mother and Father, may I present Captain Jacob Halder. Captain Halder, this is my mother and father." Both of them extended a hand to Jacob and said they were pleased he was joining them for dinner and the weekend.

"Thank you both for allowing me to barge in like this."

"It's our pleasure. Janet has told us a great deal about you, Captain." Janet's father said. Jacob glanced over at Janet. She looked down as she blushed.

"Really, there's not a lot to tell about me."

"On the contrary, an ace fighter pilot keeping the *Hun* at bay, I'd say that tells a lot about you." Jacob looked at Janet and she blushed again.

"Thank you, sir. It's been an interesting experience for me."

"I understand you were a volunteer in the RAF, and by the look of your uniform, I see you are now in the United States Army Air Forces."

"Yes, sir, that change was made just recently."

"Jarvis, take Captain Halder to his room. I suspect he would like to freshen up before dinner."

"Right this way, sir." Jarvis said, as he picked up Jacob's bag and started up the gracefully curving staircase. Jacob thought he should carry the bag instead of letting this ancient person do so. He felt a little awkward, but not knowing what to do, he just followed the butler up the stairs.

Jarvis walked down the hall quite sprightly and opened a door to a bedroom. It was huge. The furniture was off-white with gold antiquing and gray Damask upholstery, which had an oriental design woven into it. The pile on the very pale yellow carpet was so plush he removed his shoes for fear of soiling it. His toes sunk deep into the *savonnerie* carpet. The bed was massive. The sun shone through a huge window, covered with sheer off-white curtains from ceiling to floor, and washed the room in light. Jacob had never seen anything like it or even imagined being welcomed in such opulent surroundings. He was overwhelmed by it all. The bathroom was something else as well. Marble everywhere. A huge tub with gold faucets seemed to invite him to *try me*. He said, "Why not?" He ran the water while he undressed. He poured a little bath oil in the water and foam rose to the surface.

He tested the water with his fingers, stepped in and sank into the steaming cauldron. He hadn't been in a bathtub since leaving home. The feeling was wonderful. He soaked for at least half an hour. He didn't want to get out, but thought Janet might wonder what happened to him. *At least it will give her time to be alone with her parents.*

Finally the water began to cool and he got out and toweled off. The towels were thick and very soft. *I could get used to all this.*

His conversation with Ashburn and General Shaw came to his mind. It kept nagging at him. *I wish I could talk to Janet about it, but of course I can't. Well, I'm going to forget about it until morning, because tonight I have a date with the most beautiful girl I have ever met…and her parents,* he chuckled.

He dressed, checked himself in the mirror, dabbed a little shaving lotion on his freshly shaved face, and headed downstairs.

As he descended the staircase, there she was, standing just below him. She was wearing a soft white billowy dress and she couldn't have looked more beautiful.

"There you are," she said. "I wondered when I'd see you again."

"Sorry I took so long. I fell in love with a bathtub."

An enormous crystal chandelier hanging over the center of a very long table lighted the dining room. There were four place settings at one end. Sir Jones was at the head. Lady Jones was on one side and Janet and Jacob on the other.

Jarvis ladled soup into white porcelain bowls with a crest of arms staring up from the bottom. The soup was cold, which he thought strange, but very tasty.

"Umm, this is very good. What kind of soup is this?" Jacob asked.

"It's vichyssoise," Lady Jones replied.

"What kind of fish is used to make it?"

"No, it's *Vichyssoise,* not Fishyssoise," Lady Jones corrected him. Janet had to turn her head and hold her breath to keep from laughing.

Sir Arthur cleared his throat, "Harrumph, well what's on tap for the main course tonight, Jarvis?"

"Leg of Mutton, Sir."

"Again! This is the third time this week. I should get a beef or two pasturing with those sheep. A man ought to have a steak once in awhile."

"We are fortunate to have anything at all to eat during these times, dear. We should be thankful for what we have."

"Harrumph, of course you're right. This damnable war is a real nuisance."

"Dear, we have a guest."

"Quite, harrumph, sorry for the outburst, old boy." Janet looked at Jacob and stifled a snicker with her hand.

After dinner was over, Jacob thanked them profusely for the wonderful meal. It may have been common for the Joneses, but it was a feast for Jacob.

Jacob and Janet excused themselves and Janet said, "Would you like to go for a walk around the grounds?"

"Yes, I'd love that." She took Jacob by the hand and led him outside. It was still quite warm and the air was fresh.

"I want to apologize for father, sometimes he gets a little carried away."

"No apology needed. I think your parents are great. It makes me think of how much I miss my Mom and Eddie, my step dad."

"Do you hear from them often?"

"Mother writes several times a week. The letters come in batches. I may not get a letter for two weeks and then all of a sudden, I get a handful. Eddie doesn't write as often. I guess mothers are the letter writers." Janet nodded at this.

"How many acres are there on this property?"

"Heavens, I haven't the faintest idea. I've never even thought about it."

"It sure is big. I believe you could just about put the whole city of Milwaukee on it with room to spare."

"Someday, I'd like to see your home town of Milwaukee."

"Really, I'd love to take you there." By now they were far away from the mansion. Jacob still held her hand. They stopped and Jacob looked down at her. She moved closer and tilted her head up. They just looked at one another. Not a word was spoken, but they both knew what was about to happen. Jacob could hardly breathe. He put his arms around her, drew her to him and kissed her with a passion he had never felt before.

Next morning Jacob was up very early. He awoke nagged by the implications of his meeting with Ashburn and Donavan. No one else was stirring. He decided to go for a walk. The decision that he knew he had to make by noon Monday was eating at him and he couldn't sleep. Janet was a new factor in the puzzle now. He was in love for the first time in his life. Oh, he had a crush on his high school sweetheart, but this was entirely different. This was serious.

He came upon a small pond. There was a huge boulder near its bank and he sat down. He looked around at this beautiful setting. It was so tranquil. A fish jumped and the splash startled him. *Why do nations have to go to war? No doubt that question has haunted mankind from the beginning of time.*

As he sat there he was weighing all the factors in the equation of the proposal made to him by Ashburn and Donavan, so he could make a decision. He asked himself the question, A*m I up to what they are asking of me? Yes, I believe I could do it. I would have to give up flying. Am I willing to do that? I don't know. What about Janet? How long would we be separated? No doubt it would be until the war ended. That thought tore him up. Could I really affect the outcome of the war and help save lives?* That really appealed to him. *How would mother and Eddie take the news of my death? That's the most difficult part of all.*

He was so engrossed in his thought he hadn't even heard Janet come up behind him.

"Hi, there you are." Jacob, startled out of his reflections, looked up to see Janet astride a beautiful dappled gray Arabian mare, dressed in a riding habit. She sat the horse like a person that had ridden all her life, which he later learned she had.

"Oh!…hi, I didn't even hear you coming. You sneaked up on me like a phantom Me 109," Jacob said, as she got down off the horse.

"I could tell you were deep in thought. When I couldn't find you I figured you had gone for a walk. Still struggling with your decision?"

"Is it that obvious?"

"You might say so."

"I have to decide by noon Monday. It's not an easy decision."

"I realize you can't discuss it with me, but I have a pretty good idea what it involves. Our department gathers intelligence and that must be what they want you to do."

"I knew you were a mind reader. It's a little scary," Jacob chuckled.

"So, have you decided what to do yet?"

"Not a hundred percent, but I'm leaning toward accepting their proposal. It would mean an entire change in my life. Also I would be away from you for a very long time."

"I was afraid of that. I've become very fond of you, and that doesn't sound very appealing to me."

"Just fond of me?" Jacob laughed.

"Well, maybe more than fond," she grinned.

"Millions are being separated from their loved ones by this war. Why should we be any different?" Jacob asked.

"You're right, of course. But I've just found you, and I don't want to lose you."

"Well, I wouldn't be rushing off right away. There are some things I need to learn. It sounds like I'll be pretty busy, but I bet between the two of us we could persuade our Colonel Ashburn to give us a few moments together."

"He'd better or I'll go on strike," she pouted.

"About last night, I…well…it was wonderful. This may sound a little corny to you, but that kiss was even more exciting than when I soloed. I realize you can't relate to that, but soloing was the most exhilarating thing in my life until we kissed. I guess I'm trying to tell you something…I'm not very good at this sort of thing. I guess what I'm trying to say is…well, I'm in love with you," he blurted out.

"And I with you," Janet said. They kissed again for a very long time. It was a magical setting and Jacob didn't want it to end.

Finally, Jacob got on the horse behind Janet and put his arms around her waist. He wished he could hold onto her forever, and never let go. When they got back to the house Janet's parents had just finished breakfast.

"We didn't know how long you would be, so we just went ahead," Lady Jones said.

"I'm glad you did. Sorry for holding you up. It's easy to lose track of time here, everything is so peaceful."

"Jarvis will serve your breakfast in just a few minutes," Lady Jones said. Jacob and Janet sat down, held hands under the table, and just gazed at one another like a couple of moonstruck puppies. Lady Jones had a knowing smile on her face as she and Sir Arthur left the dining room.

"I believe our daughter is fond of that young Captain," Lady Jones said.

"Really, how can you tell?"

"You'd have to be blind not to see it."

"Hurump, is that so?"

"I don't mean literally. A man just does not seem to sense these things like a woman does."

"Well, these times are much too uncertain to get romantically involved."

"Really, I seem to remember a dashing young cavalry officer that became romantically involved while we were at war."

"Hurump, well that was different...anyway that was a long time ago...and I...well...I guess you're right," Sir Arthur finally admitted. "I just hope he doesn't break her heart by getting himself killed in one of those Spitfires."

"We'll just pray that doesn't happen," Lady Jones replied softly.

After the most wonderful weekend of his life, Jacob accompanied Janet back to London. They arrived at 1120 hours. As they walked into the British MI6 Military Intelligence Headquarters they were astounded by the activity. People were carrying boxes full of files, furniture, office supplies and everything imaginable. Janet stopped one of the workmen and said, "What's going on?"

"We're moving the office out of the city," he replied, "The bombing has become too dangerous here."

They rang for the lift and waited and waited for it to come. Finally just as Janet said, "let's walk up," the lift came. Two men wrestled a desk out of the lift and they got in.

"What a mess, I may be in hot water for being late, but I'm too valuable to fire, at least I hope so." They rode the elevator to the second floor, got off, and entered the outer office where Janet worked. She walked over to Ashburn's office door, knocked, and went in. She shut the door and Jacob waited. It wasn't long before Janet came out with Ashburn following right behind her.

"Ah, there you are. Janet said you had a marvelous weekend. Come on in. I'm anxious to talk to you, actually both of us are." Jacob went into Ashburn's office and he closed the door. Donavan got up and shook Jacob's hand.

"You cut it close, but it's not quite noon yet. Sit down and tell us what you have decided," Donavan said.

"Thank you Mr. Donavan. It has not been an easy decision, but I have decided to accept the assignment on two conditions."

"Really, and what might they be?" Donavan asked anxiously.

"First, that Janet...Miss Jones, that is, is not in trouble for being late to work. It was my fault."

"She is not in trouble," replied Ashburn. She is much too valuable to do without."

"And what's the second condition?" Donavan asked, hoping it would be as easy to accept as the first.

"Instead of informing my parents that I have been killed in action, report that I'm missing in action. That will be sufficient enough reason why I'm unable to write them, and it leaves them with some hope that I may still be alive."

Ashburn and Donavan looked at one another. Ashburn gave a slight nod and Donavan said, "Agreed."

CHAPTER 21

▼

William J. Donavan flew to Washington and reported to Roosevelt. "FDR's talent for intrigue was merely another weapon in the Rooseveltian arsenal, along with his vision, courage, charm and unquenchable spirit that he employed toward laudable ends."[1] Colonel Charles Ashburn reported to Churchill, and *Serendipity* was given the green light. The operation received a top priority rating, and the intelligence machinery of two nations went into high gear. Like a snowball rolling down hill, it started out slowly but soon picked up speed and mass.

Donavan returned to England after getting the OK from Roosevelt. He was a little frazzled by so many time zone changes in such a short time. He tried to sleep on the plane, but so many ideas were rattling around in his head he only caught a few catnaps.

Ashburn and Donavan had been working on the details of the operation from the beginning assuming that Jacob would accept. Experts were identified in every field in which Jacob would need training. A base of operations was secured and the necessary equipment was requisitioned.

The base was located on the outskirts of Perth in an old Scottish Inn. The Inn provided quarters for all the needed personnel and was close to the prison holding Karl Müller and Franz Vandieken. A barbed wire fence was installed around the building and guard shelters were constructed.

The skills Jacob had to master were many and varied. He would have to learn to operate a wireless, understand codes, become familiar with German military rank and protocol, be familiar with German money, recognize relatives, friends

---

1. *Roosevelt's Secret War*, by Joseph E. Persico

and fellow officers, and maybe, most of all, be able to mimic Karl's mannerisms. He must *become* Karl. These were only the obvious ones. The list seemed endless.

Donavan and Ashburn were soon interviewing prospective personnel for training. Those accepted were sworn to secrecy and warned that any breach of security would be dealt with harshly.

Word had been passed to agents already operating in Germany to provide as much information as possible about Karl Müller. They would depend on Vandieken and Müller to supply the rest.

A German Me 109 *Messerschmitt* that had crash-landed in England was restored, and Jacob would learn to fly it just in case that need arose.

Jacob and Janet were having dinner together at her apartment. Jacob was to return to Debden before entering into his new world at Perth. Knowing they would not be seeing one another very often, if at all, for quite some time, their mood was somewhat somber, and a little more restrained and quiet than they were during that idyllic weekend at her parent's home.

"I can hardly stand the thought that I may never see you again," Janet said as she cried softly.

"Hey, that sounds pretty gloomy. Of course you're going to see me again."

"When?"

"When all this is over."

"And when will that be?"

"I wish I knew. We'll just have to take it one day at a time."

"I know. I'm just feeling sorry for myself. I don't want anything to happen to you and I'm frightened."

"I'm going to be fine. Ashburn will keep you informed."

"Jacob."

"What?"

"Let's get married."

"What?"

"I said let's get married."

"That's not practical."

"For once, let's forget about being practical and do something our hearts tell us is right."

"Well, practicality tells us we haven't got time to get married because I'll be leaving tomorrow."

"We could get married tonight."

"We couldn't get married tonight. I'd have to get permission from my commanding officer. We don't have a marriage license, and all the government offices are closed this time of night. And besides, where would we find someone to perform the ceremony?"

"If a way could be found to overcome all those obstacles, would you marry me?"

Jacob felt pretty confident there was no way to solve those problems this time of night so he said, "Yes, of course. Nothing would make me happier."

Janet smiled, picked up the telephone, and dialed…"Hello, this is Janet Jones…He said yes. We'll meet you there in 20 minutes." She hung up and dialed another number…"Hello, this is Janet Jones…He said yes…We'll meet you in 45 minutes." She hung up the telephone and Jacob said, "What was that all about?"

"My dear Captain, your future wife has just outwitted you and that future is only a matter of minutes away. Remember you are an officer and a gentleman and are bound by your word."

"What are you talking about?"

"You said if a way could be found to overcome all the problems you mentioned that we could get married tonight. I have a friend at the public records office and she will meet us at her office and issue us a marriage license. The second call was to the minister of the church I attend, and he has agreed to perform the ceremony."

"But you haven't overcome all the problems I mentioned. What about my commanding officer? I have to get his permission."

"Who is your commanding officer?"

"It's…well, it must be…for crying out loud I'm not sure who my commanding officer is right now."

"If that's the case, let's just get married and you can find out later who that might be. You wouldn't let a technicality keep you from marrying me would you? What are they going to do, court martial you? I think not." Jacob made a few lame excuses, sighed and said,

"I should know better than to underestimate someone that works for the British Intelligence Service."

"You do want to marry me, don't you? I don't want you to feel like I tricked you into this."

"Of course I want to marry you. You are my whole life. I just feel the circumstances are too complicated right now."

"There are times when one must seize the moment. This is one of those times. Life is too fragile and precious to waste by putting things off. The future is too uncertain and I want a few moments of happiness, and the knowledge you are mine through what is sure to be a long separation."

"What about your parents. What will they think?"

"I'm not marrying my parents. They will accept the news with grace. They both like you very much and they know we are in love." Jacob couldn't think of anything more to say. He surrendered to this remarkable woman. He voiced every reason why they shouldn't marry at this time, and she had battled and won. As he looked at her he was happy she had. He thought he was the luckiest person in the world.

"OK, you win. Where should we go on our honeymoon?" Janet squealed, grabbed Jacob and gave him a hard kiss.

"We don't have time to go to Tahiti or your Niagara Falls, so let's just stay here tonight."

"What will your neighbors think when they see a man leaving your apartment in the morning."

"I don't care what they think. If they want to know who you are, I'll scream it from the roof top that you are my husband."

The next day Jacob returned to Debden and reported to the base commander, Major Hunter.

"Well, I see they finally sent you back to us. I'm glad you're here. It's not easy filling a Squadron Leader's slot. We have so many raw recruits coming aboard, we don't have enough veteran pilots to give them the kind of training they need. I won't ask you what happened while you were away, because I know it's none of my business, but that's all in the past now. You're back and that's all that matters."

Oh yeah, Jacob thought. *If he only knew.* He felt a little guilty about having to abandon the Major at a time he was needed so badly, but the die had been cast and he couldn't change course now. The snowball was rushing downhill at breakneck speed and the mass was fast accumulating in the form of personnel, material and intelligence.

"It's nice to be back, Commander," Jacob replied truthfully, trying to exude some enthusiasm into his voice. He almost felt like a traitor knowing what was about to happen.

"In fact, you returned just in time. Weather permitting; we will be escorting a bomber raid on targets in Le Havre in the morning. Right now the weather is marginal. Briefing is at 0430 so you better get some sleep."

"Yes sir. See you in the morning, sir"

Jacob telephoned Ashburn. "That's right…in the morning…we'll probably take off at 0500…Le Havre. It looks like it will be cloudy and foggy over the Channel…I agree…perfect for the situation. Just be sure that *pseudo* German pilot knows what he's doing. I'll have the plane marked tonight. See you soon, I hope!"

Jacob hung up, and went out to find his Spitfire. His mechanic was working on it. "Good evening, Corporal. Everything OK?"

"Yes sir, I'm just giving it a last minute check."

"Very good. I appreciate that very much. I want to thank you for taking such good care of the plane. You have been very professional and very proficient. I'll never forget how well you have taken care of the aircraft."

"Gee, thanks, Captain. That almost sounds like a farewell speech."

"You never know, Corporal."

"Shucks, Captain. Nothing is ever going to happen to you."

"Like I said, you never know. There is one thing I'd like you to do before tomorrow's operation."

"What's that sir?"

"Paint a yellow circle about thirty six inches in diameter on each side of the fuselage."

"What's that for, sir?"

"I want my squadron to be able to quickly identify their squadron leader."

"Yes sir. Consider it done."

"Thank you, Corporal. See you in the morning."

Jacob spent a fitful night and was awake when they were rousted out of bed for breakfast. He quickly got dressed and headed for the mess hall. "It looks like it's a go," Jacob said to Sellers.

"It sure does, the weather looks lousy though."

"I agree, but apparently they don't think it's too bad or we would still be in the sack." They finished breakfast in silence, each keeping his thoughts to himself. After breakfast they headed for the briefing room.

"Good morning gentlemen," said Major Hunter.

"Good morning sir," the men replied in unison.

"Today we will be flying protective escort for our bombers over Le Havre. Operations will provide you with the vector for forming up with the bombers once you are all aloft. Stay in tight and see if we can keep Jerry off of them. They have changed tactics, somewhat, by coming up to attack our underbelly. Keep a sharp look out. If you spot them coming up you should be able to clobber them. If not, you are likely to get a belly full of lead. Good hunting."

Major Hunter stepped back and Captain Johnson cried out, "Pilots man your planes."

The room exploded with the noise of scraping chairs, babbling voices, and pounding feet as they rushed out of the hall and sprinted to their planes.

Flying helmets and parachutes were adjusted as the pilots dashed for their Hurricanes and Spitfires, lovingly made ready by ground crews and mechanics. Engines started, and within seconds planes began to roll in wave after wave as they took off. The coordinates came in over the radio as the planes roared away to form up with the bombers.

Jacob heard his radio come to life and Major Hal Erickson, flight commander announced, "There are the bombers just ahead and to our port side. Move up and take your positions. Easy does it. We don't want any mid-air collisions."

Jacob was on the starboard perimeter, just where he informed Ashburn he would be. He hoped the pilot in the Me 109 could see the yellow markings and knew his job.

Jacob had a sudden pang of regret for agreeing to *Serendipity*. He wished he could finish this mission. It hit him hard as he realized how difficult it was going to be to give up flying, and the thought of his mother and Eddie getting the news that he was missing in action left an empty feeling he couldn't quite shake.

They were approaching the coast of France when over Jacob's radio a voice yelled, "Bogey, 2 o'clock high." Jacob looked up just in time to see the Me 109 come out of the clouds straight at him as tracers sliced the air under him. The 109 slid just below him and banked to the left. Jacob cranked open his canopy slightly, punctured a pressurized smoke canister, heeled over to his right and plunged toward the water below. Black smoke streamed out of the plane and to any observer the plane appeared fatally hit.

Sellers, Jacob's best friend, was so distraught when he saw Jacob's plane go down, he broke formation to follow him, screaming at the top of his voice in his radio to bail out. The flight commander ordered Sellers to get back in formation and he reluctantly pulled up and complied.

Jacob was glued to his altimeter. He was enveloped in fog and his altimeter told him the sea was rushing up fast. He had a sudden feeling of vulnerability. He would have to rely completely on his instruments since the fog was so thick he could not see the ocean surface. He fought the controls and finally leveled off so close to the water, his windshield was momentarily wet from the breaking waves. *That was a close one.* Sweat was dripping from the end of his nose. *That was almost too realistic, and it should have certainly fooled anyone that saw me go down.*

Jacob flew due east. His instructions were to go around Land's End, which was on the southeastern most tip of England, then head north and land at a remote field just north of Pembroke. The Me 109 would precede him to the same location.

Reality seeped into his consciousness. It was too late to back out now. Again realizing this was his last flight, his previous feeling of regret returned. Finally he crossed the English coast. In a few minutes he saw the field where he was to land. He spotted the Me 109 already on the ground. *I'll bet that pilot is glad to get out of that plane,* he mused.

Parked alongside of the Me 109 was a military transport plane, and a short distance away was a van painted with camouflaged markings.

Jacob slid the canopy back, banked to the left keeping the field in view as long as possible, lined up on the landing strip, and smoothly touched down in his beloved Spitfire for the last time. He taxied toward the two planes and the van, shut off the engine, and climbed out. Ashburn greeted him and hustled him into the transport plane.

"Good show. Nice of you to pop by old chap," Ashburn said grinning.

"I'm happy I'm still alive to pop by old chap," Jacob mimicked.

"Seriously, I'm glad you're safe. How did it go?"

"I believe it was realistic enough. Much too realistic, as a matter of fact."

"What do you mean?"

"Never mind, I don't even want to think about it." Jacob noticed a crew of men swarming all over his plane.

"What are they doing?"

"They're painting over all the markings that might identify it as your plane. They are also changing the serial number. After all, your plane is supposed to be on the bottom of the Channel. As soon as they get it detailed it will be flown to a new base for reassignment." This fact did not help Jacob's mood.

The transport plane, with Jacob and Ashburn aboard, taxied onto the strip, did a pre-flight check and took off. Jacob looked down longingly at his plane until he could no longer see it.

An hour and a half later they touched down at Perth. While they were in the air the pilot and co-pilot did not leave their seats. Jacob and Ashburn got off the plane and quickly got into a waiting military vehicle. Ashburn did not want anyone to get a good look at Jacob.

As they drove up to the gate of the training facility Ashburn said, "We're finally here. This will be home for the next several months. I'm afraid it's going to feel a little like a prison, but we have everything here we need. There will be no leave,"

"What about visitors?"

"Not now and maybe not at all. You're going to be so busy you won't have time to think of anything except the things being drilled into your head. At the end of the day you'll be so tired that your bed will be your best friend. Janet will come into your consciousness only when you are unconscious sleeping."

I wonder what he would say if he knew Janet and I were husband and wife. He would probably throw a fit. I hope he doesn't find out. If he does I hope it isn't until I'm in Germany.

"It sounds like sweet dreams to me."

"I suggest you get to bed early because wake up call is 0400. Your first appointment is with our elocutionist."

"Our who?"

"Elocutionist. He is an expert in the style and manner of speaking. He will train you to speak exactly like Karl Müller. While you are here, only German will be spoken, unless we have an expert that is crucial to your training who cannot speak German. After your session with the elocutionist the next person to talk to you will be a surgeon. He will explain his role. Don't worry; it's no big deal. I'll see you sometime tomorrow. Sweet dreams," Ashburn said with a sly smile on his face.

Surprisingly Jacob slept soundly. He went to bed physically and mentally drained and awoke at 0400 refreshed. He showered, dressed and made his way to the dining room. The Inn was a far cry from the military barracks he was used to being housed in. It was more like staying in a hotel.

Seated at the table was a civilian dressed in a suit and tie. He was slight of build, had a well-trimmed mustache and a receding hairline. "*Guten morgen, Hauptstrumführer* Müller. My name is Professor Hans Franke. I believe Colonel Ashburn explained my role, did he not?"

"Yes he did. He said you would teach me how to speak like Karl Müller."

"Not just speak like Karl Müller, but become Karl Müller. There is quite a difference."

They talked as they ate. The professor was listening closely as Jacob spoke. As soon as they finished eating the professor escorted Jacob into a projection room. Jacob didn't realize it then, but much of his time would be spent in that room.

"I'm going to show you some footage taken of Müller surreptitiously at the prison camp. Listen carefully to his voice and inflections."

The professor turned off the lights, started the projector, and sat down. Several symbols flashed by and then two men were shown walking briskly in the exercise yard of what was obviously the prison camp. They were talking as they walked. Jacob was fascinated and somewhat disturbed. He didn't have to be told which one was Karl. It could have been him in the picture.

"This is amazing," Jacob said. "How did you get these pictures?"

"I didn't get them. Colonel Ashburn supplied them. You will have to ask him how he got them, but I'm sure they have their ways. It's quite remarkable not only how much you resemble this Karl Müller, but also how much you sound like him."

"Really, I couldn't tell."

"That's because we hear our own voice differently than others hear it, but take it from me you sound exactly like him. It's as if you were twins." *There was that disturbing statement again.*

"There are a few differences and those we will work on. Much of the difference is in the strength of the voice. Karl is very assertive. He dominates the conversation with whomever he is with. He is used to commanding others. The difference between you and him is how you were reared. He was probably not a very pleasant child. You on the other hand no doubt were."

"You can tell all that from a voice."

"Oh yes, that and much more. Also, notice how animated he is. He uses his hands for emphasis as he talks. The man he is talking to is his roommate. He is submissive, whereas Karl is dominant. Think of this as a play. You will be playing the role of Karl Müller. I've talked to actors that become so absorbed in a role they have a difficult time returning to themselves when the play was over. That is what you must do. Wherever they are sending you, you will be on stage 24 hours a day and you must absorb the role of Karl Müller absolutely. In real life an actor may flub a line and they only throw cabbage at him. In your case the projectiles could be more deadly."

"Are you trying to scare me to death? If so you're doing a good job."

"There is nothing wrong with being a little frightened. Fear is a great motivator. Confidence will keep fear in check, however. We must get you to the point where in your own mind you are in command of any situation that may arise. When you feel that, you will actually relish the performance."

The next several hours were spent in role-playing. The film was shown over and over and Jacob began his acting career.

"That's enough for today. Everyone you talk to from now on you must talk to them the same way you think Müller would talk to them. Do not revert back to Jacob Halder. He no longer exists."

"Yes sir," Jacob replied emphatically.

"Good afternoon, I'm Doctor Harvey Lindeman. I believe Colonel Ashburn told you I would stop by to chat with you."

"Yes, he said a surgeon would be talking to me today," Jacob replied in German. "You must be that surgeon."

"I'm sorry I don't speak German. Could we converse in English?"

"Of course, doctor. Sorry, I didn't know. What can I do for you?"

"It's not what you can do for me it's what I have been asked to do to you."

"And what is that?"

"I'm to duplicate a scar on your left forearm, your head, and a very tiny one at the corner of your right eye."

"You're kidding. What kind of doctor are you?"

"I'm a plastic surgeon."

"What's this all about?"

"Apparently the man you are being made to look like has these scars on his body. Without them someone familiar with this person could tell you are not he."

"I see. I sure didn't know this was part of the deal."

"This will be a very simple procedure. You will be anesthetized and won't feel a thing."

"That's easy for you to say."

"No, really you won't know what's happening. There will be very little pain after the operation and any discomfort can be taken care of with some pain medication. The wounds will heal nicely in just a few weeks."

"When does this take place?"

"This afternoon at 5:30 PM."

"What! You don't give a guy much time to think about it."

"The longer you have to think about it the more disturbed you will become, and you seem to be quite disturbed."

"Id just like to get a little used to the idea."

"I've been told you are on a time schedule and the longer the wounds have a chance to heal the more they will appear to be authentic. Fortunately the scars on the eye and arm are not deep or they would take years of healing to appear the same. The scar on your head and the scar on Müller's head are both more recent injuries. A little alteration and they will appear the same."

Well, I guess it has to be done, but I'm not excited about it as you can tell."

"Someone will drive you to the clinic. Your prep will start at 5:00 PM. I'll see you then."

Doctor Lindeman stood over Jacob and adjusted the operating room light that flooded the operating table. The anesthesiologist monitored Jacob's vital signs as he administered the anesthetic. A photograph of Karl's scars, wrapped in sterilized plastic, lay on Jacob's chest for reference. The doctor made a small incision on the arm and one near the eye. The nurse dabbed at the incisions with gauze dipped in alcohol until the bleeding subsided. The doctor then put a butterfly bandage on the arm and let the tiny incision on the corner of the eye stay open. It was apparent Karl had not had that wound stitched or closed with a bandage because it was so small.

Now came the more difficult procedure; the cut on the forehead. The Doctor had actually examined Karl's head on one of his routine physical examinations at the prison. A nurse had photographed the scar for reference. This scar, fortunately, was more recent than the other two, and was in almost the exact same place, or it would be difficult to make it appear authentic. The doctor made an incision in such a way that made the scar look like it had been injured the same way Karl's was injured. Plastic surgeons are artists, and after 30 minutes the doctor was satisfied. He closed the wound by stitching it securely.

"There now, I believe that will do. You can have an orderly wheel him into the recovery room. I want him monitored carefully. Inform me when he is conscious."

Even though this operation was quite minor, Doctor Lindeman did not want anything to happen to what he understood to be a very important person. It didn't take much imagination for him to understand that Jacob Halder was being substituted for Karl Müller. The Colonel was quite emphatic about him or his staff ever mentioning this operation to anyone. This surgery never happened.

CHAPTER 22

▼

Karl seemed to be in a melancholy and talkative mood. He sounded a little homesick. He said, "Franz, I'm going to tell you a family secret. Promise me you will never tell anyone."

Franz: "I promise, what is it?" Robert Wiley, one of the operators monitoring the conversation between Karl and Vandieken suddenly leaned forward.

Karl: "You were an only child like me. Isn't that right?"

Franz: "Yes, that's correct."

Karl: "Have you ever wondered what it would have been like to have had a brother or sister?"

Franz: "Not really, why?"

Karl: "Well, when I was very small, about six, I overheard my mother and father talking about me when I was born. My mother said she would never get over losing her other baby. She sounded so sad. Apparently I was a twin and my twin brother died at birth."

Franz: "Did you ever ask your parents about it?"

Karl: "No, I assumed they didn't want me to know. I never let on I overheard them."

Franz: "That must have been a sad time for your parents."

Karl: "I'm sure it was." There was silence for about 30 seconds and then Karl said, "I didn't think I would miss my parents, but I do. I'm worried about my father. He's missing, you know."

Franz: "No I didn't know. What happened to him?"

Karl: "I don't know specifically, but I think the *Gestapo* arrested him."

Franz: "That *is* serious. You may never see him again."

Karl: "That's what I'm afraid of." There was silence for several minutes.

Karl: "Franz, did you ever have a secret hiding place? You know, a place where you could escape from the world?"

Franz: "No, did you?"

Karl: "Yes. It was a very unique place. The only people that knew about it besides me were my parents, my grandparents, and our housekeeper. Of course the builder knew, but no one else did.

Franz: "Where was this secret hiding place?"

Karl: "When our house was constructed my father made a private deal with the builder to build a wine cellar, unknown to the architect."

Franz: "A wine cellar, what's so secret about a wine cellar? Lots of people have wine cellars. We even have one."

Karl: "Yes, but how many have a secret entrance?"

Franz: "A secret entrance. Why would you want a secret entrance to a wine cellar?"

Karl: "It wasn't a matter of wanting one, it was because…oh forget it. It's too complicated."

Franz: "Where is this secret entrance?

Karl: "I don't think I should tell you. It wouldn't be very secret if I told you where it was located." Wiley, monitoring the conversation, yelled out loud, "Tell him where the bloody entrance is."

Franz: "I told you I wouldn't tell anyone."

Karl: "Oh well, I guess it's no big deal. It's in the library." Wiley shot his fist in the air and yelled, "Yes, tell us more."

Franz: "Did you ever drink any of the wine?"

Karl: "Not when I was little. I would have been severely punished if my father found out."

Franz: "Then what did you do in the wine cellar if you didn't drink wine?"

Karl: "I pretended I was a spy. My father let me set up a small table to use. I would write secret messages using lemon juice. My Uncle Wilhelm taught me how. When the lemon juice dries, it's invisible. When the paper is heated, the words appear like magic. It sounds childish now, but it was great fun at the time."

Franz: "But where in the library is the door?" "Tell him, my boy," Wiley shouted.

Karl: "On either side of the fireplace are carved walnut panels. Around the outside edge of the panels is a row of rosettes. When one of them is slid down, and another one below it is slid up, it unlocks the door and the door then pivots open to a landing leading down to the cellar."

"Tell him which rosettes," Wiley screamed, but Karl didn't say anything more about the wine cellar.

Karl: "Somehow we've got to get out of here. If we can escape and get to Leeds I have a contact there that can get us back to Germany."

Franz: "Really? That would be nice."

Karl: "If we do find a way out, and become separated for some reason, go to 269 Lander Street. The contact's code name is *Cato*. He lives in flat 312." Karl then told Franz the code phrases to use that would identify him as genuine.

Karl: "Can you remember all that?"

Franz: "I think so."

Karl: "You'd better or you'll be out there all alone."

Franz: "I'll remember."

Wiley started the alternate recording machine, removed the spool from the first machine and rushed out of the monitoring room. He rang up Ashburn.

"Hello, Colonel Ashburn's office. May I help you?" Janet said.

"May I speak to the Colonel please? This is an emergency."

"I'm sorry the Colonel is not in. May I ask who is calling?"

"This is Robert Wiley. I must speak with Colonel Ashburn as soon as possible."

"I'll tell him you called as soon as he comes in. Do you have a number where you can be reached?"

"He knows where I can be reached. Is there any way to contact him?"

"No, he's away on an assignment. He's been gone for quite sometime now. We expect him back soon, however. Would you like to leave a message?"

"Yes, just tell him the fox has a twin with a secret hiding place."

"What does that mean?"

"He'll know. Just tell him, and have him call me."

Janet rang up the Debden Air Field, and asked if she could speak to Captain Jacob Halder.

"To whom am I speaking?"

"My name is Janet Jones."

"What is your relationship to Captain Halder?"

"I'm a very close personal friend," Janet replied.

"Just one moment please." Corporal Guy Allen put Janet on hold and rang Major Hunter's office.

"Hunter here. What is it."

"This is Corporal Allen sir; I have a woman on the line asking for Captain Halder."

"Who is she?"

"She says she's a close personal friend of Halder's. It's probably his girl friend."

Hunter dreaded this kind of call. He took a deep breath and said, "Put her on."

"Hello, this is Major Hunter, how may I help you?"

"I…I would like to speak to Captain Halder…is that possible?"

Hunter wanted to say *If you're clairvoyant you might be able to talk to him*, but instead he said, "Miss Jones I don't know quite how to tell you this except to give it to you straight, Captain Halder was shot down over the Channel on a mission day before yesterday. He's missing and presumed dead."

Janet went numb. She wanted to scream but was paralyzed. Her whole world came crashing down. Her life was over. Darkness enveloped her as she fainted and fell to the floor, dragging the phone from the desk. Hunter heard a crash and then silence. "Hello, Hello, are you all right?"

A few minutes later, Ashburn, just returning from his mission, opened the door to the outer office and saw Janet sprawled on the floor, a telephone on the carpet beside her. He rushed in and shook her by the shoulder, trying to revive her. He heard a faint voice coming from the telephone. He picked it up and said, "Hello, this is Colonel Ashburn, who is this?"

"This is Major Hunter, commanding officer at Debden air field. Is the lady all right? I guess the bad news was quite a shock to her."

"What bad news?"

"She was inquiring about Captain Halder, and I told her he was shot down day before yesterday and was presumed dead."

"I see. Thank you Major. Sorry for the inconvenience. I've got to hang up now and take care of Miss Jones."

"Of course, I understand. Give her my condolences."

"I'll do that." Janet was starting to revive. She rolled over on her side, curled up in a fetal position and began to sob. Ashburn put his hand on her shoulder and shook her gently and said, "Can you hear me? Jacob is not dead. He's as alive as you and I." Those words slowly penetrated her mind as she emerged from the fog of unconsciousness. She leaned up on one elbow and with red eyes looked at Ashburn and said,

"What did you say?"

"I said Jacob is not dead. He's as alive as you and I"

"But that man just told me he was shot down and presumed dead."

"I don't care what he told you, Jacob is alive and well."

"Are you sure? Then why would that man say Jacob was dead?"

"Because it's important for security reasons that he appear to be dead. We faked his death. You have worked here long enough to know we do some very unusual things. Now I've told you more than I should. It is very important to this operation and to Jacobs' safety that no one knows he's alive. You must act as if he *is* dead. Can you handle that?"

"Yes, but it won't be easy now that I know he's alive."

"Well try very hard because a lot depends on it. As I said his safety could be jeopardized if it became known he is alive. Even his parents are being informed that he was shot down and is missing."

"That's terrible. Was that necessary?"

"Yes, take my word for it, it was necessary."

"Can I see him, talk to him?"

"No, you cannot."

"Please, just a phone call?"

Ashburn was getting a little perturbed and again emphatically said, "No, you cannot!"

"You're not telling me he is alive just to make me feel better are you?"

"I'm telling you the truth, and like I said I've told you more than I should. Maybe a little later on I'll let you see him, but not now."

"Thank you, Colonel, for letting me know Jacob is alive. He is very important to me."

"Yes, I understand. He's very important to me as well. But his importance to the mission we have in mind for him is far greater than any one individual, no matter how much we think of him personally. His mission is far greater than anything you can imagine. I cannot emphasize enough that under no circumstance can you let anyone know he is alive. No one. It could cost him his life. If you love him, and I suspect you do, his safety would be jeopardized if it was known he is alive. Do you understand?"

"Yes sir. You can depend on me."

"I knew I could."

Ashburn helped Janet to her feet, handed her his handkerchief, and then sat her down on a chair. Color was coming back to her face. She wiped her eyes, and blew her nose. Ashburn, looking concerned, asked her again if she was all right. "Yes, I think so."

"Good. You had me worried. I know that must have been quite a shock."

"That's putting it mildly. You will never know what a relief it was to hear you say he is alive and well."

"I didn't realize your relationship with Jacob was quite as serious as it now appears to be."

"Believe me, it is very serious," Janet said. "Colonel I almost forgot. A Mr. Robert Wiley called while you were away and said it was extremely important he got in touch with you."

"When did he call?"

"About two hours ago."

"Did he leave a message?"

"Yes sir. He said to tell the Colonel that the fox has a twin with a secret hiding place, whatever that means."

"Hmm, that's very interesting. Is that all?"

"Yes sir."

"Excuse me Janet; I need to make a phone call." Ashburn went into his office and called Wiley.

Wiley played the section of the wire about the wine cellar. When the conversation ended, Wiley said, "That's it Colonel."

"Thank you Robert. I appreciate you getting this information to me so promptly."

"Glad to be of service, sir."

"Keep up the good work, and let me know if anything else pops up I should know."

"Yes sir. I'll do that."

CHAPTER 23

Major Raymond Elsmore, an officer in the United States Army Air Forces, rang the doorbell at 223 Vine Street in Milwaukee. As he walked up to the front door he noticed the blue star in the window. He had lost count of how many times he had performed this sad duty. He thought, *Another star that will turn gold at my coming.*

Ilse opened the door, and let out a soft moan as she looked into the stern face of Major Elsmore.

"Good evening mam. My name is Major Raymond Elsmore, of the United States Army Air Forces. May I come in?"

"Of course Major, please do," Ilse tensely replied. Eddie came into the living room as the Major stepped across the threshold. He immediately went to Ilse and put his arm around her.

"Won't you please have a seat Major?" Ilse said.

"Thank you, no; I'll only be a few moments." He took a deep breath and said, "I deeply regret to inform you that advice has been received from the United States Army Air Forces casualty officer overseas that your son, Captain Jacob Halder, was reported missing in action on December 6, 1942. More complete details will follow from your son's commanding officer. Please accept my profound sympathy." Ilse sagged and Eddie had to hold her with both arms to keep her from collapsing. He guided her to the sofa and gently sat her down. She buried her face in her hands and sobbed uncontrollably.

"Thank you Major," Eddie said. "We appreciate you coming personally."

"I can find my way out, Mr. Halder. Keep in mind that missing in action does not mean he has been killed. He may only be a prisoner of war. Don't lose hope." Ilse raised her tear stained face at that comment.

A few days later, Ilse and Eddie received a letter from Major Joseph B. Hunter concluding: *Your son's aircraft was shot down over the English Channel near the coast of France. His plane disappeared into clouds and fog, which made it impossible to tell if he was able to deploy his parachute. If he did, it's possible that enemy forces may have rescued him and is still alive. The loss of your son comes as a great blow to all of us who knew him. The entire squadron would like to express our profound sympathy.*

Because of Jacob's service in the RAF, a week later a letter was received from the King of England who wrote, *The Queen and I offer you our heartfelt sympathy in your great sorrow. We express our gratitude for a life so nobly offered in the service of our country and may you find some measure of consolation from his great heroism in the defense of freedom.* (Signed) George, R.I.

Two days later, an article with a picture of Jacob in his uniform appeared in the Milwaukee Journal. The article read, *Captain Jacob Halder, of 223 Vine Street, Milwaukee, was reported missing in action over the English Channel, December 6, 1942. Captain Halder and his mother emigrated from Germany in 1923. Captain Halder was a volunteer with the RAF and flew for that organization until America entered the war, when he was transferred to the United States Army Air Forces. He is survived by his mother, Ilse Halder and his step father, Edward Halder.*

CHAPTER 24

▼

"Who is this please?"

"This is Sergeant McDonald, m'um. What can I do for you?"

"I'd like to speak to Captain Jacob Halder."

"Who is this and how did you get this number?"

"Never mind just put Captain Halder on the line."

"I'm sorry, m'um; there is no one here by that name. I insist you tell me who you are and how you got this number."

"That's unimportant since I know the number, and the fact that I know Captain Halder is at this facility should be sufficient."

"It might be from your point of view, but there is no one here by the name of Captain Jacob Halder."

"Now you listen to me, Sergeant. I know that Captain Halder is at this number and if you fail to notify him that he has a phone call you are placing yourself in a position to be severely reprimanded, and furthermore you..." The phone went dead. Janet just stared at the receiver and then slammed it down. Tears came to her eyes. *I've just got to talk to him. Why won't they let me?* She put her hands to her face and cried.

"What was that all about, Sergeant?"

"Oh...uh...hi Captain...that was...well it was someone asking for you, sir, and I told her that there was no one here by that name. She wouldn't give me her name or how she got this number. As you know this number is supposed to be secure and known only by authorized personnel.

"Thank you sergeant, you did the right thing." Jacob was fairly certain it was Janet who had called. *Ashburn would have a fit if he found out. I've got to see her some how. To hell with Ashburn!*

The telephone rang. Janet lifted the receiver and said, "Hello."

"This is Jacob, sweetheart; I've got to talk fast so listen carefully." Janet could hardly believe her ears.

"Oh Jacob darling, it's so good to hear your voice. I've missed you terribly."

"I've missed you too, sweetheart. I can only talk a few seconds so get something on which you can write down some directions."

"Just a minute, I'll get a pencil and paper...All right, I'm ready."

"Do you know where Workington is?"

"Yes, I've been there before. It's just a little further north of my parent's home"

"That's right. It's on the St. George's Channel about 350 kilometers northwest of London. There's an Inn there called the Painted Rose. It's very secluded and we won't be disturbed. Call them and make reservations for two, and be there day after tomorrow. You'll probably arrive before I do so use the name Mrs. Charles Hardwick when you register. Tell them your husband will be checking in later."

"Oh Jacob, you mean I'll get to be with you. I can hardly wait, and don't worry I'll be there. Nothing could keep me away, but I'm surprised Ashburn will let you leave the compound."

"He doesn't know, so don't say anything to him about meeting me."

"Won't you get into a lot of trouble? Ashburn will be furious."

"What can he do, cancel the mission? I don't think so. He'll fume for a few days, and then things will get back to normal. Tell him your father is very ill and you have to go home for a few days. Do you have enough petrol stamps to travel to Workington and back?"

"Yes, it isn't much further than my parent's home, and it's in the same direction, so if Ashburn has me followed it will look like I am going home."

The next night Jacob got into a staff car, rolled up the collar on his coat so it partially covered his face, put on the sergeants cap, and drove out the gate. *It's easier to get out of this place than it is to get in,* Jacob mused.

It feels good to be free of that stifling compound. Now keep left, he kept reminding himself. Jacob checked off the towns as he rolled south: Motherswell, Harwick,

Dumfries. He was getting very sleepy. He had driven all night. It was now 0900. He pulled off the road, parked in a grove of trees and slept for a couple of hours.

"Good afternoon sir, May I help you?"

"Yes, my name is Captain Charles Hardwick. I believe you have reservations for my wife and me for tonight."

"Yes sir, your wife checked in about an hour ago, she's in room 143, just down the hall. It has a beautiful view of the Channel. May I take your bag sir?"

"No, I can manage just fine, but thank you any way."

"Have a good afternoon sir. Would you like a wake up call in the morning?"

"No, we don't want to be disturbed."

"I understand, sir," the clerk said with a knowing smile.

Jacob opened the door to room 143, and there stood Janet. She rushed into his arms, and they kissed for a very long time. Jacob held her by the shoulders and said, "Let me look at you. You look more beautiful every time I see you."

"Thank you darling. It's wonderful to be in your arms." They kissed again.

"Neither one of us got much sleep last night. Don't you think we should go to bed?"

Janet smiled and said, "I think we should. I am quite tired."

"What do you mean Jacob's missing," Ashburn exploded. How do you know he isn't on the grounds somewhere? Maybe he went for a walk."

"His bed hasn't been slept in sir, and he didn't show up for breakfast."

"When did you last see him? Did you check with the gate?"

"Yes sir, I did. They said a car left last night with what looked like me driving. My cap is missing sir."

"Yes, and I bet Miss Jones's father is not ill."

"What?"

"Never mind." Ashburn was in a panic. He could see a fortune in materials and manpower going down the drain, let alone the whole mission having to be scrubbed. His career was at risk as well. *Why didn't I anticipate something like this? Where could they have gone?*

"All right Sergeant, we've got to keep this hush-hush. No one else is to know he is missing especially anyone outside this compound. He'll be back, I'm quite certain of that. Cancel all his training exercises. If inquiries are made tell them he is ill, and the doctor has ordered him to stay in his quarters and not to be disturbed."

"Yes sir."

"Good morning darling, did you sleep as well as I did?" Janet asked. She was curled up close to Jacob as they lay in bed.

He stretched and mumbled, "Yes dear, what time is it?"

"I don't know and I don't care. I'm too comfortable to worry about time. I wish the clock would just stop and we could remain together forever."

"That's a nice thought, but the clock is ticking. Let's make the most of this day, because tomorrow we had better get back to our jobs."

"I was hoping we could make it a fortnight."

"Two weeks! Ashburn would go crazy and probably have the police looking for us."

"I don't care. Tomorrow is too soon."

"All right, day after tomorrow," Jacob conceded.

"That's a little better," Janet said, as she snuggled a little closer.

CHAPTER 25

▼

Jacob drove up to the gate of the compound wondering what kind of reception he would get. The gate guard said, "Good afternoon sir. I believe Colonel Ashburn would like to see you, sir."

"What kind of mood is he in," Jacob asked.

"I would say it was much like a thunderstorm, sir."

"That's what I thought. I'd better get my umbrella out."

"Umbrellas aren't much protection against lightning, sir."

"That bad, huh?"

"I'd say so, sir." Jacob took a deep breath and drove through the gate.

"Where in the bloody hell have you been? There are no holidays during wartime!" Ashburn yelled.

"It won't happen again, sir."

"You bloody well better believe it. The gate guard has orders to shoot if you try that again."

"I won't try it again if you make me a promise," Jacob said.

"I'm in no mood for bargaining." Jacob didn't reply. He just waited until Ashburn cooled down a bit. Finally, Ashburn broke the silence and asked, "All right, what is it you want?"

"Janet is not to receive this kind of tongue lashing, and there will be no reprisals or I quit."

"You could receive a court martial for that kind of remark," Ashburn snarled.

"Is that what you want?"

"Of course not, we've gone too far with this thing to end it now, but you two have got to stop acting like a couple of love sick teenagers."

"Do we have a deal or not?" Jacob reiterated.

Ashburn was still smoldering, but finally said, "Yes if you give me your word this won't happen again."

"You have my word."

After a few days things were back to a normal routine, and Jacob's training continued.

CHAPTER 26

▼

"What is you mother's birth date?"

"October 22, 1889."

"Correct. Where was she born?"

"Berlin."

"Correct. What is your Father's birth date?"

"March 18, 1886."

"Correct. Where was your father born?"

"Leipzig."

"Correct. What is your Grandmother Von Kleist's birth date?"

"I can't remember the exact date, but I remember the tulips were in bloom when we celebrated her birthday, so it must be in April sometime."

"That's the best answer. Children seldom remember the birth date of their grandparents. You can't be perfect on every answer, or it will appear it has been rehearsed, and by not knowing the exact date of your grandmother's birth date will add to your credibility.

"What rank is equivalent to colonel?"

"*Standartenführer*"

"Correct."

"What about sergeant?"

"*Unterscharführer*."

"Correct."

"Second lieutenant?"

"It's…I believe it's…no…I can't remember."

"*Untersturmführer*. Remember, suspicion begins with small mistakes.

"Who is *Reichsführer* Walther von Reichenau?"

"He commanded the 10th Army for the invasion of Poland."

"Very good." The interrogator then held up a picture and said, "Who is this?"

"*Gruppenführer* Hans Oster, Chief of Staff to Admiral Wilhelm Canaris."

"Correct. And who is this?"

"*Obergruppenführer* Friedrich Olbricht. He is a close associate of Oster."

"Again, very good. And who is this?"

"That is *Obergruppenführer* Reinhard Heydrich, Chief of *SS Reich* Security Head Office and Protector of Bohemia and Moravia."

"That is correct. He is a very dangerous man. Steer clear of him at all costs"

"What is your Uncle Wilhelm Canaris's middle name?"

"Franz."

"Correct."

"Where did you take your flight training?"

"Hamburg."

"Who was the commanding officer?"

"*Standartenführer* Konrad Heinkel."

"When you are on the base, what do you see when you looked up?"

"The sky."

"Don't get smart. What else?"

"Do you mean the faded green water tower on the hill?"

"Yes, that's exactly what I mean. That's enough for today. You're probably a little brain weary after four hours of interrogation, but keep in mind, if they suspect you are not who you claim to be they will go at you with teams of interrogators for much longer periods of time, trying to wear you down. If so, pretend to go to sleep. This shouldn't be too difficult. They will try to revive you and may be harsh in doing so, but keep relapsing into sleep and they may give up for the time being. Sleep is important to keep you mentally tough enough to resist. They know this and will try to keep you talking beyond your will to refuse what they want."

"I know. I'll get it right the next time."

"Just keep in mind, with them there is no next time."

A weary Jacob replied, "Yes sir."

CHAPTER 27

▼

Gerhard Huber was seated at a table in his favorite restaurant in Berlin, savoring a delicious dinner of *Sauerbraten* marinated in buttermilk and *sauerkraut* cooked in pineapple juice. The vegetable of the day was a healthy portion of *Teltower Rubchen,* a delicious little root grown in a nearby suburb. A large stein of dark *Bock* beer with a frothy head sat conveniently above his plate. Large slices of dark rye bread were piled high on a side dish. As he took a bite of the tangy sweet *sauerkraut* he blessed the farmers around Stuttgart where most of the cabbage is grown in Germany.

Gerhard was a large man with a girth that reflected his eating habits. He was fifty years old and unmarried. There was little to enjoy in Berlin these days on a government employee's salary, but once a week he splurged on his favorite pastime: eating at *Kranzler's.* He was thinking about *Frau* Helldorf, a widow he met at the *Luftwaffe* offices, where they both worked. She had caught his eye, or rather his stomach, when she invited him to her flat for dinner one evening. After several dinner rendezvous' he had proposed marriage and she had accepted.

His thoughts were interrupted by a man who suddenly sat down opposite him and said, "Excuse me *Herr* Huber. I'm sorry to interrupt your meal, but may I join you for a few minutes?"

Alarmed, Gerhard said, "Who are you and what do you want?"

"My name is Erich Graff. I work at the Department of Public Records, and I noticed your application for a marriage license that came across my desk. As you know, before a marriage license can be issued we must check to be sure both applicants are of pure Aryan descent."

"Yes, I know that. What are you trying to tell me?"

"You have a problem, *Herr* Huber. Your application has been denied."

"What! On what grounds?"

"Because your grandmother was a Jew."

"Preposterous. She was a German."

"You're right, she was a German, but she was a German Jew. Have you ever checked your family genealogy?"

"No. I know nothing about such nonsense, and I have no interest."

"That's too bad. How badly did you want to marry this woman, *Frau* Helldorf, I believe her name is?" In Gerhard's mind he could see those exquisite evening meals vanish like steam over a boiling kettle.

"I love her very much. She will be as disappointed as I am to learn this."

"Maybe I can help."

"What do you mean?"

"I may be able to expunge the damaging evidence." The evening meals suddenly reappeared.

"How can you do that?"

"I could alter the record so that no one would ever know your lineage. You realize that if anyone knew of your Jewish background, you would no doubt lose your job as well as your prospect of marriage to this woman." Gerhard looked down at the remainder of his meal and suddenly lost his appetite.

"Why are you telling me all this, and how did you find me?"

"That was quite easy, and I'm telling you all this because I can help you if you do something for me in exchange."

"What do you want me to do?"

"I have a friend that requires a little alteration to his record. Nothing major mind you. Just some little thing like I can do for you. He's with the *Luftwaffe* and his records are on file where you work. Look at it as two friends helping one another without it doing any harm to anyone. What do you say?"

"Tell me what you want me to do."

Graff handed *Herr* Huber an envelope.

"Here's a substitute file. Just remove this same file in this person's folder, and put this one in its place. Can you do that?"

"I could, but what's in this file?"

"Like I said. Just a tiny alteration." *Herr* Huber thought that one over and finally said. "I'll do it. Is that all I have to do?"

"Just one more thing. Bring the file you remove back here tomorrow night, and I'll buy you dinner." This brought a smile to Gerhard's face.

"What about my marriage application?"

"You and *Frau* Helldorf are going to be happily married." Gerhard's appetite suddenly returned. He picked up his fork and continued eating as Graff left.

The man who identified himself as Erich Graff to Gerhard Huber was using a fictitious name. He is actually a British MI6 agent whose code name is *Camel*. He is the agent who recruited Emil Jellenik from the information Ashburn received about him from Jacob. *Camel* had just successfully, through Gerhard Huber, made arrangements to replaced Karl's fingerprints with Jacob's in the *Luftwaffe* files. There was one other piece of incriminating evidence that must be replaced. Dental records were as foolproof an identifier as fingerprints.

Camel looked up at the sign at 1145 *Wullenweber Srtaße in* Charlottenburg. It read *Doktor* Jurgen Streckenbach, *Zahnarzt*. It was 0110 in the morning. *Camel* looked up and down the street. No one seemed to be in sight. Allied bombers were over Berlin almost every night, and the entire city was blacked out. *One of the advantages for this kind of work, Camel* thought. He slid the pick into the lock and expertly unlocked the door. He climbed the stairs, and found the dentist's office. The door was unlocked, and he quietly entered. He turned on his small flashlight and saw he was in the waiting room. He opened the only other door in the room and there sat the dentist chair. He made a quick survey of the room, and he saw the filing cabinets. The drapes were open so he extinguished his flashlight. As he was about to close the drapes a voice said, "Don't move or I'll shoot." *Camel's* heart almost stopped. He wheeled around but couldn't clearly see the man attached to the voice.

"You about scared me to death. Don't shoot, I'm harmless."

"Who are you, and what are you doing in my office this time of night?"

"My name is Erich Graff. I'm one of your patients. I didn't have any place to stay tonight, and I thought your office sofa would be nice and comfortable."

"Then what are you doing in here? I was sleeping on my sofa tonight, and I don't have a patient named Erich Graff. The only patient I have named Graff is Max Graff."

"Of course, he's my father. He recommended you. I have a tooth that's been bothering me."

"So, Max is you Father, is he?" *Camel* thought he had hit the jackpot until the dentist said, "Max Graff is seven years old." *Camel's* brains were churning. Now what?

"Oh, that Max Graff. He's my nephew."

"Sure he is, and I'm your brother." *Camel had* about run out of ideas.

"I'll tell you what. Just let me leave and we'll just forget this whole incident. You can go back to sleep, and you'll never see me again." By this time *Camel's* eyes had adjusted to the dark room after turning off his flashlight. There was enough light from the moon and stars coming through the undraped window for *Camel* to see that the dentist was not holding a gun in his hand. It looked more like a pen.

"Shoot me if you must, but I'm leaving." *Camel* walked toward the door. As he passed the dentist, he chopped him across the throat with the side of his hand. The dentist dropped like he was shot, gasping for air. *Camel* closed the drapes, turned on his flashlight and pulled open the top file drawer. The last file was a patient named Kruger. *The M's must be in the next drawer.* He slid the drawer open and shuffled through the files. There it was, *Karl Müller.* He pulled it out, dropped the substitute file in its place, turned off the flashlight, and opened the drapes. The dentist was lying face down on the floor still gasping for air. *Camel* stepped over him and left.

CHAPTER 28

▼

"In my judgment and the judgment of the entire staff, we believe he is ready," Ashburn said.

"Good, we need to get him in place at the earliest possible moment. What is our next move?" Donavan asked.

"We'll make the switch day after tomorrow. If all goes well the escape plan will be implemented."

"Jacob I have a surprise for you," Ashburn said.

"Really, what is it?"

"You will be entertaining a very beautiful guest this evening."

Jacob's expression was hopeful as he said, "Could that beautiful guest be my wi...?" He caught himself and said, "Could it be Janet?"

"Right you are old boy. One bit of caution, however. She must not know your insertion into Germany is imminent. Talk about anything except *Serendipity*. You will be left completely alone with her while she's here. No one will interfere or will you be monitored in any way. Again, I emphasize, in no way are you to discuss any part of the operation. Is that clear?"

"Yes sir, I understand. How long can she stay?"

"I believe it would be wise to have her leave before the staff arrives. Let's say by 0600," Ashburn said with a leering smile and wink.

Jacob was overjoyed. He knew what Ashburn was thinking. *Wouldn't he be surprised if he knew we were man and wife?* Jacob smiled broadly, and Ashburn misinterpreted its meaning.

CHAPTER 29

▼

"Karl Müller, you are to come with me," the guard commanded.

"Where are we going?"

"Major Milne, the prison commander wants to see you."

"What does he want with me?"

"He very seldom confides in me. Just come along, and don't ask so many questions." The guard escorted Karl to Major Milne's office, closed the door, and waited outside.

"Ah, there you are. Have a seat. I'll be with you in a moment." Major Milne finished writing something, closed the file on his desk, and stood up.

"You are being transferred. Come with me." Karl could hardly believe his ears.

"What did you say?"

"I said you are being transferred. Stand up and come with me."

"Why am I being transferred?"

"That's none of your business, just come with me."

"I refuse to leave until you tell me why I'm being transferred and what about my belongings?"

"We will send them along shortly. You will be issued new prison clothing if needed, as well as toiletries at your new location."

"Where am I going?"

"You'll know when you get there."

"Can I say goodbye to Franz?"

"No, there is no time for that, now come along." Karl slowly got to his feet, lunged at Major Milne, knocking him down, and bolted for the door. He threw the door open and raced into the outer office. The guard sprinted after him, and tackled him just as he was about to leave the building. By this time, Major Milne had recovered and helped subdue him.

"That was a stupid thing to do. Where did you think you were going to go? You will be spending a very long time in solitary confinement at your new location for that outburst."

Two more guards were summoned, and Karl was escorted out the front door and into a waiting vehicle. They drove out of the compound and Karl was on his way to a new prison.

"What did the *Kommandant* want?" Franz asked.

"He told me to stop complaining about the food."

"What did you say?"

"I told him the English slop they feed us isn't fit for pigs."

"And, what did he say?"

"That *Dummkopf* had the gall to tell me I'd be eating *with* the pigs if I didn't stop complaining," Jacob arrogantly replied. Franz had to turn his face to keep Jacob from seeing him smile. Franz's reaction told Jacob the switch was successful.

"We won't be eating their slop much longer," Jacob said.

"What do you mean?"

"I have a plan."

"What kind of plan?"

"We're getting out of here."

"We're getting out of here? Are they letting us go?"

"No, you fool. We're going to escape this stinking prison."

"How are we going to do that?"

"They have you working in the dispensary, right?"

"Yes, of course. What do you have in mind?"

"Doctor Harris makes his weekly visit tomorrow night. I can feel a very upset stomach coming on. I'll demand to be taken to the doctor. Now this is what I want you to do." Jacob explained the plan in detail to Franz.

"You understand what you need to do, don't you?"

"I don't know about this? We have it pretty well here. If they catch us we may be put in solitary confinement until the end of the war."

"Now you listen to me. You'll do exactly as I tell you. Do you understand?" Jacob sternly warned.

"Yes, I understand."

Jacob watched from the barracks as Doctor Harris's little Austin came through the gate. Shortly after, a guard came for Franz and escorted him to the dispensary. In a few minutes, Jacob went into his act. He began to moan and was soon screaming at the top of his lungs. A guard rushed in and asked, "What's the matter?"

"My stomach is killing me. It must be that slop they feed us. Get me to the doctor quick. I feel like I'm going to die."

"All right, all right, just settle down. I'll check with the doctor." Jacob continued to moan as the guard left.

The guard returned and said, "All right, the doctor said to get you over to the dispensary right away." Jacob got up and walked stooped over holding his stomach. They entered the office, and the guard helped put him on the examination table and left the room, shutting the door behind him. Jacob was writhing and moaning as he held his stomach. The doctor bent over him and began unbuttoning his shirt when Jacob grabbed him around the neck, and put his hand over his mouth to stifle any scream. Franz slapped a chloroform-soaked piece of gauze over his nostrils until the doctor slumped over and slid to the floor. Jacob jumped off the table and hid behind the door. Franz ran to the door and yelled to the guard, saying, "Doctor Harris has fainted."

The guard rushed in and leaned over the fallen doctor. Jacob came from behind the door, grabbed the guard by the hair, and plunged a scalpel into his throat. Blood spurted out and Franz's mouth dropped open in horror. Franz was paralyzed with fear but finally found his voice and said, "Are you crazy. Why did you do that?" If they catch us now they'll shoot us. I thought you were just going to chloroform him like we did the doctor. Why this?"

"I don't want to take any chances. Now quit babbling, and let's get out of here."

Jacob went through the doctor's pockets and took his wallet and keys. He slipped the doctor's watch off and put it on his own wrist. He then put on the doctor's hat and coat, turned off the light, and closed the door as they left. They exited the building and looked around. There was no one in sight. They could see the lights glowing at the compound entrance. The night air was crisp and Jacob inhaled deeply to help relieve the tension as they walked to the Austin. Franz got in the trunk, and Jacob closed the lid as quietly as possible. He started the engine, rolled his coat collar up, and drove to the gate. He slowed as the gate was opened and waved as he drove through. *Now remember, drive on the left side of the road,* he reminded himself.

When the guard heard the muffled sound of the doctor's automobile engine start, he got up off the floor and fumbled around until he found the light switch. He looked in the mirror. He was a bloody mess, literally. He unhooked the fake scalpel from his shirt collar and put it in the sink. He reached for a towel, soaked it in water and was cleaning himself when Ashburn walked in.

"How did it go?"

"I believe Franz bought it. He sounded scared to death."

"You're a mess."

"You would be too if a bag of blood spilled all over you."

"I'm sorry, but it had to look real."

Major Milne walked in as the guard was leaving. He took in the scene at a glance. The doctor was lying unconscious on the floor, and Ashburn was turning him over and placing a pillow from the examination table under his head. Blood was all over the floor and a bloody towel was in the sink.

"Was the guard's fake murder necessary? Look at this mess."

"Yes, very much so. I want Franz to be so frightened about being caught that he doesn't do something stupid to alert the authorities. He was too comfortable here and much too willing to wait out the war. Now he thinks if they get caught it's a death sentence for them. No, I think we played it just about right. Besides, when he is interrogated on his return to Germany, the *killing* will give Jacob greater authenticity. A *plant* wouldn't murder one of his own countrymen."

Ashburn, looking down at the doctor on the floor said, "Look at him. Sleeping like a baby. What we don't do for jolly old England."

After several kilometers, Jacob pulled over to the side of the road, got out and let Franz out of the trunk.

"You can't believe how uncomfortable that is back there. The trunk in these small English automobiles is atrocious."

"Quit complaining, and get in. We need to keep moving."

"How long do you think it will take us to get to Leeds?"

"About an hour and a half."

"I hope we don't run into any road blocks."

"There shouldn't be any road blocks. They won't discover the doctor and guard until morning, and by that time we'll be safe in Leeds. We need to rip these black patches off our sleeve. There's no way to get rid of the P painted on our pant leg, however."

They drove in silence until they saw a sign that read, "Leeds 15 Kilometers". It was 2200 hours. Suddenly, they heard what sounded like thunder in the direction of the city. A red glow erupted just above the horizon.

"It looks like our planes are bombing Leeds. There are a lot of manufacturing facilities in that city. This is very fortuitous. They will be so busy fighting fires that no one will pay any attention to us."

Jacob pulled over to the side of the road, and told Franz to get back in the trunk.

"Not again. It's too cramped back there. Why can't I ride up here?" He whined.

Jacob gave Franz an icy stare and said, "I'm only going to tell you this once. Do exactly as I say without question or you'll end up like that guard. Do you understand my meaning?" Franz wasn't about to challenge Jacob after what he witnessed earlier, so he got in the trunk.

Jacob drove to the center of the city. The fires were in the industrial section, just outside the business district. People were running in the opposite direction of the fire. An elderly man ran in front of the Austin and Jacob braked hard to keep from hitting him. He rolled his window down and called out to him.

"Hey! You there. Can you give me some directions?"

"Sorry I'm in a hurry."

"Hop in and I'll give you a lift."

"Thanks mate. Don't mind if I do." He ran around the front of the Austin, opened the passenger side door and jumped in.

"Where are you headed," Jacob asked.

"Any…bloody…place…away from that fire," he said between labored breaths.

"Are you a long time resident of Leeds?" Jacob inquired.

"You might say that. Born and raised here."

"You must know where Lander Street is located then."

"I sure do. Keep going in this direction until you come to Farley and turn left. Lander is four streets from Farley. Let me out at Farley. I go the other way." At Farley, Jacob stopped and let the old man out.

"Thanks for the lift mate. These old legs ain't what they used to be."

"Thanks for the directions old timer. I hope you get home safely." Jacob turned left and slowed at Lander Street. *Which way do I turn now, I wonder?*

He turned left and began reading the numbers. 348, 351, 355. *It looks like I guessed wrong. It's the other way.* He made a U turn and headed back, crossed Farley and found number 269. It was a three-story apartment building. All the buildings looked pretty much alike. Jacob pulled over to the curb, stopped, got out, and opened the trunk. Franz crawled out, stood up slowly, placed his hands on the lower part of his back and flexed backward.

"I'm glad to get out of there. That's as cramped as a can of sardines. Too bad the doctor doesn't have a Rolls Royce," Franz said in German.

"You *Dummkopf,* we're not in Germany yet. Speak English until we leave this stinking Island," Jacob hissed between clenched teeth.

"Sorry, I forgot. Is this the place?" Franz asked in English.

"Yes it is. I just hope our contact still lives here. Bring the torch we found under the seat. We're going to need some light." They entered the building and started up the stairs.

"Let me do the talking." They were breathing hard as they reached the top floor. They stopped at 312, and Jacob knocked on the door. No one answered. He knocked louder. He thought he heard movement on the other side and finally a voice said, "Who is it? What do you want?"

"I have a message from Uncle Brewster." Slowly the door opened a crack. From the light of the torch they could see the face of a middle-aged man. He was unshaven and looked concerned.

"What's the message?"

"He sends his regards and asked us to tell *Cato* the tulips have been planted."

"When will they bloom?"

"When the nightingale sings." The tension in the man's face relaxed. He opened the door and motioned them in. They stepped inside, and *Cato* quickly closed the door. A single candle lighted the room. The flat was quite cold. *Cato* had a blanket wrapped around his shoulders and held it tightly in front to keep in the warmth.

As their eyes adjusted to the dimness of the room, they saw a man sitting on the sofa. *Cato* asked,

"Who are you and what do you want?"

"Who is that on the sofa?"

"That's *Hubert* He's one of us. He normally operates in London, but he's staying here for awhile."

"Why is he here?"

"We routinely vacate a location from time to time. If someone is getting close to us it throws him off the scent. Now you answer a few questions. Who are you and how did you know how to find me?"

"I'm *Hauptsturmführer* Karl Müller and this is *Obersturmführer* Franz-Walter Vandieken. We're with the *Luftwaffe.* We were both shot down and have been prisoners at a camp in Perth. We escaped earlier this evening." *Cato* looked a little skeptical at that statement.

"And you got here so soon. How did you manage that?"

"We stole the doctor's automobile and drove straight here and…" Jacob gave Franz a grim look and Franz quickly shut up.

"Never mind the details. We're here and need your help to get back to Germany, My uncle said you could use your wireless to get us on a submarine."

"Are you *verrückt?* They would never dispatch a submarine for just two people."

"I think they might. Do you know who my uncle is?"

"I have no idea." Jacob seemed to stand a little taller and said, "My uncle is Admiral Wilhelm Canaris. Do you know who he is?"

"Of course I do, he's the head of the *Abw…Cato* stopped in mid sentence and his eyes grew wide.

"Your uncle is Admiral Canaris?" He exclaimed.

"That's correct. How do you suppose I knew the passwords?"

"I was about to ask you that. *We* work for the Admiral."

"Don't you mean you work for Germany and report to Admiral Canaris?"

"Yes, of course, that's what I meant," *Cato* replied a little sheepishly.

"I'll send a message tonight and see what kind of response we get."

"Please do; we are both anxious to return to the *Vaterland.*"

The man on the sofa was in truth a British MI5 agent. What Franz did not know, of course, was that the escape was a charade. It had been carefully scripted and every move was calculated to make sure Jacob's insertion into Germany was seen as genuine.

Cato was a bona fide German agent who was *rolled up* by British MI5, the agency responsible for counter intelligence. The code name given to *Cato* by the British was *Garbo.* He along with two others that were captured, whose British code names became *Tricycle* and *Zig Zag,* were given a choice: work for British Intelligence as double agents or be shot. The choice was not a difficult one, and they were *turned-around.*

It was a major intelligence coup and resulted in a "steady flow of disinformation to enemy networks."[1] Their services proved to be of incalculable importance

---

1. *The McMillan Dictionary of the Second World War,* by Elizabeth-Ann Wheal & Stephen Pope

as they fed their former masters false information. The monitoring of Karl Müller paid big dividends, even before Jacob left for Germany.

Garbo (Cato) sent the message on his wireless. It was very important this *turned-around* German agent send the message. Every wireless operator has a distinct *fingerprint* or *hand* as it is sometimes called. If someone else sent a message pretending to be that person, the receiving operator would recognize him immediately as a fraud.

"We'll just have to wait for a reply," *Garbo* said.

"How long will that take, do you suppose?" Jacob asked.

"I have no way of knowing. I'm sure they do not get a request for a submarine to pick someone up in England every day. We normally receive messages at either 0800 or 2300 hours."

"How secure are we here?"

"You'll be safe as long as you remain inside."

"There's something that has to be attended to very quickly."

"And what's that?"

"The automobile parked outside at the curb is the one we stole to make our escape. It must be disposed of before someone notices it."

"You're right, and the sooner the better. No doubt an alert will go out as soon as they discover you are missing. Let me think. Where can we get rid of it permanently?"

"Is there a lake nearby?"

"None I know of, but there is a pond at the smelter not far from here."

"Is it deep enough to hide a small automobile, and is there access to it?"

"Yes, access is possible. I believe the north end is the deepest and fortunately the water is as black as tar, at least it looks black because it is so brackish. It should hide the automobile very well."

"Can you dispose of it tonight?"

"Yes, but you two stay here with *Hubert* and I'll take care of it. It's close enough that I can walk back."

"There is one other thing we need."

"And what's that?"

"We need to get out of these prison clothes."

"We'll take care of that in the morning," *Garbo* replied.

Garbo took the keys from Jacob and put on his hat and coat. "Don't leave the flat and keep quiet. It will take me about an hour. There are only two beds in the flat.

I use one and *Hubert* uses the other. One of you can sleep on the sofa and the other will have to make do on the floor. There are extra quilts in the closet. What's the make of the automobile?"

"It's the gray Austin parked just outside the steps leading into the building." *Garbo* left the flat, and they could hear his footsteps recede down the hall. Franz went to the closet, got the blankets, and curled up on the floor. Jacob smiled to himself. *Trained just like a good little dog.*

Garbo found the Austin, got in it, started the engine, and drove off. He did not drive the Austin into the smelter pond. Instead he drove it to a garage, got out, inserted a key into a padlock and unlocked it, opened the doors and drove the Austin in. He left the keys in the ignition, closed the garage doors, replaced the padlock and walked back to the flat.

At the Perth hospital, Ashburn inquired at the front desk if Doctor Harris had recovered from the chloroform yet.

"Yes he's fine. They want to keep him overnight just to be sure."

"May I see him?"

"There are no restrictions on visitors. He's in room 113, just down the hall to your right."

"Thank you, nurse." Ashburn walked down the hall and entered the room. The doctor was propped up and reading a newspaper.

"Ah, there you are old chap. You look very comfortable," Ashburn remarked as he greeted the doctor.

"I most certainly am. This is the most rest I've had in a long time. I'm really just fine, you know. The nurses are just being nice to an old man. Do you have any more assignments this pleasant?" he replied laughing.

"I can't think of any right off hand. But I'll keep you in mind if something pops up," Ashburn replied with a chuckle. "I realize all this was a very different cup of tea for you. I very much appreciate your cooperation. Everything is going smoothly. Your automobile is being retrieved as we speak. It will be back here by morning, ready for you when you check out. I've ordered it to be filled with petrol. And by the way, here's a new watch."

"Bless my soul, that jolly well is. My, oh my, it's a beauty. It's much nicer than my old one. Thank you very much, and thank you for the petrol."

"You're welcome doctor, and I'm glad you are feeling all right. I've got to get cracking now. Have a good night's rest."

"I'll try, but I slept for quite sometime already, as you know."

"Let's hope the next time you fall asleep, it won't be a chloroform induced one." Ashburn replied as he left.

CHAPTER 30

▼

The Teleprinter began to rattle and the operator walked over to the machine. When the message ended he tore it off and read it.

"Hmm, the Admiral will be personally interested in this one," he said to no one in particular.

"What is it?" said *Gruppenführer* Hans Oster, Canaris's chief of staff.

"Here, read it, sir." The operator handed Oster the message.

He scanned the page and said, "You're right, that's his nephew. See that the Admiral gets this as soon as he walks in the door in the morning. It will be interesting to see what he does."

The Head of the *Abwehr,* medium in height and squat in build, strode through the door at exactly 0700. To the casual observer, this rather insignificant looking man wouldn't warrant a second glance. However, to those who knew him well marveled at his intellectual prowess and canny instincts. Those who underrated him were likely to regret it. He had a long prominent nose and receding brow and chin; which betrayed his ascetic nature.

"*Gut Morgen,* sir. You may want to read this first thing," Oster said, handing Admiral Wilhelm Canaris the message.

Canaris read the message and said, "Get me Dönitz on the telephone."

Grand Admiral Karl Dönitz was the commander of all German U boat submarine forces. Oster turned to a clerk and gave him an order to call Dönitz.

"I'll take it in my office when the call comes in," Canaris said as he walked away.

"Yes sir."

"*Gute Morgen,* Wilhelm, it's a nice surprise to hear from you."

"*Gute Morgen,* Admiral, thank you for returning my call. Something just came up and I need your help."

"What is it, Wilhelm. You know I'll help if I can."

"We just received a message from one of our agents in England that two of our *Luftwaffe* pilots escaped from a prison in Perth and are with him in Leeds. Is there any chance that one of your submarines could pick them up? As you know we are desperate for experienced fighter pilots."

"Well, let me think about that a moment. To put a submarine and her crew at risk for two men may not be very wise. How did these pilots know how to contact one of your agents?" Canaris squirmed a little, but decided it was best to be upfront about it.

"One of the pilots is my nephew. I gave him a heads up about whom to contact for help if he was shot down."

"I see. I understand your concern. Can I get back to you in about an hour?"

"Yes, of course. I know it's a lot to ask. Anything you can do will be reciprocally appreciated.

"Hans, can you come in here a moment?"

"What can I do for you sir?"

"I talked to Dönitz about picking up those two flyers in a sub. He's hesitant about doing so. In a way I can't say I blame him, although I don't believe the risk is as great as he imagines. I want a staff meeting in ten minutes. We need two plans. One by air and one by sea." Canaris, a history buff, commented, "That sounds a little like an incident in the American Revolutionary War."

An orderly tapped on the conference room door and Canaris said, "Come."

The orderly entered and said, "Admiral Dönitz is on the telephone for you sir."

"*Vielen Dank,* I'll take it here." Canaris picked up the phone and said, "Canaris here, thank you for getting back to me so soon Admiral. What have you decided?"

"I've got a submarine that's due to rotate back to the pens at Brest in three days. It will mean a pretty sizable detour, but we can do it. There's a stretch of beach about 100 kilometers long that is fairly desolate between Torquay and Weymouth just east of Plymouth."

"Just a moment, Admiral. Hans, hand me the detail map of the south coast of England. Yes, that's the one. All right, Admiral, I have a map in front of me now."

"There's a little town by the name of Exeter about ten kilometers inland at the apex of the ninety degree angle formed by that stretch of beach."

"Yes, I see it."

"My sub will surface at exactly 0300 hours three days from today. They'll surface two kilometers offshore. At exactly 0305, your agent will signal with three blinks from a powerful flashlight followed by two blinks after a two second interval. The sub will acknowledge with one short blink. Your agent will confirm with one blink. If we don't see a signal we will assume the operation is aborted and the sub will leave. If they receive the one blink acknowledgement, a rubber raft will be launched and rowed to shore. Your agent is to signal with a single blink every ten seconds so the raft will have a bearing point all the way in. If those ten second interval blinks cease, we'll know something is wrong and the raft will return to the sub as fast as the crew can row. It should take them about thirty minutes to reach shore unless it's rough. If it's foggy, forget it. Have you got all that?"

"Yes sir. I've got it all down and *danke*. I owe you one."

"I'll hold you to that," Dönitz replied.

Jacob and Franz sat eating a breakfast of stale toast, marmalade, and day old coffee. Jacob grumpily commented, "We might as well be back in Perth." Franz turned his head and smiled.

"The 0800 incoming signal time passed two hours ago and no message. What's the problem?" Jacob asked *Garbo*.

"Patience, I suspect a lot has been happening since they received my message. Like I said, they don't get a request for a submarine every day. We'll see how much influence your uncle has." Jacob hoped they would get the sub. The alternate plan to *steal* a plane and fly to France would be much more dangerous.

"Something's coming through now." *Garbo* had his headset on and he began writing on the pad in front of him. After a few minutes, he stopped writing and sent a quick acknowledgement. He took off the headset and opened his codebook. "This will take me a few minutes to decode." Time dragged, and finally he said, "Well, it looks like you got your submarine. It seems it pays to have friends in high places. Here read this." Jacob took the decoded message and read it.

"It looks like we're heading home, Franz."

"*Wunderbar.* I can hardly wait."

"We'll have to wait three days just to get started, and that's going to seem like an eternity holed up here. I hope the food gets better at this bed and breakfast." *Garbo* gave Jacob a dirty look, which didn't go unnoticed by Franz. *This performance still had three days to run, and the supporting cast remained very convincing,* Jacob mused.

"We're in luck, no fog. What time is it *Cato?*"

"It's 0301, four minutes before we signal." At exactly 0305 *Garbo(Cato)* flashed three blinks, waited two seconds and blinked the flashlight two more times. Keep a sharp eye out for their signal." Everyone was straining so as to not miss that one single light blink from the submarine. A light coming from the direction of the channel can be seen by anyone on shore and some of those eyes might be the wrong ones. There are coast watchers all up and down the coast, particularly on the Channel side. Someone on shore might never see one quick blink unless they were expecting it, and a light directed toward the Channel could not be seen by anyone on shore.

"There it is," Franz excitedly whispered.

"I see it," *Garbo* replied. *Garbo* blinked the prearranged signal. The sub replied with a single acknowledgement blink. *Garbo* flashed one more single blink.

In his mind's eye, Jacob could see sailors jumping into a raft and plowing toward shore, their oars digging into the surf with powerful strokes. In the time it took the raft to reach shore, Jacob thought about all the circumstances that had brought him to this moment in his life. He was about to enter the unknown. All his preparation might be wasted as well as his life if he failed in the next few days. Little doubts begin to invade his mind, and he was tempted to turn and run. *Steady old boy,* he could hear Ashburn say. His mind turned to Janet and his heart ached.

He was abruptly brought back to reality as Franz said, "I see the raft." There it was, almost on top of them. In a black raft were six men in black turtleneck sweaters, black pants and black sneakers. Their faces were smeared black. The two men in front jumped into the shallow surf and pulled the tip of the raft onto the sand.

Jacob whispered to *Garbo,* "Thanks for your help," and he and Franz jumped aboard. *Garbo* helped the two sailors push the raft back into the water, the two sailors jumped in and they paddled away from the shore.

Unseen by those in the raft was the MI5 agent as he walked out of the darkness to stands alongside *Garbo*. The agent said, "That's all we can do. They're safely on their way. It's up to the American now."

Jacob had never been on a submarine before. He was a little concerned about going under the water. They climbed down the ladder into the Command Center. The *Kapitän* greeted Jacob and Franz with an out stretched hand.

"Welcome aboard, gentlemen. We'll try to make you as comfortable as possible. My first mate will show you to your quarters."

"*Danke sehr, Kapitän.* Your hospitality is very much appreciated." *Forget English, only German is spoken from now on,* Jacob reminded himself.

"Steer 195, full speed ahead. The smoking lamp is lit," The *Kapitän* sang out.

"Right this way gentleman," said the first mate.

"Will we be diving?" Jacob asked.

"*Nein,* we will stay on the surface at night. We can travel much faster using our diesel engines, and at the same time we will be charging our batteries. Can I get you some coffee?"

"That would be nice. We haven't eaten since breakfast. Is there any chance of getting a snack before we turn in?"

"Certainly. I'll have the cook prepare something for you. *Gute Nacht.*"

"*Gute Nacht,*" Jacob replied.

Jacob awoke and looked at his watch, or rather looked at Doctor Harris's watch. It was 0738. *I hope Ashburn reimburses the doctor or gets him another watch. If he doesn't I'll buy him one when I get back, if I get back. That's enough of that,* he thought. *I don't want any negative self-fulfilling prophesies.* He could hear the hum of the battery-powered engines as he made his way forward.

"*Guten Morgen, Hauptsturmführer Müller,*" the *Kapitän* said as Jacob stepped into the command center.

"*Guten Morgan Kapitän.* Are we under the water yet?"

"*Ja,* that we are, seventy meters in fact. Does that bother you?"

"A little. I've always flown above the water."

"Now that sounds dangerous."

"Where are we now, *Kapitän?*"

"We're approximately 160 Kilometers from the point we picked you up. We have 125 kilometers to go until we arrive at Brest. Did you sleep…?"

"*Kapitän,*" a crewman shouted," Screws bearing 095, 500 meters, and closing fast."

"Right rudder to 290, depth 200 meters. Sound general alarm."

"*Jawohl*, my *Kaptiän*!" Jacob grabbed a stanchion and caught himself as the sub turned. Disciplined pandemonium broke out all around him as men rushed to their battle stations.

"The Sonar operator sang out, "400 meters…300 meters…200 meters." Jacob noticed everyone gripping just a little tighter on their hand holds, and he could feel the tension rising.

"100 meters…50 meters…he's on top of us, sir"

"Splashes, sir." The sonar operator shouted.

"Left rudder to 240," the *Kapitän* ordered. The sub tilted as it turned. All of a sudden Jacob heard two massive explosions followed by four more at about three second intervals. The sub bounced around like a toy, and water squirted from several pipes. Then two more explosions followed, but not as close this time. Two more were heard as the destroyer moved off.

"All stop," the *Kapitän* ordered. The sub went silent. "Release 200 liters of diesel and stuff a torpedo tube with as many life jackets, clothing, blankets, garbage or anything handy you can find and shoot it out. Quickly now."

Jacob heard a whoosh as the compressed air in the torpedo tube was released sending the material to the surface, along with the diesel fuel. Jacob hoped this ruse worked.

"Everyone, be very quiet now," the *Kapitän* ordered. The helmsman let the sub sink to the bottom. Jacob was praying silently. He couldn't remember when he had been so frightened. The *Kapitän* looked at him and smiled weakly.

"Are you all right," he whispered. Jacob just nodded.

"You never get used to it so don't feel ashamed if you wet your pants." Jacob grabbed his crotch. The *Kapitän* chuckled. *Thank goodness it's still dry.* He felt a little embarrassed. *Wouldn't it be ironic if I drowned in a German sub before I even reached Germany?*

"He's coming back, sir," the sonar operator whispered. The *Kapitän* just nodded. They could hear the destroyer's screws getting louder and louder and Jacob braced for another attack. Suddenly, the sound of the destroyer's screws stopped.

"They're checking our garbage and oil slick," the *Kapitän* whispered. We'll soon know if they think they killed us." Jacob saw the men looking up as if they could see the destroyer. In his mind's eye he could.

After an excruciating ten minutes they heard the Destroyer's screws start slowly, and their sound gradually receded until they could no longer be heard. No one moved, except to slip quietly to the floor and sit very still. Jacob joined them. Again he heard the screws and he wondered if this time depth charges would be dropped. The destroyer passed overhead again and the noise from the screws finally receded until they could no longer be heard. Still no one moved. It was getting cold and Jacob wished he had a blanket.

The *Kapitän* whispered something to one of the crew and he removed his shoes and tip toed out of the compartment. In about five minutes he returned with an armload of blankets. *The Kapitän must be clairvoyant,* Jacob thought. *On the other hand this is probably just standard procedure.* No one moved and no one spoke for three hours. Quite a few fell asleep.

Finally the *Kapitän* said, "All right take her up to periscope depth and let's take a peek. The sub floated up and stopped. The *Kapitän* raised the periscope, peered through the lens and made a fast 360 degree sweep of the horizon.

"It's all clear he announced." You could hear more than just a few breaths quietly escape, including Jacob's.

"Take her down to 30 meters and steer heading 160." the *Kapitän* ordered. Jacob decided to check on Franz. He met him in the gangway. He was as white as a sheet.

"Quite a ride," Jacob said. Franz could hardly speak. He finally found his voice and said, "I wish we would have flown home."

"That would have been nice, but may have been even more dangerous. Can you imagine a British plane trying to land in Germany?"

"I'd take my chances. There are no parachutes on submarines."

At 1700 hours, the *Kapitän* ordered the sub up to periscope depth. He again swept the horizon 360 degrees, and lowered the periscope.

"Steer two points to port." The helmsman made the adjustment and the *Kapitän* ordered the sub to the surface. "We're almost home gentlemen," the *Kapitän* announced.

The sub broke water and a crewman climbed the ladder and opened the deck hatch. The *Kapitän* followed. Another crewman handed the *Kapitän* a headset and saluted. Deck hands emerged and went to their stations. Jacob climbed up and watched as the submarine slid gracefully through the water. They entered a mammoth concrete opening in the hillside like a whale swallowing a fish. These were the submarine pens at Brest.

"We're home and safe," the *Kapitän* said to no one in particular.

"Thanks to you, *Kapitän.* You did a fine job," Jacob sincerely replied.

Jacob and Franz were put on a plane to Berlin. As they landed at Tempelhof *Flughafen* Franz said, "I'm certainly glad you didn't listen to me in Perth or we'd still be in prison. Now look, we're home. I wonder what will happen to us now?"

"I'm not sure, we'll just have to wait and see." As they stepped off the aircraft a *Gestapo* agent greeted them.

"Welcome home gentlemen, please come with me." They were put in an automobile and driven to *Gestapo* Headquarters at 8 *Prinz-Albrecht-Straße,* probably the most feared address in the *Third Reich.* Nothing was spoken during the entire ride. Jacob was reviewing in his mind all the memorized details he had practiced at Perth. It was final examination time, and he hoped for a passing grade. The building was a foreboding structure, and Jacob wondered if he would walk out of there alive. He remembered what the elocutionist said to him about absorbing the role and being on stage, and that he would have to give the performance of his life, but maybe he should have said, *I'm about to give the performance for my life.*

Jacob's thoughts were interrupted when the *Gestapo* agent said, "Here we are gentlemen." They got out of the automobile and walked into the building. Jacob strode in with as confidant a stride as he could manage. *The curtain just went up,* he realized.

"Why have we been brought here? Why aren't we being taken to *Luftwaffe* Headquarters?" Jacob asked.

"Settle down. All in good time. We'd like to ask you some questions about your confinement in England." Jacob was escorted to an office and another man took Franz down the hall. As Jacob entered the room a short, stocky, man with a shaved head greeted him. His jowls hung in fleshy layers. He reminded Jacob of a bulldog.

"*Heil* Hitler. My name is *Obersturmbannführer* Bruno Redder. Have a seat." Jacob seated himself, and sat very erect. He took an instant dislike to Redder.

"Tell me where you were confined?" Redder asked.

"It was in Perth, Scotland." The questions droned on for several hours. Where were you trained, who were your commanding officers, and where were you born? The questions were those anticipated, and Jacob had no trouble answering them. He had been well prepared. Some were repeated, no doubt to see if the answers were consistent. A few of the questions he did not know and admitted it. He wondered what affect that had on Redder.

"When will you be through with me? I've been out of Germany for over a year and I'm anxious to see my family."

"Soon, but first we need to take your fingerprints. Later a *Doktor* will examine you."

"My fingerprints are on file at the *Luftwaffe* Headquarters. This is nonsense," Jacob testily replied.

Redder glared at Jacob and snapped, "We can be more demanding if you like. We have certain procedures we must follow, and if you are not more cooperative I can keep you here all night and beyond if necessary."

"If it has to be done, let's get on with it, so we can get this over with as soon as possible."

"Come this way then." He was led to another room where a technician took his fingerprints. That done. Redder said, "You will be taken to the hospital for a complete physical examination. We want to be sure you are in good health and haven't picked up any diseases while in England. Only then will you be taken to *Luftwaffe* Headquarters."

The same driver that brought Franz and Jacob to *Gestapo* Headquarters escorted him out of the building and into a waiting automobile.

"Where's Franz?" Jacob asked.

"He was taken to the *Doktor* over an hour ago." Jacob was concerned. *Why had he been kept so much longer? Was Franz more convincing?*

The two interrogators got together after Jacob left and compared notes. Redder said, "There's something fishy about Müller. I can't put my finger on it, but something just doesn't seem right."

"Really? Their stories seem to be consistent. Did you know Müller killed one of the guards when they escaped? He stabbed him in the throat with a scalpel."

"No, I didn't know that. He never mentioned it. All the same, I trust my instincts. I'm going to keep my eye on him."

At the hospital, Jacob took off all his clothes except his underwear. The *Doktor* probed and listened and questioned Jacob thoroughly. He was given a complete and very intense examination from head to toe.

"You're in excellent physical condition. You must have been exercising and eating well," the *Doktor* said.

"We were able to exercise in our quarters all we wanted, and we were given the privilege of walking an hour a day outside in the prison yard. As for the food, it may have been nourishing, but I didn't like it at all."

"That's what your fellow prisoner, Vandieken, told me. Tell me, how did you get that cut on your head?"

"Oh, that. I hit my head on the cockpit frame when I bailed out. I was unconscious for a short time, but fortunately I recovered in time to open my parachute. It bled for a while, and an English *Doktor* stitched it up."

"You say you lost consciousness?"

"Yes, just for a short time, however. I was conscious when I hit the ground."

"Did you have any problems after that?"

"I probably shouldn't mention this, but you can keep a confidence, can't you? I believe *Doktors* take an oath to do so, isn't that correct?"

"A *Doktor* keeps all kinds of things confidential."

"Well, sometimes I forget things, and I passed out a couple of times, but I haven't had any problems lately. I don't think it will be a problem in the future."

"I see. Does anything you do bring on these fainting spells?"

"Nothing special I can think of. I just never know when it's going to happen. Don't get me wrong it's no big problem."

"I see. You can get dressed now."

"Can I leave after I'm dressed?"

"Not until we X-ray your mouth. We want to be sure you have no cavities."

I'll *bet,* Jacob thought. After they took the X-rays, Jacob said, "Are you finally through with me. I'd like to leave."

"Yes, of course. Someone will be in touch with you. We have your home address and telephone number."

"Danke schön, Herr Doktor."

The driver drove Jacob to the *Oberbefehlshaber der Luftwaffe* offices on *Knesebeck Straße* just outside Charlottenburg. Jacob realized the building that housed the Supreme Command of the German Air Force was not very far away from Karl's home. He was more nervous about going home than he had been going to *Gestapo* Headquarters. He felt it might be more difficult to fool Karl's mother than the *Gestapo.* She knew Karl much more intimately.

He was not too worried about the debriefing at the *Luftwaffe* Headquarters. It should be pretty straight forward, and he knew he had all the answers; at least he hoped he did.

The driver let him out at the curb, and Jacob told him to wait. The guard at the building challenged him, and upon identifying himself, he was ushered inside. He was still in the clothes given him aboard the submarine and felt out of place,

"*Heil* Hitler, *Hauptsturmführer* Müller. My name is *Standarttenführer* Zingler, Welcome back to Germany. We were informed of your escape and would like to talk to you about your experience in England."

"*Heil* Hitler. I'm anxious to supply whatever information I can that will help *der Vaterland.*"

"Tell me about the conditions in the English prison." Jacob told them what the routine was like, describing the conditions in the best light, but complaining about the food. At the end of two hours of questioning, Ziggler said, "The *Doktor* informed us you are prone to fainting spells as a result of a head injury." Jacob feigned outrage at the *Doktor's* revelation.

"That was supposed to be kept confidential. The *Doktor* had no right informing you what I told him. What kind of *Doktors* do we have that break their oath of confidentially?"

"The kind that has the best interest of the *Luftwaffe* at heart. We can't have a pilot endangering his *Flugzeug* and mission by losing consciousness while flying. I can understand how you feel, but we are grounding you. We'll find something besides flying that will be more suitable." Jacob acted angry and disappointed but was elated. So far the plan was working. *I've got to see Uncle Wilhelm as soon as I can before the Luftwaffe reassigns me.*

"We're giving you a week's leave. You deserve some time off after your experience." Ziggler handed Jacob a sheet of paper. "Here's a requisition for a new uniform. Report back to me one week from today at 0800." Jacob was dismissed, and he left the building.

As he walked outside, he looked for the automobile that was supposed to be waiting for him. It was nowhere in sight. In its place was a large black Mercedes Benz parked at the curb. An *Unterscharführer* was standing beside it, and when he saw Jacob, he began motioning to him. *Now what,* Jacob wondered. As he approached the Mercedes the sergeant opened the back door and out stepped a thin faced, slender, squat, officer. Jacob was stunned. It was Canaris. He stopped, stiffened, and saluted. Canaris had a big smile on his face; which gave Jacob enough confidence to greet him.

"Uncle Wilhelm, what a wonderful surprise. How did you know where to find me?" Canaris just laughed.

"Come on, get in. I'll give you a ride home." Jacob got in the back seat with his uncle and they drove away.

"It's good to see you my boy. You've had quite an experience. Your *Mutter* will be very happy to see you."

"It will be nice to see her. Does she know I'm back? How is she?"

"*Ja,* I let her know you arrived. I'm afraid there's not very good news about your *Mutter.* She suffered a stroke when your father was arrested. I don't even know if your father is alive or dead. I've talked to Kaltenbrunner about him, but he claims he doesn't know where he is. He's lying of course, but he won't tell me anything. I'm still trying to find him, or what happened to him, through my own sources." Jacob remembered Karl's recorded conversation with Vandieken about him reporting his father to the *Gestapo*. He wondered if Canaris knew of Karl's involvement. He decided to test the waters.

"So, he was arrested. He must have deserved it or that wouldn't have happened." Canaris didn't reply. They rode in silence for several minutes.

Canaris broke the silence and asked, "What do they have in mind for you now that you are back?"

"I don't know yet. They've grounded me for now. That squealing *Doktor* that examined me told them about my fainting spells as a result of the bump I received to my head when I bailed out. He has ruined my flying career."

Canaris looked over at Jacob and said, "It seems there are many in Germany who are willing to inform on others." With that statement, Jacob was sure Canaris knew of Karl's duplicity.

"By the way, I want to thank you for rescuing Franz and me. It feels good to be back in Germany. I hate the English now even more than I did before getting shot down. They are a weak race. Why haven't we invaded them by now?"

"They don't appear as weak as the *Führer* imagined. We've got a real fight on our hands."

"We will win. There's no doubt in my mind about that," Jacob said. He was sincere about that statement, and realized Canaris did not understand what he meant by *we*.

"I hope you're right." Again there was that awkward silence as they drove.

"Uncle Canaris, do you remember teaching me to write invisible messages with lemon juice when I was a little boy?"

"Yes, I do remember. That was certainly a long time ago. I'm pleased you remember."

"I used to dream about becoming a secret agent. It was a childhood fantasy. I was wondering if you could use your influence to have me transferred to the *Abwehr* where my childhood fantasy would become a reality. If I can't fly any more, I'd like to pursue my second dream."

"Hmm, I'll have to ponder that one over. I don't know how you would fit in. I demand absolute loyalty from the people that work for me." This statement was not lost on Jacob.

"If you let me work for you, I'll do anything you ask to prove my loyalty."

"I'll give that some thought. When do you report back for duty? They gave you some time off, didn't they?"

"Yes. I report back one week from today."

"I'll talk to you before then. In the meantime enjoy your leave." The Mercedes pulled into the driveway of Karl's home. He recognized it immediately. It looked exactly like the one they built in Perth. An Allied agent in Berlin had secreted plans of the house out of Germany. Jacob had become so familiar with this house he knew every room intimately.

"Here we are. Tell your *Mutter* hello for me."

"Aren't you coming in?"

"*Nein.* I've been away from the office too long. Give your *Mutter* my regards and apologize for my having to rush off." Jacob got out and the automobile drove away. He watched it until it turned back onto the street, then turned around, looked up at the house and took a deep breath. He didn't know what to expect when he faced Karl's mother. *Remember now, you're Karl, not Jacob. You can't let your feelings give you away.*

He walked up the steps, opened the door, and stepped inside. Again it looked exactly like the house in Perth, except this one was furnished. He was struck by its lavishness compared to the home in which he was raised. *That brat Karl didn't realize how lucky he was.*

The house was filled with the aroma of food. He was very hungry. He hadn't eaten since breakfast on the sub. *The Gestapo wouldn't care if you starved to death,* he thought.

"Anybody home?" Jacob shouted. Martha appeared down the hall. She was startled.

"So, you're here," she said in an icy tone.

"Yes, Martha, it's me. Is *Mutter* home?"

"Yes, she's expecting you. We're just having supper. She's in the kitchen." Jacob walked toward the kitchen and pushed open the swinging door. His mother looked up and began to cry. No sound came from her, but she was crying. She was also smiling.

"Hello *Mutter,*" Jacob said.

"Your *Mutter* can't talk. She had a stroke after your father was arrested," Martha said icily.

"Yes, I know. Uncle Wilhelm told me. He also told me about father. He asked me to give you his regards, *Mutter,* and he apologized for not coming in. He said he had to get back to the office."

Freya held out her arms and Jacob put his around her and kissed her on both cheeks. It was a strange feeling. His emotions were complicated. He didn't know what to say. He didn't want to get out of character, so he didn't say anything.

Freya motioned for him to sit down at the table. She scribbled a note with her left hand on a pad lying on the table. It said, *Welcome home dear. I'm thrilled you're home safe.*

"*Danke, Mutter.* It's good to be home." Freya motioned to Martha and then to the stove. Martha got up and ladled some food onto a plate and handed it to Jacob.

"*Danke schön,* Martha. I certainly missed your home cooking when I was in that stinking prison in England. You could teach them a thing or two about cooking. No one can cook like you." Jacob thought it wouldn't hurt to butter up Martha a little.

Martha said, "*Danke schön,*" and it sounded a little warmer.

"I've been grounded, *Mutter.* I bumped my head when I parachuted and I had a few fainting spells afterward." Freya looked alarmed. "It's nothing serious, but those fools at *Luftwaffe* Headquarters said my flying days are over. I asked Uncle Wilhelm if he could get me transferred to the *Abwehr.* He said he'd think about it." Freya wrote on her pad: *that would be wonderful. I'll have your grandmother talk to him.*

Jacob spent the evening talking to Karl's mother. Martha hovered over Freya like a protective hen. Finally Martha said, "Don't you think it's about your bedtime *Frau* Müller? You look very tired." With sad eyes, Freya, nodded her head in agreement.

"Your room is just as you left it," Martha said. Jacob just grunted.

"I think I'll just roam around the house for awhile before I retire. Maybe even read a little." Martha wheeled Freya to her bedroom, and Jacob headed for the library.

The room was just as Karl had described it to Franz. He walked around the room reading the titles on some of the books. It was a strange feeling seeing the real thing after only imagining what it would look like.

He stopped in front of the fireplace and looked at the carved panels. *The panel on the left side was the important one,* he remembered. *Why didn't Karl tell Franz which rosettes were the key to the door?*

He looked around to be sure he was alone. He moved closer to the panel, and ran his fingers over the rosettes. He noticed a very small scrape under one of the rosettes. It wouldn't even be noticed unless its significance was understood. He grasped the rosette and slid it down. It moved about an inch. He pushed the one under it up. It didn't move. He tried the next one. It didn't move. He tried the next one and it slid up. He then pushed the panel inward, and it rotated open revealing the landing and stairs. He stepped onto the landing. There were two light switches on the wall. He flipped them both. A light turned on over the stairs and in the room below. He closed the panel and locked it. He looked up along side the chimney and then descended to the room below.

Wine racks stood against the walls. They were empty except for about a dozen bottles. He picked one up, blew off the dust, and looked at the label. It read *Rheingau Cabinet, Eltville, Deutschland, 1918.* "Wow, 24 years old." He picked up another one. It read *Spatlesen, Bad Durkheim, Deutschland, 1922. This must have been some wine cellar in its hey day.* A table and a single chair sat on one side of the room. He wondered if this was the table Karl used when playing secret agent. *How ironic,* he thought.

He awoke the next morning and looked at his watch. It was 0813. He could hardly believe he had slept so late and so soundly. He got up and ran a tub full of water and bathed. He looked for a safety razor, but couldn't find one. A straight razor lay on the counter by the sink. *O boy. I didn't anticipate this. I've never used one of these before.*

He opened the cabinet and saw a soap dish and brush. The soap was dry and cracked. He let a little water drip into the bowl, wet the brush, and swirled it around. He brushed the lather on his face, and opened the razor. *I hope I don't cut my throat.* He'd seen men shave with a straight razor in movies and it looked so simple. He suspected the actors were already shaved and the razor was as dull as a tongue depressor.

He angled the blade to his face, starting at his sideburn, and carefully dragged the razor down his cheek. It slid smoothly, and he was surprised how easily it moved. Before he was through he had nicked himself a couple of times, but his whiskers were gone. He dabbed at the blood with the towel until his face stopped bleeding.

He dressed and went downstairs. He could smell bacon. He was starved and the aroma was delicious. He swung the kitchen door open and saw Martha at the stove and his mother sitting at the table. *"Guten Morgen Mutter,"* Jacob said. Freya mouthed the words, *"Guten Morgen,"* in reply.

"Guten Morgen, Martha." Martha ignored him. Freya patted the empty chair seat by her and Jacob sat down. Martha slid two over-easy eggs and slices of bacon on a plate, and set it in front of him, and poured him a cup of coffee. Freya touched her cheek and pointed at Jacob's.

"Ja, I haven't shaved with a straight razor for so long I'm a little out of practice. This breakfast looks delicious, Martha. Where are you getting this kind of

food during such hard times?" Freya scribbled: *Your grandfather is taking good care of us. We haven't wanted* for anything. Jacob marveled how well she could write left-handed. *She must have had a lot of practice.*

"Good for him. How are he and grandmother?"

Just fine, she wrote. *They will be happy to see you. Martha called them this Morgen and they will stop by tonight.*

Martha said, "Can I get anything else for you *Frau* Müller." Freya shook her head no.

"Martha, is the automobile in running condition?" Jacob asked.

"I don't know. It hasn't been driven since your father was taken away." She looked sternly at Jacob. *Oops. I struck a raw nerve.*

"I'll call a *Mechaniker* to look at it. I'm going to need transportation. Looking at his mother he asked, "Is Albert still in business?" Freya looked at Martha and pantomimed thumbing through a book. Martha got the telephone book and handed it to Jacob. He looked up the number in the business section.

"Here it is. I'll give him a call." Jacob dialed and the phone rang…Hello, is this Albert's *Mechaniker?*…It is? Good. This is the Müller residence. Would you please come by and check out our automobile. It hasn't been driven for quite some time. I'm sure the battery is dead, and what else isn't working I'm not sure…Yes, it's still the '39 Mercedes…Yes, we're at the same address…In about an hour?…I'll see you then." Jacob hung up the phone.

"I'll need some money for the automobile repair, *Mutter.*" Freya motioned Jacob to follow her. She started to propel the wheelchair, but Jacob took over and pushed it. "Where to, *Mutter?*"

Martha said, "She wants to go to her bedroom." Freya opened a dresser drawer, and retrieved an envelope and handed it to Jacob. It was filled with *Reichmarks.* He folded it and shoved it into his pants pocket without any acknowledgement or thanks. Right in character.

The *Mechaniker* put a new battery in the Mercedes, worked on the carburetor, and got it running. The tank was half full of *Benzin.* The *Mechaniker* told him the fuel was sour and he should get some fresh *Benzin* in the tank as soon as possible. Freya gave Jacob a *Benzin* ration book. None of the coupons had been used.

"I've got to go to the military supply depot and get a new uniform," Jacob told his *Mutter.* "I'll be back in time for dinner."

The address on the requisition paper was 2143 *Goethe Straße* in Charlottenburg. He found a Berlin street map in the glove compartment of the Mercedes. *This will come in handy,* he thought. The map showed the supply depot to be even closer to Karl's home than the *Luftwaffe* headquarters. It proved to be only 20 minutes away. He found the building and went inside and handed the requisition to the *Rottenführer.*

"Write your sizes next to the items, and I'll start pulling the clothes. Jacob had memorized the correct European sizes. He penciled them in next to each garment and handed it back to the *Rottenführer.* When everything was collected he said, "I'd like to change into my uniform here."

"There's a room with a mirror right over there. Help yourself." Jacob took the clothes to the room and tried them on. The pants were a little too tight and the shoes were too big, but everything else was just right. He asked for a size larger pant and smaller size shoes. When he was fully dressed he looked at himself in the mirror, and everything seemed to be suitable.

"These will do. I'll need the insignia of a *Hauptsturmführer.*" The clerk went to a drawer and put the items on the counter. Jacob attached the metal insignia to his uniform and put the cloth patches in his pocket. I'll *have Martha sew these on tonight.* The clerk had him sign the form that indicated the items he had received, and stapled it to the requisition. Jacob gathered up the clothes he had been wearing and left.

As he drove away, Redder, the *Gestapo* agent, entered the building and approached the *Rottenführer.*

"Let me see the paper work on that officer that just left."

"Yes sir. Here it is." Redder looked it over and asked, "Did you see anything unusual about this man?"

"Not really. He seemed quite normal to me."

"I see. If he should come back, do not mention my inquiry. Do you understand?" Redder scowled.

"Yes sir. Perfectly, sir."

"*Heil* Hitler."

"*Heil* Hitler," the *Rottenfhürer* replied.

The receptionist looked up and seeing a *Gestapo* officer, nervously asked, "M…May I help you, sir? Do you have an appointment? What is your name?" Redder just scowled at her. Alarmed, she stood up and backed slightly toward the inner office door.

"I don't need an appointment. Get out of my way." Redder roughly pushed the receptionist aside and barged into the inner office. Startled, the dentist looked up and almost dropped his drill. The patient, who did not like going to the dentist in the first place, looked even more frightened than he did when he first sat down in the chair.

"What is the meaning of this? Can't you see I'm with a patient? Who are you and what do you want?" Redder said to the patient, "Get out of here."

"Now see here, you can't just barge in here and order my patients around."

"Shut up and listen to me, or would you rather we talk at *Gestapo* headquarters?"

"There's no need for that," the dentist replied in a more conciliatory tone. A devilish smile creased Redder's face. He had horrible teeth, and the dentist thought he was there to have his teeth examined.

"I believe I can help you. Are you having any pain?"

"I'm not here about my teeth. I'm here about someone else's teeth. I want the file on Karl Müller."

"What do you want with his file? He hasn't been in for an examination for a very long time."

"That's none of your business, just get it." The dentist opened the file cabinet drawer, retrieved the file, and handed it to Redder.

"A patient's medical record is confidential. I shouldn't be giving that to you."

Redder just ignored him and said, "This file hasn't been tampered with in any way, has it?"

"Not to my knowledge, however there was an unusual incident that happened several weeks ago."

"What incident?"

"A man broke into my office and assaulted me. I heard him open the file drawer, and then he just left."

"Were any of your files missing?"

"Not that I could tell."

"You'll get this file back when I'm through with it. Under no circumstances are you to say anything to Müller about this visit. Do you understand?"

"I have no idea when I will see *Herr* Müller again."

"Just keep your mouth shut if and when you see him. If I hear differently, I'll be back."

"Yes sir," the dentist replied. Redder stalked out, and the patient timidly crept back into the *torture chamber*.

"*Guten Abend, G*randmother and Grandfather. It's nice to see you both again."

"Don't be so formal, Karl. Give me a hug and kiss," Inge said. His grandfather's greeting was more reserved.

"Let me take a good look at you. A little more mature, maybe. It appears those barbarians treated you quite civilly," his grandmother said.

"I feel like the same person."

"Too bad," his grandfather replied.

"Now Max, keep a civil tongue. Don't spoil Karl's homecoming." Max ignored the comment.

"I understand you want to work for the *Abwehr*."

"Yes, I approached Uncle Wilhelm about working for him. I believe I would enjoy that since I'm unable to fly anymore."

"Good, it's much too dangerous up in those *Klugzeugen* any way. I'm sure your mother agrees." Freya nodded her head in the affirmative.

"If Uncle Wilhelm accepts me, I will give him my loyalty and best effort. I believe I can do the job."

"I know you can, and I have a hunch he will welcome you," his grandmother said with a wink.

"My name is Friedrich Olbricht, *Obergruppenführer* Friedrich Olbricht. The Admiral has asked me to show you around the offices and introduce you to the *Abweherstellen*." As they walked, Olbricht went on to explain that the *Abwehr was* divided into three main groups; Group I; Secret Intelligence Service; Group II; Cipher Service; Group III; Counterespionage. "Group III is the most extensive and better organized. I don't know what the chief has in mind for you, but it would be well if you were to become associated with Group III.

"You will learn that the *Abwehr* does not have the power to make arrests. It depends on the *Gestapo* for that. It's a galling point with us, but that's the way it is."

CHAPTER 31

▼

Jacob and Franz-Walter Vandieken were having dinner at Felix's, a well-patronized restaurant. Jacob had learned from the eavesdroppers at the prison that it was Karl's favorite eating establishment.

"It's good seeing you again Karl; did you enjoy your leave?"

"It was all right. How about you?"

"It was too short. I was not thrilled to report back to duty," Franz replied.

"I wouldn't say that where the wrong people might hear you. There are ears everywhere."

"I trust you wouldn't report me, would you Karl?"

"Of course not, but be careful."

"I was told that you have been reassigned to the *Abwehr*. Is that true," Franz inquired.

"That's true. I was grounded by the *Luftwaffe*, as you probably heard."

"Yes, too bad. You will be missed."

"I'll miss flying, but I'm enjoying my new assignment." They continued to talk as they ate. It was an excellent meal. Jacob had ordered *Linsensuppe*; a soup made from lentils, followed by *Königsberger Klopse*, poached meatballs in lemon and caper sauce, and washed down with a chilled *Rheingau Cabinet* wine. He understood why this was Karl's favorite restaurant. The food and service were excellent.

After they were through eating, the waiter cleared the table and asked, "May I get anything else for you this evening gentlemen?"

"No, that will be all. Just bring me the *Rechnung*," Jacob replied.

"Excuse me, Karl, I've got to use the *Toilette*."

"Go ahead. I'll take care of the check." The waiter returned with the *Rechnung* and laid it in front of Jacob. He looked at the amount and noticed at the bottom there was a small drawing of a camel. Jacob looked up, surprised. The waiter gave a slight nod. Jacob tried to remain calm, but his heart was pounding. He gave the waiter enough *Reishmarks* to cover the *Rechnung* and gratuity. The waiter thanked him, picked up the money and check, and shuffled off.

Jacob anxiously waited for Franz. *Now what do I do? How do I make contact?* Franz interrupted his thoughts as he returned. "Let's get out of here," Jacob said as he got up from the table.

They left the restaurant and Franz said, "Thanks for dinner, let's do it again soon."

"Sure. Why not," Jacob replied absently as he walked away. *Same old Karl,* Franz thought.

Jacob was trying to decide what he should do now that contact with his handler had been made. He went outside and got into his Mercedes and turned on the engine. As he sat there contemplating his next move he glanced into his rear view mirror and noticed a car pulling out that did not turn on its lights. *Could Camel have followed me so soon?* He wondered. On impulse he turned the car around and his headlights bathed a startled Bruno Redder. Jacob stopped his automobile in front of Redder's, got out and slammed the door. He jerked Redder's door open, grabbed him by the lapels, and yanked him out of the car.

"What are you doing following me?" Jacob shouted, the veins on his neck bulging.

"I'm *not* following you."

"Then what are you doing here?"

"That's none of your business."

"I'm only going to tell you this once. Stay away from me. I'm tired of seeing your ugly face." He roughly pushed him back into the automobile and headed back to his own. He watched until Redder left. He was seething to the boiling point. *Redder is a nuisance I hadn't counted on.*

Jacob sat in his automobile and watched as patron after patron left until there were no more cars. The restaurant's blackout curtains hid any light from inside, and he didn't know if anyone was still there. It was now 0120 and he was about to leave when an automobile appeared from behind the building. He picked up his binoculars and strained to see who it was. It *was* the waiter. Jacob quickly turned on his dome lights as the waiter passed. *He didn't stop. I'm sure he could see me, why didn't he stop?* Jacob decided to follow.

He followed the car until they were outside the city. It was very dark. Jacob had to drive very close because the headlights were designed to light the road only a short distance, and were covered on top so the light could not be seen by enemy aircraft. Suddenly, the waiter accelerated and made a turn at an intersecting road. Jacob followed, but after he turned, the car was nowhere in sight. He stopped, straining to see where he might have gone. Suddenly the door was yanked open and he felt the cold steel of the end of a revolver under his chin.

"Who are you, and why are you following me?"

"Surely you know who I am."

"If I knew, I wouldn't be asking. I don't recall ever having seen you before." Jacob began to wonder if he had misinterpreted the drawing.

"I thought I knew who *you* were, but now I'm not so sure. The gun was still under his chin and he was getting nervous. Jacob asked, "Have you ever been fox hunting?" The gun lowered just a bit and Jacob relaxed a little.

"Yes, I've been fox hunting, and I may have just found one."

"Couldn't you see me back at the restaurant parking area? Why didn't you stop?" Jacob replied.

"I saw you, but I don't take chances. Amateurs. How do I know you weren't followed?"

"I wasn't followed. I did learn a few things at Perth." Jacob then remembered Redder and knew *Camel* was right.

"You made a mistake. You should have waited for me to approach you."

"I guess so, but I needed to make contact as soon as possible, because I have vital information that must reach London. Do you have the transmitter?"

"Yes, it's in the boot, I'll get it." Jacob followed *Camel* to his vehicle, which had been driven off the road into some bushes. *Camel* lifted the boot lid and picked up the wireless transmitter. He handled it almost reverently.

"It was not easy getting this into Germany. It was hand carried from Switzerland into Austria, then over the mountains at Innsbruck, and on into Berlin. It cost one agent his life. Take good care of it. It's an exact duplicate of the one you used at Perth, with one additional feature."

"And what's that?"

"See this red switch. It's a destruct switch. Thirty seconds after it's activated, you will hear a very loud noise. That is you'll hear it if you're far enough away when it goes off. It has a wad of plastic explosive in it the size of your fist. It will blow it and anything else around it into a million pieces. It's way ahead of the competition and we can't afford to let it fall into enemy hands."

"Or it's operator. Is that the plan?"

"Don't be so cynical. Just be careful with it."

"I think careful every waking minute."

"Keep thinking that way and you'll live longer."

"It's very late and I need to get home. I have to be at the office by 0630. How do we make contact in the future?"

"Eat at Felix's as often as you can. If I have a message for you, I'll point the tines of the fork toward you when I lay out your silverware. That's the signal for you to use the toilet. A message will be taped to the underside of the toilet water tank lid. Read the message and flush it. If you leave a message there for me, lay your knife across the top of the plate. Can you remember that?" *Camel* remarked sarcastically.

"Yes, I'll remember."

"All right, I'll see you when you next visit Felix's. You'd better get going."

Jacob arrived home at 0250. He quietly tip toed into the library and opened the panel door. He went down the stairs and deposited the wireless on the table. He retraced his steps and headed for his bedroom. A pair of unseen eyes followed his every movement.

At exactly 0630 Admiral Wilhelm Canaris walked through the door of the building at *72-76 Tirpit Ufer Straße.* The guard stiffened to attention as he passed. He entered the rickety elevator, which deposited him on the third floor of this gloomy building. He made his way down the poorly lighted hall passing several darkened, uninspiring offices. Most were unoccupied at this early hour.

His own office, which overlooked the *Landwehr Canal,* contained "a leather couch, a desk and conference table, a few document stands, the inevitable camp bed, numerous books, a model of the light cruiser *Dresden* and a trio of bronze monkeys from Japan symbolizing the cardinal virtues of the secret serviceman *(see all, hear all, say nothing)*"[1] A large portrait of Hitler adorned one wall. Secreted behind the portrait was Canaris's personal safe.

Jacob, upon seeing Canaris arrive, waited a few minutes for him to get settled, and then entered the outer office where Canaris's senior secretary, Vera Scharte, greeted him.

"*Guten Morgen, Hauptsturmführer* Müller."

"*Guten Morgen, Frau* Scharte. I see the chief has arrived."

"*Ja, go right* in. He's expecting you."

Jacob stood in front of the office door and knocked. A voice said, "Come".

---

1. *Canaris, Hitler's Master Spy,* by Heinz Höhne

Jacob entered and said, "*Guten Morgen* uncle."

"Don't ever call me uncle in these offices, understand?"

"Yes sir, perfectly sir."

"Be seated. I want to talk to you."

"Yes sir." Jacob sat down, sitting very erect.

"I've appointed you to be my adjutant."

"Yes sir. *Obergruppenführer* Olbricht informed me of such."

"You will attend all the staff meetings and meetings of the High Command whenever I attend. Hitler usually attends all the High Command meetings. You are to take notes; particularly of any questions I'm unable to give an answer to at the time that will require some research. Do not speak unless you are spoken to. If you are asked a question and don't know what to say, I'll step in and answer for you. At the end of these meetings prepare a summary of your notes of the meeting for future reference. Are there any questions?"

"No sir, I think I understand perfectly sir." Jacob was elated. He was now in a position to know just about everything Canaris would know. The *Fox* was literally in the hen house. It then struck him that he was also where Canaris could keep a close eye on his yet to be trusted nephew.

He reminded himself not to get overconfident and careless.

The next day, Jacob was summoned to Canaris' office.

"I want you to call a staff meeting for 0900 tomorrow morning. Here's a list of all those who should attend. See that they are informed."

"Yes sir." Jacob took the list and read the names as he walked back to his own office.

At 0900 the following morning, seated around the conference table in Canaris's office were the following department heads: *Gruppenführer* Hans Oster; *Abteilung Z, Standartenführer* Georg Hansen; *Abteilung I; Standartenführer* Wessel von Freytag-Loringboven; *Abteilung II; Sturmbannführer* Rudolf Bambler; *Abteilung III; Obersturmbannführer* Werner Best; legal adviser, Richard Protze, head of sub group IIIF; Canaris and Jacob. All eyes were on the chief.

"Gentlemen, we have been too pacifist regarding counterespionage. We are now going on the offensive. I want our agents "to penetrate foreign intelligence agencies and investigate their operations against Germany from within, or cause disruption by feeding them *Spielmaterial* {doctored information}."[2]

2. Ibid

"Our agents will be joined by a second group of informants comprised of waiters, porters, and chambermaids who work in hotels in the vicinity of each of our *Abwehrstellen*. Their job is to keep watch on suspected agents, but also to prospect for foreigners who might lend themselves to employment abroad on behalf of German counterespionage. Also concentrate on diplomatic establishments in Berlin, where foreign intentions can be gauged by agents insinuated into legations and embassies."[3] Are there any questions?" *Sturmbannführer* Bambler spoke up.

"Yes sir. I have one. Are there any budget constraints on hiring additional personnel if we feel it necessary to meet these objectives?"

"None. I want results. Do whatever it takes. Any more questions?"

"Yes sir," said *Gruppenführer* Oster. "Do we finally have the authority to order any arrest we think is necessary?"

"No, Oster! We do not! You know the power to arrest lies solely within the jurisdiction of the *Gestapo*."

"But what if a suspect is in danger of getting out of our reach before we can contact the *Gestapo* and get them on the scene?"

"In such cases unavoidable accidents might be necessary." Heads nod as the meaning sinks in.

"I expect a report on your progress one week from today. That will be all, gentlemen." They arose as a body and filed out of the office. As Jacob was about to leave, Canaris said in a somber tone, "*Hauptsturmführer* Müller, would you stay just a moment." Every nerve in his body jumped. *What now,* he wondered.

When the others had gone and they were left alone, Canaris said, "I received a complaint from the *Gestapo* that you roughed up one of their agents." Jacob knew he couldn't lie. There would be an investigation, and that's the last thing he wanted.

"Yes sir, I did, but let me explain. Ever since I returned to Germany this agent, his name is Bruno Redder, has been following me. I just got sick and tired of it and lost my temper."

"Is there any reason why he should be following you?"

"None that I'm aware of, sir."

"I don't want any more of that kind of behavior. We must keep good relations with the *Gestapo*. They can be frustrating, but we need them. I'll speak to Kaltenbrunner about Redder."

"*Vielen Danke,* that would be most appreciated. It won't happen again, sir."

---

3. Ibid

On his way home from the office, Jacob stopped at a material supply store. He purchased an automobile antennae, a coil of insulated copper wire, solder, a rubber grommet and a drill. He nervously looked around to be sure he wasn't being observed. He especially looked for Redder. He wouldn't be able to explain the purchase of such items. Satisfied that no one was watching, he paid the clerk and left. He was anxious to get the wireless operative, but cautious in doing so.

He stood in front of the walnut panel about to slide the rosettes to open the door. Suddenly the hair on the back of his head felt prickly and he unconsciously took a deep breath as fear enveloped him. The hair he had placed under the rosette was missing.

Someone has been in the cellar since I deposited the wireless. Slowly he turned around, expecting someone to be watching. No one was in sight. He sat down in a winged chair, his brain whirling. He looked around at the innocuous surroundings. Books stacked on shelves clear to the ceiling, a fireplace, and comfortable chairs. It was an inviting and peaceful atmosphere in contrast to the turmoil that raged within him. *Who has been in the cellar? Who was it that has seen the wireless? Having seen it what will they do, or what might they have done already?* He broke out in a cold sweat as he pondered this dilemma. *How many people know about the cellar? Freya knew, but she could not have negotiated the steps in her condition. Karl's father, Friedrich, knew, but he was either dead or in a concentration camp. Karl's grandparents knew, but it was unlikely they had been in the house, and if they had been here they would not likely have gone to the cellar. The builder knew, but it was out of reason he would have been in the house. It had to be Martha.*

All during dinner that night, Jacob watched Martha very closely. Everything seemed normal. They had the usual conversation. *How were things at the office? The bombing is deplorable; food is getting ever more scarce.* Martha did seem a little more subdued than usual. She wouldn't look Jacob in the eye when he spoke to her. But she had never been very friendly, so that may not mean anything.

After dinner was over and dishes washed, and Freya put to bed, Jacob stood in front of Martha's room door and knocked softly. A voice said, "Who is it?"

"It's Karl. May I come in?"

"Just a moment." Martha got out of bed, put on a robe, and opened the door.

"What do you want?" she asked sharply. Jacob entered the room and sat on the edge of the bed.

"Sit down Martha; I'd like to talk to you." She sat down in her bedside chair and folded her hands in front of her.

"What do you want to talk to *me* about?"

"What were you doing in the wine cellar today, Martha?"

"I haven't been in the wine cellar for over a year."

"We both know that's not true. What were you doing in the wine cellar, Martha?" Martha began to squirm a little and just stared at her hands. Finally she said, "I went down to fetch some wine."

"Where is the wine, Martha? We didn't have any with dinner tonight."

After a long silence, Martha defiantly looked Jacob square in the eye and said, "Who are you?" This was a defining moment. Jacob knew what he should do. She had to be eliminated. She knew too much. He stared at his hand as he wrestled with his conscience. His training said act and act fast. Everything may hinge on what happens in the next few moments. The whole operation could be blown. His life could be in jeopardy, but he was loath to take the life of this woman on whose care Freya was dependant. He was churning inside, but he answered as calmly as he could,

"You know who I am, Martha. I'm Karl."

"You are *not* Karl. Karl would have slit my throat by now." She was right. That's probably what he should do, but even with all his training he could not bring himself to do it. It's one thing to go through the motions while preparing for the mission, but quite another thing when confronted with a real situation. If it was Redder, he could have done it without a moment's hesitation.

They both just sat in silence, each with their own thoughts. Finally Martha broke the silence; she looked Jacob directly in the eye and said, "Until the end of the war, you are Karl Müller."

Jacob smiled, extended his hand and said, "It's a deal." They both visibly relaxed and Jacob got up and left the room.

Jacob descended the steps to the wine cellar. He was still reeling from his confrontation with Martha. *Could he trust her? Did he have a choice?* Yes, and he had made that choice. He felt that Martha would not risk putting Freya and herself in danger by exposing him. *No need upsetting the status quo* he decided. *I'll let it ride for a while and see what happens. It might even be an advantage having a willing accomplice.*

He laid out the items he had purchased at the material supply store on the table by the wireless. He attached one end of the copper wire to the wireless. He soldered the other end to the antennae. He then climbed the ladder alongside the chimney and drilled a hole in the roof, and inserted the rubber grommet. He slid the antennae through the grommet out into the space above the roof.

He was now ready to broadcast. The wireless had a unique feature that would make it almost impossible to be detected by enemy eavesdroppers. The message was stored in a memory bank and then broadcast in a *blast* signal. This speeded up signal was of such a short duration that it would be almost impossible for the enemy to pinpoint its location. When it was received in London and recorded, the recorder slowed the coded message to normal speed and then deciphered it.

Jacob entered his report into the wireless, and hit the send button. A short whirring sound and the message was in the airwaves.

Hunched over powerful receivers were several men with earphones on their heads. They were monitoring Allied radio traffic. One of them looked up, startled, and said out loud, "What was that?"

Another operator just as startled said, "I heard something too. What was it? I've never heard anything like that before." They looked at one another, puzzled. "Probably just an anomaly," one said as he shrugged.

"I'm not so sure," the other replied. "It may be important."

"It was so short it would be almost impossible to get a fix on its location."

"We've got to try if it happens again."

In London the message was decoded and delivered to Colonel Ashburn. He read the message and yelled at the top of his voice. "FINALLY!"

Janet came rushing into his office, startled at the outburst. "What's wrong? Are you all right?"

"I've never felt better in all my life," he replied, grinning from ear to ear.

"I'm happy to hear that. I thought something had happened to you."

"I guess I should share this news with you, but remember you cannot repeat what I tell you to anyone."

"What is it? Is it about Jacob?" Janet anxiously asked.

"Yes it's about Jacob. The message is from him. All I can tell you is that he is safe." Janet began to cry. The relief was overwhelming. Ashburn sat her down and handed her a tissue.

"What's he doing? Where is he? Can I send him a message?"

"I can't tell you any more than I've told you. And no you cannot send him a message. I'll keep him apprised of your interest from time to time."

"My interest! He bloody well knows my interest. I want to communicate with him."

"The less distraction he has, the safer he will be. You've got to trust my judgment on this."

Janet pouted a little, but finally said, "I suppose you're right." She sighed, "But please let him know that I think of him every minute of every day."

"I'll let him know you are in good health. Now send in a courier."

"Yes sir."

"And don't look so happy. Remember you're supposed to still be in mourning."

"Yes sir, I'll try".

Ashburn licked the flap of the envelope and stamped the front, "Eyes Only, PM." He handed the envelope to the courier and said, "Get this to the Prime Minister as fast as you can and don't lose it or you'll be shot. Understand?"

The courier gave Ashburn a nervous look and said, "Yes sir." He placed the envelope in the leather dispatch pouch, slung the strap over his head, and briskly walked out.

CHAPTER 32

▼

Jacob again sat in Karl's favorite restaurant, Felix's, waiting to be served. *Camel* approached the table and said, "*Guten Abend Hauptsturmführer* Müller. You haven't been in for some time."

Jacob ignored the mild rebuke and said, "*Guten Abend,* Josef. You're looking fit tonight for such an elderly waiter." *Camel* just smiled. Jacob enjoyed the banter between them.

"What do you recommend this evening, Josef?" *Camel* shrugged off the insult and laid out the silverware. The tines of the forks were pointed toward Jacob. "Excuse me, Josef. I'd like to wash up before ordering."

"Of course, I'll return when you're seated." Jacob got up and went straight to the toilet. He locked the door, lifted the water closet lid and removed the message. It read, *You are still being followed by the Gestapo. They're using several different agents so it will be less likely you would spot them. Redder is probably still directing the surveillance but is staying in the background so you won't spot him. BE CAREFUL.* Jacob tore up the message and flushed it down the toilet. He returned to his table and seated at it was a very attractive woman, looking a little apprehensive.

"I'm sorry *Fräulein,* but this is my table."

"I know it is. I've been waiting for a friend of mine, but it looks like he's not coming. I felt very uncomfortable sitting alone. It seemed like everyone was staring at me. I noticed you were alone and wondered if I might take my meal at your table."

Jacob was suspicious. *Could she be part of Redder's surveillance team? It may be safer having her close by rather than skulking in the background.*

Jacob clicked his heals and bowed. "I'd be delighted for the company, *Fräulein*. I'm *Hauptsturmführer* Karl Müller."

She extended her hand and said, "*Danke, Herr Müller*. That's very gallant of you." Jacob took her hand, clicked his heels, and lightly kissed it.

"May I inquire *your* name?"

"How stupid of me. I'm so sorry; my name is Edith Fletcher."

"I'm glad to make your acquaintance, *Fräulein* Fletcher," Jacob replied. He sat down and *Camel* approached the table with a scowl on his face.

"Are you ready to order, sir?"

"What do you recommend this evening, Josef? By the way, this is *Fräulein* Fletcher. She has joined me for dinner."

"I can see that," *Camel* replied, looking down his nose. "Our special this evening is *Bratwurst mit saurer Sahnensosse*. I'd recommend a *Rote Rübensalat* topped off with a *Zitronencreme* for desert."

"And what wine do you recommend this evening?"

"You may need a clear head this evening, *Herr Müller*," *Camel* replied as he looked directly at *Fräulein* Fletcher.

"I see…hmm…Well the entrée sounds quite good. What do you think, *Fräulein?*"

"It sounds delicious, and I may need a clear head this evening also, so no wine for me either Josef." Josef left with the order and headed toward the kitchen.

So she needs a clear head too. Jacob carefully began asking probing questions, and a verbal dance between the two began. It had been a long time since he had been this near a woman. His thoughts drifted to Janet. This woman reminded him of her in many ways: articulate, self assured, pretty, yet different. A nostalgic mood settled over him as his thoughts drifted toward his former life. He was jarred back to reality as Josef brought their dinner.

It smelled delicious, and he was ravenous. As they ate and talked, his suspicions softened, and he began to relax. He was enjoying the company in spite of the possible danger. The meal was delicious, *Fräulein* Fletcher was enchanting, and he hated to see it all end.

"*Herr Müller,* I'm stranded here. A friend dropped me off, and I was depending on my companion to escort me home. Do you suppose you could drop me off at my flat?" Jacob knew he should say no, but his sense of chivalry overcame his good judgment. He felt it would be very rude to refuse.

"I'd be delighted," he replied, but felt uneasy as he made the commitment. *Camel's* eyes bore into them as they made their way out of the restaurant together.

Edith gave Jacob directions, and they eventually arrived in front of an upscale apartment complex. He opened the door for her and led her into the lobby. She greeted the attendant at the desk. "*Guten Abend,* Siegfried. This is *Hauptsturm-führer* Müller. He is going to escort me to my room." Jacob had no intention of doing that but felt trapped.

They entered the elevator and stopped on the second floor. She put her key in the door lock, swung the door open, and walked in. Jacob stood outside, looking very uncomfortable.

What's the matter, *Hauptsturmführer*? Afraid to come in? I won't bite you. Come on in, and I'll fix you a drink." She walked into her bedroom and sat on the bed. He could see her kick off her shoes.

The next thing he heard was pfft! pfft! It was the unmistakable sound of a silenced gun. A silencer on a gun deadens the sound of the explosion of the cartridge, but the sound of the bullet speeding through the air, although muffled, is distinct. Instinctively he drew his revolver, crouched, and scooted behind the sofa. Peeking over the top he looked quickly in every direction, ready to shoot.

He heard movement in the bedroom and ran to the door, keeping very low. He peered in and could see Edith lying on her back, blood oozing from two holes in her chest. The window was open, and the curtains wafted in the breeze. He ran to the window and looked down the fire escape. A man was near the bottom and moving fast. It was too dark to see his features. His first inclination was to give chase, but on second thought he knew it would be hopeless to overtake him.

He turned around and went to the bed. He felt for a pulse on Edith's neck, but there was none. Blood from the two bullet wounds saturated her blouse. He could smell the hot, metallic scent of blood mixed with her perfume. The mingling odors created a sense of remembrance and revulsion. Her open eyes stared up accusingly, and he gently closed them. It was a grizzly sight. A beautiful human being had been snuffed out in an instant. He felt sick. *How could something like this have happened?* One minute she was a vivacious, living, breathing soul. In an instant she was gone as if she never existed.

Quickly he went to the apartment entrance, looked up and down the hall, and closed the door. He went back to the body. *Who is she, really?* He wondered. *Why was she killed?* Jacob's brain was whirling. *Was it meant to look like I killed her? I was foolish to* have *escorted her to her flat. The man in the lobby can identify me. She had even given him my name.*

He slid the body to the edge of the bed and rolled it up in the bedding. He threw her over his shoulder, climbed out the window, and carried her down the fire escape.

"That was a pretty dumb thing to do," a voice out of the dark said. Jacob almost dropped the corpse as he whirled around. It was *Camel.*

"What are you doing here?" Jacob almost shouted. "You scared the bejabbers out of me."

"It serves you right. What have you got there?"

"It's the woman I was with tonight. Someone shot her."

"A fine mess you've gotten yourself into."

"I agree. I should have known better, but it's too late now for recriminations. I've got to get rid of her body."

"Put her in the boot of my automobile. I'll take care of her" Jacob carried the body to the car. *Camel* opened the boot and a dead man was lying there looking up at him.

"Who's that?"

"The guy that came down the fire escape ahead of you."

"What happened?"

"I was a little faster getting off a shot than he was."

"He must be the one that killed the girl."

"Then he deserved what he got. Put the woman on top of him and get back up the fire escape as fast as you can. Go out of the building the way you came in. This may have been a set up. You were probably meant to take the blame for this woman's murder."

"That crossed my mind too," Jacob said.

"The *Gestapo* is probably already on their way," *Camel* warned.

Jacob unceremoniously dropped the body in the boot and sprinted to the fire escape. *Camel* slammed the boot lid shut and took off, burning rubber as he accelerated.

Jacob climbed back into the room and left the window open. He went out into the hall, closed the door to the flat, and headed for the elevator. He was breathing hard from the exertion. He took deep breaths to slow his heart rate and calm himself. He pressed the button for the elevator. It emitted a faint ping as the door opened. He stepped in and pressed the button for the lobby. He exited into the lobby and walked toward the front door. Siegfried said, "*Gute Nacht,*" *Herr* Müller."

Jacob replied, "*Gute Nacht,*" and stepped out into the night air. Two automobiles skidded to a stop in front of the building. Eight men jumped out and surrounded him with drawn guns.

"What is the meaning of this?" Jacob blurted out.

"We received a report of gun fire coming from this building." *Camel* was right. This was a setup. No one could have heard gunfire from a silenced gun.

"I didn't hear any gunfire."

"I'm sure," the one who appeared to be in charge said with a sneer.

"You are coming with us." They walked Jacob back into the lobby. When Siegfried saw the *Gestapo* the blood drained from his face.

"Did this man come in here tonight with anyone?" the agent growled.

"Yes sir. He was with *Fräulein* Fletcher. She's in room 202. Should I ring her for you?"

"That won't be necessary; we'll see for ourselves." They pushed Jacob into the elevator and went to the second floor. At apartment 202, they banged on the door. No one stirred inside. Jacob knew no one would be coming to the door and thought the *Gestapo* also knew this. The *Gestapo* agent turned the doorknob and cautiously peered inside. They pushed Jacob into the room and followed him in. They walked from the sitting room to the bedroom. No one was there.

"Check the kitchen."

"There is no one there, sir."

"Where is *Fräulein* Fletcher?" The agent demanded.

"I have no idea. She was here when I left," he lied with as much conviction as he could muster. The agent walked over to the open window and peered down. Jacob said, "Maybe she went out the window."

"And took all her bedding with her? You must think I'm a *dumbkoff.*"

"You have my vote." A blow to the side of his head almost made him black out.

"Don't get smart with me." Jacob shook his head to clear the cobwebs.

"What other explanation is there."

"You tell me. What were you doing here tonight?"

"I met *Fräulein* Fletcher at a restaurant, Felix's, in Charlottenburg. We had dinner together. She asked me for a ride back to her flat and I obliged."

"How long have you known her?"

"About two hours."

"That' a likely story. How long were you in her apartment?"

"About ten minutes, and no one could have heard gun shots, because there were none. Ask Siegfried, the lobby attendant."

"Don't tell me how to investigate this incident. You are coming with us." They led Jacob out of the building to one of the automobiles. He was put in the back seat between two burly agents, and they sped off. He noticed the other automobile stayed behind.

"Where are you taking me?" Jacob asked.

"Shut up. You'll see soon enough."

In about thirty minutes they pulled up in front of *Gestapo* Headquarters. A chill went up Jacob's spine. The two agents he had sat between roughly dragged him out of the automobile and practically carried him into the building.

Inside waiting was Bruno Redder, a smirk on his ugly face. Jacob struggled to free himself and received a chop to the back of his neck. He went out like a light. They dragged him to a cell in the basement, shoved him to the floor, and slammed the door shut.

"Where's my adjutant, *Frau* Scharte?"

"I don't know, sir. He's never been late before."

"Call his home. Maybe he overslept."

"Yes sir." *Frau* Scharte dialed the telephone and waited. Martha answered.

"This is *Frau* Scharte, Admiral Canaris's secretary. Is Karl in?"

"No, he isn't. He didn't come home last night, and we're very worried."

"When did you last see him?"

"Yesterday morning. He had breakfast and left for his office."

"I see. *Danke.* If you hear from him, have him call Admiral Canaris."

"Yes of course. If you hear from him, please have him call home."

"I'll do that. *Guten Tag.*"

"He didn't come home last night, sir, and they are very worried about him."

"Hmm, that's not like Karl. Call the hospitals and make inquiries."

"Yes sir."

Jacob rolled over and moaned. He had a splitting headache and was stiff and cold. It was very dark, but he could tell he was in a cell. A cot stood against the wall. It had only a thin mattress and no blanket. He struggled to his feet and headed for the cot and sat down. The mattress felt clammy and it stank. He began to shiver from the cold. He wrapped his arms around himself and curled up in a ball, trying to get warm. It didn't help much.

He didn't know how long he had been lying there, but it seemed like an eternity. He shivered uncontrollably. He was startled out of his funk by the sound of the cell door opening. Two men grabbed him under his arms and escorted him out of the cell and down the hall. They passed other cells, and he could dimly see human forms in some of them. No sound came from them. The odor of human waste burned his nostrils. They entered a room, bare except for a table with a chair on each side. A single light bulb hung from the ceiling. They pushed him into one of the chairs and stood aside. He was aware of someone entering the room. He looked up and saw Redder taking the seat across from him.

"Well, did you have a nice nap?" Redder asked. Jacob didn't answer. Someone hit him on the side of the head and knocked him to the floor. He was picked up and sat back in the chair. His head throbbed.

"I'd suggest you answer my questions. These two gentlemen love to inflict pain. Now tell me what you were doing at *Fräulein* Fletcher's apartment." Jacob didn't answer. A fist caught him flush in the face, and blood ran out of his nose into his mouth. They picked him up off the floor and put him back in the chair.

"We can keep this up all day if you like. Now tell me, what were you doing in *Fräulein* Fletcher's flat?"

Jacob hesitated, expecting another blow, but before they hit him again he said, "She invited me into her flat after I escorted her from the restaurant where we had dinner together."

"How long have you known this woman?"

"The first time I laid eyes on her was at the restaurant."

"Do you expect me to believe that?" Redder sneered.

Jacob angrily replied, "I don't care if you do or not, it's…" He didn't get to finish the sentence. Another blow to the side of the head and down he went. They picked him up and slammed him into the chair.

"I'd suggest a little more cooperation and respect. Now, what did you do in her flat?"

"We just talked. She wanted to fix me a drink, but I declined."

"How long were you in her flat?"

"Just a few minutes."

"Wasn't this a lover's tryst?"

"No it was not. I was only there a short time."

"Long enough, I'm sure."

"Maybe for you, but not…" Another blow to the head and down he went. This time he was unconscious. He woke up in the same smelly cell with a worse headache than before. He was still cold and clammy.

"Sir, I just received an anonymous call saying that Karl has been arrested and is at *Gestapo* Headquarters." Canaris looked stunned. Then a scowl crept over his face.

"Get me my limousine," He growled.

"Yes sir. I'll have it brought around immediately."

"Where to sir," the chauffeur asked cheerfully.

"*Gestapo* Headquarters." The chauffeur's mood abruptly changed.

"Yes sir," he replied with little enthusiasm. No one in Germany who was familiar with that address wanted to be anywhere near it. They rode in silence until they arrived at *8 Prinz-Albrecht-Straße.*

The chauffeur stopped the automobile, ran to the other side, and opened the door of the limousine for Canaris. He stiffened to attention as Canaris emerged. The guard at the door to the building snapped to attention and saluted. Canaris acknowledged with a casual salute as he passed inside.

The officer at the desk about knocked his chair over as he jumped to his feet when Canaris approached. "Where is Kaltenbrünner?" Canaris demanded.

"He's not in today, sir. Can I help you sir."

"You certainly can; you can bring my adjutant here immediately."

"What is his name sir?"

"*Hauptsturmführer* Karl Müller." The officer blanched.

"I…I'm sorry sir, but he is under arrest. I have no authority to release him."

"I'm giving you an order. You will release him immediately."

"I…I…I'm sorry sir. I can only do that with permission of the proper authority," he stammered. "I have my orders sir."

"And who might that be?"

"It would be *Herr* Kaltenbrünner himself, sir."

"Tell *Herr* Kaltenbrünner I'm here, and I demand to speak with him straight away."

"I'm sorry sir. Like I told you, he is not here, sir."

"And when will he be here?"

"I don't know, sir. He doesn't share his schedule with me, sir."

"What is *Hauptsturmführer* Müller charged with?" Canaris snarled.

"I'll have you talk with the arresting agent, and you can ask him, sir." Relief spread across the officer's face as Redder entered the foyer. Canaris scowled when he saw who it was. Redder was taken aback when he saw Canaris.

"Why was *Hauptsturmführer* Müller arrested?" Canaris demanded. Redder hesitated. Canaris, red faced, shouted the question again. Redder finally found his voice and blurted out that he was suspected of shooting a woman last night.

"What woman?" Canaris again demanded.

"A *Fräulein* Fletcher, sir."

"And where did this take place?"

"At her flat, number *10 Kirch Straße,* sir."

"Were there any witnesses to this so called shooting?"

"The lobby attendant heard the shots and called us, sir."

"That isn't what I asked you. Did anyone see *Hauptstrumführer* Müller shoot someone?"

"Well not exactly. The..."

Canaris cut him off and with controlled fury said, "Either someone saw him shoot this woman or they did not. Which is it?"

Redder was pale and sweating. "It's like I said, the man at the desk heard shots and called us."

"Why would he call the *Gestapo* instead of the *polizei?*" Redder hesitated and Canaris knew he was lying. "Where did they take this woman's body?"

Redder knew he was trapped. He squirmed and replied, "We didn't find a body. We're not sure what he did with it, sir."

"YOU DON'T KNOW WHAT HE DID WITH IT!" Canaris shouted. "IF YOU DIDN'T FIND A BODY HOW DO YOU KNOW SOMEONE WAS MURDERED?" Redder was silent. Canaris was apoplectic.

"When Kaltenbrunner returns have him call me immediately, do you understand? Immediately!" Canaris fumed and stomped out.

Redder, shaken by the confrontation, weakly replied, "Yes sir. *Heil* Hitler"

When Kaltenbrunner returned he was told of Canaris's visit. He was informed of Jacob's arrest and the circumstances surrounding it. He was so concerned by the political implications of the incident that he telephoned Himmler.

At this time, Himmler controlled the "vast administrative and police network, the *Gestapo,* the concentration camp system, the feared *Einsatzgruppen, and a vast Waffen SS* army of 40 divisions. In addition the *SS* had developed a hugely profitable economic section, which owned its own industries, and had embarked on a human breeding programme based on the *Lebensborn* maternity homes serviced by chosen *SS* men that was designed to perfect a future German élite."[1]

When Himmler got this news he was livid. The *Gestapo* had forged a cordial relationship with Canaris and the *Abwehr,* and Himmler did not want anything to jeopardize it. He had always treated Canaris with courtesy and respect. He was intrigued by Canaris's reputation as a spy *par excellence.* This romantic image of Canaris appealed to this power-hungry, mystical *Reichsführer.* Himmler telephoned Canaris.

---

1. *The Macmillan Dictionary Of The Second World War* by Elizabeth Anne Wheal & Steven Pope.

"My dear Admiral, I have just been informed of the arrest of your adjutant. I've ordered his immediate release. Those responsible have been put on restrictive leave and will be harshly dealt with. I'm so very sorry for this incident."

"*Danke Sehr,* Heinrich. These things happen, but I'm not very happy about it."

"I understand. What can I say? I can only try to make amends. Let's do the opera and dinner soon."

"That would be nice," Canaris icily replied.

A Gestapo agent drove Jacob home. He slowly got out of the automobile and painfully made his way up the steps. As he stepped inside the house, Martha was coming out of the kitchen. When she saw him she gasped, "What happened to you? Have you been in an accident?"

"It was no accident."

"I'll let your *Mutter* know you are home. She has been sick with worry."

"Not now. I would like to get cleaned up first." Jacob struggled up the stairs to his room. He undressed and put his clothes in a hamper. They smelled so bad he put the hamper in the hall. He filled the tub with steaming hot water, and climbed in. *Oooooh that feels good.* He laid back and rested his head on the tub. He closed his eyes. The warmth penetrated his aching muscles. As he lay there his thoughts returned to the *Gestapo* prison. *Something has got to be done about Bruno Redder. I'll think of something appropriate.*

Freya's speech had been slowly returning. She called out as loud as she could. "Who…is…that?…Is it…Karl?"

Martha went into her bedroom and said, "Yes, Karl is home."

"I…want…see him. Take…me…to him."

"He's gone up stairs to clean up."

"What…do…you…mean…clean…up? Is…he…all right?"

Martha hesitantly replied, "He was a little soiled…and…and he has a few cuts and bruises, but he is all right."

"What…happened? How…did…he…get hurt?"

"He didn't tell me, but I'm sure he will explain in good time. Now don't fret, he's home and safe."

Jacob drove to Felix's. He entered the restaurant and was seated by the *maitre d'.* Josef came to the table, and when he saw Jacob he said, "You look like you have been in a fight. How does the other fellow look?"

"Ugly, but not because of me. His parents are responsible."

"I see," Josef said with a knowing nod. Jacob noticed that Josef had laid the tines of the fork pointing toward him.

"Excuse me Josef, I'd like to wash up before dinner. I'll be right back."

"Yes sir, I'll return when you are seated." Jacob went into the toilet, locked the door and lifted the water closet lid. The note read, I'll *take care of Bruno Redder. Don't do anything foolish; it's too dangerous.* Jacob scribbled a note saying, *what do you have in mind? I know what I'm going to do,* and placed the note under the lid and returned to his table. *Camel* came back and Jacob said, "What do you recommend this evening, Josef?"

"We have a *delikate* veal steak sautéed to a golden blush, and prettied up with a *béarnaise* sauce and served with snowy, buttery asparagus on toast."

"My mouth is watering. That sounds just fine, Josef."

"Your usual *Spatlesen.* wine, sir?"

"Perfect, Josef. A large bottle please, I'm very thirsty tonight"

"As you wish, sir."

Jacob left the restaurant with his stomach pleasantly satisfied and a warm glow from the wine. *There is no place like Felix's. Thank you again Karl for the recommendation.* When Josef cleared the table he noticed the knife was placed across the top of the plate.

When Jacob got home he went to the wine cellar to see if any messages had come. There was one. He decoded it and it read, *URGENT. Lt. General Thomas Marsh, US Army Air Forces made unauthorized flight on bombing raid over Berlin. B17 he was on shot down. Parachutes were observed. Important we know if he survived and is captured. He has sensitive information concerning Overlord. Vital that information regarding this operation not be extracted from him. Use extreme measures if required to eliminate possibility of any leak.* Jacob read the message several times. The words *extreme measures* jumped out at him and made his head throb. *Eliminate* made his mouth go dry. This is one message he wished he had never seen.

CHAPTER 33

▼

So much secret information was being absorbed by Jacob that it was difficult to know what to prioritize for relay to London. He made copious notes and smuggled them out of the *Abwehr* on paper rolled up inside his fountain pen.

On 29 August 1943, he learned from a cable sent by an Abwehr agent (code number RR 3174) reporting to his controller at *Abwehrstelle* Hamburg, that the Russians might be amenable to a negotiated settlement with Germany. This impending Russo-German peace settlement was confirmed by a telegram to the Foreign Ministry in Lisbon.

According to Canaris, Hitler was not interested in a settlement but instead wanted to crush Russia and Bolshevism. Jacob included in his report that this may only have been Canaris' assessment of the situation because of *his* anti-communist feelings, and that there may be an interest at the very highest level in Germany for a negotiated settlement.

If the Russians made peace with Germany, it would allow Germany to transfer massive forces from the east to the west front to face the Allies.

Ever since Jacob learned of the existence of a safe in Canaris's office, he had been curious as to what it might contain. Canaris never attempted to keep Jacob from knowing about the safe, but he never shared the combination either.

Jacob's office joined Canaris', and a door between Jacob's office and Canaris' provided easy access when Canaris summoned his adjutant. A button on Canaris's desk activated a buzzer in Jacob's office and was the signal for Jacob to drop anything he might be doing and rush to his master. It was an irritant that Jacob had to endure.

Access to both offices from the hallway was through an outer lobby occupied by *Frau V*era Scharte, Canaris' secretary.

It was 2130 hours and most of the *Abwehr* offices were deserted for the night. Canaris was to leave the next morning for Madrid. Jacob made sure *Frau* Scharte's office was empty. The lights were out. *She must be gone for the night,* he surmised. He then entered Canaris's office and switched on the light.

He brought with him a folder with several sheets of paper in it on which he had typed the minutes of a meeting that day with *the Abteilung II* chief Colonel Wessel von Freytag-Loringhoven and his staff. He laid them on Canaris's desk and walked over to Hitler's picture. He looked to see if there was a latch or lock that would release the picture and allow it to swing away from the wall. He couldn't see any, so he just pulled on it and it swung from the wall on hidden hinges. The safe was now exposed. It measured about 18 x 24 inches, had a combination lock, and door handle. *How am I going to open this monster,* Jacob thought to himself. *Unfortunately safe cracking was not part of my training.* He tried the handle hoping it was set to open. The door didn't budge. He turned the dial hoping he may be able to detect something that would reveal the combination. It turned smoothly. *Nothing there. It's no use.*

As he reached for the picture frame to swing it back against the wall, something caught his eye. Etched faintly into the bottom rung of the frame were the numbers 39, 12, 23, 6. Jacob was stunned. *Could that be the combination,* he asked himself. *Would Canaris, the master spy, be so careless as to leave the combination to his safe exposed for anyone to see?* He then remembered the nightmares he used to have while in high school about forgetting the combination to his school locker. *Could Canaris have that same fear?* It didn't seem too unreasonable that Canaris would have the combination at his disposal for quick reference. The building was heavily guarded. Probably very few people knew of the safe or had access to it since Canaris kept his office locked.

Jacob turned the dial right 39, left 12, right 23, and left 6. He turned the handle, pulled, and to his delight, the safe door swung open. He peered inside. There were numerous bundles of currency held together by an elastic band. He saw *Reichsmarks,* English pound notes, US dollars, Spanish peseta, and Rubles.

Standing upright were about a dozen folders and a spiral notebook. He removed the notebook and turned to the first page. There were several columns. The first column was a set of numbers succeeded by a column of names. He quickly glanced through these names: *Cicero, Don Antonio, Drummond, Eva,*

Cato, Gutemann, Hubert. There were many more. *These are probably the agent's code names,* Jacob surmised, because he recognized the names of *Cato* and *Hubert.*

The next Column must be their real names, he thought. Another column listed the names of cities. *No doubt the location where they operate. The currency amount must be the agent's salary.* The last column showed a full name, and Jacob thought this might be their real name or their handler's name.

Jacob was very excited over having stumbled onto such a gold mine of information. He could hardly believe he had in his hands the worldwide network of spies employed by the *Abwehr.* He wished it showed the address of the agent, *but there is probably enough information here to find them, especially if the agent is using his real name instead of an alias,* Jacob reasoned.

Realizing it would take more time to copy all the information than he wanted to linger in Canaris' office, and that Canaris would be in Spain for three days, he decided to take the notebook with him. He would have plenty of time to copy and return it before *Canaris* returned. He lifted his tunic and tucked it under the waistband of his trousers.

Just then he heard a door open and he froze. A sliver of light came on under the door, and he knew someone had entered the foyer office. *Could it be Frau Scharte,* Jacob wondered. He just had time to slam the door to the safe shut, twirl the dial, and swing the picture back against the wall.

A key turned in Canaris' office door as Jacob hurriedly picked up the folder he had earlier set on Canaris' desk. In walked Canaris. Jacob tried to remain calm. Canaris was startled to see Jacob in his office and asked, "What are you doing in here this time of night?"

Jacob handed Canaris the folder and replied, "I just finished typing the *Abteilung* II report and was about to lay it on your desk when I heard you unlock your door."

"*Danke Hauptsturmführer,* just leave it on my desk. I'll review it when I return. Canaris walked over to Hitler's picture, swung it away from the wall and began to turn the combination dial.

Jacob was frantic. His heart was pounding so fast he felt faint. The notebook was like a hot iron against his stomach…*If he notices the notebook is missing I wonder how he will react,* Jacob asked himself. He noticed Canaris surreptitiously peek at the picture frame after dialing the first two numbers. Jacob would have laughed if he hadn't been so frightened. *So you forgot the combination,* Jacob would like to have said, but he couldn't have spoken if he wanted to his mouth was so dry.

Canaris surveyed the interior of the safe for several seconds while Jacob held his breath. Finally he picked up a stack of Pesetas and closed the safe door. Jacob was so relieved he almost collapsed. *I guess he wants to purchase his usual box of strawberries while in Lisbon,* Jacob thought.

"I hope you have a successful trip, sir," Jacob said as he made his way back to his own office.

"*Danke, Hauptsturmführer.* Stay out of mischief while I'm away."

"Yes sir. I most certainly will."

Jacob spent the next two evenings sending the contents of the spiral notebook to London.

That should keep MI5 and the FBI busy for a very long time.

He returned the notebook to the safe, locked it and swung the portrait of Hitler back in place.

It seemed to Jacob that Hitler was glaring down at him with indignant disapproval. Jacob just glared back defiantly and began singing the popular song everyone in America and England was singing.

"When the *Fuhrer* says *ve* are the master race, than we'll *heil* pfft, *heil* pfft, right in the *Fuhrer's* face."

"Not to love the *Fuhrer* is a big disgrace, so we'll *heil* pfft, *heil* pfft, right in the *Fuhrer's* face."

Jacob left Canaris's office in high spirits.

▼

"*Guten Abend Fräulein.* My name is *Herr* Eigruber. I'm with the *Vaterland Heim Wache.* This document will identify me as such. I've been ordered to inspect all of the residences assigned to me by *Gauleiter* Sauckel to be sure they meet the requirements specified in the *Heim* code." Jacob wore a dingy suit with matching vest, a wide brimmed hat and sported a beard and droopy mustache. His girth, with the help of some padding, gave him the appearance of a well-fed penguin. He was the epitome of the German civil servant. An irritated *Fräulein* Isolde Kettler retorted,

"Can you come back another time? I'm expecting someone."

"I'm sorry *Fräulein,* but I have my schedule."

"Didn't you hear me? I'm going to be busy."

"I heard you, *Fräulein,* but I must insist on coming in."

"Well then hurry up and get on with it. I'm going to be busy tonight." Jacob entered the flat, looked around, and walked over to the drapes and adjusted them.

"It is your duty to keep these drawn tight each night so no light escapes."

"*Ja ja,* I always keep them drawn at night," she sarcastically replied. Jacob continued looking around the room as though looking for infractions to the *Heim* code rules.

"Hmm, everything seems in order here." He walked into the bedroom. He noticed the bed had the covers turned down. There was a dressing table and chair against the opposite wall. A candle on the table burned with a small steady flame. *Very romantic.* A container with several artificial houseplants stood at the base of the window. Jacob walked over to the window and as he leaned over to adjust the drapes he slipped a wire recorder in among the plants and pressed the record button.

"Where is the kitchen, *Fräulein?*"

"Right this way and please hurry."

Jacob walked over to the gas stove and checked the connections. He turned on and off the water faucets and smiled at *Fräulein* Kettler. "A very nice kitchen *Fräulein,* but you must have the gas connections checked for leaks. They seem to be quite rusty."

"*Ja ja,* sure, anything you say." She shooed him toward the door like a sheepdog maneuvering its charges to their pen.

Jacob tipped his hat and said, "*Gute Nacht, Fräulein, and danke sehr* for your cooperation."

"*Gute Nacht, Herr* Eigruber," and good riddance, she wanted to say but bit her tongue.

Jacob slouched down in his Mercedes and waited. He didn't have to wait long. An automobile stopped in front of *Fräulein* Kettler's residence and out stepped Bruno Redder. *Gotcha,* Jacob silently mouthed.

I'm *Oberführer* Erich von Manstein and this is *Hauptscharführer* Rudolf Ilgner. We have orders to retrieve the American prisoner, General Thomas Marsh, and take him to *Brigadeführer* Jodl. Here are the papers."

"Just one moment sir." The *Gestapo* clerk took the papers, left the lobby, and disappeared into an adjoining room. Jacob was dressed in an *Oberführer* uniform with a monocle pressed in his right eye. He had a fake mustache and goatee glued to his face. *Camel* was in the uniform of a *Hauptscharführer. Camel* nervously paced up and down the floor as they waited for the clerk's return.

"I don't like the feel of this. He's been gone much too long," *Camel* whispered.

"Patience. Can't lose our nerve now."

"It's not my nerve I'm worried about losing."

Just then the clerk returned and said, "Follow me sir." He led them down the hall and into another office.

"Be seated, someone will be with you in just a moment." Both Jacob and *Camel* remained standing. Suddenly the door opened and Redder and two men entered the room. They held Luger pistols in their hands.

"Put your hands on top of your head and don't make any sudden moves." Jacob and *Camel* slowly raised their hands.

"What is the meaning of this? How dare you…"

"Save the theatrics. Take their side arms Klaus," Redder ordered.

"Now sit down and tell me who you are and where you got these fake papers?"

"I'm *Oberführer* Erich vo…"

"*Unsinn!* If you're an *Oberführer,* then I'm a *Reichführer!* Now tell me who you are," Redder snorted. Jacob and *Camel* remained silent.

"I called Jodl and he's never heard of you. You must think we are *Dummkopf's.*" *You have my vote again,* Jacob thought.

"Search them," Redder ordered. Klaus and Albert went through their pockets. Klaus pulled the recorder from Jacob's pocket and handed it to Redder.

"What's this?"

"Nothing important. It's a recorder I use to make notes for later reference," Jacob replied.

"Oh really. Let's see what you have been referring to lately." Redder pushed the play button. *Where is the kitchen, Fräulein? Right this way and please hurry.* There was the sound of water running and a voice again said, *A very nice kitchen Fräulein, but you must have the gas connections checked for leaks. They seem to be quite rusty. Ja ja, sure anything you say,* came the reply.

Redder looked confused. *Gute nacht Fräulein, and danke sehr for your cooperation.* A female voice replied, *Gute nacht Herr Eigruber.* Redder's face went pale as it finally dawned on him who the female voice belonged to. He slammed a finger on the stop button, and ordered Klaus and Albert to leave the room. They gave puzzled looks at one another as they left. As the door closed behind them Redder demanded, "Where did you get this?" Jacob didn't answer. Redder pushed the play button again. There was the sound of a door opening and a female voice said, *come in my little Häschen. What did you bring me?* Redder's face went purple with rage as he recognized his voice. He quickly pushed the stop button.

"I'll kill you both for this."

"Before you do anything rash, maybe you should listen to the rest of the wire." Redder just stared at the recorder. He looked reluctant, but did as Jacob suggested. *You look tired tonight my little Süsser. Have they been working you too hard? That weak chinned, lame-brained Himmler doesn't know up from…*Redder slammed his hand on the stop button.

You can play the rest, but I believe you know what's on it," Jacob said.

"How did you record this? We were alone."

"That's not important. The important thing is we have the recording and I don't think you want it to fall in the hands of Himmler." A smug grin spread across Redder's face as he pointed the Luger at Jacob's head.

"I believe you are mistaken. I have the recording and I have you."

"Do you think that is the only copy? The original and several copies are in very competent hands. If anything happens to us, Himmler gets the original." Redder sagged as he lowered the Luger.

"I'm a dead man," Redder whispered.

"Not quite yet. Let me ask you a question. How come you seem to have so much authority around here? I thought Himmler disciplined you over the incident with Karl Müller." Redder had a surprised look on his face.

"How do you know about that?"

"Never mind. What we want to know is where you are holding General Thomas Marsh?"

"He's not here, and as far as my being disciplined, that was all an act for Canaris' benefit. Himmler doesn't mind a little rough stuff. In fact he enjoys it. He appreciates my skills."

"It doesn't take much skill to beat someone. Now just tell us where General Marsh is being held." Redder's lips tightened. It was obvious he did not want to say anything.

"Let me remind you about the recording. If we are not back safe by midnight with General Marsh the wire will be delivered to Himmler. Time is growing short, so I'd suggest you tell us where they are holding him."

After a long pause and a deep breath Redder finally said, "He's not here. He's at another location." Unknown to Redder, Klaus and Albert's ears were pressed to the door, listening. Klaus fingered his *Luger.*

"We want you to take us to him." Redder just sat there looking glum.

"NOW!" Jacob demanded. Redder jumped. He looked miserable.

"If we try to leave, we'll be stopped. You are supposed to be under arrest."

"We'll walk out of here with our hands on our heads and you with a gun at our backs. An unloaded gun, of course. If anyone says anything tell them Jodl ordered you to take us to his headquarters so he can question us personally. We have an automobile parked out front. I'll drive and my associate will sit in the passenger seat. You will get in the back seat with your Luger. Be very convincing. Your life depends on it."

"Yours also," Redder replied.

"That's why I hope you are very convincing." Jacob retrieved his pistol and the release papers and put them in his briefcase. *Camel* tucked his gun into his waistband under his tunic. They walked out and were immediately confronted by Klaus and Albert. They had smug grins on their faces.

"Where are you taking them, *Herr* Redder?"

"To Jodl's headquarters. Get out of my way."

"Not so fast. That was a very interesting conversation you were having with these two, and the recording is very enlightening. You seem to have some explaining to do. Let's put these two in a detention cell in the basement until we can determine what is going on here."

"Are you questioning my authority? I'll have your hides!" While this distracting exchange was going on, Jacob slowly lowered his arms and reached into his brief case. His hand wrapped around the pistol. The handle felt warm and reassuring. He fired two shots through the briefcase. Both Klaus and Albert dropped. Klaus got off a shot as he fell and it hit Redder in the chest. Jacob reached to help Redder, putting Redder's arm around his shoulder and half-dragged, half-walked him toward the entrance door. Redder was bleeding badly down the front of his tunic. The coppery smell of blood mixed with Redder's bad breath was nauseating.

Another *Gestapo* agent burst into the foyer, gun in his hand. *Camel* fired, and he pitched forward. Jacob shouldered his way through the front door and made for the Mercedes. *Camel* came out, walking backward; ready for anyone that might follow. Jacob put Redder in the back seat and *Camel* jumped in beside him. Jacob then climbed into the driver's seat and started the Mercedes. He pushed the gas pedal to the floor and tires screeched as they wildly careened down the street. Redder was moaning. *Camel* said, "I'm asking you for the last time, where is General Marsh being held?"

"If you take me to a *Doktor*, I'll tell you."

"You tell us and then we'll take you to a *Doktor*." *Camel* pressed a handkerchief over the wound. *No bloody bubbles were coming from Redder's mouth. A good sign, Camel thought. The bullet apparently missed the lungs.*

"I'm hurt bad. We may not have time."

"That's just too bad. No information, no *Doktor*." Redder remained silent. "Time's wasting, and you're bleeding badly."

"OK! OK! He's being held in a sanitarium. They've probably pumped him full of sodium pentothal by now."

"Where is this sanitarium?"

"It's on *Kurfürsten Allee* in Charlottenburg."

"I know that location," Jacob said as he made a U-turn. Redder slid hard into *Camel and* screamed with pain.

"I told you where the lousy general is; now take me to a *Doktor!*"

"I think we'll wait until your information is verified," *Camel* replied. Redder just moaned.

Jacob stopped in front of the sanitarium. "I'll check it out. You stay here with our ugly friend," Jacob said to *Camel*. He got out of the Mercedes, briefcase in hand, and his sidearm back in its holster. He straightened his uniform and hat and strode up to the entrance. A nurse behind a desk looked up as he entered.

"May I help you sir?"

"I would like to talk to whoever it is that is in charge of this facility."

"I'm sorry, but *Doktor* Höpner is with a patient and cannot be disturbed. Can anyone else help you?"

"Is the patient he is with an American officer?" The nurse's face flushed and the look told Jacob what he wanted to know.

"I'm here regarding that officer. Take me to him immediately."

"I'll go and see *if Doktor* Höpner can see you."

Jacob slowly withdrew his gun from its holster and said, "You would be wise to take me to *Doktor* Höepner now." The nurse's eyes grew wide as she slowly got up from her chair.

"This way, sir. Under the circumstances I'm sure the *Doktor* will see you."

"I'm sure he will. Don't try anything foolish. I don't like firing my revolver. It makes a very loud noise and necessitates me having to clean it at the end of the day, and I detest having to do that"

The nurse stared at the revolver, her mouth slightly open. She swallowed and began to walk down the hall, Jacob following. He put his revolver back in its holster, but kept the flap unfastened. The nurse stopped in front of a door, hesitated and looked back at Jacob.

"Just act natural. I'll introduce myself. Stay in front of me no matter where I go. I won't hesitate to use my gun if I have to." The nurse opened the door and Jacob walked in behind her. Three heads turned to look at them.

"What…who…what's the meaning of this? Who are you? Can't you see I'm with a patient?" Jacob quickly absorbed the scene. A man lay on a gurney; a sheet covered him to his chin. A bag full of yellowish white liquid ran down IV tubes attached to his arm.

"I'm sorry to interrupt you like this *Doktor* Höpner, but I have orders to take your patient to General Jodl's headquarters. Here are the papers." Jacob opened his briefcase and handed the papers to the *Doktor*. The *Doktor* took the papers and scanned them.

"This is *verrückt*. Our orders are to interrogate this man. What does Jodl want with him anyway?"

"I didn't ask. I'm just following orders."

"You must give me time to finish our procedure and…interrogation."

"How can you interrogate this man when he's unconscious?" A sly grin spread across the *Doktor's* face.

"He is only partially unconscious. He will talk to us in due time,"

"Has he given you any information yet?"

"We have just started the process, and I do not appreciate being interrupted like this."

"So he hasn't told you anything?"

"I just told you we have just started. It takes a few minutes for the sodium pentothal to loosen the tongue."

"I see. Do you mind if I stay and watch?"

"I would prefer it if you would leave, but if you insist."

"I insist."

"All right, I will continue with my duties."

The nurse said, "*Doktor,* I'll go back to my station now."

"No! You will stay right here," Jacob demanded.

"What is going on here? Why are you interfering with everyone's duties? I'm going to call Jodl and see what this is all about." The *Doktor* began to walk toward the door.

Jacob drew his revolver and said, "I don't think so *Doktor.* Everyone just remain calm and no one will get hurt. Everyone put your hands on the top of your heads." Hesitantly they all raised their hands.

"What is the meaning of this? Who are you?" the *Doktor* demanded.

"Someone that is giving you an order, and I strongly suggest you obey it."

"Again I demand an answer, what is the meaning of this?"

"Never mind, is there a room nearby with a lock on it?" No one answered. Jacob fired the revolver into the ceiling. The explosion reverberated in the room like thunder.

"The next shot may not be so harmless." This got a quick response from one of the attendants.

"There is a supply closet right over there," he said pointing at a door in the opposite wall.

"*Danke.* All of you get in that closet!" They about stumbled over one another as they moved in the direction of the closet. It must have seemed like a sanctuary to them.

"Everyone get inside except *Doktor* Höpner." They crowded into the closet and Jacob said, "Don't make any noise or I'll have to shoot *Doktor* Höpner." He ordered the *Doktor* to close and lock the door, which he did. Jacob tried the door to be sure it was really locked. It was.

"Now *Doctor,* I want that IV removed from this man." The *Doktor* walked over to the general, slid the IV needle out of the general's arm, and taped a patch of cotton over the puncture.

"Now wheel the gurney to the front entrance." The *Doktor* hesitated, but finally the gurney began to move. Jacob held the door open and they went down the hall.

They met a nurse rushing their way and she asked, "What was that noise, and where is Nurse Hess? No one is at the front desk." The *Doktor* looked back at Jacob, who gave him a stern look.

"She...She's checking on a patient. She'll be back soon. As for the noise it was..."

Jacob interrupted finishing his reply. "We heard it also. It must have been an automobile backfiring." Satisfied, the nurse continued down the hall. As they exited the building *Camel* got out of the automobile. The *Doktor* wheeled the gurney to the car.

"Put the general in the back seat. *Camel* picked him up under the armpits and with the *Doktor* helping, struggled to hold onto his ankles as they guided him into the back seat.

"All right *Doktor,* roll the gurney to the other side of the automobile. We have a patient for you. It seems like a fair exchange. This man has been shot and we promised to take him to a *Doktor.*"

"We are not equipped to treat bullet wounds."

"Do the best you can. Our obligation to him is over."

"Do you think he will survive?" *Camel* asked.

"Do we really care? If he succumbs we don't have to worry about him any more. If he survives he could be useful to us. Either way it's a win win situation. I don't think he will talk. We've got him by the *Kugel's.*"

Jacob let *Camel* off at his automobile and then drove home. The general was still unconscious. Jacob didn't know how long it would take for the drug to wear off. He drove into the garage, got out, and closed the door. He glanced at his watch. It was after midnight. He opened the back door of the Mercedes and felt the general's pulse. It seemed strong enough, but he was no judge of what it should feel like, considering the effects of the drug. *Well pal lets see if I can get you inside.* Jacob grasped him by the wrist, stooped and slid his other arm around his leg and lifted him onto his shoulder into a firemen's carrying position. He was heavy, but Jacob was able to manage. As he struggled into the house he almost bumped into Martha.

"For crying out loud, what are you doing up this time of night?" Jacob blurted.

"We have been worried about you. Who is this?"

"Someone who needs to sleep off a little too much to drink." Jacob whispered, not wanting to wake Freya.

"Open the cellar door for me so I can take him down stairs."

"Why don't you put him in the spare bedroom? He will be much more comfortable there."

"I'd prefer no one knows he is our guest, including *Mutter.*"

"I see." Jacob was pretty sure Martha did see that this was no ordinary drunk by the look she gave him, but she made no comment.

"Please hurry, Martha. This guy isn't getting any lighter." Martha opened the panel door, and Jacob walked in. "Close the door Martha, and go to bed. I'll see you in the morning." He carried the general down the stairs, kneeled down beside the cot, and rolled the general onto it. He was sweating and panting from the exertion.

"Whew, I'm glad to get you off my back pal." The general didn't reply. He was still unconscious. Jacob covered him with a blanket and curled himself up in the chair with another blanket tucked around his shoulders.

"We both need some shut-eye, General. Pleasant dreams."

Jacob began to stir. His limbs were stiff and aching. A voice intruded on his dream. Slowly the fog began to lift. The voice said, "Where am I?" Jacob's head was still fuzzy, but he jerked upright at the sound. It was dark. It was as black as ink.

"You're safe and in good hands, general," Jacob said to calm him. He fumbled for the light switch that lit the stairs. The light was a startling contrast to the total darkness. The general squinted, and tried to sit up.

"Take it easy pal, not too fast. You've been drugged." The general's eyes widened with alarm when he saw Jacob's uniform. He looked around the room, confused and in a panic. Trying to reassure the general Jacob said, "Don't let the uniform fool you, General. I'm an American."

"You are? Where am I?"

"This is my home. Well I mean…not this wine cellar, but upstairs is my home…well it's not really *my* home…I guess I had better start from the beginning."

Jacob spent the next half hour giving the general the *Readers Digest* version of his circumstances and the general's rescue from the sanitarium. He sat motionless listening intently as Jacob spoke. He just slowly shook his head and said," Well I'll be damned."

"What made you get on that B17, General? I believe you are in big trouble with the brass back home. You'll probably lose a star over this escapade."

"It'll be worth it. I couldn't stand sending those young men up day after day while I sat back safe, waiting for them to return. Too many didn't. It just tore me up."

"There are lots of things we don't like to do. I could write a book about it. You've put a lot of other people's lives in danger, including yours truly."

After a few seconds of silence he raised his head and said, "I get your point. What do we do now?"

"I've still got to figure out how to get you back into Allied hands, and it *ain't goin'* to be easy." The general looked a little chagrined as he stared at the floor.

"Let me chew on it for a few days. I'll try to figure something out. Are you hungry?"

"I'm starved. Anything to eat around here?"

"I'm going upstairs and have breakfast. I'll have Martha, our cook, fix something for you, and I'll bring it down here. I don't want my mother, Freya that is, to know you're here. Martha knows, but I don't think she will say anything to anyone."

"If you have aspirin I could use a couple. My head is splitting."

"Coming right up…or rather, right down."

While the general was eating, Jacob entered a message into the wireless. It read, *Package retrieved and safe. Contents did not leak. Will ship package back as soon as I determine routing. Fox.* He hit the send button. In a fraction of a second the message was gone.

"How are you feeling, General?"

"Much better with food in my stomach. The aspirin helped a lot too. Thanks."

"You're going to have to stay down here until I can figure out how to get you out of Germany. Martha fixed you a sandwich for lunch and here are some books from our library to keep you occupied. I found a few written in English."

"Thanks, I'll make do."

"I'll be back around 1800 hours. Get some rest. It should be plenty quiet down here."

"You can count on that. That drug is still having its affect on me. See you tonight."

Helmut Bock was a professional make-up artist who worked for the *Abwehr*. If a disguise for an agent was required, he was their man. He was the best and had worked in Hollywood before the war. He could make a woman more beautiful, a man more handsome, or create a monster out of a normal human being.

"*Herr* Bock, I wonder if I could persuade you to do me a little favor."

"What is it *Hauptsturmführer?*"

"My uncle, a brother to my father, has cancer of the larynx, and there is a *Doktor* in Zurich that is world renowned for treating this kind of disease. His name is *Doktor* Ulrich Reber. I believe I can provide my uncle the necessary papers to get him across the border for treatment."

"That's good, then why do you need my help?"

"The problem is this; he cannot talk because the cancer has affected his vocal cords. I'm going to go with him if I can arrange it. I'm sure you know the mentality of the *Gestapo*. They're suspicious of everyone. If he is traveling alone, and they ask him a question, he won't be able to answer them. This will make them even more suspicious. If I'm with him, and I tell them he has cancer of the larynx and cannot talk, they may not believe me."

"What do you want *me* to do? I don't want to get involved with the *Gestapo.*"

"You won't be involved. What I want is for you to create the appearance of a freshly healed bullet wound on his throat. I can point to that as the reason he cannot talk and they will have visual proof of the problem. Also I believe it would be a good idea if you could make him appear older. Anything that would make him unrecognizable to anyone that might know him. If someone recognized him they may say something to my Uncle Wilhelm."

"Surely Admiral Canaris could smooth the way with the *Gestapo.*"

"I don't want Uncle Wilhelm to know about this. My uncle with the cancer and Uncle Wilhelm have not been on speaking terms for years. There was a little misunderstanding some time ago between them and I don't want the family feud to be rekindled."

"Hmm…I'm not sure I want to get mixed up in your family's problems. If the Admiral found out I'd be in big trouble, and so would you."

"He won't find out because neither of us will say anything about this to anyone." Jacob removed a bottle of wine from the sack he was holding and set it on the table. Bock's eyes bulged at the sight.

"I heard you were quite a connoisseur of fine wines, *Herr* Bock. Could you give me your expert opinion on this one?"

Bock gingerly picked up the bottle and read the label. *Rheingau Cabinet aus Eltville, Deutschland, 1908.* He slowly looked up and said, "*Mein Gott, Herr Hauptsturmführer,* do you know what you have here?"

"Of course. It's a bottle of wine"

"This is not just any bottle of wine; this is a very old and very rare bottle of wine. Where did you get it?"

"From our wine cellar. I don't have any use for it. Would you like it?"

"Would I like it? What a question. That's like asking a person if they would like to keep breathing. Are you offering this to me?"

"Of course. It's my gift to you."

"*Shönen Dank, Hauptsturmführer.* I'm overwhelmed, and I'd be most pleased to help you with your little project. When can I see your uncle?"

"Give me a few days to arrange everything. I don't dare bring him here. Uncle Wilhelm may see him. Could you come to my home?"

"Of course. Where do you live?"

"This is my address. It's in Charlottenburg. Is 2200 hours all right with you?"

"2200 hours! Why so late?"

"I'd prefer my mother doesn't know about this. She will be in bed by then."

Looking longingly at the bottle of wine Bock finally said, "I guess I can arrange to come at that time."

"OK General, here's the plan. We have train tickets leaving Berlin Friday at 0800. The train will travel south through Leipzig, Frankfurt, Mannheim, Stuttgart, Ulm and on into Konstanz, where you will cross the border into Switzerland. There may be delays en route because military trains have priority. It's possible we may have to sit on a siding for hours until they clear our train to continue. Here are your papers. Your name is Manfred Manstein. Remember you cannot talk. The *Gestapo* has a little trick they use. They may be questioning us in German, and everything is going along just fine, and they send us on our way. As we walk away they will ask us a question in English. Unless we are under complete control, if we flinch even a little, they will suspect we are not German. It is extremely difficult not to react. You must be on your toes every second. Any questions you are asked I'll answer because, of course, you are not supposed to be able to speak. The questions will be in German, and you won't understand them anyway. Even though you cannot understand what is being said, act as though you are following the conversation. The man I told you about, Helmut Bock, will be here at 2200 to do your make-up. Do not speak, and act a little tired. Remember you are supposed to have cancer of the larynx. Martha and Freya will be in bed. We'll do this in the library. I do not want *Herr* Bock wandering around in the wine cellar or even knowing of its existence. One last thing, General. I wonder if I could impose upon you to do me a favor when you get back to London."

"Certainly. You've done so much for me that I would be pleased to be able to return the favor. What do you want me to do?"

"There is a certain person in London that I would like to be able to communicate with occasionally. Her name is Janet Jones, and she is the secretary to my handler, Colonel Charles Ashburn, at MI6. She has access to the radio receiver and transmitter of my wireless at the MI6 offices. Ask her to send me a message without the colonel being aware she is doing so, and have her let me know the best time to reply without Ashburn knowing."

"Hmm…are you sure you know what you're doing? You could get yourself and Miss Jones into more trouble than I am in if Colonel Ashburn found out. What is your relationship to Miss Jones?"

"She is my wi…my fiancée. It gets a little lonely out here without even knowing what she is doing…and well, I miss her…Would you mind contacting her for me?"

"Of course. That's the least I can do. I hope everything goes well."

"Thank you, General. I very much appreciate it."

"Well, what do you think, *Herr Hauptsturmführer? Gut* enough to pass inspection?"

"You are a genius, Helmut. It's so realistic I couldn't tell it from the real thing. And the aging, he looks at least ten years older. How can I thank you?"

"You already have. The wine, remember?"

"Of course. I'm pleased you are enjoying it."

"I have not tasted it yet. It's still unopened, but nevertheless I'm enjoying it very much. I just sit and look at it. I'm torn between opening it or letting it age a bit longer. It will take a lot of courage to pop that cork. I don't know if I have the nerve to do it. It's a slice of history and very valuable."

"That might be true, but it will be worthless if an Allied bomb lands on it."

"Perish the thought. If that happens, I hope I go the way of the wine. I couldn't bear to survive if the wine did not."

Jacob chuckled and said, "Then let's hope you both survive."

"Good luck on your trip to Switzerland."

"*Danke die,* Helmut. Remember to forget this evening."

"*Jawohl,* I was never here."

CHAPTER 35

▼

"Colonel Ashburn, I have a Major McKenzie on the line for you, sir," Janet said as she handed him the phone.

"Yes Colonel, Ashburn here. What can I do for you?"

"Colonel, I'm the Commanding Officer at the Edinburgh prison camp, and I understand from Major David Milne at Perth that you have some interest in a German prisoner of war by the name of Karl Müller."

"Yes, but my interest in him has been satisfied."

"Well, he thought you might want to know that Karl Müller escaped this compound ten days ago."

"WHAT! Why was I not informed of this immediately? Do you have any idea the consequences that could result from this escape?"

"No, not really. It seemed like a routine matter. He'll be caught eventually. What harm could just one German do running around the countryside?"

"You have no idea. Of course I understand you could not possibly know. I can't believe Major Milne did not inform me immediately of the escape."

"He didn't know anything about it until I happened to mention it to him during one of our routine conversations concerning common problems overseeing a prison camp. He asked me to notify you immediately."

"Thank you, Major. I don't want to seem abrupt but I must ring off and take care of some urgent business. Thank you for calling."

"JANET!! Get Cooper and Coleman in here as fast as you can round them up!"

"Yes sir. Are you all right, sir?"

"I'm fine, but just hurry. After you find Cooper and Coleman get the PM on the phone. Tell his secretary it's most urgent."

"Prime Minister, I have some disturbing news. The German prisoner, Karl Müller, has escaped. It's for real this time, sir."

"WHAT! How did that happen?"

"I'm not sure sir. I've just been informed, and I don't have all the details yet."

"What are you doing about it?"

"I've sent two of our people to surveillance the flat in Perth. Of course *Garbo* is no longer there. If Müller has already been there and finds out he no longer has a contact at that location, he may go looking for others we have not yet *rolled up*. If that's the case he may be able to get word to Germany and *Fox* will be compromised. Should we pull him out?"

"I think not, and I believe it would be wise not to inform *Fox*. No need adding to his pressure. Let's just hope we can find Müller before he does any harm."

"We're putting *Fox's* life on the line by leaving him in place and in the dark, sir."

"We're putting men's lives on the line by the tens of thousands every day. He is much too valuable to risk losing unnecessarily. Get cracking and see to it that you use every resource at your disposal."

"Yes sir. I'm already doing that."

Ashburn informed every police unit in the United Kingdom of the escape. Flyers were printed with Müller's picture on it, and they were being displayed in every city, town, and hamlet. Surveillance at the Leeds apartment house came up empty thus far. Ashburn was very worried.

Janet saw the flyers and realized Jacob was in extreme danger. She begged Ashburn to pull him out, but of course he could not. She was frantic.

Five days after his escape, Karl made his way to the Leeds apartment house. He had stolen clothes from a clothesline at a farm. He was far from the most stylish dressed Englishman, but the clothes were typical of the working class in that area, and he blended in in such a way as to make him almost invisible. He worried about being stopped and questioned about why he was not in a uniform. He had no identification, and most men his age were in the military. He was depending on his contact to rectify that problem. He climbed the stairs and knocked on the door. A woman opened the door. Karl was surprised, but said to her, "Is *Cato* in?"

"Cato? There ain't no Cato here. You must have the wrong place."

"I have a message for him from Uncle Brewster."

"Well ain't that sweet. I don't have no Uncle Brewster."

"Are you sure? I'm supposed to tell him the tulips have been planted."

"Are you daft? Tell him he should have planted crocus."

By this time Karl had lost his patience and said, "Madam you are a crazy old bitch."

"And you are a bloody cheeky upstart." At that she slammed the door.

CHAPTER 36

▼

After the pressure of the last few days, Jacob was looking forward to a relaxing dinner at Felix's. The *maitre d'* seated him at his usual table and handed him a menu. Soon *Camel* came to the table and said, "Guten *Abend, Herr Hauptsturm-führer.* How may I serve you this evening?"

"Josef, I'm very hungry tonight. What do you recommend?"

"Well, let's see. Why don't we start you off with *Linsensuppe,* followed with *Falscher Wildschweinbraten* and a side dish of *Blumenkohl.* For desert we have *Apfel torte* or a luscious *Schwarzwälder Kirschtorte.* Maybe a tall glass of *Steinbager* might be a refreshing change instead of your usual wine."

"That sounds *wunderbar,* and I'll have the *Schwarzwälder Kirschtorte* for dessert."

"Very well, sir." *Camel* left for the kitchen and Jacob headed to the toilet. He left a note that read, *I'm unable to take package to Swiss border. I've been ordered to accompany Canaris to a meeting of the High Command. You will have to deliver the package. We need to meet to discuss details. Advise time and place.* Jacob returned to his seat just as *Camel* was delivering his soup.

"Ah, that smells delicious, Josef."

"I think you will enjoy it, sir." Jacob did just that, and the *Falscher Wildschein-bratenh* was superb as usual.

When *Camel* brought the *Schwarzwälder Kirschtorte Camel* noticed Jacob had placed his knife across the top of the plate. He delivered the dirty dishes to the kitchen and headed to the toilet to retrieve the message.

After reading the message, he left Jacob the following note. *Meet me the day after tomorrow at 2300 hour at the location where we first met. Be certain you are not followed. If that is acceptable rub your nose with your right hand as you leave the premise. If you cannot meet, rub your nose with the left hand. I'll be watching.*

Camel brought the *Rechnung,* and Jacob left enough *Reichmarks* to cover it and the gratuity. He went into the toilet and read *Camel's* message. As he left the restaurant he rubbed his nose with his right hand.

CHAPTER 37

▼

Jacob checked for messages on the wireless. There was one. He decoded it and quickly read it. It said: *we have received word through diplomatic channels of a plan to assassinate Hitler. The code name is Werewolf. We need a detail schedule of Hitler's itinerary next 30 days. Urgent.*

Jacob was stunned. He entered the following message in the wireless. *Strongly advise operation Werewolf be scrubbed. It is far better to have a corporal acting like a general than have the real generals in charge of the war. Hitler has several doubles. It would be extremely difficult to identify real target.* Jacob hit the send button.

Ashburn read the message and rang for Janet. "Get the Prime Minister's secretary on the phone."

"Yes sir." Janet went to her desk and dialed. The Prime Minister's secretary came on the line.

"Colonel Ashburn would like to speak with you, sir. Just a moment and I'll connect you"

"The secretary is on the line, sir."

"Thank you Janet."

"Hello, Colonel, Ashburn here. I need an appointment with the PM. It's very urgent…No, it cannot wait; it's extremely important…Yes, I can come any time, but the sooner the better. Tell him I have a message from *Fox* regarding *Werewolf*…He'll know what it means. Just inform him as soon as possible."

Ashburn was pacing the floor when Janet told him the Prime Minister's secretary was on the phone.

"Hello, Ashburn here."

"Hello sir, the Prime Minister will see you at 2200 hours."

"Thank you. Tell him I'll be there."

"Now what is this about *Fox* and *Werewolf?*" Churchill asked. Ashburn handed Churchill Jacob's message. He read the report.

"Hmm, I tend to agree with *Fox,* but how can we stop *Werewolf?* Some of his own officers are set on his elimination."

"The question is, are these officers trying to eliminate him to make peace or to gain control of the conduct of the war, sir?"

"We are getting mixed signals on that aspect of *Werewolf,*" Churchill replied.

"Then what should we do, sir?"

Churchill contemplated that question and finally said, "Nothing. Let it run its course. It's out of our hands anyway."

Jacob read Ashburn's reply about *Werewolf. Regarding Werewolf, take no action. Since this operation originates with officers inside the Wehrmacht, we are unable to influence its outcome. Let it run its course.* Jacob pondered this reply. *Should he inform Canaris of the plot? Maybe Canaris is involved. I know Canaris has become skeptical of Hitler's conduct of the war. If I alerted him, how could I explain how I knew? Maybe Ashburn's right. Let it run its course.*

Jacob drove to the location where he first met *Camel* and parked in the shrubbery just off the lane. A cold shiver went up his spine as he remembered the feel of the pistol *Camel* held under his chin. He now knew *Camel* was not timid about using it. An automobile pulled in next to his. It was *Camel.* Jacob got out of his automobile as *Camel* got out of his. They shook hands.

"It sounds like we have a problem," *Camel* remarked.

"Yes we do. I can't accompany the general to the Swiss border like I planned. You will have to go with him. Canaris has ordered me to go with him to a meeting of the High Command. You are to leave at 0800 day after tomorrow from *Lehrer Hauptbahnhof.* Here are the tickets, itinerary and your papers." Jacob briefed *Camel* on everything he had discussed with General Marsh.

"Everything should go smoothly," Jacob commented.

"Don't give me that bull. In this business things rarely go smoothly."

"Well, we've done everything we can do, so let's hope for the best." *Camel* didn't reply. He took the papers and tickets from Jacob, got in his car, and drove away. Jacob had an uneasy feeling.

CHAPTER 38

▼

"Are you ready to leave for the Ukraine in the morning?" Canaris asked.

"Yes sir, I am. My bags are packed."

"The High Command will be assembled at Supreme Headquarters near the Eastern front, a few miles east of Vinnitsa. The Russians are proving to be more difficult than Hitler expected, and I suppose we will be forced to listen to his usual tirade."

Jacob was very excited over this development, but at the same time worried about the necessity of leaving *Camel* to escort General Marsh to Switzerland.

However, this would allow him to travel through Germany and assess first-hand the effectiveness of Allied bombing. He had not been in the presence of Hitler yet and was excited about that prospect.

Jacob was hoping they would go by train, but Canaris explained that trains were too slow to arrive in time for the meeting. They flew instead, and were escorted by two Me 109 fighters. Jacob got a bird's eye view of the devastation below, but it was impossible to determine the extent of the damage of any particular industry. Allied daytime bombers had the same view. His only chance for any detailed information would take place at Hitler's Headquarters.

Generals and a few lesser officers filed into the room. The meeting was being held in Hitler's concrete bunker, constructed at enormous cost. A large table with chairs surrounding it seemed squeezed in the tight space, and the low ceiling and overhead lights gave one a claustrophobic feeling. A babble of voices echoed off the harsh walls as they waited for Hitler's arrival. Several large maps lay face up in front of what was obviously Hitler's chair. Jacob strained to get a look at them, but they were too far away to decipher.

Suddenly, Hitler entered the bunker followed by Martin Bormann. The bunker became as silent as a tomb. Jacob could hardly breathe. Every eye was on Hitler as he walked to his chair.

"Be seated gentlemen, and thank you for coming." Jacob smiled to himself at this pronouncement. Did he think anyone would have dared not be here, having been summoned by the person that held their very lives in his hands.

As Jacob looked around the room and saw Hitler surrounded by the highest members of the *Wehrmacht,* it reminded him of a recurring dream he had as a child. In the dream he was in a crowd, completely naked, and everyone was staring at him. No matter how hard he tried to hide he was unable to do so.

Here he stood, a spy, in the midst of Hitler and his cronies. He felt naked, exposed, the same as in the dream and imagined everyone was looking at him. He grappled with his emotion by taking several deep breaths to calm himself. Even though the temperature was cool in this concrete bunker, he wiped the perspiration off his forehead. He finally relaxed as he looked around the room and realized that every eye was on *der Führer,* and no one was paying any attention to him.

"The dictator was now at the height of his power and his authority was unfettered."[1] He held complete political and military control in Germany as well as the conquered nations. He had proclaimed himself Supreme Commander of the *Wehrmacht,* and he alone decided all political, military and strategic matters in the conduct of the war, to the consternation of his generals. In his own eyes, he was the only one capable of directing the war. Almost all his military hierarchy disagreed with him, but they were too afraid to challenge him.

With brooding eyes and scowling face, he demanded to know why they had not yet captured Stalingrad. He growled, "This eastern campaign is bleeding us dry. We must turn our attention to England and America straight away."[2]

Everyone in the bunker except Hitler knew he had underestimated the resolve and resilience of the Russians, and made the fatal mistake of ignoring history. Russian winters were the equal of a hundred divisions. They thought he was mad to have attacked the Soviet Union, but to voice that opinion would have cost them their positions and probably their lives.

---

1. *Inside Hitler's Headquarters,* by Walter Warlimont
2. Ibid

Oberstgruppenführer Jodl spoke up. "In solemn tones he stated that the fate of the Caucasus will be decided at Stalingrad. He made some other general remarks and sat down."[3]

Hitler stood and began to speak. His voice began softly, slowly and deliberately. He reviewed his earlier successes as if he were giving a history lesson to school children. He reminded them how quickly they had overrun Poland and had caused the collapse of the Baltic States. He boasted about how they had routed France, one of the most powerful European nations, in just six weeks. The defeat of Denmark and Norway took even less time. Germany now controlled most of Europe. The tempo of his speech began to rise and his voice became a shout as he berated his generals for their lack of vision, their cowardice, and their defeatist attitude. He singled out officers by name, and you could see the indignation on their faces, and feel the tension rise like a thermometer in a blistering sun.

"Chief of Staff Franz Halder, interrupted, and urged that Ninth Army, which was fighting at *Rzhev,* should be allowed the necessary freedom of maneuver and authorized to withdraw to a shorter line which could be held by its dwindling force."[4]

Hitler, red faced and eyes bulging, shouted, "You always come here with the same proposal, that of withdrawal."[5] He ended his tirade with the words: "I expect commanders to be as tough as the fighting troops."[6]

Halder was now furious and he raised his voice as he replied: "I am tough enough, *mein Führer.* But out there brave men and young officers are falling in the thousands simply because their commanders are not allowed to make the only reasonable decisions and have their hands tied behind their backs."[7]

Hitler recoiled. He fixed Halder with a long stare, and ground out hoarsely: "Colonel-General Halder, how dare you use language like that to me! Do you think you can teach me what the man at the front is thinking? What do you know about what goes on at the front? Where were you in the First World War? And you try to pretend to me that I don't understand what its like at the front. I won't stand that! It's outrageous!"[8]

---

3. Ibid
4. Ibid
5. Ibid
6. Ibid
7. Ibid
8. Ibid

Hitler was livid. No one else dared speak. Everyone was stunned into silence. Some shifted uneasily in their chairs. They all knew what fate awaited Halder.

Hitler would not tolerate anyone challenging his authority, particularly in front of the entire High Command. Any worthwhile suggestions that might have been proposed at this meeting dissolved like children's sandcastles in a rising tide. The High Command was like a circle of limp rope.

Jacob sent a report to London of this meeting, detailing the exchange between Hitler and Halder, the harangue of his officers, and the disarray of the High Command in regard to the war on the eastern front.

In addition to Hitler's problems on the eastern front, he faced another crisis in the south. There were indications Italy might withdraw from the war and make a separate peace with the Allies. Hitler was so worried about an attack on the Balkans that he ordered a "survey of the situation should Italy withdraw from the war. OKW Operations Staff felt that this was the most likely target for Western strategy in the Mediterranean: the coasts were barely defended, the population was in revolt, the area contained valuable raw material and last but not least, it offered the possibility of breaking into Fortress Europe from the south east with all the strategic and political consequence that implied."[9] Hitler assigned Field Marshal Erwin Rommel to take charge of the Mediterranean field of operations.

The fear was that if a collapse in Italy occurred, the Italians would seal the border in the Alps. In late 1943, fortification on the Italian side of the Alps frontier only led to Hitler's paranoia that this was directed against Germany. If this occurred it would then be difficult to get reinforcements into Italy and the troops already there would be trapped.

If Italy surrendered, the Allies would be able to land with minimal opposition and would have a wide open field of operations. Hitler was intent on getting the largest number of German forces into Italy in case they defected, which caused great alarm and suspicions by the Italians. Hitler's offer to send three divisions into Italy was met with a rebuff by Mussolini. He demanded additional tanks, anti-aircraft batteries, and aircraft instead. In spite of Mussolini's protests and demands, Hitler was able to send three newly formed German divisions, two German armored divisions and two Panzer Grenadier Divisions into Italy.

Fearing for his personal safety, Hitler refused to travel to Italy for a meeting with Mussolini. However, his military and political advisers seemed to have con-

---

9. Ibid

vinced him that the Axis was disintegrating and "that Germany was now alone in the Mediterranean and could not do more than defend Northern Italy."[10]

Hitler decided "to seek final clarification by reviving the meeting with Mussolini which had been postponed since Tunis. Hitler now set aside his worry over his personal security"[11] and traveled to Italy to a meeting known as the *Feltre Meeting*, named after the town in which it took place. Hitler's purpose was to keep Italy in the Axis and stiffen the resolve of his Fascist partner.

"Subsequent accounts have shown that immediately on returning from Feltre, Mussolini accepted the views of his advisers and as early as 20 July informed the King that he hoped by the middle of September 1943 to have dissolved the alliance with Germany. Hitler on the other hand returned from the meeting convinced that he had once more brought his friend and ally back on the rails"[12]

However, on 20 July 1943, King Victor Emmanuel III forced the resignation and arrest of Mussolini. He then appointed Marshal Pietro Badoglio to form a new government. When an angry Hitler received news of this change in government, he set in motion a flurry of contingency plans. It was first to be established whether or not Italy planned to continue the fight. Hitler suspected they would not. He considered having the 3 Panzer Grenadier Division occupy Rome and seize the government by arresting the King, the Crown Prince, the entire Royal House, Badoglio, and all the members of the Grand Council.

He ordered trains sent to Northern Italy as far as the Brenner Pass in preparation to evacuate troops from Italy. The Italians had been stopping German trains from entering Italy beyond this point. He ordered the seizure of all the passes "in the Alps, all travel and private communications to Italy be stopped and all persons of importance must call off their visits and no further authorization will be given."[13] After the new Italian government was seized, a Fascist government would be installed and "Fascist soldiers and officers must join the National Socialist formations."[14]

On 3 September, following the capture of Sicily, General Castellano signed the Italian surrender which was kept secret to prevent Germany from taking over political and military control of the country.

---

10. Ibid
11. Ibid
12. Ibid
13. Ibid
14. Ibid

On 9 September, the Allies landed Eighth Army's 1st Airborne Division at Taranto and General Mark Clark's US Fifth Army landed at Salerno.

On 12 September, a daring raid by Otto Skorzeny and a team of elite paratroopers rescued Mussolini who was being held at the *Campo Imperatore* ski lodge in the Abruzzi Mountains and took him to Germany.

On 13 October, Badoglio declared war on Germany from his government's temporary base at Brindisi. This was to show support for Allied operations in Italy and to give the Italian people "a clear understanding of their position as the war flows around them."[15]

15.Ibid

CHAPTER 39

▼

The train pulled out of the *Lehrter Hauptbahnhof* station and *Camel* heaved a sigh of relief. General Marsh was mute, staring straight ahead, but alert for any danger. They were in a compartment that seated six, but only three other passengers were accompanying them. One was reading a newspaper and another was reading what looked like a technical manual and making notes in the margin with a pencil. The third man addressed himself to General Marsh.

"My name is *Herr* Lehrgang. May I inquire your destination?" Marsh smiled and pointed to *Camel.*

"*Herr* Manstein cannot speak. He received a wound to his throat that has affected his larynx."

"Oh, I'm sorry. Where did this happen?"

"At, ah…at El Alamein."

"What Division was he with?" *Camel* was not prepared for these questions. He made a wild guess, believing this fellow wouldn't know one division from another.

"He was with the 21st Infantry Division. He received the Iron Cross for rescuing 14 fellow infantrymen that had been captured. He killed six Americans and made his way back to Axis lines."

"Such a brave man." Addressing Marsh he said, "The *Vaterland* has need of more men like you." Marsh just smiled.

"I'm sure he would thank you if he could speak." Lehrgang just grunted and opened a book. The five rode in silence until they reached Leipzig, for which *Camel* and Marsh were thankful. The train pulled into the Leipzig station.

"I'm getting off to stretch my legs," *Herr* Lehrgang announced as he stood up. "Anyone else interested?"

"I think we'll just remain aboard," *Camel* replied. The other two passengers said this was their destination, and they got up and left. When *Camel* was sure they were out of earshot he whispered to General Marsh, "I wish that busybody Lehrgang was getting off to stay. He asks too many questions."

"I wish I could understand German. It's nerve-wracking not knowing what is being said."

"You're doing just fine. Keep smiling and I'll do the talking."

Herr Lehrgang returned as well as three other passengers. *Camel* sensed something was different about the three new passengers, and it wasn't long before his suspicions were confirmed. Two of them stood up and stood in front of the door. The third, addressing both *Camel* and Marsh said, "Show me your identification papers please."

"Who are you, and why do you want to see our papers?"

"My name is Dieter Rattenhuber, and I demand to see your papers." *Camel* retrieved his identification papers and travel permit from his coat pocket and handed them over. Marsh seeing what *Camel* had done reached into his coat pocket and did the same. Rattenhuber looked them over carefully and then stood up.

"You will remain here for the time being. My men will remain with you."

"What is the meaning of this? Our papers are in order. Why are we being detained?"

The 21st Infantry Division has been fighting at Novgorod and Volkhov in the Ukraine. That's a long way from El Alamein." *Camel* looked at Lehrgang who was looking straight ahead. He had a faint smile on his face.

About a half hour had gone by when Rattenhuber returned. The train began to move. Rattenhuber sat down across from them and said," You two will be returning to Berlin with us."

"What do you mean? Why are we returning to Berlin? Are we under arrest?"

"For the time being, yes you are. We will do some further checking."

"This man is suffering from cancer of the larynx, and we have permission to travel to Zurich for treatment. We must make that appointment without delay. It could prove fatal if he doesn't get treated right away."

"It may prove fatal for both of you if we learn these papers have been forged. We will be returning to Berlin."

The next stop was Frankfurt. *Camel* and Marsh were taken to the local *Gestapo* office and locked in a room.

"Now what do we do?" Marsh whispered.

"We just wait and see what develops." They didn't have to wait long. The door opened and Rattenhuber with the other two agents came into the room.

"We will be leaving for Berlin within the hour. We've arranged passage on a munitions train that will pass through Berlin on its way west."

"I object most strenuously. I have friends in high places and you will be reprimanded for this delay."

"I doubt that. You have a lot of explaining to do. The addresses on your papers are false. In Berlin I believe you will tell us what we want to know."

They were shoved into a boxcar full of small arms ammunition, and the door was slid shut and locked. They were squeezed between crates so tightly they could barely move.

"Quite a difference in accommodations from the other train," General Marsh complained.

"I'm not as worried about these accommodations as I am about the ones that await us in Berlin."

"You're a cheerful sort of fellow."

"And I'm not your typical tourist guide either. *Gestapo* headquarters is the last place on earth you want to visit."

"It's that bad, huh?"

"Just wait and see. It will be no picnic."

The train moved along with the familiar clickity click as the wheels rolled over the rail connections. The hypnotic rhythmic sound made them drowsy and their eyelids began to droop.

Suddenly there was a terrific explosion. They were thrown out of the boxcar as the door blew out and crates spilled on top of them. Bombs were falling all around them and they expected to be blown to bits any second. Smoke and dust were so thick they could hardly see or breathe. *Camel's* arm and leg was bleeding. General Marsh suffered a deep gash to his forehead and blood ran into his eyes. His arm hung limp, and he suspected it was broken. He called out for *Camel. Camel* crawled to him and put his hand over his mouth.

"Quiet! Don't speak English, remember?" It flashed through Marsh's mind the saying *speak no evil, see no evil and hear no evil.* He wasn't supposed to speak, he couldn't see, and the explosions had made him almost deaf.

"What happened?" Marsh whispered.

"It seems your bombers came at a fortuitous time."

"We could have been killed by our own Air Forces. Pretty ironic, don't you think?"

"The irony I see in it is that we may have been *saved* by our own Air Forces. How badly are you hurt?"

In a sarcastic tone the general replied, "Nothing serious; I'm blind, I think my arm is broken, and my body feels like the first day of football practice. Every muscle in my body is screaming."

"I don't think you're blind. Just blood in your eyes from the head cut, but I believe you're right about the arm though." *Camel* wiped the blood from Marsh's eyes with a handkerchief and tied it around his head to stem the flow.

"Can you walk?"

"I don't know; I'll try." *Camel* helped him to his feet and they began to move away from the carnage.

"Where are Rattenhuber and his thugs?"

"I don't know. Let's hope they're beyond this world."

"That sounds good to me. What do we do now?"

"We get away from this train as fast as we can. I'm sure this place will be crawling with troops and emergency vehicles very soon."

"Where are we?"

"I'm not sure. Probably some place just outside of Frankfurt. It looks like farmland. I don't see any houses, but with cows in the field it tells me there must be some nearby."

A small stream flowed parallel to the tracks. It had to be crossed and they waded in. They were about to step up onto the opposite bank when *Camel* said, "Let's walk down stream a ways. If they bring in dogs it will take them more time to get on our tracks."

They waded for about five minutes and then headed for a clump of trees that stood like sentinels over the cows grazing in the meadow.

Sirens were wailing in the distance, and they knew they needed to get out of sight. They reached the seclusion of the trees so completely exhausted they both dropped to their knees and rolled over on their backs. In a few minutes they slowly sat up. They could see the train, what was left of it. Fire and smoke were still billowing above it like red and gray ghosts. Ammunition was popping like popcorn, and an occasional large explosion erupted.

Camel removed his shirt and made a sling for the general's arm. The cuts on *Camel* had coagulated, but his body was bruised and battered.

"I believe we should get as far away from this place as fast as we can move. If Rattenhuber or his henchmen are still alive, they will be looking for us. There must be a farmhouse nearby. Like I said, the cows are a good sign of that."

General Marsh said, "Lead the way; you're the guide."

"Right, the blind leading the blind. How's the arm?"

"It hurts like the blazes, but it'll do for the time being."

"It needs to be set and a cast put on it."

"Sure, why don't we just walk into the nearest hospital and say Hi, I'm your friendly American. Could you take a look at my broken arm? We just got blown off a munitions train. It's more likely they would put us in the psychiatric ward."

"One thing for sure, we can't stay in the open all night. It's too cold." They walked for half an hour in the opposite direction of the train. By now it was dusk.

"Look, up ahead. There's a farmhouse. I see smoke coming from the chimney."

"I see it. What kind of reception do you suppose we'll get?"

"I don't know, but remember you still can't talk." They walked directly toward the house. No one was in sight. A dog began to bark. A door opened and an old man stepped out. He was cursing the dog and keeping a wary eye on Marsh and *Camel.*

"*Guten Tag,* I guess you are wondering who we are. We must look a real mess. Did you hear the explosion in the distance?" *Camel* pointed in the direction of the train.

"*Ja, ja,* American bombers flew over our house. What did they bomb?"

"It was a munitions train. We were in our automobile on the road next to the tracks, and one of the bombs hit so close it destroyed it. It's now a pile of junk. It was unlucky we were passing so close by, but lucky to be alive. My friend, *Herr* Manstein, has a broken arm. We both have a few cuts and bruises, but we survived." An elderly woman, probably the man's wife, had come out of the house and heard *Camel's* last comment.

"Luther, don't just stand there. Have them come into the house and get warm."

"Of course, please do come in. You both look very tired."

"*Danke Schön,* that's very kind of you." They entered the house and looked around. The floor was stone, on which braided rugs were randomly placed. A large wood-burning stove stood against one wall. Something cooking in a large black pot gave off a wonderful aroma, and it reminded *Camel* and Marsh how hungry they were.

"We were about to have supper. Would you care to join us?"

"*Danke,* we are very hungry. Let me introduce ourselves. My name is Josef Ebert, and this is *Herr* Manfred Manstein. *Herr* Manstein suffered a bullet wound to his throat and it tore up his vocal cords so badly he cannot speak. It's very frustrating for him. May I inquire your names?"

"*Ja,* my name is Luther Löhr and this is my wife."

Frau Löhr carried a pan of hot water to the table and set it down. She said, "Let me dress those cuts. They are likely to get infected if they are left untreated."

"That's very thoughtful of you, Frau Löhr," *Camel* replied. Using a washcloth, she cleaned the cut on Marsh's head and the cuts on *Camel's* leg and arm. She spread salve on the cuts and tied clean cloth strips around them.

"Your head wound should have stitches. I can sew it up. I've done it often on Luther, but I do not have anything to deaden the pain. Your arm is another matter. You should see a *Doktor* about that."

Camel said," I believe if you could just wrap his arm tightly until we can see a *Doktor* that will be good enough. I believe he can hold still long enough for a few stitches"

"There is a *Doktor* in the village. Luther could fetch him."

"*Keinen, Doktor.* Let me explain our situation. When our automobile was blown up it destroyed our luggage, our papers, our passports, and all our identification. A *Doktor* most likely must make a report of those he treats as a result of this kind of accident. There would be reams of red tape, all kinds of inquiries, and endless delays. We were traveling to Zurich where *Herr* Manstein is to be treated by a *Doktor* who is a world-renowned surgeon, in the hopes he can repair the vocal cords and restore some of his speech. Crossing the Swiss border at Schaffhausen now is out of the question without our papers. If we could get to Belfort, I believe we could travel through occupied France much easier than we could through Germany. Then we could probably find a border crossing into Switzerland near Basel. The Swiss border on the French side is not as heavily guarded as it is on the German side. Do you know of someone that could guide us to the border at Belfort? I can pay them very well."

Marsh gave *Camel* a quizzical look. *Camel* removed his belt, spread open a seam on the inside, and spilled several diamonds onto the table. The light from the wick lamp reflected off the facets and they sparkled brilliantly. There was a gasp from *Frau* Röhr. *Herr* Röhr looked at his wife and there seemed to be some unspoken thought pass between them.

"We would like to discuss this privately. Would you excuse us please?"

"Of course," *Camel* replied. The Röhrs went into their bedroom and closed the door. Marsh was about to say something when *Camel* put his finger to his lips. *Camel* put his mouth close to Marsh's ear and whispered to him what he had proposed.

"You are full of surprises. The idea is as brilliant as the diamonds. Where did you get them?"

"Don't ask. Let's hope the Röhrs have a greedy streak." The bedroom door opened and the Röhrs returned.

"We think our son-in-law might be interested in your proposal. He is familiar with that area and has a team of horses and wagon. After dinner, Luther will fetch him, but first let me stitch up *Herr* Manstein's head." Quickly, *Camel* pointed to Marsh's cut forehead and pantomimed a sewing motion, all the while telling him in German what *Frau* Röhr was about to do. Marsh's eyes widened as he saw *Frau* Röhr threading her needle. He couldn't protest. He couldn't even make a sound.

After a supper of beef stew, homemade bread with lots of butter, and a stein of beer, life was looking brighter. Marsh's arm was feeling better since *Frau* Röhr had wrapped it, and a full stomach helped relieve his apprehension. The stitching was painful, but tolerable.

Luther went to get his son-in-law while *Camel* chatted with *Frau* Röhr. General Marsh tried to act interested, but kept dozing off.

The Röhr's dog, Caesar, a name they gave him to provide a little dignity, since his mixed breeding gave him none, was asleep on the floor. Suddenly he raised his head and came to his feet. The hair on the back of his neck stood up like porcupine quills. He walked to the door and emitted a low growl.

Frau Röhr went to the window, parted the curtain slightly, and peered out. She saw several flashlights in the distance, their beams crisscrossing back and forth, penetrating the night like a lighthouse beacon. She sensed danger.

"Someone is coming. Quickly, help me fold this rug back," she said pointing to the floor. *Camel* grabbed the rug and folded it in half, exposing a door flush with the floor.

"Open it and get down below," she ordered. Both *Camel* and Marsh scampered down the wood steps. *Frau* Röhr dropped the door shut and spread the rug back over it.

It was completely dark and had a musty smell. *Camel* stumbled over what felt like bags of potatoes. He realized they were in a root cellar.

Frau Röhr took hold of Caesar's collar and pulled him away from the door. He was snarling and began to bark. The door to the cottage opened and several men, two of whom held dogs on a leash, burst into the room.

"What is the meaning of this? Who are you?" *Frau* Röhr demanded.

Rattenhuber, a bandage wrapped around his head, said, "Never mind who we are, who are you?"

"I am *Frau* Dagmar Röhr and this is my home that you have invaded. You have no right coming in here like this. What do you want?"

"We have the right to do anything we please when treason is suspected. We are looking for two men and our dogs led us to this house."

"My stew is probably what led your dogs to my house. I'm the only one here, now get out. You are upsetting my dog as well as me."

Ignoring her, Rattenhuber yelled, "Search the house." Men and dogs combed through every room, including the loft.

"There's no one here, sir."

Rattenhuber looked grim and tired. The dogs were snarling at one another and *Frau* Röhr was struggling to keep Caesar under control.

Rattenhuber's attention was drawn to the remains of the meal on the table. He gave *Frau* Röhr a hard look and in a menacing tone asked, "How many people live in this house?"

"My husband and myself. Why?"

"It appears four people had supper here tonight. Where are the other three?" He demanded.

"My husband and our son-in-law are out looking for one of our milk cows that is missing. Our daughter went home."

Rattenhuber gave her a skeptical look. Surveying the room with a sweep of his head, he walked over to where a basin of water sat on the counter. He picked up a needle with thread still hanging from it, and said,

"What is this?"

"Have you never seen a needle and thread before?" She answered sarcastically.

"What have you been stitching, *Frau* Rohr?" Rattenhuber replied smugly.

"I sewed a button on my husband's shirt that had come loose. Is that against the law?"

"Don't get smart with me or you'll regret it."

Caesar, with curled lips and teeth bared, rose up on his hind legs and lunged toward the black dog. *Frau* Röhr lost her balance and reached for the table to steady herself, but instead caught the oil cloth table covering. Bowls, spoons and the remains of the stew went crashing to the floor. The black dog pulled his leash free from his handler, snatched the stew bone in his teeth, darted through the door and disappeared into the night.

The other dog broke free and began lapping up the remains of the stew. His handler, cursing, kicked him in the ribs. He yelped and darted out the door.

Caesar was going crazy. It was pandemonium. *Frau* Röhr was sprawled on the floor, still clinging to Caesar's collar. She was being dragged across the floor as Caesar tried to get loose.

Camel and Marsh looked up, straining to hear what was happening, but couldn't make any sense of it. They felt helpless and trapped.

Frau Röhr struggled to her feet and screamed at Rattenhuber to get out of her house. Frustrated, he turned on his heels and left, cursing his men and dogs.

Frau Röhr slammed the door shut and bolted it.

It became very quiet. *Camel* and Marsh couldn't hear anything, but were afraid to open the trap door. They just sat, quietly whispering. *Frau* Röhr began cleaning up the mess.

In about half an hour, Luther returned with his son-in-law. He tried to open the door, but it was locked. Puzzled, he banged on the door and shouted to his wife. She unlocked the door and they entered the house. Caesar wagged his tail and nuzzled Luther as if nothing concerned him.

"Why was the door locked and where are our guests?" She put a finger to her lips and pointed to the floor.

"Did you see anyone on your way home?" *Frau* Röhr whispered.

"No, we didn't. What is going on here? Is something wrong?" *Frau* Röhr told Luther and her son-in-law what had happened.

"They may be watching the house. I told them you, Fritz and Grettle were here for supper, and that you and Fritz went looking for a lost milk cow. I said Grettle went home. You need to know that in case they come back."

"What are we going to do about them?" Luther asked pointing to the floor.

"We can't turn them in to the authorities since I have already denied knowing them," *Frau* Röhr replied.

"Who do you think they are? This changes everything. I don't like messing with the *Gestapo* or the *Polizei*," Luther exclaimed.

"I don't either. I hate them both…but the *diamants*…let's not forget about them."

"Check to be sure the curtains are drawn tight and turn the lamp down a bit. Fritz, help me fold the rug back and let's get our guests out of the cellar."

When *Camel* and March were brought up, Luther made the introductions.

"This is our *Schwiegersohn*, Fritz Brehm. Fritz, meet *Herr* Ebert and *Herr* Manstein. I have told Fritz about your proposal."

"*Gute.* Can you do it *Herr* Brehm?"

"Let me see the *diamants* please." *Camel* let them slip out of his hand onto the table. They rolled like dice and when they came to a stop, Fritz leaned over them to get a closer look.

"*Ja*, I can do it, but only for all the *diamants.*"

"I believe three should be sufficient," *Camel* replied.

"Now that the *Gestapo* and *Polizei* are involved the risk is much greater," Fritz countered. *Camel* let that statement sink in and finally replied, "I'll give you three before we start and three when you get us to Belfort."

"You don't trust me?"

"That's right. I don't trust anyone I've known for only five minutes. Trust comes with performance." Fritz was silent, deep in thought. Finally, he said, "I'll do it. The terms are acceptable."

"*Gute.* When can we get started?"

"I think we need about two days to get ready. We will need food and water, bedding and hay in the wagon. I want to reconnoiter the area to make sure we are not being watched. We must get you into some proper clothing; something more suitable to make you look like a farmer. You would stand out like a searchlight in those clothes. *Ja*, I think two days is about right."

"I don't see a telephone. I need to call someone badly. Do you know where there is one I can use?" *Camel* asked.

"There are none in this area, only in the city, but we should steer clear of Frankfurt. Too many *Gestapo* agents. They check every stranger they see. If you don't have the proper identification they will detain you. We will pass near Mannheim on the way. That's a possibility although I would prefer we didn't go into a city."

"It's imperative I make a telephone call before we get to Belfort, so we must stop in Mannheim."

"If you insist."

"I insist."

CHAPTER 40

"Anything new on Müller, Colonel?"

"Not yet Prime Minister. We're still receiving our regular traffic from *Fox,* so apparently Müller hasn't been able to alert anyone in Germany."

"We must find him before he does. Keep me informed."

"Yes sir. That I will do."

Karl was frustrated and humiliated. He has to beg for food and he combed through garbage cans for enough to eat. The pickings were very slim. Food was rationed in England and not much of it was being thrown away. He was afraid to be seen during daylight hours for fear someone would recognize him. Everywhere he turned he saw his face on a wanted poster. It seemed like it rained all the time. He was constantly cold and wet. He knew it was only a matter of time before someone spotted him unless he did something soon. He was so cold and hungry he thought about giving himself up. Then he remembered what it would be like to be back in Germany and his determination was rekindled.

He was now just outside Liverpool. From the ditch in which he had concealed himself, he had been watching aircraft take off and land all day. Slowly he worked his way to the edge of the field. A barbed wire fence encircled the perimeter. Several planes were lined up on the tarmac. He recognized them as Bristol Beaufighters. He ticked off their capabilities in his mind. *Speed 335 mph, ceiling 20,000 feet, range 1,100 miles, armament four 20mm cannon and six .303 machine guns. Perfect.* He salivated at the sight of this formidable aircraft. He thanked his ground instructors for cramming enemy aircraft information into his head. *If I can just get into the cockpit without being seen I can fly out of this diesem abscheulichen Ort.*

He squeezed himself under the barbwire and crawled toward the nearest aircraft. A petrol truck was filling a plane two planes from it.

He boosted himself onto the wing and climbed into the open cockpit. He feverishly studied the instrument panel. Satisfied, he hit the start button and the prop began to spin. He knew he didn't have time to warm up the engines. He would just have to take his chances. He pulled onto the strip and gave it full throttle. As he raced past the petrol operator he saw him waving his arms. What he couldn't hear was him yelling, "I HAVEN'T FUELED THAT PLANE YET!"

The Beaufighter lifted off the runway and Karl banked left to a heading of 270 until he was over water. He then turned to 180, and skimming low over the water flew down the St. George's strait. He knew that Land's End was the southerly most point in England and when he reached that he would turn southeast and France would be only a quick hop over the English Channel.

He struggled to get his arms into the safety harness while skimming low over the water to avoid radar. He would worry about German fighters and German anti-aircraft when he got to France. He knew he couldn't just land at a German held airfield in a British plane without some reason. He would use the plane's radio to try and convince them he was friendly. Suddenly his radio came on.

"Calling BF 163 please come in, over." *I'm not biting on that one.* He didn't reply.

"BF 163, your aircraft should be running out of fuel any minute now, over." Karl glanced at his fuel gauge. He had been concentrating on flying and had not even looked at the fuel gauge. The needle showed empty. He went cold. He veered left toward land. *If I can just reach land I may be able to set this down in a field. Why didn't I wait until that fuel truck got to this plane instead of assuming he had started with this plane?*

Karl screamed a stream of profanities. He was beside himself. Just then the engine sputtered and coughed and in a few seconds it stopped. He let it glide into the water with the nose held high, the tail hitting the water first and the fuselage finally splashing into the waves. The force slammed him forward and he was glad he had put on the safety harness.

The plane settled into the water and the swells rocked it back and forth. He released the safety harness and slid the canopy back. The plane began to settle and he climbed onto the wing. He reached into the cockpit and grabbed the seat cushion that doubled as a life preserver. He thought to himself, *that's not going to do me much good. I'll die of hypothermia in this cold* water *if I don't drown first.* The plane stayed afloat for about ten minutes and finally was swallowed by the sea.

Karl was still standing on the wing when it went down and the suction pulled him under water. He popped back up still holding onto the cushion. He could see land, but it was too far to reach. He knew he was about to die. Resignation mercifully swept over him and he acquiesced to the inevitable. Even the cold seemed to be lifted from his misery. He thought about home, and as many men often do when they know there is no time left to repair the damage they may have wrought, he cringed with regret.

As a swell lifted him to its highest point he saw a ship. It was headed straight toward him. He began frantically waving his arm and yelling as loud as he could. The ship was about on top of him when it slowed, turned slightly, and its side coasted toward him. It was a British destroyer. He was never so glad to see an enemy ship in his life. Two sailors jumped into the water and grabbed him. They tied a line around his waist and he was hauled aboard. The two sailors climbed the net hanging on the side of the ship. He was shivering violently. A blanket was thrown around his shoulders, and he was hustled inside.

His teeth were chattering so hard he could hardly speak. Someone shoved a cup of hot coffee in his hand. He wrapped both hands around it, savoring the warmth. His stomach was thankful as well.

Questions began to fly at him. *Why did you have to ditch? Where were you headed? Why the civilian clothes? What outfit are you with?* He realized no one knew who he was. In his best English accent he replied, "I was giving that Beau-fighter a trial run after some repairs. Apparently the repairs were inadequate. The engine gave out on me. Thanks for picking me up; it was a Jolly good show. You guys are my heroes. I'd be shark bait about now except for you." A small cheer erupted from the crew.

"Where's your uniform, mate?" One sailor sang out.

Avoiding a direct answer Karl said, "I'm glad I didn't have it on or it would be soaking wet and ruined." That got a few chuckles.

"What's your name, mate?" Another called out.

"Captain David Conklin, what's yours?"

Before the sailor could answer an officer said, "OK, everyone back to your stations." The men drifted out of the compartment and Karl was left alone with the officer.

"Come with me, and I'll get you out of those wet clothes into some dry ones. They're Navy, but they're dry."

"Thank you sir, I'm most appreciative."

"Permission to see the captain, sir."

"And what do you want with the captain, Higgins?"

"It's a private matter sir."

"OK follow me," the lieutenant replied. They went down a passageway and stopped in front of the captain's cabin. The lieutenant knocked and a voice said, "Come." He opened the door and said, "Seaman Higgins would like to speak with you, sir."

"Thank you, Paul, show him in." Higgins entered the captain's quarters, removed his hat, and saluted.

"What is it, Higgins?"

"Beggin' your pardon, sir, but that bloke we fished out of the drink 'little while ago is a *Jerry.*"

"A what? What do you mean?"

"A *Jerry,* sir, you know, a '*einy,* sir"

"Are you trying to tell me he's a German?"

"Yes sir. That's what I said, sir."

"And what makes you think he's a German?"

"When I was on shore leave I seen his picture plastered in every pub I visited, and I was in quite a few, sir."

"What kind of picture?"

"A wanted poster, sir, and there is a reward too. It said the bloke was an escaped German prisoner of war. They must want him awful bad, sir. The reward is 5,000 pounds."

"Are you absolutely sure, Higgins? I heard him talking and he sounded British to me."

"I ain't lyin' sir. I 'ad me share of tall ones in those pubs, but I was sober enough to be able to read, sir."

"Thank you Higgins. Please have Lieutenant Cunningham report to me at once. Under no circumstances are you to say anything about this matter to anyone, and you are to steer clear of this man. Do you understand?"

"Yes sir. Ah…ah…beggin' your pardon sir, 'bout that reward."

"Don't worry, Higgins. If this is that man, I'll recommend you get the reward."

"Thank you, sir." Seaman Higgins left with a huge smile on his face.

When Lieutenant Cunningham entered the captain's quarters, the captain was checking his revolver. Staring at the gun, Cunningham asked, "Is anything wrong, sir. Higgins said you wanted to see me."

"That's right, lieutenant. I want you to find Warrant Officer Murphy, Chief Petty Officer Hill, and Chief Bo's'n Mate Delaney, and have them report to me as quickly as you can get them here. They are to have their side arms with them. Yours also. They are not to speak to any of the crew about this"

"What's up sir?"

"I'll brief you when everyone is here. Where is the man we rescued?"

"He's in the mess hall, sir, getting a bite to eat."

"All right, get the men here as quickly as you can round them up."

"Aye aye, sir."

The men the captain requested were crowded into his quarters. Each one had his side arm strapped to his hip.

"Now listen up. The man we rescued this morning may be an escaped German prisoner of war. That's what Seaman Higgins thinks, and I tend to believe him. In any event we are not going to take any chances. He's in the mess hall right now. We will confront him, and arrest him. If he bolts we will physically subdue him. I don't want him shot. The side arms are to intimidate him only. Is that understood?"

The men replied in unison, "Aye-aye, sir."

"All right, let's get on with it." Cunningham followed the captain and the others got in line behind him. They entered the mess hall and surrounded Karl. He was just finishing his food. He looked up, mouth open in surprise. His demeanor immediately changed from the jovial camaraderie he had enjoyed with these men to a sullen expression that hardened the captain's suspicions.

"Is there something wrong captain? What's up?"

"I believe you know. Please stand up; you are under arrest."

"Under arrest. What for?"

"What is your real name?"

"My name is David Conklin, Captain David Conklin, British Royal Air Force."

"I doubt that, but we'll get it all sorted out in time." Karl grabbed for Cunningham's side arm. The Bo's'n mate hit Karl with a right hook that sent him sprawling.

"Pick him up and get him to the brig," the captain ordered. They picked him up, escorted him to the brig and locked the door. Karl realized his freedom had just come to an end.

Colonel Ashburn called the Prime Minister, and in a relieved voice said, "I have just been informed that Karl Müller was captured this afternoon and is being taken to Military Headquarters in Bristol. He is now aboard HMS Broadsword."

"That *is* very good news. I don't think we should put him back in that same prison Too risky. What do you suggest Colonel?"

"The Tower, sir."

"Hmm, good idea. I'll inform them to expect him. I want maximum security twenty-four hours a day. I don't want a repeat of what we've been through."

"Me either, sir, and thank you, sir."

"Good show, Colonel. No more worry about him upsetting *Serendipity* and jeopardizing *Fox.*"

"I believe you're right sir. That asset is safe for the time being."

CHAPTER 41

▼

The wagon full of hay carrying Fritz, *Camel* and General Marsh lumbered along on what appeared to be two separate, but ill-marked roads. It reminded Marsh of Robert Frost's poem *THE ROAD NOT TAKEN*. The words of the final stanza crept into his mind like a lengthening shadow as they bounced along, jostled by the uneven terrain.

> *I shall be telling this with a sigh*
> *Somewhere ages and ages hence:*
> *Two roads diverged in a wood, and I—*
> *I took the one less traveled by,*
> *And that has made all the difference.*

I hope Fritz chooses the road that makes all the difference for us, Marsh thought. The wagon continued to move along at a steady pace. The only sounds that disturbed the silence were an occasional snort or sneeze from the horses or the trill of a meadowlark. The wagon creaked as it swayed back and forth, and the hardware on the harnesses softly clinked and rattled. *Camel* and General Marsh, decked out in clothes loaned them by Fritz and *Herr* Röhr, swayed in sync with the wagon as it slowly rolled through meadows and groves of trees.

They got started very early in the morning. Mannheim was forty-five miles as the crow flies from the Röhr's farm. They were not crows, so they had to follow the meandering road. It would take two long days to reach Mannheim. The only people they saw, and only at a distance, was an occasional farmer or sheepherder. So far it seemed safe enough.

The sun went down over the hills to the west and dusk enveloped the meadows. They looked for a place to camp and settled on a clearing alongside a small brook. Fritz strongly recommended they not build a fire. *Camel* agreed. It felt good to stretch their legs and *Camel* walked downstream a few hundred yards. Fritz unloaded their bedrolls, and General Marsh helped lay them out. Fritz said something to Marsh and he pointed to his throat. He wished *Camel* would get back. Fritz hobbled the horses and threw them down an armload of hay.

When *Camel* returned, Fritz laid out a meal of homemade bread, Röhr farm stuffed *Schlachtwurst,* and cheese. General Marsh savored every bite. He was very hungry and couldn't remember when he had tasted anything quite as good. He loved German food. *Too bad the Nazis had to spoil it.* They passed a bottle of wine around to wash it all down.

A full moon bathed the serene landscape as they crawled into their bedrolls. It was quiet and peaceful. *Camel* hoped it remained that way.

Fritz was up at dawn and harnessed the horses. He roused *Camel* and Marsh out of their slumber, handed them a few sticks of jerky, and said they had better get started. They all climbed aboard the wagon for another long day's ride.

It was almost dark when they reached the outskirts of Mannheim. Even from a distance you could tell this city had been badly damaged from Allied bombing. General Marsh had ordered many a raid on this very target.

Fritz said, "I believe this is as close to the city as I should go. You'll have to go the rest of the way on foot."

"All right, listen up. It will take me about half an hour to get where I might find a telephone. Hopefully it will take only fifteen minutes to reach my party, and if I'm lucky, the same time to return. Let say a maximum of an hour and a half to two hours, if everything goes well. If I run into a problem it may take longer so don't give up on me and leave. If I don't return before sun up you can assume I'm not coming back, and you had better move on." It was a good thing General Marsh didn't know what he said.

"What about the *diamanten?* Shouldn't you leave them with *Herr* Manstein for safe keeping?"

"They will be safe with me," a suspicious *Camel* replied.

Camel reached the city proper without incident. It was heavily damaged. He walked quickly down the street looking for some business establishment that was still open. It was dark now, and no lights were on in the streets. The city was in a total blackout.

He came to a tavern and could hear music inside mingled with boisterous laughter. It seemed like a dichotomy to the dismal surroundings. He stepped inside and quickly surveyed the room. It was crowded and noisy. Beer was flowing freely and it made for a jovial atmosphere. He went to the bar and ordered a mug. It seemed the natural thing to do, and he *was* thirsty. When the bartender sat the beer in front of him *Camel* said, "Do you have a telephone?"

"*Ja,* but it's only for my use."

"I need to call someone in Berlin. If you will let me use it I'll give you a hundred Reichmarks."

"Let's see the money." *Camel* laid the money on the counter. The bartender deftly crumpled it in his hand and put it in his pocket."

"Behind the curtain at the end of the counter." *Camel* slid off the stool and walked to the end of the counter, parted the drapes, and stepped behind them. He lifted the receiver and the operator said, "die nummer bitte." *Camel* gave her Jacob's home phone number. It was now 1950 hours and he hoped *Fox* was home.

"Hello, the Müller residence."

"Hello, I'd like to speak to *Hauptsturmführer* Karl Müller, please."

"I'm sorry he's not at home. We expect him soon." *Camel* let out a low groan.

"Is everything all right?" Martha asked. *Camel* swore under his breath and replied, "May I leave a message for him?"

"*Ja,* of course."

"Listen very carefully; I'm calling from Mannheim. Tell him the camel and package were sidetracked at Frankfurt, and that they are proceeding to Belfort, France by horse drawn wagon. Have him provide secure transportation at the border. Use password *Gold Braid.* Can you remember all that?"

"I'm writing it down. Just one moment please."

Martha read the message back as she had written it and *Camel* said, "That's fine, be sure to give it to him the minute he gets home."

"Who should I say called?"

"Tell him it was the camel's keeper."

"Anything else?" she asked.

"*Nein,* just give him the message as soon as you see him." *Camel* hung up the receiver and went back to the bar. He finished his beer and left.

He was heading back to the wagon when he saw two individuals walking toward him. As they came closer he could see they were soldiers. One had a rifle slung over his shoulder, and the other carried a *Mauser* machine gun. They stopped him, and the one with the machine gun snarled, "Where are you going?"

"I'm on my way home. I just stopped at the Boar's Den for a quick beer."

"Let me see your identification."

Camel tried to remain calm and answered, "I left it in my other trousers at home."

"Don't you know you must have your identification paper with you at all times?"

"Yes, I know that, but like I just told you, I left it in my other trousers."

"Maybe a few nights in custody will improve your memory."

"Come on now, give a guy a break. It's late and the *Frau* isn't going to be too happy as it is when I get home this late."

The soldier with the rifle said, "Let him go, Gustav. We haven't got time to mess around with this guy."

Camel was hopeful, but "*machine gun* Gustav" said, "No, we're taking him in. I don't like the looks of this one."

"I know I'm not the best looking guy in town, but I'm not a bad sort either."

"Get moving," Gustav barked as he motioned with the machine gun. *Camel* reluctantly began walking in front of them.

Suddenly air raid sirens filled the night air. Their piercing wailing sound sent chills up *Camel's* spine. It apparently had the same effect on his two captors. They bolted and ran. *Camel* ran in the opposite direction toward the wagon. Just as he reached the outskirts of the city, bombs began to fall. He thought, *This is the second time Allied bombers have rescued me, assuming I can get out of here fast enough.*

He ran as fast as he could. Bombs were falling in the area he had just abandoned. The noise was deafening. He stopped to catch his breath and looked back. Explosions and flames lit up the city like Roman candles. He was doubled over and could hardly breathe. *I'm getting too old for this nonsense.*

He didn't rest long. He turned and continued running, arriving at the wagon completely out of breath. He literally collapsed and rolled over on his back beside the wagon, his chest heaving. Fritz and Marsh picked him up and boosted him up onto the seat. They climbed aboard. Fritz grabbed the reins, and smacked the frantic horses on their rumps with a whip. They didn't need much encouragement. They wanted away from the noise as much as their passengers. When they were a safe distance away, Fritz slowed the horses to a walk.

"That was mighty close, *Herr* Ebert. Did you get your phone call made?"

"Yes, just barely."

General Marsh later learned that on this date, 20 December 1943, that approximately 1,000 Allied aircraft dropped 2,000 tons of bombs on Frankfurt and Mannheim.

When Jacob arrived home, Martha gave him the message she had written down. He was upset that he had missed the call.

"Is this all, Martha?" he asked.

"*Ja, Ja.* I read the message back to him, and he said it was fine."

"*Danke schön,* Martha."

"Why are they taking a camel to Belfort? That must have been quite a chore getting it into a wagon." It was hard for Jacob to keep from laughing.

"I suppose the Belfort Zoo needs a camel."

"Why do they need a password for a camel?"

"It's just an inside joke, Martha." Jacob excused himself and went to the wine cellar. He sent the following message to London. *Change of plans. Scrub meet at Zurich. Camel and package proceeding to Belfort, France, by wagon. It will probably take two days to reach border. Have partisans make contact at border and retrieve package. The password is Gold Braid. Fox.*

CHAPTER 42

▼

The wagon carrying Fritz, *Camel,* and General Marsh was nearing the French border. They had seen a German patrol earlier in the day in the distance, but they either didn't see the wagon or were not interested in them.

"How will we know when we are in France?" *Camel* inquired.

"I know we're close, but it's hard to determine. There is no fence or barrier to define it," Fritz replied. General Marsh pointed ahead and to the left. Both Fritz and *Camel* turned to look. Off in the distance was what looked like a sign. Fritz turned the wagon in that direction. The horses plodded ahead until they were close enough for them to read what it said. The sign was badly weathered and was tilted almost to the ground. They could barely make out the words *Deutschland-Frankreich Grenze.*

"This is it," Fritz said.

"*Gut,* It shouldn't be long until we are in Belfort." Marsh began frantically pointing off to their right. An armored personnel carrier full of German soldiers was headed straight toward them.

"That looks like the patrol we saw earlier in the day. What should we do?" Fritz asked.

"Just keep moving and act natural. Let me handle this," *Camel* replied.

The patrol vehicle pulled up alongside the wagon and an officer yelled, "HALT!" Fritz reined the horse in and the wagon stopped. The officer stepped out of the vehicle and approached the wagon. Several soldiers climbed down with their weapons at ready.

"Who are you and where do you think you're going?" the officer demanded.

"We're farmers. We're delivering a load of hay to our cousin in Belfort," *Camel* replied.

"And who gave you permission to cross the border into France?"

"I didn't think permission was required, now that we control that country."

"You are badly mistaken. Let me see your identification papers." Fritz retrieved his and handed them to the German officer. After scanning them he looked at *Camel* and Marsh and said, "Where are your papers?" Marsh looked at *Camel* and wondered what was being said.

"Our papers were lost in the raid on Frankfurt."

"Let me see your hands."

"What do you want with our hands?" *Camel* asked.

"Never mind. All of you hold out your hands, palms up." All three reluctantly obeyed. *Camel knew* what he was looking for.

"You two are not farmers. You haven't done a days work on a farm in your life." *Camel* made a quick decision. He grabbed the switch and cracked it across the startled horse's flanks. They bolted and it almost threw an unprepared Fritz and Marsh over backwards. Several shots were fired, but fortunately none found their mark. The German officer and men jumped into their vehicle and roared after them.

"We can't outrun them," Fritz screamed.

"Just keep moving as fast as these horses can run." The wagon was bouncing crazily and hay was flying out the back. Suddenly gunfire and grenades exploded behind them. Fritz reined the horses in and the wagon stopped. They all stood up and looked back. The German vehicle was on its side and in flames. Several soldiers were running, but not for long. Gunfire cut them down and then it was quiet. Only the crackling of the burning vehicle violated the quiet of the countryside. A dozen men seemed to appear out of nowhere; each of them carried a rifle. As they approached the wagon *Camel* stepped down and waited.

"Thank you for taking care of those Germans," *Camel* said.

"Our pleasure *Monsieur*. What are you doing here and where are you going?"

"Our *Gold Braid* has become a little tattered. We are taking it to Bern for repair" *Camel* replied. General Marsh got down off the wagon.

"*Oui Monsieur*. Maybe we can help."

"It would be most appreciated," *Camel* replied.

"What's going on here, *Herr* Ebert? Who are these people? What's all this about a gold braid." *Camel* slipped the belt off his pants and handed it to Fritz.

"Thank you Fritz. I believe you had better get started back to the farm."

"What is going…?"

"Better not to ask, Fritz," *Camel* interrupted. "Just go." A puzzled Fritz looked at *Camel,* then at General Marsh. He shrugged his shoulders, picked up the reins and urged the horses forward. They watched as the wagon rumbled off.

"What's with the belt, *Monsieur?*" one of them asked.

"Payment for services rendered," *Camel* replied.

"He must work very cheap." *Camel* just smiled.

"We had better get away from here. Another patrol might have heard the commotion," commented the partisan leader.

"Lead the way, we're ready. By the way, what is your name?" *Camel* inquired.

"Just call me *Corbeau,* and your name *Monsieur?*"

"Just call me *Camel.*" A knowing smile crossed both their faces.

The partisans escorted *Camel* and General Marsh across the Swiss border just east of the little town of Ferrette without any more incidents. They traveled by night and slept during the day. Their guides moved like ghosts, silent and invisible to the outside world.

"We are here, *Monsieur Camel.* This is as far as we can go. You will be safe now. Ahead of you are the Jura Mountains. They are not very high and you will have no difficulty if you keep to the pass. The pass is not high enough for snow, even at this time of the year. Continue east for about ten kilometers and you will come to a small village called Delemon. There you can purchase bus tickets to Bern. Do you have money?"

"Only *Reichmarks.*"

"They are practically worthless in Switzerland. Here are some *Franken.* It should be enough to get you to Bern."

"Thank you, *Corbeau.* How can we ever repay you?"

"By getting the *Nazi cochons* out of France."

"That, I can promise you," *Camel* replied.

The partisans evaporated into the forest like steam disappearing over a hot kettle. The silence was like a tomb. It was still nighttime. They walked until they came to a sharp rise in the slope. *Camel* said, "We probably should remain here until daybreak. It might be too dangerous to proceed in unfamiliar terrain in the dark."

"That sounds good to me, I'm pooped," Marsh replied. They untied the rope around their bedrolls and crawled in. They had become used to sleeping on hard ground under the stars. The fresh air was a catalyst for sleep, and they were both soon oblivious to the night.

General Marsh was roused out of a deep sleep by a kick in the ribs. The pain caused a loud yelp and immediate consciousness. He looked up, squinting, and there stood two uniformed soldiers. *Camel* sat bolt upright at the noise. Speaking German, one of the soldiers demanded, "Who are you? What are you doing here?"

Camel could tell by their uniforms that they were Swiss. He replied, "I'm English and this is an American. We are trying to get to our embassies in Bern."

"Let me see you identification papers."

"I'm sorry, but they were lost when our vehicle and luggage were destroyed in a bombing raid on Frankfurt."

"What were you doing in Germany if you are British and American?"

"That is information we cannot divulge. Our embassies will vouch for us. We demand to be taken to Bern."

"You are in no position to demand anything. You will have to come with us to Basel."

"Basel! We need to get to Bern," *Camel* replied.

"That's just too bad, because our headquarters are in Basel. You can tell your story to our commander."

"But it's quite urgent we get to Bern."

"If our commander says you can go to Bern, you can go to Bern, but we're going to Basel first."

"What's the deal? Are these guys German or Swiss?" Marsh asked.

"They're Swiss and they're taking us to Basel."

"Basel! Tell them we want to go to Bern."

"I already have. Apparently they need to verify that we are who we say we are at their headquarters in Basel. We had better do what they say. No use arguing with them, they have the guns."

"So, you have no identification and your appearance belies your claim as to who you say you are, so why should I believe you?" Major Staheli asked.

"If you will contact our embassies in Bern, they will vouch for us."

"What are you doing entering this country illegally?"

"We had no other choice. As I explained to your border guards, our papers were destroyed near Frankfurt in an Allied bombing raid on a munitions train."

"What are your real names, it will be much better for you if you tell me the truth."

"We have been telling you the truth. I repeat, this *is* General Thomas Marsh, United States Army Air Forces, and my name is Joseph Ebert a British subject. General Marsh was shot down in a raid over Berlin. He parachuted safely from the doomed aircraft, and I helped him escape from Germany. If you will contact either the British or American Embassies in Bern they will verify our identification and the facts as I have related them to you."

"You claim to have been living in Berlin, *Herr* Ebert. What is a British subject doing in Berlin?"

"I cannot divulge anything more about myself than I have already told you. It would save you a lot of time and energy, and a great deal of anxiety on our part, if you would contact our embassies in Bern."

"I *have* already contacted them, and they are sending representatives to Basel."

"Why didn't you tell us that in the first place? It would have saved a bloody lot of chit chat and your bloody lot of questions," *Camel* said testily.

"Take them back to their cells," Major Staheli sternly replied.

"Major Staheli, we are from the American and British Embassies. This is Mr. Robert Sutton from the American Embassy and I am Gordon Sandstrom from the British Embassy. The two men you have detained are American and British subjects. We have photographs, documents, and sworn statements by our ambassadors as to their identities. It would be most appreciated by our governments if you would release these men into our custody."

"And if I release them what will you do with them?"

"General Marsh will be flown to England, and Josef Ebert will return to Berlin."

"I thought Mr. Ebert was a British subject. Why would he return to Berlin?"

"We would rather not say. It's a delicate matter."

"Yes it is. We must be careful to maintain our neutrality and not anger the German government."

"You might be better served by not angering our governments. This war will not last much longer, and Germany will be a defeated nation. Would you rather be friends to the victors or the vanquished?"

Major Staheli pondered that question and after a few moments replied, "You can have them, and good riddance."

"Good luck general. It has been an interesting experience."

"Thank you Josef. I once had a real estate agent tell me the word "interesting" was a code word they used when describing a really ugly piece of property in front of a client. I guess I'm that ugly piece of property, but I am most grateful to you for saving my life."

"It comes with the territory. Keep those bombers flying, and no more hitch hiking."

"You can count on that. I believe I've learned my lesson."

"Josef, the Embassy has prepared these documents for you. Here is a passport. It has been stamped with the Swiss seal showing the date you legally entered Switzerland. In your wallet are *Reichmarks* and *Franken* as well as a hotel receipt for your stay in Zurich. In the briefcase are papers and correspondence, which indicates you were here on a procurement trip for instruments to be used in guidance systems for rockets. It doesn't say that directly, but the inference is there. The Swiss are masters at manufacturing delicate instruments so this would be the logical place for you to come. Here is a forged unlimited-travel rail warrant. It allows you priority passage on any train in Germany. Your train leaves at 0900."

"It looks like your people have been very busy. Thank you very much for your help. Maybe we'll meet when the war is over."

"That would be nice. By the way, good show and good luck."

"Thank you, but I don't believe in luck."

After an uneventful trip, *Camel* returned to Berlin and resumed his duties at Felix's.

"Josef, I've missed you. Have you been on vacation?" Jacob teased.

"Some vacation," Camel sneered.

"The food has just not been the same since you left."

"I had some very good food on my *vacation*."

"Really. I'm happy to hear that, and I'm happy you are back. What do you recommended this evening, Josef?"

"Chef has prepared some delicious *Mastgefügel*. They have been browned gently in butter and stewed in their own juice with diced smoke bacon, shallots and mushrooms. This will be served with little new potatoes browned in butter."

"This is torture, Josef. Stop talking and just serve it. I'm starved."

"You lead such a rough life. Good job, nice food, no worries."

"You're wasting time, Josef, the kitchen's that way," Jacob pointed. He had missed this banter with *Camel*. He was happy to see him back safe and sound.

CHAPTER 43

▼

On 1 June, 1944 the *Abwehr* was removed from the control of the *Wermacht* and placed in the hands of Heinrich Himmler, the SS leader. Admiral Wilhelm Canaris was suspected of clandestinely conspiring against Hitler.

This news was a devastating blow to Jacob. He wondered if his relationship to Canaris might put him in danger. *Should he run or stay put,* he wondered. After an excruciating day pondering what to do he decided to weather the storm. If he was on the front line fighting, he could not cut and run when it got dangerous.

Before Canaris left the *Abwehr,* he changed Jacob's status from adjutant to a junior officer in the *Abwehr's* section III, Counter-espionage. Jacob felt he was still in business as long as Himmler did not interfere.

Hitler gave orders for Canaris to be removed from active duty on 10 June, but this order was rescinded several days later. He was reinstated as an admiral *z V* or *zur Verfügung,* meaning available for duty. He soon received word "that the Führer had appointed him head of the *OKW's Sonderstab fur Handelskrig ünd wirtschaftliche Kampfmassnahmen* or HWK-Special Staff for Mercantile Warfare and Economic Combat Measures."[1] His former position of power was gone, but he was still alive.

The responsibility of this new office began to shrink as country after country stopped shipments of vital material to the *Third Reich.* He was left with little to do except hold conferences with his staff, shuffle paper, which he despised, and try to stay busy.

---

1. *Canaris, Hitler's Master Spy,* by Heinz Höhne

▼

Jacob received the message on his wireless with excitement. The Allied landing in France was to begin on 6 June 1944. The original date had been set for 5 June, but inclement weather, which almost cancelled it until July, was rescheduled for 6 June. On 1 June, the BBC sent the first half of a coded message about the landing to the French Resistance. "The message consisted of two completely innocent sounding lines of poetry from Verlaine's *Chanson d' Automme;* the first; *Les sanglots longs des violons de l'automne,'* formed the warning order to be given on the 1ˢᵗ or 15ᵗʰ of the invasion month; the second, *'Blessent mon coeur d'une longueur monotone;'* the more immediate warning to be given forty-eight hours before the start of the invasion."[1] The second half of the coded signal was broadcast to the Resistance on 5 June. This was the signal for them to begin a massive sabotage campaign in France.

The Allies had used all kinds of ploys to convince the Germans that the landing would come by way of the short sea route to Calais. To reinforce this misconception, an exercise called *Operation Fortitude* was initiated. General George S. Patton had been ostentatiously recalled to England from the Mediterranean and given command of a phantom First US Army Group. Dummy encampments were set up, fake radio traffic was broadcast, imitation landing craft was fabricated and false reports were sent to Germany by *turned,* captured German spies. Jacob had been able to also reinforce this evaluation by influencing the thinking of the *Abwehr* staff. Ironically, the Germans had received reports of the real landing site, even the day and the hour from *Gestapo* agents that had penetrated the

---

1. *Inside Hitler's Headquarters* by General Walter Warlimont

French Resistance forces, but Hitler felt the enemy had deliberately planted this information to deceive him, and this only buttressed his view that Normandy was only a feint.

There was pandemonium in the *Abwehr* offices when it became clear that Normandy, not Calais was the real invasion site. They realized heads could roll because of their miscalculation. Ironically Hitler stubbornly held to the belief that Calais was the target, and that the landing at Normandy *was* only a feint to draw his strength from Calais.

Rommel desperately pleaded for more armor to be diverted to Normandy. Of the six panzer divisions available, Hitler agreed to release only three, but not the best three. He refused to divert any of the army divisions from the Calais area whose reinforcements were critically needed at the ultimate invasion site.

It was some time before Hitler realized his mistake. Fortress Europe had been penetrated by the Allies, but the Germans fought back furiously.

One of the most strategic objectives, led by Lieutenant General Omar Bradley, was the capture of the port of Cherbourg at the tip of the Cotentin peninsula, west of the Normandy beaches. This port would allow the supply by ship of the invasion forces, and its capture was crucial to the success of *Overlord*.

Gold Beach proved to be thinly defended and Montgomery's British 50th Infantry Division secured this beach relatively easy and began to move inland toward Caen.

At Utah Beach, Brigadier General Theodore Roosevelt, who had originally been refused to go in with the first wave because of a bad heart, realized the tides had landed them a mile south of their target. He found himself in a shell hole with Commodore James Arnold, the navy control officer assigned to the Utah Beach invasion force. They conferred and wondered if they should shift their forces a mile down the beach to the original site or proceed from the position they now found themselves in. It's reported that Roosevelt said, *We'll start the war from here.*

The battle for Omaha Beach proved to be the bloodiest site of the invasion. Allied planners knew it would be rough but necessary. It was a very narrow battlefield. It had fixed fortification and trenches connected by tunnels. The water and beaches had been heavily mined. Every square inch of the beach had been pre-sighted for Mortars, 88's, and 77's. The firing positions for all types of weapons were laid out at angles to the beaches to provide cross firing, grazing and plunging fire for maximum destruction. It was literally a killing field and many men were slaughtered before they even had a chance to return fire. In spite of all this, those that did survive the initial thrust, succeeded in getting up the bluffs and beyond. They had done their job.

If the British 3rd Infantry Division landing at Sword Beach was to be successful it depended on the British 6th Airborne Division, who had landed during the night to secure the Orne Canal and Orne River bridges. Major John Howard was concerned about what he knew would be an inevitable counter attack by German armor, which he knew was capable of driving his forces from the bridges. The fate of the entire 3rd Infantry Division hung in the balance if those two bridges were retaken; maybe even the fate of the entire invasion. If Tiger tanks could reach the beach over these bridges, they would be able to unleash unimaginable havoc on the invasion force.

In the dark, Sergeant Wagger Thorton nervously fingered his Piat, the only weapon available at that juncture that could penetrate a tank. His superb training told him to wait until the tank was close enough so he would not miss. If he missed he would not have time to reload before the tank killed him. The tank kept inching forward and Thorton patiently waited. As the tank turned, Thorton fired, and hit it broadside. The Piat bomb penetrated the tank setting off ammunition inside. The night sky was lit up with what looked like fireworks at a 4th of July celebration. It went on for over an hour and convinced the German company commanders that the British were present in such great strength that they had their forces fall back and wait for daylight to assess the situation.

At Juno Beach the defenders were to be softened up by intense air bombardment and naval gunfire. Unfortunately, the bombs fell too far inland and none of the fortifications at Juno were hit. Naval guns were woefully inaccurate and few shells hit their targets. Fortunately, the Canadian force outnumbered the German six to one. The defenders were made up of boys under eighteen years of age, and men over thirty five, and Eastern Front veterans with disabling wounds. The Canadians were made up of tough outdoorsman, all volunteers.

Before the landing craft hit the beaches an eerie quiet settled over the battleground. They received no gunfire while they were approaching the beaches. It felt more like an exercise than the real thing. They didn't realize it at first, but all the German guns were sighted to fire only down the beaches. After fierce fighting the concrete emplacements, machine guns, and pillboxes fell silent. Villagers began streaming into the street greeting the Canadians with flowers. Of the 29,000 men that went ashore at Sword, there were only 630 casualties. They inflicted far more than this upon the defenders.

The *Overlord* landing operation had been successful, but at an enormous cost of men and equipment, and tough fighting still lay ahead.

Jacob followed the invasion reports with great interest. He sent a flood of information on his wireless to London from information he felt pertinent gleaned from *Abwehr* reports of the fighting.

CHAPTER 45

▼

On 20 July, 1944, a rumor spread like wildfire throughout the Abwehr of the attempted assassination of Hitler. Reports at first were sketchy, but as time went by it became clear it was an attempted military putsch.

During a conference at Hitler's headquarters in Rastenburg, a bomb had been planted by Colonel Count von Stauffenberg. It exploded, and when the dust settled a shaken, but still alive Führer emerged with only cuts and bruises. Before the end of the day many of the conspirators were arrested and executed. Others were subsequently hanged with piano wire and their grisly executions filmed.

Others, such as Rommel, Halder, von Kluge, Witzleben and Canaris were aware of the plot, but took no active part in the conspiracy, and they were not immediately arrested. Canaris had already been sacked, and all the others but Rommel were relieved of their commands. Because Rommel was so enormously popular with the German people, Hitler was afraid to execute him. However, in August 1944, he was finally confronted and given the choice of standing trial or taking poison. He chose poison.

The paranoia that Hitler had always exhibited was magnified by these events, and the circle of those he trusted grew smaller and smaller. Ever since he had come to power Hitler had employed three look-alike doubles. One was in Frankfurt, one was at Obersalzberg, and another was in Berlin. The double in Berlin looked so much like Hitler that even when standing next to one another, his close associates had a hard time telling them apart unless they spoke. The attempt on Hitler's life so exacerbated his paranoia that he resolved to always place one of these doubles in harm's way before he took center stage.

He lamented to his inner circle that these traitors, meaning those that plotted his murder, were responsible for Germany's apparent coming defeat. It was always someone else's fault. It was an exhibition of human weakness that was exaggerated by his grandiosity.

CHAPTER 46

▼

General Marsh, waiting outside MI6 Headquarters, approached the first person that exited the building.

"Excuse me Miss, do you happen to know a Miss Janet Jones who works in this building?"

"I might," she cautiously answered.

"I'm trying to get a message to Miss Jones. Would you mind giving her this envelope?"

"I can do that. What's in it?"

"It's a private matter. Please just give her the envelope."

"Excuse me, Colonel Ashburn; may I have a word with you?"

"Of course, Mrs. Crawford, won't you please come into my office...Now, what can I do for you?"

"I was approached by a high-ranking American officer, at least he was in the uniform of a high-ranking American officer, who asked me to deliver this envelope to your secretary, Miss Jones. It seemed quite suspicious to me, and I thought you should know."

Ashburn took the envelope and said, "Thank you, Mrs. Crawford; we can't be too careful, can we? You did the right thing by letting me know of this incident."

Ashburn steamed the envelope open and read the message. It said, "I have a message for you from your fiancé, Captain Jacob Halder. Meet me at the Oxbow Restaurant, 1629 Parish Avenue, tomorrow, Tuesday the 16th, at 1900 hours. Come alone and do not let anyone know of this meeting. My name is General

Thomas Marsh. Give the maitre d' your name, and he will direct you to my table."

Hmm…General Marsh what are you up to? Why didn't you just walk into the office and give Janet the message? I know you were in Germany with Fox. Why the secrecy?

An MI6 officer was seated at the table next to General Marsh's when Janet was brought to Marsh's table. The general stood up and introduced himself to Janet as she sat down. Unknown to either of them, a microphone had been planted in the small flower arrangement in the center of the table.

"Thank you for coming, Miss Jones; it's a pleasure meeting you after hearing so much about you from Jacob."

"It's nice to meet you too, General Marsh. I'm happy you were able to get out of Germany safely. How is Jacob, how does he look, is he all right? How I envy you having seen him so recently. How does he…?"

"He was just fine the last time I saw him," General Marsh interrupted. "He sends you his love and asked me to give you this message." General Marsh handed Janet an envelope.

"Thank you, General. I can't tell you how much I appreciate this. I miss Jacob so much I…I…it's hard to explain…It's been so long…and I worry about him every minute of the day, and…I want him back so badly…" Janet broke down and held a handkerchief to her face as she cried.

Trying to give Janet a measure of assurance, General Marsh said, "I wouldn't be too concerned Miss Jones. He's very good at what he does, and Germany can't hold out much longer. I'm sure he will get back safely, and the both of you will live happily ever after."

"Thank you, General. I hope you're right. I just couldn't live without Jacob."

The MI6 officer handed Ashburn the recorder. "I do not want to be disturbed, Miss Jones. Hold all my calls and no visitors," Ashburn said as he disappeared into his office.

He seated himself at his desk and pressed the start button. *Thank you for coming Miss Jones. It's a pleasure meeting you after hearing so much…*

When the recording ended, Ashburn leaned back in his chair and reflected on this conversation…*It sounds innocent enough to me, but I wish he had given Janet the message verbally.*

When Janet got back to her flat at the end of the workday, she frantically tore open the envelope that Marsh had given her. Breathlessly, she read the instruction Jacob had given her via General Marsh about contacting him…*I can do it,* she thought. *I'm glad Ashburn had me send some of his messages to Jacob because now I'm familiar enough with the wireless transmitter to operate it.*

As Colonel Ashburn Left his office for the day, he noticed that Janet was still at her desk. He said, "I see you're still here, Miss Jones. Are you working late tonight?"

"Yes sir. I have some typing to catch up on. It shouldn't take me more than an hour or two to finish up."

"Well, don't work too late. I want you to be bright and fresh for the conference tomorrow regarding *Operation Marta.*"

I won't sir. Have a good evening, and I'll see you in the morning."

"Good evening, Janet."

Janet waited a half hour to be sure Ashburn was gone for the night and then let herself into the secure vault that held the transmitter. *It has an eerie feeling being in here alone. I hope no one comes while I'm sending my message.*

She set the transmitter to the proper frequency and began to speak. "Hello out there, darling. I'm sure you know who this is. There are a million things I'd like to say to you, but I must keep this short. I hope you are well and safe, and I love you so much it hurts. The best time to reply is midnight, Friday the 19th, London time. I can hardly wait. With all my love, J."

She turned the transmitter off, closed and locked the vault, covered her typewriter, and left as fast as she could move. *That was nerve-wracking, but worth it. I'll be on pins and needles until Friday.*

"Did you hear that, Gustav?" One of the radio traffic monitors asked.

"I did, what did you make of it, Herbert"

"A very strange message. I've never heard anything quite like it before. It's in a code different from any other I've come across."

"Play it back and let's see if we can make any sense out of it." Herbert rewound the wire and started the recorder. The two of them analyzed the message sentence by sentence.

"*Darling* must be the agent's code name, and if he is getting messages on a regular basis, he would know who is transmitting."

"That's right, and the phrase *I hope you are well and safe* may mean his handler is very worried that he may be close to being exposed, and this is a warning."

"I believe you've got it, Gustav, and when she said *I love you so much it hurts,* that might mean that if they lose this agent it would do great harm to their operation. We must be alert for the message when this agent replies on Friday the 19th."

"Yes, and we had better pass this information on to *Sturmbannführer* Stuckart."

Sturmbannführer Markis Stuckart listened intently to the recorded message. After listening to the whole conversation he rolled his eyes and said, "You must be a couple of *Dummköpfe.* This just sounds to me like a lovesick girl contacting her boy friend. Have either of you two ever heard this voice before?"

Both Gustav and Herbert shook their heads, and Gustav said, "No sir, we haven't. This is the first time I've heard it."

"Have either of you heard any other traffic on that same frequency?"

Herbert hesitated and then said, "Well sir, not exactly; however, we both have heard a short *squeal* sound that happens quite regularly, but it's so short we have not been able to get a fix on it."

"Do you have a recording of this so called *squeal* sound," An irritated Stuckart demanded.

"No sir, I do not. Do you Gustav?"

"No, it's of such a short duration; I didn't think it would have any value."

"Let me be the judge of that! I want a recording of that *squeal* the next time you hear it, is that clear?"

"Yes sir," they both replied.

Friday the 19th came and Jacob descended the stairs to the wine cellar, prepared to transmit his reply to Janet. He entered the following message into the transmitter.

It was wonderful to hear from you, darling. I wish you could be transported here by wireless, but since that's not possible your voice is the next best thing. I'm just fine and in good shape, except I miss you terribly. Don't worry about me because everything is going smoothly. As you know Allied forces are making good progress and Germany's defeat is in sight. Hang in there, and take good care of yourself. Love ya. J. Jacob pressed the transmit button, and with a short squeal the message was on its way.

"There it is Herbert, did you hear it?"

"I did, and I was able to record it this time. You had better get this over to Stuckart straight away. Let me know what he thinks it is."

Gustav played the recording, and Stuckart listened intently. "So that's what you two have been hearing for months, is that right?"

"Yes sir, pretty strange, don't you think?"

"Can you slow that recording down?" Stuckart asked.

"Yes sir."

"Well do it!" Stuckart ordered. Gustav wound the wire back, turned a dial, and started the recorder again. The squeal now turned into something that sounded more like words, but they were too fast to be discernable.

"Can you slow it down any more?"

"Yes sir." Gustav turned the dial as far as it would go, and started the recording again. This time the words came through clearly, but they were slower than a person would speak so Gustav adjusted the dial until the speech was normal.

"Play it again from the beginning." Stuckart said. Gustav did as he was ordered.

"That is very interesting. It sounds like two lovers corresponding with one another. He's obviously an enemy agent located somewhere nearby, and he's an American. The girl sounds British. I want half a dozen trucks scattered around section 16 until they get a fix on the location of that transmitter."

"That won't be easy sir. The signal is so short we will hardly be able to turn the antennas before it stops.

I don't give a damn how long it takes, just get it done! That's an order!"

"Yes sir," Gustav replied.

CHAPTER 47

▼

"Uncle Wilhelm, how have you been, sir? It's been quite some time since we've seen one another."

"I've seen better days, my boy, but for the time being, I'm still alive. How long that lasts is up to Hitler. How are things at the *Abwehr?*"

"It's been a mad house around there. It hasn't been the same since you left, sir."

"How is Oster?"

"The same old worry wart. What's happening at HWK? You never did tell me why you were dismissed from the *Abwehr* and transferred there."

"My boy, you must distance yourself from me. It may be bad for you to even be seen with me. I've been accused of committing *Landesverrat* as well as *Hochverrat*." (Betraying my country to the enemy in addition to plotting the government's downfall). Hitler has always suspected me of being an accomplice in the attempt on his life. He has never had proof, but when has he ever needed proof? I believe my arrest is imminent."

"Are you guilty of such things?" Canaris's only reaction was a wry smile.

"Go! Save yourself and your parents. Use everything you have learned and anything you might need at the *Abwehr* that will facilitate your escape. You don't have much time."

"What about you, and Grandmother and Grandfather."

"I've taken care of them. I still have a few tricks up my sleeve. They're on their way west. They have the necessary passes and documents. I still have a few friends in the department. I wanted your mother to go with them, but she wouldn't go without your father. I was unable to secure his release in time."

"His release! Do you know where he is?"

"Yes, I finally traced him. He's in Luckenwald. Himmler put him in a forced labor camp in a munitions plant there. I was unable to secure his release before I was dismissed. You must go and do that now."

"What will he think when he sees *me?* I'm responsible for him being there."

"He'll be so happy to get out of that hell hole he would go with the Devil himself."

"I'm afraid he may think that's who I am."

"Here, take these documents. They are orders to release your father into your custody. They are signed by Himmler. They're forgeries, of course, but they are good ones," he chuckled "You shouldn't have any trouble getting him out. The other documents are travel passes for your parents and Martha. Himmler also signed them. They're necessary to get them past any checkpoints going west. Instruct your father to pose as a diplomatic emissary for Himmler. He supposedly has been ordered to make contact with the Allies. Himmler, always the conniver, hopes to save his skin by negotiating behind Hitler's back. Count Folke Bernadotte, the King of Sweden's nephew, will try to convince the Allies that Himmler is the heir apparent, and wants to make a separate peace."

"How do you know all this?"

Canaris again chuckled. "As you know, it's has always been my business to know such things. I may not be head of the *Abwehr* anymore, but I have my sources. There are very few things that happen in Germany of which I'm not aware. Here are the keys to my personal limousine. Take it, it's a very imposing automobile and will lend authenticity to your movement. Also it is bulletproof. There is extra *benzin* in containers in the trunk."

"What about you, why don't you leave with us?"

"I'm of no importance now, and I would only add to your danger. It's a race to see who kills me first, Hitler or the Allies. I don't care which. Go now, that's an order."

"Yes sir." Jacob took the documents, shook hands with his uncle, saluted, turned and left.

Jacob drove directly to the factory where Friedrich was being held. He presented the release papers to Ulrich Graf, the plant manager.

"What is this, a release order? What does Himmler want with this man?"

"I don't know. My orders are to fetch him as quickly as possible."

"We can't spare even one man. This is ridiculous. I'll call Himmler myself and object." Jacob tried to remain calm, but was churning inside. *What to do? If he talks to Himmler the charade is over with disastrous consequences.*

Jacob summoned every ounce of energy in his body. He put his face within inches of the manager's face, and in a tone of controlled fury, and between clenched teeth said, "Go ahead and call Himmler. I can just see his reaction. When he finally calms down he will probably order you shipped east with a rifle in your hands." The manager cringed at this suggestion, and Jacob knew he had won.

"Deitrich, find this man and bring him here at once!" Graf yelled at one of his subordinates as he handed him the order. The man took the order, saw the name, and went to a file cabinet. He pulled a file and disappeared into the cavernous munitions factory.

"May I get you a cup of tea or coffee while you're waiting?"

"I'm not thirsty," Jacob snapped. The manager could tell Jacob was still furious, and he was trying to mollify him.

"Please have a seat. I'm sure they won't be long."

"I prefer to stand."

The manager fidgeted and shuffled through some papers trying to look busy. Jacob kept glancing at the clock over *Herr* Graf's desk. The only sound was the soft click of the sweep hand as the seconds ticked by.

Finally, the underling with a man in tow came into the room. Jacob was shocked by his appearance. His features were gaunt, and he was obviously malnourished. His clothes were ragged and looked several sizes too large for him. Friedrich was looking down as if staring at his feet.

"*Herr* Müller, you are to go with this man." Friedrich slowly raised his eyes. Upon seeing who he thought was Karl, started to open his mouth. Everyone was looking at Friedrich when Jacob gave an almost imperceptible shake of the head and Friedrich's mouth closed. Jacob stepped forward and took Friedrich by the arm.

"You are to come with me." Having said that, he roughly escorted Friedrich out of the room and made his way to the limousine. Jacob gently helped him into the front seat, shut the door and went around the limo and climbed into the drivers' seat. He turned the key and the automobile roared to life. In his haste to leave he depressed the accelerator so hard the wheels spun, kicking up gravel as they sped away.

Both were silent for several minutes. Jacob didn't know how his, or rather Karl's father, would react to him. Friedrich finally broke the silence by asking in a weak voice, "How did you manage it, *Sohn*?"

"With Uncle Wilhelm's help. He located you and provided the necessary papers."

"Good old Wilhelm. I must thank him." Jacob didn't reply. *No need to burden him with Uncle Wilhelm's problems.*

"Here, open this," Jacob said softly as he handed Friedrich a package wrapped in paper. Friedrich tore it open and saw more food than he had seen in years. There was a large sausage, cheese, bread, an apple and some chocolate. His hands trembled as he picked up the sausage. He began to weep. Finally getting control of his emotions he stuffed it into his mouth.

"Slow down, Father, or it will make you sick. Eat slowly. I can only imagine how hungry you must be. You look terrible. Those bastards will pay for this inhumanity, I promise you."

"That doesn't sound like you, Karl. I thought you were a devoted disciple of the *Nazis*." Jacob had a pained look on his face.

"That was before I finally realized they are nothing but filth and murderers. I'm sure you can understand how hard it is for me to admit that. I've grown up a lot since the day I...since the day I harmed you so badly. I hope you can forgive me. I wouldn't blame you if you didn't."

"To admit error is a sign of character, *mein Sohn*. You certainly seem to have changed. I accept your apology with all my heart."

They drove several more kilometers, when up ahead they saw soldiers standing in the road. One of them, a *Unterscharführer,* was signaling them to stop. The other soldiers stood with guns ready.

"Hide the food. It looks like a check point." Friedrich stuffed the food under his coat and swallowed hard. Jacob brought the car to a stop, rolled the window down and gruffly snapped, "What do you want, I'm in a hurry?"

The soldier saluted and said, "May I see your papers sir?" Jacob handed him the passes signed by Himmler.

"Who is this man with you?"

"He's a prisoner."

"Where are you taking him?"

"That's none of your business. If you want to ask *Reichsführer* Himmler that question, be my guest, but I wouldn't recommend it. Now get out of the way I'm in a hurry." The soldier handed back the passes, stepped back, saluted and waved them on.

"That was close," Friedrich said.

"Not really, there is so much confusion right now you could bluff your way into Hitler's bunker."

They could hear artillery fire in the distance. The Russians were driving hard toward Berlin. It was only a matter of days before all escape routes would be blocked. Berlin was almost completely pulverized from the Allied bombing and Russian artillery. It was fortunate their home was outside the city.

They drove in silence for a time and then Friedrich said, "How is your *Mutter?* It seems like forever since I've seen her." Jacob had dreaded this moment, but knew he had to prepare Karl's father before they got home.

"She's had her problems. She will be very concerned when she sees you."

"I can hardly wait to see her."

"About *Mutter,* try not to let her see you are shocked at her appearance. She had a stroke, which left her right arm paralyzed. She cannot walk and cannot speak very well. The *Doktor* says she will improve in time with proper therapy. She's in a wheelchair."

Tears rolled down Friedrich's cheeks as he quietly cried. Jacob handed him a clean handkerchief.

It was dusk as Jacob turned into the driveway and pulled up to the entrance. Friedrich just stared at the home he had built so many years ago. It was terribly run down and in need of repair and paint, but it never looked better to him.

"I never thought I would ever see this place again. Thank you, *mein Sohn.* What would I have done without you?"

"You would have done much better without me." Jacob quickly ran to the other side of the automobile and helped Friedrich out.

"We have to hurry. We've got to get a few things together before we leave."

"Where are we going?"

"West, away from the Russians. I want to get you all into the hands of the Americans as quickly as possible."

"You're coming with us aren't you?"

"No, there are things I must do."

Jacob took Friedrich's arm and helped him up the stairs. A dim light glowed through the cut glass door windows. Friedrich thought of happier times when guests were welcomed through those same doors.

Jacob inserted his key, unlocked the door and they went in. Everything was quiet. Jacob called out "Is anyone home?" He heard a rustle and footsteps and Martha appeared. Seeing Friedrich she let out a scream and rushed forward and hugged him. She was crying like a baby.

"Sorry sir to be so forward, but I'm so happy you're home. I'll get *Frau* Müller." She disappeared into the hall and ran to the bedroom.

Freya, hearing the scream, was struggling to propel the wheelchair with her one good arm to see what had happened. Martha rushed to help her and said, "You will never guess who just came home." Freya thought it had to be Friedrich, but she didn't dare believe it was possible, because the disappointment would kill her if it weren't.

Martha pushed the wheelchair into the living room and there stood Friedrich. Freya almost fainted. The astonished look on her face turned to joy as Friedrich rushed to her; fell to his knees and took her in his arms. They held one another, both crying.

"I've dreamed of this moment for a very long time," Friedrich said as he wiped the tears from her cheeks." Freya opened her mouth, struggling to say something, but no sound came out.

"I know exactly what you want to say. You're asking me why I've been away so long?" Freya nodded her head up and down…"and, you probably want to tell me how handsome I am." Freya again nodded her head up and down as she struggled to laugh.

"Well, I've looked better, but you have never looked more beautiful." Jacob didn't want to ruin the mood but knew they had to get moving.

"I hate to break up this reunion, and I know this is short notice, but you are all leaving as soon as we can get some things together."

Freya had a puzzled look on her face. Friedrich spoke gently to Freya and said, "Karl feels it wise we go west and come under the jurisdiction of the Americans, and I agree. I know it will be a tremendous disruption in our lives, but if we wait until the Russians occupy Berlin, we will regret it. After what they have suffered, they will no doubt take out their revenge on any German they find. They will assume we are all *Nazis.*"

"Martha, pack some clothes for mother and you. Also pack some food. Take all the jewelry and any other small valuables. We need to travel light. Father, we have time for you to bathe, shave and put on your best suit. You need to look presentable. Pack anything you think you might need, but keep it small."

Freya began to wave her good arm for attention. She mimicked writing something. Martha understood and ran to her bedroom to get her writing pad and pencil. Freya took the pencil in her left hand and laboriously printed the word "*FOTOGRAFIE.*"

"Of course, mother, we'll take the albums and any other *fotografie* we can squeeze in." Freya visible relaxed.

"We got a fix on that transmission sir. It's coming from a house in Charlottenburg."

"*Gut,* get the *Gestapo* over there as fast as they can move. I want that agent, do you hear!" Stuckart yelled.

"Yes sir, right away, sir."

The sound of a motorcycle in the driveway brought a concerned look to their faces. Jacob went to the door and peered out.

"It's OK. It's someone I'm expecting." Jacob motioned for the motorcycle rider to come in. He waited for him at the door as he came up the steps two at a time.

"Thank you for coming, Hans, it's good to see you again. Everyone, this is *Sturmbannführer* Hans Steiner, a very close friend. Hans, may I present my mother, Freya Müller, my father, Friedrich Müller, and Martha Kramer, our housekeeper, cook and my nanny as a child, whom we all love and adore."

Freya smiled and nodded her head at Hans. He clicked his heels and bowed slightly, Martha curtsied, and Friedrich approached him and shook his hand.

"It's very nice to meet all of you," Hans said.

"Hans will be driving you west, and you couldn't be in better hands. Now everyone get busy packing; we don't have much time."

Martha wheeled Freya to the bedroom; Friedrich followed to get his clothes and made his way into the bathroom. He turned the water on in the tub and undressed. He stepped in and sunk into its warmth. The luxury of it was exquisite. He wished he could stay under the scalding water until it cooled, but knew he had to hurry. He toweled off and was lathering his face when Jacob poked his head in and told him to be sure he kept his mustache when he shaved as his identification photograph showed him with one.

He carefully opened his straight razor and began slicing through several months' growth of beard. He trimmed his mustache and his hair the best he could and splashed some after-shave lotion on his face. He vowed he would never again take for granted what he once thought as trivial amenities.

He quickly dressed and looked in the mirror. The transformation was startling. He looked, smelled and felt like a new man. It was a wonderful feeling.

He stepped into the bedroom and Freya looked up. She smiled and mouthed the words, "You look *wunderbar*."

"Thank you, my dear. I feel *wunderbar*." Freya was thrilled that he had understood what she had said.

The automobile Wilhelm Canaris had given Jacob was the largest limousine manufactured by Mercedes Benz. It was black and highly polished and was as imposing as his uncle had said it was. It *was* very official looking.

Jacob removed one of the metal containers from the huge trunk and poured the contents into the *Benzin* tank. He and Hans then packed the belongings in the trunk alongside the remaining 76-liter *Benzin* container. Jacob carried his mother down the steps and placed her in the back seat. Hans folded the wheelchair, carried it down the steps, laid it on top of the luggage in the trunk, and slammed the lid closed. Martha got in the back alongside Freya. Jacob gave each of them their identification papers and a diplomatic passport for his father. He instructed them to let Hans do the talking at any checkpoint. If asked, they were to say Reichsführer Heinrich Himmler had ordered them to Hannover.

"The orders are signed by Himmler. Actually they are forgeries, but very good ones." Jacob smiled to himself as he thought of Canaris's retort.

"It will be very unlikely anyone will interfere with someone associated with Himmler. Father, you are a diplomatic emissary and have been instructed by Himmler to make contact with the Allies." He then told him what Canaris told him about Himmler trying to negotiate a separate peace.

"Of course you will not reveal that to anyone. That is just for your information. Like I said, let Hans do the talking. Just look imposing and important. A little haughty, even." He gave his mother a hug and a kiss and closed the door.

"Be careful," she mouthed.

Jacob took Friedrich's hand. Friedrich hesitated then grabbed Jacob and held him close to him and whispered, "Take care of yourself *Sohn*. I hope we can be reunited soon."

"Of course, Father. I'll be all right. Don't worry about me." He helped his father into the front seat, closed the door, and waved them on.

CHAPTER 48

▼

Redder, having finally recovered from his chest wound, was back with the *Gestapo*. As his body healed his mind deteriorated. He was filled with such hatred for Jacob that he threw caution to the wind. Heinrich Himmler, having replaced Canaris, now controlled the *Abwehr* and was Jacob's superior. Jacob had done everything he could to steer clear of Himmler.

Redder sought an audience with Himmler and was ushered into his presence.

"What is it *Herr* Redder? What do you want?"

"Do you know a man by the name of Karl Müller, sir?"

"*Nein*, should I?"

"He holds a minor position here at the *Abwehr*. I once had him arrested for killing a girl in her flat. She was…"

"Ah, yes. I do remember that incident," Himmler interrupted. "You made a complete ass of yourself, and as I recall, Canaris was very upset over his adjutant being arrested."

"You may also recall, sir, that you released him after the arrest because he was Canaris's nephew," Redder commented.

"I released him because of your *Dummheit*! You couldn't even produce the alleged murdered girls' body!"

"Müller must have disposed of it somehow, sir."

"Is that so? The next thing you'll tell me is that he's Houdini."

"I strongly believe he is a traitor, sir."

"Let me tell you something you probably don't know, *Herr* Redder. Müller turned his father into the *Gestapo* for spreading lies about NSDAP to his students at the university. Does that sound like someone who would betray the Party?"

"People can change, sir. I've had him under surveillance for some time now, and he has been engaged in some very peculiar practices. He has not been seen for several days. Has he been at his desk here lately?"

"How do I know? I don't keep track of every minor employee in the *Abwehr*. I have more important things to do?"

"You may want to check on him, sir. He seems to have disappeared." Himmler pressed a button and an orderly responded immediately.

"Find Karl Müller, one of our staff, and have him report to me immediately."

"Yes sir, right away sir."

"Now what are these peculiar practices to which you refer?"

"Well sir, he goes home each day from his office, and then goes back to work the next morning. It's the same day after day. Once in awhile he goes to dinner at a restaurant named Felix's."

"So what's so peculiar about that? I eat at Felix's myself. They have excellent food. Is it so strange that a man takes his duties so seriously that he shows up for work every day?"

"But he never goes out with women. He doesn't seem to have any bad habits. It's just not natural. He cannot be up to any good, sir."

Himmler exploded. "Get out of my office you imbecile! You're wasting my time!" Redder got up to leave when the orderly returned.

"Yes, what is it Fritz?"

"It seems Karl Müller has not been seen for two days, sir, and you have an urgent call from Radio Traffic Control."

Himmler picked up the telephone and said, "Himmler here, what do you want?"

"Sir, we have a fix on a house in Charlottenburg that has been sending illegal signal traffic to London. Can you get some of your men out there straight away?"

"What's the address?" Himmler wrote the address down on a memo pad and handed it to Redder.

"Here make yourself useful and arrest the occupants of this residence."

Redder looked at the paper and exclaimed, "THAT'S WHERE MÜLLER LIVES!"

"Get going then! Find him!"

▼

CHAPTER 49

After the limousine left, Jacob locked the door, turned off the lights, and headed for the library. He opened the secret door to the wine cellar, stepped in, closed the door, and locked it. He went down the stairs and sent a long message to London. He was very tired, so he turned off the lights and lay down on the cot to rest. In a few minutes he was sound asleep.

He was awakened with a start by glass breaking, wood splintering, and men shouting. He sat up in a daze and crept up the stairs. He was about to open the door but thought better of it. He pressed his ear to the door and heard a coarse voice shouting, "Search every room! We want him alive!" Jacob froze; it was Redder. His skin crawled as he thought of how close the entire household had come to being arrested. He could hear furniture overturned and glass breaking as the intruders swarmed through the house.

He struggled to hear what was being said. He could only catch a phrase or two when someone shouted…"Not in here,"…"Look again"…A motorcycle outside"…and a lot of swearing.

After a while the noise subsided and he could hear voices and booted footsteps receding as they left the house. The house became as quiet as a tomb.

This after-thought wine cellar has been a godsend, Jacob thought. *I wonder if Father had any inkling of its future importance. Probably not.*

Jacob suddenly realized how natural it was to think of Friedrich as his father. And his feelings for Freya, as his mother, were far more than the counterfeit relationship he had assumed. He began to realize his subconscious feelings were encroaching on his conscious thoughts. The word "twin" kept surfacing in his mind, and he was becoming troubled by its implication. He was suddenly jarred back to reality as he realized how precarious his position was now that the *Gestapo* was looking for him. I *haven't got time for these feelings. I'd better to let sleeping dogs lie. I've got to start thinking survival.*

He went to his wireless and sent another message to London.

That night Jacob slept in the wine cellar. No one returned to the house looking for him as far as he could tell. He had no way of knowing if the house was under surveillance but suspected it might be. The next morning he quietly let himself out of the cellar and proceeded to inspect the house. It was a mess. He knew he had to leave and find a safe place to hide. Whom could he trust?

He remembered that he and Walther Werner, one of Hitler's private pilots, had talked about getting together for dinner some night. Walther had made some derogatory remarks about the regime in Jacob's presence, which displayed a measure of trust in Karl. *Certainly this good friend would not give me away,* Jacob felt.

Jacob reached for the telephone, but jerked his hand back as if it was a poisonous snake. I *don't dare call from here. They probably have the phone tapped by now. What to do?* He tiptoed through the house trying to decide what to do next.

He carefully moved the curtain back ever so slightly and peeked out the front window. He couldn't see anyone, but naturally any surveillance would be out of sight. *The Gestapo is very professional at surveillance.* He noticed Hans' motorcycle was still in the driveway, lying on its side. The key was still in the ignition. *Strange they would leave that. Did they just overlook it or are they tempting me to use it. But they don't think I am here, so my guess is they aren't concerned about it.*

Jacob decided to take a chance on leaving. He put on his uniform coat and buttoned it. He strapped the Luger pistol to his waist and pulled his hat tight down on his head. He stepped sideways through the front door panel. The glass had been completely broken out. *What a shame,* he thought. *Friedrich and Freya would be appalled if they saw how their beautiful home had been so contemptuously treated.*

Every muscle in his body was as tight as a coiled spring, ready to unravel at the first sign of danger. He walked slowly across the landing, the broken glass crunching under his feet. The noise made him cringe with every step. He tiptoed down the steps and walked briskly to the motorcycle. He wondered if any moment the *Gestapo* would appear and arrest him. The adrenalin was flowing and it took little effort to lift the motorcycle to an upright position. He looked around. No one had challenged him so far. If anyone were watching the house they would be parked on the street a discreet distance away. If they were, this would give him a fighting chance.

He turned on the ignition, placed his foot on the starting pedal and pushed down with all his strength. The engine roared to life. *Thank goodness Hans kept his cycle in tiptop shape.* He threw it in gear, twisted the handgrip accelerator, and with gravel flying behind him, he darted for the entrance. At the entrance he slowed enough to look up and down the street. Sure enough, to his left, an automobile was pulling away from the curb. Jacob turned right and sped away with all the power he could coax out of the motorcycle. He felt that he could outrun the automobile, but he knew the occupants were no doubt already on the radio calling for others to interdict. A motorcycle had the advantage of being able to go where an automobile could not, and Jacob began to think in those terms. He was also more familiar with the neighborhood than his pursuers.

He turned off onto another street and headed for a heavily wooded park with its innumerable meandering walking paths. The automobile was still behind him. When he reached the park, he left the road and raced across the lawn heading for the dense trees and shrubbery. The automobile followed, but could not continue when he began picking his way through the underbrush.

Most of the trails were overgrown from neglect, and it was difficult to traverse even on a motorcycle. Deep in the park, Jacob stopped and turned off the engine. He listened but could not hear anything except birds chirping. He sat for about fifteen minutes, just listening. He tried to analyze where they might be. What would I do if I were in their shoes? He recalled his experience with the *Dornier* 17 when he was flying convoy patrol over the North Sea. He had anticipated the enemy's move and guessed right. *The obvious thing for these goons to do is to go around the other side of the park and wait for me to come out, since they cannot follow me through this dense underbrush. That is so obvious; they are probably waiting for me to double back, so I'm going straight through.*

He kick started the cycle and continued through the brush. He emerged from the cover of the brush and shrubbery onto a lawn. Not seeing anyone, he spun his wheels and darted out onto the road. The *Gestapo* was nowhere in sight. He had guessed right.

He needed a safe place to hide until evening and a place to make telephone call to Walther. He was sure every man in the *Gestapo* would be on the alert and have his description. A motorcycle stands out like a sore thumb.

An idea dawned on him. *If I can just get there undetected, I'll be safe,* he thought. It took him thirty excruciating minutes to get to his destination. He rode the motorcycle through the yard and stopped behind the house. He turned off the engine, pushed the kickstand down and got off. He quickly strode to the back door and knocked loudly.

A large buxom woman opened the door. She looked terrified when she saw a uniformed German officer. Especially when she looked down at the sidearm strapped to his waist.

"Who are you and what do you want?" She nervously asked.

Jacob said, "Don't be frightened, Lisa. I'm Jacob Kelm. May I come in, please?"

Lisa's jaw dropped open and her eyes were wide with fear.

"I don't know anyone by that name," she lied.

"Of course you do, Lisa. How are Emil and the children?" he asked. Jacob was frantically trying to establish his identity by giving Lisa facts about her family.

"Eric must be twenty-seven years old now; Hanna should be about twenty-four and little Otto, who is probably not so little any more, should be about nineteen. My *Mutter,* Ilse, rented a room from you and we lived here for years. *Mutter* worked at the hospital. Ask me anything you like. I really am Jacob"

Lisa didn't know what to think. Jacob saw she was still puzzled and frightened.

"One more thing. *Mutter* took me to the zoo on my seventh birthday. Beside myself, only my Mutter and you would know that."

"Just one moment please." Lisa closed the door. Jacob was getting frustrated and desperate to get inside. The door opened again and there stood Emil with Lisa at his side.

"Emil, thank goodness you're here. Please may I come in?"

"Lisa said you claim to be Jacob Kelm."

"That's right, I am."

"Do you have any proof?"

"Does the word *fox* mean anything to you?"

"It might."

"What about *Camel?*" Upon hearing his controller's code name, he threw the door open and pulled Jacob inside.

"Jacob, is it really you?"

"That's what I've been trying to tell you for the last ten minutes."

"We cannot be too careful."

"Yes, I understand. You're right, we cannot be too careful. I'm not really a German officer, as you probably know. I'm an undercover agent working for the American OSS and British M16. I also know that you work at the Ministry of Public Records, Emil, and that you have been supplying us with valuable information through our agent, code name *Camel.* I dared not reveal myself to you sooner for security reasons. The *Gestapo* is searching for me and I need a place to hide for a few hours. I haven't been followed, so you're safe."

"You're welcome to stay here as long as you like," Emil said.

"How is your *Mutter?*" Lisa asked.

"I don't know." Jacob proceeded to tell them the whole story about his life in Milwaukee, his stint in the RAF, and his recruitment and insertion into Germany, including the fact that his mother remarried and thinks he is missing in action. When Lisa and Emil heard about him being substituted for Karl Müller because they looked exactly like each other, they didn't quite know what to say.

Does he know they are twins? Lisa wondered. *Has Ilse told him the whole story or has she never revealed what happened?* Lisa decided to tiptoe around that subject and asked, "How come you look exactly like this Karl Müller?"

"I really don't know. It is strange. People kept asking me if we are twins. Do you know why I look exactly like this person?"

Lisa's face flushed as she turned away and said, "How would we know?" Jacob thought Lisa might be lying, but decided not to pursue it further.

"May I use the telephone?"

"Of course; it's still in the same place." Jacob walked directly to its location in the living room. If they had any doubts about this being Jacob, this removed them.

Jacob dialed Walther's office at *Tempelhof.* It rang three times and a male voice said, "This is Tempelhof *Flughafen.*"

"Is *Sturmbannführer* Walther Werner there?"

"He's around here someplace. Who's calling?"

"This is *Oberstgruppenführer* Alfred Jodl. I want you to find *Sturmbannführer* Werner and be quick about it."

"Yes sir, right away, sir." In less than a minute an out of breath voice came on the line.

"This is *Sturmbannführer* Werner, sir. How can I help you sir?"

"Relax Walther, this is Karl Müller. I used Jodl's name to get you on the telephone fast. Don't let on to whom you are speaking if anyone can overhear you. I don't want anyone to know where I am."

"That's easy; I don't know where you are. By the way, where are you?"

"I'm not far away. Since we have often talked about getting together for dinner, I thought it had better be soon, with the situation as it is. Are you free tonight?"

"Yes, I think so. What do you have in mind?"

"There's a little place in Charlottenburg at 445 Goethe *Straße,* just East of Stein Place. It's called Felix's. They serve excellent spaghetti and their *Beetensuppe* is mouth watering."

"You're making my mouth water just talking about it. Are you sure they're open? Not many restaurants are these days, you know. Where are they getting their supplies? There's hardly any food left in the Berlin area."

"Felix will no doubt be serving the Russians and Americans when they come marching in without missing a beat. I have no idea where he gets his supplies. Probably the black-market and financed by some corrupt officials. Who cares as long as the food is good?"

"It sounds good to me. Talk about marching in. They expect *Tempelhof Flughafen* to fall in three or four days. I'm getting out of Berlin tomorrow night"

"Really. Where are you going?"

"I don't think I should say."

"Walther, the war is almost over. The time for secrets has past."

"I guess you're right. I'm flying a couple of VIP's to Obersalzberg. We start out in a *Storch* that is already parked between the Brandenburg Gate and the Victory Column. It's being heavily guarded. I'm to fly them to *Tempelhof* where we will transfer to a *Focke-Wulf* 200 Condor."

"That will be a dangerous trip. By the way, you must be kidding. There is no *Flughafen* by the Brandenburg Gate."

"There is now. Actually it's only a street, but sufficient for the *Storch.* We'll barely get off the ground before we land at *Tempelhof.*"

"Why don't they motor there?"

"I don't ask questions, I just obey orders." Walther replied.

"I'll see you tonight. 1900 hours at Felix's. You can tell me more about this assignment then. By the way, do not mention to anyone you have talked with me or that we are having dinner together tonight."

"What's the big secret?"

"I'll tell you tonight."

"No problem. See you later." Jacob hung up the phone and just sat there, deep in thought. Finally, he said, "Emil, is there an *Apotheke* nearby?"

"Yes, there is."

"Would you mind going there and buying me a bottle of Ipecac?"

"Of course. What do you want that for?"

"I have something in mind." Jacob peeled off several *Reichsmarks* from his money clip and handed them to Emil. Emil left on his bicycle.

"Lisa, I need to borrow some of your clothing."

"Mine? Don't you mean Emil's?"

"No, I mean yours."

"Don't tell me you are a cross-dresser." Jacob just chuckled.

"No, I need a disguise. Can you make me up to look like a woman?"

Lisa gave Jacob a skeptical look and said, "I'll give it a try."

She went into the bedroom, picked out a dress, semi-low heeled shoes, stockings, brassiere, purse, and makeup.

"I've laid everything out on the bed, but first use Emil's razor and shave. Jacob went into the bathroom, found the razor and brushed on some shaving soap. Lisa walked in just as he was finishing.

"That's much better. Not too many women have five o'clock shadow. Take your pants off. I need to widen your hips."

"What!"

"A woman has wider hips than a man. I'll wrap some towels around your hips and pin them so they stay in place." Jacob took off his pants, but felt a little embarrassed in Lisa's presence.

"Don't act so squeamish. I've seen men undressed before." Jacob didn't think he should pursue that comment further.

After the towels were in place, Lisa picked up the brassiere and strapped it around his chest. Now he really felt weird.

"I'll stuff these with toilet paper. I hope I have enough." She laughed. "It takes a lot to fill *my* cups." Jacob was amused, but again didn't reply. He was completely dressed when Emil returned.

"What in the world…Jacob is that you?"

"What do you think, Emil? Can he pass for a woman?" Lisa asked.

"He fooled me, except for the hair."

"Stay put, I'll be back in a minute." Lisa said as she rushed out the front door.

"Where's she going?" Emil just shrugged.

"Why the sex change, Jacob?"

"I need a disguise."

"Well, that's a good one. I don't think I'd recognize you except for the hair. Here is the Ipecac and change."

"Thank you Emil. I appreciate you getting this for me." Shortly, Lisa came bouncing back into the house waving a wig.

"Borrowed it from my neighbor." She spread it open with her fingers and slipped it on Jacob's head and fussed with it.

"Now that's much better." Emil commented. "I like it."

"Stand up and walk across the room," Lisa ordered. "But first put on the shoes." Jacob struggled to get them on.

"They're a little tight."

"Emil, get a shoehorn." Emil jumped up and went into the bedroom. *Nothing has changed in this household,* Jacob thought. *Lisa is still the boss.*

"Here, try this," Emil said handing the shoehorn to Jacob. Jacob slipped it behind his heel, pushed hard and finally got the shoes on.

"Now walk across the room." Jacob got up and walked. "No, no, no. You walk like a man."

"I am a man."

"I know that, but do you want everyone else to know you are a man or do you want them to think you are a woman?"

"A woman, of course," Jacob replied a little sheepishly.

"Watch me walk." Lisa sauntered across the room, her hips swaying.

"Now you try it." Jacob made another attempt.

"That's better, but not good enough. Don't stride. Use more of a mincing step. Think *woman.* You've probably ogled plenty of them in your young life. Think how they look when they walk. Swing your hips a little. Try it again." Jacob walked again. Emil gave a little low *wolf* whistle.

"Not bad. Emil just gave you the stamp of approval. Right, Emil?"

"I like it. He…she would turn my head." Emil replied, a little embarrassed by his comment.

"If you have to talk to anyone, just whisper in a voice as high as you can, and complain that you lost your voice because of a cold."

"Good idea, thanks. Do you have a small bag I can borrow to carry my uniform in?" Jacob asked.

"I've got just the thing." Lisa left and came back with a small flowered bag that zippered across the top.

"Here, I'll fold your clothes for you. What do you want to do with the gun?"

"Put it in the purse. I may need it. Oh, I almost forgot. Put the Ipecac in with the pistol."

"By the way, I haven't even inquired about the children. Where are they?"

"Eric and Otto are in the army," Lisa replied. "They were in France the last we heard. Heavens knows where they are now. We haven't heard from them for a very long time. We only hope…," Lisa broke down as she struggled to continue.

"Sorry. We have been so worried about them. Hanna was working at the Ministry in Emil's section, but everything is in such disarray there, that no one goes in any more. She's been caring for an elderly woman not far from here. Her little bit of income is what we have been living on for the last three months. No one at the Ministry has been paid since March, and the building is in shambles from the bombing."

"I'm so glad to hear Eric and Otto are in France. The Americans and British will treat them much better than the Russians if they are captured."

"We pray they have been captured and not ki…injured."

"Just assume that's the case. You need to survive so the family can be united when this is all over. Emil, do you have something to write on? You may want to take some notes." Jacob waited while Emil got a pencil and paper.

"Now this is what I want you to do. Tomorrow, both of you go to 72-76 *Tirpitz Ufer*. That's the address of the *Reichweher* Ministry. It's on the corner of *Tirpitz Ufer* and *Bendler Strasse*. The *Landwehr Kanal* runs right in front of it. There you will find the offices of the *Abwehr*…"

"I know where it is," Emil interrupted.

"Good. Get there at least by 0900. That's 9:00 AM for you civilians. Ask for *Obergruppenführer* Friedrich Olbricht. He will provide you with passes that will protect you from arrest and allow you to move quite freely. Take your civilian identification papers with you and hope no one harasses you on the way there. The security at the *Abwehr* is very tight. I'll call right now and let Friedrich know you're coming. I'll try to arrange for both of you and Hanna to be flown out of Berlin. I'll have the pilot call you tomorrow afternoon and let you know for sure. The pilot's name is *Strumbannführer* Walther Werner. If he says, *Come to work, the office is open,* you will know the flight is on. He will tell you the time you should report for work. That will be the time you must be at *Temlelhof Flughafen*. The day for the flight will be the day after tomorrow, Thursday, unless he tells you differently. If Walther tells you, *The offices are closed,* stay home, you will know the flight is off. If that happens, bicycle west. Try to reach the American or British lines. Your passes should get you through any German checkpoint. Lisa, you can tell anyone who asks, that your *Mutter* in *Stendal* is gravely ill, and you are trying to get to see her before she passes away. Emil, write your telephone number down for me." Emil penciled the number on a piece of paper.

"Now, let me use the telephone again." Jacob dialed and waited while it rang. A female voice said, "Hello, may I help you?"

"Yes, this is *Oberstgruppenführer* Jodl, I need to speak to *Obergruppenführer* Olbricht."

"Just one moment please." Olbricht almost immediately came on the line.

"Yes, *Oberstgruppenführer* Olbricht here, what can I do for you, sir?"

"Are we on a secure line?"

"Yes sir, we are."

"Friedrich, this is Karl Müller."

"Karl, where are you? The *Gestapo* has been here looking for you and they've got men stationed all around the building."

"I figured as much."

"Did you know your uncle Wilhelm was arrested."

"No, I didn't know. He told me he thought his arrest was imminent."

"There are a lot of nervous people around here, particularly Oster."

"I can imagine. Listen Friedrich, I need a favor or two. Can you help me?"

"If I can, of course I will."

"I'm coming in today."

"Are you *verrückt,* the *Gestapo* will arrest you before you get through the front door."

"Maybe not, I'll be dressed as a woman." Olbricht laughed and said, "I can hardly wait to see that."

"Just don't laugh when you see me. This is serious."

"Of course, I'm sorry. I'll try to control myself."

"My name will be Gertrude Günter. I need to get inside to pick up some supplies. Alert the guards to let me pass. If they need a description, tell them I'm tall and very buxom. Another thing, would you please prepare passes for three people? I'm going to put Emil Jellinek on the line. He will give you their vital statistics. You can photograph them when they arrive. They will be in by 0900. I appreciate your help Friedrich; I'll see you in a little while. Here is Emil." Jacob handed Emil the telephone, shook his hand, and bid him farewell. He gave Lisa a big hug, took one last look in the mirror, straightened his dress and patted his hair.

"I put a comb as well as some makeup items in the purse. It will be pretty breezy on the motorcycle. Hang onto the hair piece."

"Thanks again for all your help, Lisa. I couldn't have managed without you." Jacob took Lisa's hand, put a wad of *Reichmarks* in it, and wrapped her fingers around them. She began to object and Jacob put his fingers to her lips. Tears came to her eyes and she grabbed him and gave him a big bear hug.

"Careful, you'll squash my…you know what."

Lisa giggled and said, "tell Ilse hello for us when you see her."

"You bet I will." With that he left the house and headed for the motorcycle. He strapped the bag to the rear rack, threw the purse over his shoulder, and straddled the seat. He jump started the cycle, tucked his dress under him as tight as possible to keep it from billowing up over his head, and took off, his wig whipping in the breeze. *This ought to be interesting.*

He kept his speed low. He passed very little foot traffic but plenty of military vehicles, however. What people he did pass, stopped walking and just stared. If he had been naked he couldn't have attracted any more attention. He got a few catcalls from the soldiers. He hoped he wouldn't pass any *Gestapo.*

It seemed like an eternity, but he was getting close to the *Reichweher* Ministry. He thought of how many times he had reported for duty there. He knew the neighborhood like the back of his hand. He decided to park the motorcycle behind the Italian Embassy, which was close by the *Abwehr* offices.

He strained to see if he could see any suspicious automobiles or individuals, but thought everything looked normal. He got off the motorcycle and recovered his bag from the rack. He retrieved the mirror from his purse and combed his hairpiece, touched up his lipstick, straightened his dress and began mincing his way toward the Ministry building.

As he walked down *Hildebrand Straße* toward *Tirpitz Ufer,* he passed a black Mercedes parked at the curb. Two men in black leather coats and black hats were sitting in the front seat. The windows were rolled down. *Why does every Gestapo agent wear black leather coats, he wondered? It's like a uniform. They're not very subtle. They no doubt understand their very presence is intimidating and it's a way of reminding people they are being watched.*

As he passed the Mercedes, the driver looked over at him and gave him a soft *wolf* whistle, and it reminded him of Emil who had done the same thing just about an hour ago. He almost broke out laughing but forced a straight face and a posture of indifference. He did exaggerate the swaying of his hips, however, in silent acknowledgement of the compliment. *Knock it off; I don't want to send the wrong message. They might try to pick me up.*

As he turned onto *Bendler Strasse* he saw another black Mercedes parked a block away from the Ministry building. Several men were working on the grounds. Another group was trying to look busy painting a *U-Bahn* facility opposite the entrance to the Ministry. It looked pretty phony. In times like this, that kind of work is not being done. He wondered if the *Gestapo* was getting sloppy. Don't get careless, he reminded himself. These thugs are dangerous.

Two armed sentries were standing guard outside the entry. They challenged Jacob and he was about to say who he had come to see, when to his relief, Olbricht opened the entrance door and said, "It's all right, I'm expecting her." He held the door open and Jacob walked in.

"Right this way *Fräulein*. You must sign the registry. He led Jacob to a desk, manned by another armed military guard sitting behind a desk. The guard swung the registry book around and handed Jacob a pen. Jacob signed, *Gertrude Günter* with a flourish.

"Come with me *Fräulein*. We'll take the lift." Jacob had been in this building so many times he could find his way around it blindfolded, but he pretended to let Olbricht act as his guide. They got off at the second floor and Olbricht said, "This way, *Fräulein*." They proceeded to Olbricht's office.

"You look very authentic. You would have fooled me if I didn't know."

"*Danke*, Friedrich. Just don't ask me for a date." Olbricht chuckled at the thought.

The *Abwehr* conducted all kinds of spying and intelligence gathering operations all over the world, directed from this building, and their supply and variety of material and equipment was varied and immense.

"Now what can I do for you, Karl?"

"First of all, put this recorded wire on Himmler's desk where he will find it."

"What's on the wire?"

"The voice of a man that has been very close to me. Too close in fact. I believe Himmler will find it interesting." *Goodbye Herr Redder,* Jacob thought.

"Is that all?"

"No, I need the following supplies: a bottle of Chloral Hydrate, fifty milligrams of Phenol Barbital, a syringe, a rubber arm strap, four pairs of handcuffs, four coffee cups, a large thermos of coffee and another of hot chocolate. Also identification papers and a special pass in the name of Gertrude Günter, with my photo as I now appear, identification papers, and a special pass with my photograph in my military uniform. There's one on file, but indicate my rank and name as *Standartenführer* Karl Kaufmann. I'll need insignia for that rank as well as a new hat to match, size 7 1/4. Throw in a Knights Cross with swords as well. I want 5,000 *Reichmarks* and 5,000 American dollars."

"Is that all?" Olbricht said, a little too sarcastically. "So, now you're giving yourself a promotion, a hero's medal, and a pay raise." Jacob ignored the comment.

"I hope you'll cooperate with me, Friedrich. You and I know that I know where all the bodies are buried around here and quite a few are in your graveyard."

Olbricht's tone changed as he said, "We'd better get busy. It's going to take quite some time to get all this together."

Finally, at 1800 hours, everything Jacob asked for was ready. He had to get going or he would be late for his dinner date with Walther.

"Thank you, Friedrich. You have been most helpful. There is one more thing I need you to do."

"And what might that be?"

"Order your automobile brought to the entrance, escort me out of the building, help me into your limousine, and drive me to the location I'll give you once we are on our way."

"What! Are you insane? What will people think?"

"They'll probably be a little jealous," Jacob said with a chuckle.

"That's the restaurant just up ahead on the right." Jacob looked at his watch. It was 1905.

"I'm only five minutes late for my date," Olbricht rolled his eyes and gave him a funny look.

"Don't tell me you're dating someone. Wait until he makes a pass at you."

"It's not that kind of a date, Friedrich." The automobile stopped at the curb. Jacob picked up his bag and purse, opened the door, and slid out.

"Thanks again, Friedrich. You know it's all going to be over very soon. What are your plans?"

"I've got some ideas. You should know better than anyone that we are survivors. It looks like you have your plans, also."

"Yes, I have. Good luck, Friedrich. Maybe we'll meet again sometime."

"I don't believe in luck, and yes, maybe our paths will cross some time in the future. Let's hope it isn't at *Gestapo* headquarters."

"I'll drink to that." Jacob closed the door, and Olbricht drove away. *Well, let's see how Walther reacts to me,* Jacob thought as he opened the door to the restaurant and stepped in. The restaurant was sparsely occupied. There were several military officers, most with female companions. It seemed to him that everyone looked his way, especially the men. Felix welcomed Jacob and started to lead him to a table, when he whispered, "I see my date. I can seat myself. Sorry for the voice, I have a cold."

"That's all right, *Fräulein*. Enjoy your dinner." *How many times has Felix seated me in the last three years?* Jacob wondered. *If he doesn't recognize me no one will.* Jacob walked directly toward Walther's table, hips swinging. It was located in a quiet discreet corner. *Perfect,* Jacob thought. Walther peered over his menu at Jacob as he approached. Jacob sat down as Walther stood up.

"Sit down Walther and close your mouth." Jacob whispered. "And smile. You're supposed to be pleased to see me." Walther slowly sank to his seat, his mouth still open. A few people were glancing their way.

"Yes, it's me, Walther. Please close your mouth and smile." Walther smiled weakly, still confused.

"Are you who I think you might be?"

"Yes Walther, it's me, your date. By the way, my name is Gertrude Günter. How do you like my dress?"

"Lovely. You look very nice."

"That's better. You're getting the idea."

Felix came to the table and said, "Are you ready to order, sir, and you *Fräulein?*"

"Where is Josef?"

"I don't know. He seems to have disappeared."

"Really? I will miss him. Why don't you order for both of us, Walther? My voice, you know."

"*Ja, ja*…let's see. Why don't we start with your *Beetensuppe*. I've been told it's very good."

"You have been correctly informed, sir. It's one of our specialties."

"We'll have the spaghetti with an asparagus salad, plenty of pumpernickel bread and butter. Oh yes, and bring us a bottle of your best Rhine wine; a *Spatle-sen* or a *Trockenbeerenauslesen*."

"Yes sir. You have excellent taste."

After Felix had withdrawn, Walther said, "Since you invited me to dinner, I hope you're paying."

"Relax. Walther, I've got plenty of money." Jacob slipped Walther a wad of bills under the table.

"By the way, what's going on? Why the getup?"

"The *Gestapo* is looking for me."

"What!" Walther nervously looked around the room as if expecting to be arrested on the spot.

"Why are they after *you?*"

"I'm not sure, but it may have something to do with the fact that my Uncle Wilhelm Canaris has been arrested."

"What! He's your uncle. Why has he been arrested? If he can be arrested, then anyone can be arrested."

"That's right Walther. Keep that in mind." The waiter brought the soup. Steam rose from the bowls.

"It smells good," Walther commented.

"Walther, would you get me a tissue. I'd like to wipe some of this lipstick off before I eat."

"I'll see what I can find." Walther got up and walked toward the kitchen. Jacob opened his purse, held the compact mirror Lisa had provided him, in front of his face and fussed with his hair, all the while watching Walther to be sure he was far enough away so as not to see what he was about to do. Satisfied Walther or any of the other diners were not watching, he unscrewed the lid off the Ipecac bottle, and poured about a tablespoon of the liquid into Walther's soup. He stirred it in, and wiped the spoon off on his napkin. Walther returned and handed Jacob another napkin.

"This is all they could find."

"That's perfect dear," Jacob said with a smile.

Both of them began to eat their soup. After a few spoonfuls, Walther commented, "Does your soup taste all right? After the big buildup I thought it would be better than this."

"Mine is just fine. Maybe your nervousness has affected your taste buds." It dawned on Jacob that he hadn't eaten all day, and he was very hungry. It was difficult to eat like a woman would eat; small spoonfuls ladled to the mouth slowly, when he was so hungry. Everything was as good as he remembered. The wine was superb. They ate mostly in silence. What do you talk about when the situation is so strange?

They were about finished when Walther said, "I don't feel very good. It feels like I have an upset stomach. I wonder if I'm coming down with the flu, or could it be the food is bad? That *Beetensuppe* didn't taste right. Do you feel all right, Kar...I mean Gertrude?"

"I'm fine. If you're getting sick we should leave right now. We don't want to make a scene. It will draw too much attention."

Walther signaled the waiter and said, "Please let me have the *Rechung*. We have to leave immediately." The waiter laid the *Rechung* on the table. Walther glanced at the amount, peeled off more than enough to cover the meal and gratuity and said, "Let's get out of here fast." They got up and Jacob slipped his arm through Walters' and they walked rapidly out.

Felix, noting their quick departure, ran after them and yelled, "I hope everything was all right, please come again." Walther just raised his hand in a weak wave without turning around.

"Here are the keys—you drive. It feels like I'm going to lose it." In fact, that is exactly what he did. He vomited just before they reached the automobile. He

kept retching even after losing the entire contents of his stomach. He kept spitting, trying to clear the foul taste from his mouth. Jacob helped him into the
automobile and drove to Walther's flat.

"How are you feeling now?"

"Terrible. I think I might die, which sounds like a good idea right now."

"Better get out of those clothes and get in bed." Jacob turned down the covers
while Walther undressed. He crawled in the bed and Jacob tucked him in.

Walther weakly rose up on one elbow and said, "I'm in big trouble. I just
remembered I'm supposed to fly tomorrow, and I don't think I'm going to be up
to it."

"I've been thinking about that. I've got a suggestion. I'll cover for you if you
cover for me. You've already told me the plan. I know exactly how to get to the
Storch. I'm checked out on it, as well as the Condor," Jacob lied. "Who's the
co-pilot on the Condor?"

"Manfred Fischer. He's a good man."

"Where are the charts?"

"Manfred will have them. He's your navigator as well as co-pilot."

"Any passwords I should know?"

"It's *Wolf* at the *Storch* and *Wolf* at the Condor, if you're challenged."

"Who are the passengers and how many?"

"Two passengers, and I don't know who they are. They must be very high
ranking to requisition two planes. It's all very secretive."

"I'm used to dealing with secrets. What is the departure time?"

"There is none. I was ordered to be at the *Storch* by 0900 and standby."

"Fine. Now listen to me. I need a favor in return. I'm scheduled to fly three
people west and set them down someplace where they can surrender to the Americans or British. The *Storch* is the perfect plane for that. As you know that plane
can skip along the ground at a very slow speed under radar and land in a pasture
if need be. It's all over for us, Walther. You know where I work and what I do. I
know all the secrets and, believe me, the *Führer,* the *Reichsführer,* the *Gauleiter*
and other high-ranking officials don't give a twit for the likes of you and me.
They're scattering like rats. The two you are scheduled to fly out are probably
some of them. You need to think about saving your own skin. The people I'm
asking you to take with you are very special to me. They're just ordinary people
like you and me. I know I can trust them to your care. I'm going to write down
all the instructions you need to know to carry this off; names, times, phone numbers, everything. Do this for them as well as for yourself, and I promise you will
never regret it. See that flowered bag? Take it with you and give it to *Frau* Lisa

Jellinek. She's one of the passengers. By the way, I'll have to take your automobile in the morning to get to the *Storch* on time. You'll have all day tomorrow to figure out how to get to *Tempelhof.* Will that be a problem?"

"No, I can manage. *Danke* Karl, and good luck."

"Good luck to you too, Walther. By the way, do you have an alarm clock?" Walther pointed to the dresser. The clock was on top.

"Also, do you have a small bag?"

"There's a duffle bag in the closet."

"Pillow and blankets?"

"In the closet."

"*Danke.* Get some sleep now. I hope you're feeling better in the morning." Walther groaned and rolled over on his side and closed his eyes. Jacob switched on a lamp, and turned the ceiling light off. Soon Walther was snoring softly. Jacob wrote down all the information he had given Emil and Lisa regarding the evacuation plan and laid it on the table. He undressed, ran a tub full of water and bathed. It took some hard scrubbing to get all the make-up off. He changed the insignia on his uniform, and hung it up to get some of the wrinkles out. He put all of Lisa's clothing and her other items in the flowered bag. He placed the 5,000 dollars and the remainder of the *Reichmarks* in the bottom under the clothes.

Next he poured a generous quantity of Chloral Hydrate into one of the coffee cups and swirled it around until it covered the entire inside surface. He repeated this on two more cups. Then he poured the excess back into the bottle and let the cups sit until the liquid dried. He then picked up the fourth cup, and with the barrel of his pistol, tapped the bottom edge until it chipped.

Jacob spread out the blankets on the sofa, set the alarm clock, and put it under his pillow. He climbed in between the blankets and tried to unwind. He reviewed everything in his mind that had happened that day and went over his plans for the next day. He thought about Walther and felt a little twinge of guilt for *doctoring* his soup, but he needed the Condor. *I sure spoiled an excellent dinner for him, but he'll be better off getting out with the Jellineks.* This thought seemed to salve his conscience.

Sleep overcomes consciousness without our even realizing it, and in a few minutes Jacob was sound asleep.

CHAPTER 50

▼

Hitler, along with his mistress Eva Braun, his personal secretary, Gertrude Junge, Martin Bormann, Josef Göbbels and his wife and six children, as well as other members of the military staff, were ensconced in Hitler's fortified bunker that was built to protect him from Allied bombing and Russian artillery.

Hitler, the once dynamic and charismatic leader had been reduced to a shell of his former self. His eyes were bloodshot and glazed. His hair had turned from brown to ashen gray. His vigorous walk had been reduced to a pitiful shuffle. His left arm hung useless at his side, the result of the assassination attempt during the conference at his headquarters in Rastenburg in East Prussia. His limbs trembled, and he walked stooped over. His complexion was sallow, and his face swollen. He had just turned 56 years old on April 20th but had shriveled up to look like a sick old man of seventy or more.

The Third *Reich* was in its death throes. The Battle for Berlin was nearing its climax. The Russians, one million strong, were encircling the city, and the Americans and British were not far away to the west. Germany had less than twenty five thousand trained troops, as well as a few old men of the *Volkssturm Heim Wache,* and a few teenagers from the Hitler Youth, to defend the city.

Most of the population of Berlin lived underground in cellars and *U-Bahn* tunnels. They emerged only long enough to scurry through the streets between air raids, looking for food and water. *SS* troops roamed the streets conducting roadside court-martials, arresting and executing anyone accused of cowardice by refusing to carry on the hopeless battle. Corpses dangled from lampposts and trees as a warning to others.

In a staff meeting, Hitler's generals informed him they cannot hold out much longer, and that the war was lost. This threw Hitler into a tirade, accusing them of treason and betrayal. He seemed unable to admit defeat and was constantly ordering the reallocation of phantom troops that existed only in his imagination.

Finally, realizing all was lost and the end was near, Hitler issued what became known as the *Nero Decree.* It ordered the destruction of "All military, transportation, communications and supply facilities, as well as all resources within the *Reich* that the enemy might use immediately or in the foreseeable future for continuing the war."[1] This meant that everything in Germany still under their control was to be dynamited, torched, and razed. "Everything that was essential to the maintenance of an organized society; telephones, sewage system and electric facilities were to be destroyed."[2] This scorched earth order, if carried out, would have disastrous consequences on post war Germany.

At great personal risk, Albert Speer, Hitler's personal architect and War Production Minister, was so incensed by this order that he wrote a 22-page memorandum to Hitler. In part it read, "In four to eight weeks, the final collapse of the German economy must be expected with certainty. We must do everything to maintain, even if only in the most primitive manner, a basis for existence of the nation to the last."[3]

Hitler's icy reply was, "If the war is lost, the people will be lost also. It is not necessary to worry about what the German people will need for elemental survival. On the contrary, it is best for us to destroy even these things, for the nation has proved itself weaker, and the future belongs solely to the stronger eastern nation. In any case, only those who are inferior will remain after the struggle, for the good have already been killed."[4]

This reply revolted Speer to the core. He threw caution to the wind, and began countermanding Hitler's scorched earth order. This amounted to treason and, if found out, would have resulted in his execution. Using Hitler's personal chauffeur as his driver, he rushed around the countryside, pleading with the *Gauleiter,* generals, and plant managers to ignore Hitler's order. He even contemplated assassinating the *Führer* by introducing poison gas into the ventilating system of the bunker but was thwarted by the unexpected construction of a protective chimney that put the airshaft out of reach.

---

1. *Inside the Third Reich*, by Albert Speer
2. Ibid
3. Ibid
4. Ibid

Government ministry personnel were leaving Berlin like rats scurrying off a sinking ship. A partial evacuation of the bunker was ordered. Under heavy fire, ten planes carrying eighty Chancellery personnel flew out of Berlin, headed for the relative safety of the Berchtesgaden in the Austrian Alps. This location concealed an underground railway system, several months worth of supplies and ammunition, as well as the entire stock of Germany's poison gas. Hitler himself had made plans to make a last stand at Obersalzberg in the so-called Alpine Redoubt. Here he has assembled 25,000 of his most loyal SS troops and other specially picked units. Only a very few knew of this plan and its details. A whole corps of men and woman, each one of whom met the Aryan trait prescribed by Hitler, had been secreted there. Their survival was to eventually promulgate and direct an underground army for the resurrection of the Third Reich. This area was practically impenetrable. It would take a massive effort to dislodge them and the cost in lives and material would be staggering.

On Hitler's birthday, in the situation room in Hitler's bunker, the discussion centered on whether or not to defend the metropolis or retreat to the Alpine Redoubt and shift headquarters to Obersalzberg. In past years, dignitaries and foreign ministers would have been lining up to offer birthday congratulations and bringing greetings and gifts to the *Führer*. But on this occasion there would be no such formal celebration. For a short time Hitler, and those accompanying him, moved to the upper rooms, and a delegation of Hitler Youth that had been fighting heroically was presented to him in the garden. After patting a few of them on the head and cheek, he thanked them in a low voice. Eventually, he sensed his appearance was leaving them with a bad impression, so he cut the ceremony short and returned to the situation room.

Göring pointed out that the last escape route might be cut off at any time and if they were to retreat to Obersalzberg it should be done soon. Hitler expressed his opinion that it might appear to be cowardly of him to abandon the troops defending Berlin and flee to safety. He said, "I will leave it to fate whether I die in the capital or fly to Obersalzberg at the last moment."[5]

As soon as the meeting broke up and the generals left, a distraught Göring remained, and turning to Hitler said, "I have urgent tasks awaiting me in South Germany and will have to leave Berlin this very night."[6] Hitler absent-mindedly

---

5. Ibid
6. Ibid

shook hands with Göring, giving no sign that he saw through his weak excuse to flee.

Finally, it seemed apparent to those left in the bunker that Hitler had decided to remain in Berlin and meet his fate there. Göbbels moved into the bunker on 22 April, with his wife and six children. He was the only Minister willing to remain with Hitler. He expressed a desire to join him, along with his family, in committing suicide.

CHAPTER 51

▼

The alarm clock rang, and Jacob reached under his pillow and turned it off. Walther hadn't moved. He pulled it out and looked at the time. It was 0601. He stretched, sat up, and swung his legs onto the floor. He got up and lit the two propane burners on the stove, found two pans, and poured the coffee in one and the chocolate in the other. The liquid was still slightly warm from the previous day. He put the pans on the burners and turned them down very low. He went to the bathroom and borrowed Walther's razor. After shaving, he picked out one of the several toothbrushes in the mug on the counter. He chose one that looked the newest. *Can't be too fussy at a time like this,* he thought.

After finishing his toilet, he dressed. By this time both the coffee and chocolate were steaming hot. He turned off the burners and poured himself a cup of coffee, using the chipped cup, and sipped it while he packed his bag. The remaining coffee and chocolate he poured into their respective thermoses. He then wrapped the bottle of Chloral Hydrate, the bottle of Phenol Barbital, the syringe and elastic armband in dish towels to keep them from getting broken, and laid them in the bottom of the bag. He wrapped the cups separately in towels so they wouldn't get broken, and placed them in next. He rinsed out the cup from which he had been drinking and wrapped it in a separate dishtowel. He stowed the pistol in one end of the bag and the handcuffs in the other end. *Walther won't need those towels after today,* Jacob surmised, but he left some *Reichmarks* on the table anyway. He next slid the ribbon that held the Knights Cross under his collar and fastened it at his throat. He put on his hat and inspected himself in the mirror. Satisfied, he picked up the bag, looked around to be sure he had everything and quietly left.

He still had the keys to the automobile. He unlocked the door, climbed in, and drove away. He looked at his watch. It was 0735. *Everything is on schedule if the roads are clear.*

He could hear the rumble of heavy artillery not too far away. He hoped his passengers were ready to leave when he got to the improvised airfield. The Russians were no doubt very close, and he didn't want to be trapped.

Debris from the bombing littered the roads everywhere. Every building he passed was in ruins. Several times he had to backtrack and find another route. Finally he came to one of the main thoroughfares, *Unter Den Linden.* This led him under the Brandenburg Gate and onto Herman Göring *Straße,* which ran parallel to the *Reich* Chancellery. Just across the street from the Chancellery, connecting at a forty-five degree angle to Herman Göring *Straße* was the makeshift airstrip. Jacob looked up at the road sign. It read *Lenne Straße.*

He spotted the *Storch* parked on the street. It reminded him of the bird for which it was named. It looked forlorn and forbidding, and out of place in this setting. Twelve soldiers stood guard around it like so many vultures waiting for it to die. He pulled the automobile along side the *Flugzeug* and the soldiers immediately surrounded him. The officer in command ordered him out of the automobile. Jacob got out with his bag in his hand. The officer ordered him to drop the bag and raise his hands over his head. Jacob noticed the officer was a *Hauptsturmführer.* Jacob's new rank was three grades higher.

"*Hauptsturmführer,* what is your name?" Jacob asked.

"It's none of your business."

"Don't you mean it's none of your business, *sir?*"

"It's none of your business, sir," the *Hauptsturmführer* repeated.

"I'll ask you again, what is your name?"

"My name is Hans Stakker."

"Do you know who I am?"

"No I do not," Stakker replied.

"Don't you mean, no I do not, *sir?*"

"No, I do not, sir," Stakker repeated. "Sir, I have been ordered by a higher authority than you, that no one and I mean no one, is permitted to get near this *Flugzeug* and I have the authority to shoot anyone that tries."

"Now you listen to me Stakker, I'm going to get in that *Flugzeug* and check it out. You can shoot me if you want, but when whoever it is that requisitioned this *Flugzeug* finds the pilot dead and no one else qualified to fly it, I venture to say they will have you all shot."

The soldiers began to murmur and Stakker looked uneasy. He stared at the Knights Cross at Jacobs's throat and saw the resolve in his eyes. Jacob could tell this officer was trying to make a decision. Finally Jacob said, "*Hauptsturmführer,* were you not told to ask for a password from anyone approaching this *Flugzeug?*" Stakker went red in the face.

"Y…Y…Yes sir, I was, sir," he stammered. "I just forgot."

"And is that password *Wolf?*"

"Yes sir, it is."

"Then get out of my way." Stakker stepped aside and snapped to attention. The others lowered their rifles and did the same. As Jacob was about to board the *Storch,* Stakker said,

"Sir, what's in the bag?"

"My personal belongings, why?"

"I'll have to inspect it, sir."

"If I refuse are still you going to shoot me?" Noticing the hesitation, Jacob swung the bag aboard and climbed in the *Storch.* Stakker didn't say anything more.

Time dragged and Jacob kept glancing in the direction of the *Reich* Chancellery. Hours went by and no one appeared. Jacob looked at his watch. It was 1435. He was getting hungry and thirsty. He asked the officer if there was any food or water.

"Just water sir. Here have some of mine." Jacob took the canteen and took a long drink. He had been waiting for six hours and knew the soldiers had been there much longer; probably overnight. He began to review everything in his mind that Walther told him. *Do I have the time wrong? Is it today? I'm sure it is. Walther did say there was no scheduled departure time. Whoever we are waiting for could at least send a message to let us know what's going on, but this is typical of the arrogance of these people.*

The soldiers finally gave up and were sprawled out on the ground in the shade of the *Storch's* wing. Most were asleep in spite of the noise of battle just beyond the Chancellery. Stakker ignored this lack of discipline.

Hauptsturmführer Hans Stakker was nervously pacing back and forth. He too kept a watchful eye in the direction of the *Reich* Chancellery.

I'm sure Stakker is ready to snap his men to attention the minute someone approaches, Jacob thought. He could sympathize with this officer's predicament. How to keep his men rested, but not looking slothful. He thought about the coffee and hot chocolate, but if he helped himself to that, he would be expected to share with the men, and he couldn't do that.

The shelling and small arms fire was getting closer. Suddenly, the familiar whistling sound of an incoming round forced everyone to hit the ground. It exploded about fifty meters beyond them and showered them with dirt and rocks. That woke everyone up. Jacob walked around the *Storch* to see if there was any damage. There didn't appear to be any.

"*Hauptsturmführer* Stakker, if you and your men care to leave, I'll take full responsibility for your dismissal."

"No sir, we could be shot if we left."

"You may get shot if you stay. The Russians are going to be coming down that street very soon. Whoever it is we are waiting for may not even be coming. If the Russians show up, I'm in that plane and out of here if I can make it. You and your men will be at their mercy, and they don't show any." Jacob waited for a reply. He could see the conflict going on in his mind, between obeying the orders he had been given to remain with the *Flugzeug* and the desire to leave.

"No sir, I'm staying," he replied firmly. Jacob thought that might be his answer. The compulsion to obey orders, no matter the consequences, was so engrained in the German mentality, that logical persuasion seemed to have no effect on reason.

Time continued to drag, and it was getting dark. Jacob ordered the men to disperse up and down the street and light the lanterns lining the street with their cigarette lighters. Soon, two parallel dotted lines began to take shape as the glow from each red lantern connected to the other.

CHAPTER 52

▼

On 29 April 1945, just after midnight, Hitler, with a courtly gesture, took Eva Braun by the hand and escorted her to the map-room of the bunker. A minor Municipal Party official was pulled from his unit and ordered to go with them to Hitler's bunker. He was terrified at first, but to his surprise, was informed he was to officiate at the *Führer's* wedding. He brought with him to the bunker the necessary legal paperwork and notary.

The official nervously waited while final preparations were being made. Finally, Martin Bormann escorted him into Hitler's presence. Eva Braum wore Hitler's favorite dress. It was a low cut black and pink gown with roses on the bodice. Accessories were pistols and cyanide capsules that lay within easy reach on a side table. They swore to the official they were of pure *Aryan* decent. While Berlin burned above them they exchanged simple wedding vows. Martin Bormann and Josef Göbbels signed the registry as witnesses.

After the ceremony, Eva served sweet cakes and tried desperately to keep everyone's spirit up. After all, this was her crowning achievement, to become the wife of *der Führer,* but she was to enjoy one of the shortest and saddest honeymoons in history. Walter Wagner, the official who had performed the wedding ceremony, was killed on his way back to his unit by a Russian artillery shell.

Hitler summoned his secretary, Gertrude Junge, and left the small wedding reception party and went into an adjoining room to dictate his last will and testament. In it he claimed the war was the fault of the Jews. He expressed no remorse for the terrible bloodshed and destruction the war had caused and blamed his generals for Germany's defeat, even though he himself had assumed total military and political control.

He stated, "If the German people lose this war, then they have shown themselves to be unworthy of me."[1] Here was a megalomaniac with a giant ego; a combination of destructive forces that had come together in this depraved individual to cause the death and injury of tens of millions and the destruction of property of unparalleled proportions.

As to the matter of his successors, Göring and Himmler were dropped because of their illicit attempts to seize power. Speer and Ribbontrop were not included in the cabinet. Göebbels was named Chancellor and Bormann, "my faithful Party comrade"[2] was appointed head of the Nazi Party and executor of his will. Hitler chose Grand Admiral Karl Dönitz as head of State and Supreme Commander of the armed forces.

On the morning of Monday, 30 April, Hitler held a routine military briefing, then shared a lunch of spaghetti and tossed salad with his cook and two secretaries. He called his associates together and he and Eva shook everyone's hand. Then they retired to their private apartment.

"They sat down on the blue and white velvet sofa in the study, only to be interrupted"[3] by a hysterical Magna Göebbels. She pleaded with Hitler not to take his life. She thought if she could persuade him to relent and not take this drastic step, she and her children would be spared the same fate. Hitler appeared to have not changed his mind, and she tearfully emerged from the study as hysterical as when she entered.

At a slightly ajar door at the rear of the private apartment stood two figures. They peered into the room at Hitler and Eva. One of them was Martin Bormann and the other was indistinguishable. He wore a long black cape and hood, which covered his entire body and face. They watched as Hitler picked up a cyanide capsule and handed it to Eva. The two heard him say, "It's time my dear." Eva smiled nervously and looked up at her husband. She placed the cyanide capsule between her teeth and bit down hard. She stiffened and collapsed back onto the sofa and was dead. Hitler seemed indifferent to her death.

Bormann and his companion entered the chamber. Hitler, grim faced, stared intently at them as they entered and said, "*Willkommen Ehrenmann.*"

---

1. *The Mammoth Book of the Third Reich*, by Michael Veranov
2. Ibid
3. Ibid

Bormann, clicking his heels and raising his arm in the *Nazi* salute, asked, "Are you ready *mein Führer?*"

"*Ja.* History will remember this occasion." The man in the cape pulled the hood back to reveal his face and the cape dropped to the floor. His eyes met Hitler's and fear, admiration, and wonder passed silently between them. A sly smirk creased Hitler's face as a pistol shot reverberated off the harsh walls. The bunker then became deathly silent as a limp body fell to the sofa. A trickle of blood ran down a silent cheek and the pistol dropped to the sofa seat by his hand. Bormann, faithful as ever, had continued to prove his loyalty. A cloaked figure stealthily slinked out of the room away from this grisly scene.

Led by Bormann, a detail of *SS* soldiers entered the study. The *SS* men looked down at the two familiar lifeless bodies on the sofa. The enormity of what they saw was staggering. They stood there, transfixed, as if frozen to the floor and stared.

Bormann shattered the silence with an order to wrap the two bodies in blankets and carry them up the fifty-odd stairs. The *SS* contingent emerged from the bunker entrance behind Bormann. He led them to a shallow grave in the garden and the two bodies were dumped into it like so much garbage. The bodies were then saturated with *Benzin*. Bormann crumpled up a piece of paper, lit it with his cigarette lighter, and threw it on the bodies. The *Benzin* exploded in a burst of orange flames. The intense heat forced everyone to retreat a step or two. The detail spontaneously snapped to attention and raised their arms in the *Nazi* salute and shouted, "*Heil* Hitler." One might wonder what emotions this scene evoked. These few men had just witnessed the end of the so called, *Thousand Year Reich.* It had come to an end in just twelve years.

The cloaked and hooded figure silently emerged from the shadows of the concrete bunker where he had witnessed this scene. A bemused smile crossed his unseen face. The flames threw weird and dancing shadows on the nearby structures. Anyone looking down on this bizarre scene might have thought they were peering into Dante's Inferno.

Bormann dismissed the detail and they reentered the bunker. He waited until they disappeared and then joined the cloaked figure. The two men walked past the *Reich* Chancellery onto Herman Goring *Straße*. They saw two rows of lanterns glowing in the distance and made their way toward them.

Jacob and Stakker noticed an orange glow just beyond the *Reich* Chancellery.

"It looks like something is burning," Stakker said.

"It sure does," Jacob replied. They watched and waited. Stakker thought he saw something.

"I believe someone is coming,"

"I think you're right. I hope it isn't the Russians," Jacob commented.

"All right men, be ready for anything," Stakker yelled. Jacob could see the men were very tense.

"I suggest you remind your men not to shoot until ordered. We don't want any trigger-happy mishaps."

"Yes sir. Do not fire unless I give the order," Stakker shouted to his men.

The two figures were getting closer and became more distinct. They were dark silhouettes against the glow of the fire behind them.

"I hope these are my two passengers." Jacob said. They kept moving closer and their shapes became more sharply defined.

"I can almost assure you they are not Russians," Stakker commented.

"I believe you're right," Jacob replied.

As the two figures approached, Stakker cried out, "Attention!" His men straightened and stood erect. They looked like statues in a surreal painting. Stakker challenged the two shadowy figures by shouting, "Who goes there."

A voice replied, "*Wolf.*"

"Finally," Jacob said to no one in particular. He was curious to see who these men were. He noticed that one had on a long black cape with a hood that hid his face. In the glow of the lanterns Jacob saw the face of the other man. He almost choked when he saw who it was. "Martin Bormann," he silently breathed. Jacob had been in many meetings of the Supreme Command with Canaris when Bormann had been present. Wherever Hitler was you were sure to find Martin Bormann. This Mephisophelean fiend seemed always to be at Hitler's side. Jacob lowered the brim of his hat and kept his head down.

"Are you piloting this *Flugzeug?*" Bormann demanded.

"Yes sir, I am."

"You look familiar. Don't I know you?"

"I don't believe so, sir."

"Get us aboard and let's get out of here."

"Yes sir." Jacob opened the passenger side door, tilted the step down and they boarded. The person with the cape got in the back. As Jacob ran around to get in the other side he told Stakker, "If I were you I'd get out of here." Stakker and his men were already moving out, away from the fighting.

"Look at those cowards. They're running away!" Bormann shouted. "They ought to be shot." Jacob was tempted to say, *so are you,* but bit his tongue.

He started the engine, checked the instruments, wagged the ailerons and rudder and pushed the throttle forward. They rolled down the street in between the lanterns, and in a very short distance the *Storch* jumped into the air. They gained only about 200 meters altitude before they were landing at *Tempelhof.*

Jacob saw the Condor and taxied alongside it. He braked and turned off the engine. He got out and ran around the other side to open the passenger door. He lowered the step and was about to help them out when Bormann ordered him to get aboard the Condor.

Jacob grabbed his bag and sprinted to the Condor. Inside the luxuriously appointed passenger compartment was a rack used for holding refreshments. Jacob zipped open the bag and placed the cups and thermoses in the rack, and went forward to the cockpit. Manfred Fischer was in the co-pilot seat studying the maps.

"*Guten Abend,* I'm Karl Kaufmann," Jacob said as he extended his hand.

"Where's Walther?" The co-pilot replied.

"He's quite ill, so I'm taking his place. He spoke very highly of you. Are we ready to go?"

"I am, but where are the passengers?"

"I think I hear them getting aboard now." Jacob looked over his shoulder and saw them disappear into the passenger lounge.

"Shut that damn door, and be quick about it." Bormann yelled. Jacob flipped the switch that retracted the steps, and then locked the entry door. Bormann had closed the door that separated the passenger suite from the cockpit.

"Who's that?" Manfred asked.

"Martin Bormann and one other person. I can't tell who he is because I can't see his face."

"You're kidding. You say it's Bormann?"

"That's right, big as life."

"I understand he's the crudest person in the Party. And you don't know who's with him?"

"That's right I don't know. Are you ready for this flight Manfred?" Jacob asked.

"As ready as I'll ever be," Manfred nervously replied. "This is going to be a very dangerous flight. The *Luftwaffe* is *kaput,* so we can't depend on any help from them. The Allies have total air superiority, and although we have four MG15 7.9 mm machine guns on this aircraft, we have no gunners. What do *you* think our chances are?"

"I'm a little more optimistic than you, but not much," Jacob admitted. They both fastened their safety harness and Jacob said, "All right let's go." He started the two port engines, then the starboard ones. He scanned his instruments. The oil pressure was normal and the fuel tanks registered full. Everything seemed to be in order. He radioed the control tower to turn on the runway lights. They came on with a brilliance that made him squint until his eyes adjusted to the light. He pushed the throttles slowly forward and the plane inched onto the runway. Once on the runway he depressed the left brake until the Condor swung around and was pointing straight down the runway.

"All right, Manfred, let's do it." Manfred, grim-faced, nodded. Jacob pushed the throttles forward until the engines were delivering maximum power. They picked up speed and left the ground smoothly. It suddenly went dark below as the runway lights were extinguished. His eyes now had to dilate and adjust to the darkness.

Manfred said, "Your waypoint is 185." Jacob searched for a gap in the artillery fire. He saw an area that seemed tranquil, and headed for it. They were still flying very low. A quarter crescent moon was in the sky on their starboard side at a thirty-degree angle, which provided enough light to see the ground dimly, but remained dark enough so that anyone on the ground would have a difficult time seeing them clearly. He felt it would be safer to fly very low, so as to stay under radar, as well as providing a target from the ground for a shorter period of time. However, he had hunted pheasants enough to know that the easiest target to hit is a bird flying directly away from you. It's like shooting at a stationary target. Even small arms fire at this low altitude could be deadly, and it wouldn't take long for someone to put a rifle to their shoulder and shoot. He was depending on surprise.

The Condor was handling beautifully. *It felt good to be flying again,* Jacob longingly thought.

"Manfred, take over while I check on our passengers."

"All right, I've got it." Jacob let go of the controls, unsnapped his harness, slid out of his seat and went back to the passenger lounge. He knocked and opened the door. The cloaked figure quickly lowered his head and snapped the hood over his face. Bormann angrily yelled,

"Get out of here and stay in your seat."

"Yes sir, I just wanted to mention that there is hot chocolate and coffee in the thermoses. May I serve you some?"

"No! I said get out of here and stay out!"

"Yes sir. Do you mind if I help myself to some hot chocolate? I haven't had anything to eat all day."

"Go ahead, but be quick about it." Jacob picked up the chipped cup and poured it full of the steaming liquid and took a sip. The aroma filled the cabin. He replaced the thermos and started back to his seat. Bormann yelled, "Close that damn door you idiot!"

"Yes, sir," Jacob replied as he left and went back to his seat.

"That hot chocolate smells quite delicious, Martin, and it appears to be safe. Would you pour me a cup and get one for yourself if you like?" Bormann was out of his seat in an instant. He poured the hot chocolate and served it.

"It does smell good. I think I *will* join you," He poured himself a cupful and sat down.

They leaned back in their seats as they sipped the hot chocolate. The hum of the engines was tranquilizing. Neither of them spoke. Both reflected on the events of the day, but neither one seemed willing to reveal his hidden thoughts to the other.

The hot liquid dissolved the Chloral Hydrate on the inside surface of the cup. It mixed with the hot chocolate, and was quickly absorbed into the blood stream. Chloral Hydrate is a colorless crystalline compound used as a powerful sedative. It is sometimes referred to as *knockout drops.*

Bormann's speech began to slur as he spoke. "I feel…very…sleepy." He received no answer. "Are you all ri…?" The question was never finished. The cup slipped from his hand, and fell to the floor with a thud, spilling the remaining contents.

When flying, a pilot's ears are constantly alert to any sound that is out of the ordinary.

"What was that?" Manfred asked anxiously.

"I don't know. I'll go check." Jacob picked up his bag and made his way to the lounge. Bormann was tilted to one side and the hooded figure was slumped forward. Jacob shut the door and asked, "Is there any thing I can do for you Gentlemen?" No response. They were both unconscious. He quickly zipped open the bag, found the handcuffs and secured their right wrists to the armrest. He wrapped the elastic strip around Bormann's upper arm, pulled up his sleeve, filled the syringe with 10 milligrams of Phenol Barbital and slid the needle into a vein. He slowly depressed the plunger until the syringe was empty. He repeated this procedure on the hooded figure. *That should keep you both asleep for a very long time.*

He leaned the hooded figure back in his seat and slid the hood away from his face. He gasped at what he saw. He thought his eyes were deceiving him. He blinked and just stared, mesmerized. Finally he pulled the hood back over the face, poured a cup of coffee for Manfred, closed the door and returned to his seat.

"Here drink this. I'll take over."

"*Danke*," Manfred said as he took the cup. "What was that noise? Is everything all right back there?"

"Everything is fine. Bormann, the slob, dropped his cup." Manfred sipped his coffee while Jacob watched him out of the corner of his eye. It wasn't long before Manfred began to wobble.

Jacob relieved him of the cup as he slumped forward. He quickly trimmed the controls for level flight, retrieved the syringe, and gave Manfred 10 milligrams of Phenol Barbital, and handcuffed each wrist to the armrest. He couldn't chance having Manfred regain consciousness, and wrestle him for control of the plane.

Jacob put the Condor in a tight turn, and straightened out at a heading of 260.

He then turned on his radio and adjusted it to the same frequency he used when he broadcast from the wine cellar.

"Mother Goose, Mother Goose, do you read me? Over." He waited, nothing but static.

"Mother Goose, Mother Goose, please come in, over." More static, he adjusted the dial slightly, and tried again. Nothing.

"Where are you Mother Goose?" he implored.

The radio operator in England heard a faint voice over the crackling in his headset. He tweaked the setting, slightly turning the dial to see if he could improve the reception. He strained to hear what was being broadcast. He could catch a word or two, but nothing distinguishable.

Jacob was becoming increasingly anxious. His luck had held so far, but he was a long way from England.

Suddenly a stream of tracers flashed in front of the plane. His mouth went dry. A fighter pulled up alongside of him and turned on his cockpit light. Jacob could see the pilot was talking into his radiophone and pointing at his earphones. Jacob frantically dialed to the frequency he knew Allied planes were using, and heard a voice say: "…in the twin-engine aircraft, can you hear me? *Hey Kraut*, wake up. *Sprechen Englisch?*"

"Yes, I hear you and I do speak English," Jacob replied in his best American voice.

"Identify yourself."

"This is *Luftwaffe Focke-Wulf 200* Condor *00168.* To whom am I speaking?"

"I'll ask the questions. Who are you?"

"My name is Captain Jacob Halder. I'm a member of the United States Army Air Forces. I'm also an OSS agent operating behind enemy lines."

"Sure you are, and I'm Herman Göring, out for a little spin in my P51."

"I'm telling you I *am* an American. Can't you tell by my voice?"

"That doesn't mean a thing. They caught a whole platoon of American-speaking Germans in American uniforms, changing sign, blowing up bridges, and causing all kinds of havoc. They executed them on the spot."

"But I'm telling you the truth, I really am an American. I'm from Milwaukee."

"Oh yeah, well I'm from Madison. What's the capitol of Wisconsin?"

"Your hometown; Madison."

"You could have been taught that. If you're an American, what are you doing in a German aircraft?"

"Because they only have German aircraft in Germany. I hijacked this plane."

"A likely story. What's your destination?"

"England."

"Yeah. I'm sure. This all sounds pretty fishy to me, and you're one fish that isn't going to get away."

"Hold on for just a few more minutes. What are your call letters?"

"Why?"

"I'd like to try London again and have them contact you to verify that I am who I say I am."

"All right you've got five minutes. If I don't hear anything by then I'll be painting another *Swastika* on my cowling. My call signature is P51694."

Jacob looked at his watch and turned the radio dial to the London frequency and began to broadcast.

"Mother Goose, Mother Goose, please come in. Over," Jacob pleaded.

"This is Mother Goose. I'm reading you loud and clear. Is that you, *Fox?*"

"Yes, this is *Fox*. I need…"

"We have been very worried about you *Fox*," the voice interrupted. "We haven't heard from you in days. Why are you broadcasting in the clear?"

"Listen, this is an emergency. I don't have much time. I'm in a German *Focke-Wulf* Condor 200, just north of Nuremberg. I'm trying to return to the nest. I have a P51, call signature P51694, on frequency 1370 that is itching to add me to his collection. Can you have someone call him and tell him I'm on his side?"

"Hold tight, *Fox*. I'll see what I can do." Jacob turned his dial to the 1370 frequency and held his breath. He glanced at his watch. *Three minutes left,...*

Jacob thought about Janet and his mother and Eddie. Oh, how he yearned to see them. *It's true,* he thought, *your life does pass before your eyes when you think you are about to die. I hate to have it end like this, after being in the lion's mouth for over three years.*

Thirty seconds to go. He noticed the P51 slow and fade behind him. *He's setting up for a shot. Well, Ashburn told me the odds of coming out of this alive may not be that good, and it looks like they just dropped to zero.* Jacob counted the seconds. *Twenty, nineteen, eighteen...I'm not going to just sit like a fish in a barrel.* He tightened his grip on the steering yoke; ready to take evasive action, although he didn't think it would do much good. He glanced at Manfred and felt a rush of guilt. For the two in the back, he had no such feelings. *Ten, nine, eight, seven six...*

"P51694, this is General Henry Arnold. Do you read me? Over."

"Yes sir, loud and clear." Jacob let out a pent up breath of air, and wiped the sweat off his forehead with his sleeve"

"Very good. Now listen carefully. The German Condor you are shadowing is friendly. Do not fire. I repeat, do not fire. Is that clear? Over."

"Affirmative, sir. I hear you loud and clear. Over." Jacob suddenly felt very tired, as the adrenalin subsided in his body.

General Arnold continued, "Condor, what's your destination? Over."

"I'd like to land at Debden, sir, if that's acceptable? Over."

"Do you have enough fuel to make Debden? Over."

"I believe I do sir, but it wouldn't hurt to top off some place along the way, just to be sure. Over."

"If that's the case, land at Antwerp and refuel. We'll notify them you're coming. A squadron of fighters will meet you there and escort you to Debden. We'll notify all Allied aircraft operating in the sectors you will pass through, all the way to Debden, that you are friendly. Over."

"Thank you sir. That will be a relief."

"P51694 do you have enough fuel to escort Condor to Antwerp? That's 200 miles from your present position. Over"

"Yes sir that will be no problem, over."

"One more thing general, would you please inform Colonel Charles Ashburn of MI6 that the *Fox* has the *Wolf*? Over."

"What does that mean? Over."

"He will know what it means, sir. Ask him to have a doctor in attendance when we land as well as an ambulance. There must be complete security and secrecy. He will understand why that is vital, sir. Over."

"I'll pass that information on. Anything else we can do for you? Over." General Arnold asked.

"No sir, that's about it, and thank you sir. Over and out."

Jacob glanced over at Manfred. *Is he in for a big surprise when he wakes up? He'll no doubt thank me. I wonder how our two guests are doing.* Jacob re-trimmed the controls for level flight, and went back to check on his passengers. *They're still asleep or dead.* He checked their pulses. *Just asleep.*

"P51694, this is *Focke-Wulf Condo. D*o you read me? Over."

"I read you Condor. You seem to have friends in very high places. General *Hap* Arnold? Good golly, I never dreamed I'd be talking to him. Over."

"I'm very happy you had that conversation. You had me sweating for a few minutes. By the way, I do not know General Arnold personally, but I'm glad he got through to you. Over"

"I'm glad he did too. I was sure you were a *Kraut.* Over."

"I can understand why you might think that, being in a German plane and all. Why don't we gain a little altitude? Let's say 5,000 feet? Over."

"Sounds OK to me. Over and out."

Jacob felt his skin crawl, when he thought about how close he had come to being shot down. *Wouldn't that have been ironic, shot down by a P51 instead of being in a P51 shooting down a German plane? I'm glad this mission is almost over. No more subterfuge, no more lying and no more killing…and Janet.* He sighed at the thought.

"That's Antwerp up ahead sir," the P51 pilot announced. Jacob had been in the air four hours since he left Berlin. It was now almost midnight and he was getting very tired.

"I see it," Jacob replied.

"Antwerp airfield, this is *Focke-Wulf Condor* escorted by P51694, requesting landing instructions."

A monotone voice replied. "This is Antwerp airfield; we have been expecting you Condor. You are to land first on runway 3. It is the only one lighted. The wind is out of the northwest at 7 knots with gusts up to 12 knots. There is a slight crosswind from the south. Welcome to Antwerp."

Jacob made a slight curving approach, lowered his landing gear, straightened out his flight path in line with the runway and made a smooth landing. He pulled off onto a connecting runway. A vehicle swung around in front of him with a sign that read, *follow me.* It reminded him of his landing at Halifax, Nova Scotia, on his way to England in 1940. *Has it really been five years,* he thought?

The vehicle stopped and Jacob applied the brakes until the Condor came to a stop. The driver of the vehicle jumped out, looked up at Jacob, and ran the tips of his fingers across his throat in a slashing motion; the universal sign to cut the engines.

A refueling truck pulled along side the Condor. The driver set up a stepladder, and climbed up looking for the fuel lid. Jacob left his seat, tilted Manfred's seat back as far as it would go so he would be difficult to see from the ground and made sure the passengers were still asleep. He poured himself a cup of coffee, making sure he used the chipped cup. He checked the drapes inside the passenger compartment to be sure no one could see inside, opened the door, lowered the stairs and descended to the Tarmac. He saw the P51 taxiing toward him. It parked next to the Condor.

A crowd of curious American servicemen had gathered near the Condor. It must have been an oddity for them to see a German aircraft in their front yard. When they spotted Jacob in his German uniform, a murmur went through the crowd. He heard someone yell, "We ought to lynch the bastard." They began moving toward Jacob.

The P51 pilot moved in between them, drew his 45 caliber side arm and said, "I'll shoot the first SOB that comes any closer. This is an American officer. Don't let the uniform fool you."

That stopped the crowd and they began to thin out as most of them wandered back toward the hangars. The P51 pilot holstered his gun and walked over to Jacob with a big smile on his face and offered his hand. He was fair skinned, had red hair and a freckled face.

"I'm Lieutenant James Parker, sir."

"It's a pleasure to make your acquaintance, Lieutenant. Thank you for the help. I'm Colonel Karl Kaufmann."

"But, you said you were an American. That's a German name."

"For now, I'm Colonel Kaufmann. Tomorrow I may be someone else," Jacob said with a smile.

"That's right. You said you were with the OSS."

"May I ask you not to reveal that to anyone? I'm still supposed to be under-cover. I wouldn't have made known the fact that I'm with the OSS except to keep you from shooting me down."

"Sorry about that, sir."

"You were only doing your job. Do you think you could rustle me up a sand-wich and some water before I take off?"

"Let's go inside and see what we can find."

"It's probably wiser if I stay clear of everyone in there. They're a little on edge, and I shouldn't leave the aircraft unattended."

"Who you got in there, Hermann Göring, sir?" Parker said jokingly.

"I thought you said *you* were Hermann Göring," Jacob replied with a big smile on his face. Parker grinned, as he remembered his flippant remark.

"Let's see what I can find."

"Hey…you there, whatever your name is. Where do you Germans hide the fuel lids?"

"They're in the wing, just in front of the aileron."

"OK, I see them now, thanks." It was strange to hear Americans talking. He hadn't spoken anything but German for over three years.

Jacob heard aircraft engines in the distance and watched as twelve fighters landed one after another. They pulled in near him, and stopped side by side, forming a line. He saw several fuel trucks roll out to service them. Pilots climbed out and stretched their legs. The closest fighter was a Spitfire. It was all Jacob could do to keep from going over and getting a closer look. What he wouldn't give to trade places with that pilot.

He saw Parker coming out of the hangar. The fighter pilots were heading Parker's way. They surrounded him and Jacob saw some of them pointing toward the Condor. They were in an animated discussion. I *wonder what kind of tale Parker is giving them,* Jacob thought. Finally the fighter pilots headed for the han-gar and Parker headed for Jacob. He had a sandwich and canteen in his hands.

"I hope you like Spam," Parker said apprehensively.

"That sounds wonderful."

"You sure you're an American?" Parker inquired.

Jacob took a big bite, and with mouth full replied, "True Blue."

After the plane was refueled Jacob entered the Condor, checked on the two in back, and then went forward to the cockpit. Manfred was still asleep.

He flipped the switch that retracted the stairs and went back to close the door. He started the engines and taxied to just off the runway. He checked all the instruments, noticed with satisfaction that the fuel gauge read *full*. He radioed the control tower for permission to take off.

"Permission granted," came the reply. He eased the throttles forward and turned the plane until it was pointing down the runway. He released the brakes, gave it full throttle, and the Condor began to roll. It gained speed and gently lifted into the air.

The fighters had been lined up on the tarmac ready to follow, and in just a few minutes all were airborne. In a very short time Jacob looked around and was comforted by the sight of the fighters as they formed a protective shield around him. This was the first time since taking off from *Tempelhof* that he felt completely relaxed and secure. He again thought about the odds Ashburn had given him of successfully coming out of his mission alive and the doubts Manfred had about them making it to Obersalzberg.

"Well Manfred. I believe the odds are now in our favor. In fact I believe they are now one hundred percent." Manfred didn't reply because he was still unconscious.

The weather was perfect. It was a clear night, and the stars stretched out as far as the eye could see in a brilliant canopy. The moon looked close enough to touch. He began thinking about Janet. The excitement and anticipation of seeing her and being back in England was almost more than he could bear. He hadn't even been able to take a picture of her to Germany with him, and he wondered what she looked like now. He knew she was all right as Ashburn had kept him informed to keep up his morale. He wondered if Ashburn told her he was on his way home. He also thought about the Jellineks and wondered if Walther had gotten them out safely. And what about the Mueller's? *I must call Mom and Eddie as soon as possible. Won't they be surprised?* He was tingling with excitement as a hundred random thoughts raced through his mind.

The coastline of England brought him out of his reverie. What a beautiful sight. The sun was just peaking over the horizon to his left and the mist was already beginning to dissipate. The fighters and the Condor descended to a little over 500 meters as the channel disappeared from under them, replaced by land. The fields and farms were a patchwork quilt of many shades. It reminded him of his first flight with Eddie when he was a boy. He saw a small farmhouse and barn directly ahead. A man walked out of the barn and looked up. *This must be a strange sight. I would love to know what he's thinking. Wouldn't he be surprised if he knew the whole story, but of course he will never know? Very few people will.*

It was not long before he saw the Debden airfield. It was a sweet sight. He had taken off and landed here many times in his Spitfire before that fateful flight the day he faked his crash.

Jacob radioed, "This is *Focke-Wulf* Condor 200 requesting landing instructions. Over."

"This is Debden control, use runway 2. Wind is out of the southeast at four knots. You are cleared for landing. Welcome to England. Over."

"Roger, Debden. Thank you. Over and out." Jacob over flew the airfield, made a U turn, descended, touched down smoothly, and taxied onto an intersecting strip. The typical *follow me* vehicle came into view, and Jacob taxied behind it. He saw the fighters land as he moved away from the main runway. The vehicle led him into a large hangar. It then turned around and exited as an ambulance entered through the same doorway. The doors were slid shut as Jacob braked and turned off the engines. He unbuckled his harness and opened the entry door. He went back to the cockpit and engaged the switch that extended the stairs. Out of habit he put on his hat, took a last look at Manfred, peeked in at the two in back, and walked down the steps.

There stood Colonel Ashburn. A uniformed officer with a black bag was with him. His insignia identified him as a doctor. An ambulance and two attendants stood nearby.

Jacob walked toward Ashburn, saluted and said, "Captain Jacob Halder reporting, sir."

Ashburn saluted in return. He was smiling broadly. "Welcome home, Colonel.

It's good to see you again after all these years."

"Thank you, sir. It's wonderful to be back in England." Addressing the doctor, Jacob said, "The two men in the passenger suite should be searched thoroughly for cyanide. I gave each of them 10 milligrams of Phenol Barbital about seven hours ago, and they were still asleep when I last looked in on them. I did the same to the co-pilot. He's harmless, and I believe he'll be happy to wake up safely in England, whereas the other two will be quite upset. Here are the keys to the handcuffs with which I restrained them."

The doctor boarded the Condor. Ashburn said, "Good show old boy. I'm jolly well happy for your safe return. Being responsible for sending you into harm's way was not an easy thing to do. I'm ecstatic you are back safely, and I know Janet will be also."

"Does she know I'm back?"

"Not yet. If she knew, alligators couldn't have kept her away. I thought it might be more appropriate if you met her alone at another location."

"I agree, but please tell me, is she OK? Where's she staying? When can I see her?"

"Slow down. She's just fine. I'll take you to her as soon as we get those two off the plane."

"By the way, you called me Colonel. Have you forgotten my rank?" Jacob asked.

"Not at all. You have been a Colonel for some time now. I just didn't mention your promotion. I thought you had enough on your mind."

"Well, I'll be darned."

The doctor poked his head out of the airplane door, and motioned to the two ambulance drivers instructing them to bring a stretcher. In a few minutes they emerged from the Condor carrying what looked like a corpse. A white sheet covered the body from head to toe. They slid the stretcher into the ambulance and went back to retrieve the other *body*.

"Where are they taking them?"

"To the most secure prison in all England; the Tower of London. That's where they put Rudolph Hess when he parachuted into England in 1941. That's where they keep the Crown Jewels. There is no more secure place in the British Empire."

"What's to become of them? Will they be hanged do you think?"

"I doubt it. That's too quick and easy. Their punishment will require torture," Ashburn replied.

"Torture! You're kidding. We haven't stooped to the level of the *Nazi's* have we?"

"Of course not. *We* won't torture them. *They* will torture themselves."

"What! How will they do that?"

"Can you imagine what it will be like to have been in the positions of power they enjoyed and then be reduced to irrelevance? To be locked up in a poorly lighted cell for the rest of their lives, never again to hear the sound of a human voice except their own mad ravings, never again able to smell the fragrance of a lilac in the springtime, or hear birds sing or see a rainbow or a sunset. What if you could never be with Janet or your parents again? What if you were deprived of everything and everyone you ever loved? What if you couldn't do the things you loved to do? What if you couldn't fly, Jacob?"

"Deprived of all those things it would be hell."

"Do you think the punishment fits the crime?"

"It will do until they stand before God."

After the ambulance left, Jacob and Ashburn got into Ashburn's automobile, and drove out of the hangar.

"Can I see Janet now? Where is she?"

"She's home. That's where we're going now. By the way, Janet isn't living in the same flat where you spent your honeymoon." Jacob almost choked.

"How long have you known? When did you find out?"

"Don't you know it's my business uncovering secrets? It became pretty obvious after a while."

"What do you mean?"

"You'll understand when you get home."

"Then you weren't upset when you found out?"

"A little annoyed at first. I thought it might be a distraction, but the more I thought about it, the more I felt it might give you greater incentive to do whatever was necessary to return safely. Anyway that's all in the past. You have a great future ahead of you."

"How soon will I be home?"

Ashburn looked at his watch and said, "In about 45 minutes." Jacob was so excited he could hardly contain himself. He hadn't slept since 0600 the previous morning and it was now 0500 the following day, but he was too excited to feel tired.

"You realize you'll probably be waking Janet up. It's quite early, but I bet she won't mind."

"I hope not, because even if she's asleep, I'm going to wake her." Ashburn turned off the paved road onto a country lane. It meandered through newly leafed trees and ended in front of a little English cottage with a thatched roof. In front of the house was a low white picket fence. Small flowers were in profusion along its perimeter. It looked like the picture on a postcard a tourist might find at an English gift shop. Jacob got out and said,

"When do I have to report?"

"The day after tomorrow at 0900. I wish I could give you more time, but we need to talk. You can go home every evening until something changes. Janet has your old uniform. I doubt you'll want to keep wearing that German one. Here's a pair of colonel's birds for your shoulders. We'll get you outfitted in a new uniform as soon as we can get your measurements."

"I've worn a German uniform for so long it will feel strange in an American one, but I'm anxious to change."

"We're going to get you the finest tailor-made uniform in all of England. You know we have the finest wool and the most professional tailors in the world. You need to be presentable for what lies ahead."

"And what might that be?"

"You'll see. Remember, day after tomorrow 0900 sharp at MI6 Headquarters."

"I'll be there. See you then, and thanks for the lift."

Jacob walked up to the front door and knocked. He waited anxiously for the door to open. He knocked again a little louder. The door opened a crack and then it was flung open as Janet recognized him. She squealed and fell into his arms. She cried as she kissed him. Jacob held her tight, soaking up the moment. Finally, after a long kiss, he held her at arms length and looked at her.

"You're even more beautiful than I remember."

"You sure know how to surprise a girl. I can hardly believe it's you,"

"It's me all right. How are you sweetheart and when did you move here?"

"Not long after you left. I thought I would need more room as well as…" she was interrupted by a small voice that said,

"Mummy, who's that?" A little girl, with long blond hair came into the room rubbing her eyes.

"This is your daddy, Caroline, and Daddy, this is your daughter."

Jacob was stunned. He finally found his voice and said, "Is this *really* our daughter?"

"Yes dear, this is our daughter. You remember the honeymoon don't you?"

"How could I forget it?" Jacob picked the little girl up and tenderly kissed her cheek.

"She looks just like you."

"Mum and Dad both say she resembles you."

"How are they, by the way?"

"They're just fine. They'll be overjoyed to know you're home safely. I'll have to keep pinching myself to realize this is all real."

"Why don't I do the pinching?"

Janet laughed and said, "Go right ahead."

CHAPTER 53

▼

Admiral Dönitz, into whose hands Hitler had bequeathed the leadership of *Nazi* Germany, realized that Germany could hold out no longer. To preserve his troops fighting the Russians in the east he dispatched Admiral Hans von Freideburg to Eisenhower's headquarters with an appeal to accept the surrender of the remaining forces in the west while they continued to fight the Russians in the east. Eisenhower refused. He insisted on a simultaneous surrender of all German forces and told Freideburg to sign the surrender document. Freideburg replied that he had no power to sign without the permission of Dönitz. When Dönitz was informed of Eisenhower's position he sent *Oberstgruppenführer* Alfred Jodl. The answer was the same, but Eisenhower did give them forty-eight hours so as to give them time to inform their outlying forces.

German troops began surrendering in the west while continuing to fight in the east. The forty-eight hour reprieve saved thousands of German forces from being taken prisoners by the Russians. The civilian population flooded the west to avoid the same fate. At the end of the forty-eight hour period, Dönitz gave Jodl permission to sign. Representatives from the United States, Great Britain, France, and Russia met at Eisenhower's headquarters, and on 7 May 1945, at 2:41 PM, General Jodl and Admiral Freideburg signed the unconditional German surrender documents, and the war in Europe was over.

This set off a worldwide celebration that was best exemplified by the words of Winston Churchill, who said it was, "the signal for the greatest outburst of joy in the history of mankind."[1]

---

1. *Eisenhower Soldier and President*, by Stephen E. Ambrose

CHAPTER 54

▼

Major Raymond Elsmore, the same United States Army Air Forces officer who had informed Ilse and Eddie about Jacob being shot down, walked up the walkway to the entrance of the home at 223 Vine Street in Milwaukee and rang the doorbell. He looked at the gold star in the window and remembered his visit three years ago when the star was blue. This was a strange assignment, and he wasn't quite sure what to make of it. Ilse came to the door, and when she saw Major Elsmore sudden fear gripped her.

"Good afternoon, Mrs. Halder. I'm Major Elsmore. Do you remember me?"

"Yes, I do. You brought the news about my son. Has he been found?"

"I don't know. My visit today is a little unusual, to say the least."

"What do you mean?" Ilse asked with a foreboding fear.

"Is Mr. Halder home?"

"No, he's at the airport where he works."

"When will he be home?"

"He gets home at different times of the day, depending on his customers. He's an instructor, you know."

"Could you telephone him and ask him to come home now? I have some important information for both of you." Ilse's hopes soared.

"Yes, I'll call him right now. Please have a seat." Ilse called Eddie and told him what was happening.

"I'll be right home. Let's hope its good news."

"From the look on Major Elsmore's face, I'm hopeful it is." It took Eddie 20 minutes to get home. He exceeded a few speed limits, but made it home without any incidents.

"Thank you for coming home, Mr. Halder. I'm here to ask both of you if you would be willing to receive a visitor this afternoon, quite an important one as a matter of fact." Ilse and Eddie looked at one another.

"It's fine with us. Who is it?" Eddie asked.

"President Harry S. Truman," Major Elsmore replied. Ilse and Eddie were stunned.

"You're kidding, of course," Eddie said.

"No, I'm dead serious."

"It's incredulous to me that the President of the United States would want to visit us. He doesn't even know who we are. What does he want?"

"I wasn't told. I was just asked to make the appointment. I'm sure he must know who you are. He arrived in Milwaukee at 1600 hours. May I use your telephone?"

"Yes, of course," Ilse replied. "It's there on the table." Major Elsmore picked up the telephone and dialed.

"This is Major Elsmore, sir. Mr. and Mrs. Halder will be pleased to receive the President...yes, 1630 hours, I'll let them know. Thank you sir."

"The President is on his way. He'll be here in 30 minutes." Ilse was in a panic. She began picking things up and ordered Eddie to vacuum the carpet. She rushed to the kitchen and made a pitcher of lemonade. Her head was spinning. She wished she had more time to clean the house and prepare a dessert. She was glad she had some cookies left. *What a way to entertain the President of the United States,* she thought. Eddie finished vacuuming and tried to calm Ilse.

Major Elsmore said, "President Truman is not a pretentious man. He was raised in a house much like this one and I'm sure he will feel right at home."

It seemed like an eternity waiting. Ilse kept watch at the curtained window. Finally the motorcade arrived. A large black limousine accompanied by several other cars and a dozen or so state troopers on motorcycles roared to a stop in front of the house. Eddie joined Ilse at the window. Secret Service agents crowded around the limousine as the President stepped out. Neighbors poured out of their houses to see what was causing all the commotion. The President wore a brown suit and his trademark wide brimmed hat. Ilse remembered reading that he was once a haberdasher. The President strode up the walk followed by a military officer carrying a black satchel. Secret Service agents surrounded him. Eddie opened the door.

"Welcome, Mr. President. I'm Eddie Halder, and this is my wife Ilse. It's an honor and a wonderful surprise to have you in our home."

"Thank you Mr. Halder, and it's an honor to meet you Mrs. Halder. I apologize for the short notice. I'm on my way to San Francisco and decided to stop by. I have some very good news for you both, and I wanted to deliver it personally."

"Won't you please be seated, Mr. President?" Ilse said.

"Thank you. I suggest you sit down also." Everyone took a seat except the officer with the satchel and two Secret Service agents.

"First, let me introduce you to Doctor Harriman." *That explains the bag,* Ilse thought. "He's along just as a precaution." *A precaution for what,* Eddie wondered.

"Mr. and Mrs. Halder, I mentioned that I had some good news for you. It's my pleasure to inform you that your son, Colonel Jacob Halder, is alive and safe in London as we speak." Ilse could hardly breathe. The room began to swim. Her mouth opened, but no words came out. The doctor sat down by her and took her arm. He passed something under her nose, and the acrid odor jolted her.

"Are you all right, Mrs. Halder?" The doctor asked.

"I think so."

"I know this news must come as a shock," President Truman continued. "I can't even begin to imagine how you must feel, but it's true, your son is alive." Ilse was quietly crying. Eddie put his arm around her. He was as stunned as Ilse. How many times a day had they prayed for Jacob's safe return? After such a long time it seemed like they prayed out of habit rather than hope.

"I'm all right now. I'm so happy I don't know what to say, except to thank you for letting us know," Ilse said as she dabbed at her eyes with a handkerchief.

"I'd like to explain something to you. Your son has been on a very special and secret mission in Germany since August of 1942. I didn't even know about it myself until I was briefed after President Roosevelt passed away. It was so secret that only three other Americans besides President Roosevelt knew of its existence. It was extremely important for your sons' safety and the success of the mission that he appear to be dead. You see, your son took the place of a German officer who had been shot down over London and captured. It turned out that your son and this German officer looked so much alike they could have passed for twins." Ilse went cold with fear. The President continued, "The mission was so successful that I'm sure it helped shorten the war and saved countless lives. Your son is quite a hero, Mrs. Halder." Ilse hardly heard those words she was so shaken by this revelation. "Are you all right Mrs. Halder?"

"Y…yes, I think so. It has been quite a shock. I can't tell you how happy I am. When can we see him? When can he come home?"

"He can't come home right away, but he will be telephoning you tonight. He's just outside London with his wife and daughter."

"With his what! He has a wife and daughter?

"Yes, he does. His wife is English. Their little girl is a little over two years old. You're a grandmother, Mrs. Halder." Ilse thought she must be dreaming, but there sat the President of the United States in her living room talking to her like they were old friends.

Ilse finally recovered enough to remember the refreshments. "I have some lemonade and cookies, Mr. President; would you care for some?"

"Are the cookies homemade?"

"Yes sir, they are?"

"Then I'd love to have some." Ilse got up and went to the kitchen. The President followed and sat down at the kitchen table. Ilse served President Truman and poured lemonade for the others.

"Umm, these are delicious. Just like Bess makes."

"I'm glad you like them, sir. I'll send some with you."

"Wonderful, and I do have to get going. Do you have any questions before I leave?"

Ilse and Eddie looked at one another, and Eddie said, "I guess not, Mr. President. We'll probably think of something after you leave."

"In that case, let Major Elsmore know what you need, and he'll get the answers to you as quickly as we can supply them." With that statement the President got up and said, "I have to go now. It was an honor to meet both of you."

"The honor was ours, Mr. President, and thank you for letting us know about our son," Ilse said. After the President and his party left, Major Elsmore stayed behind.

"Here's my card, Mrs. Halder. Call me if there is anything I can do for you."

"One more thing, Major. The President called Jacob, *Colonel*. He was a captain the last we heard," Eddie remarked.

"Well he's a colonel now. By the way, you can take down that gold star and put the blue one back up."

The next day, Jacob and Janet spent hours talking. They had a lot of catching up to do. They reveled in one another's company. Jacob held Caroline every chance he got. He had never been as happy and content as he was at this moment.

"It's 1700 hours in Milwaukee. It's time to call Mom and Eddie. Can you believe it? The President of the United States visiting them and letting them know I'm alive. What a wonderful gesture."

"That's because you're so wonderful, but I'll bet they *were* surprised."

"Hold Caroline while I get an operator."

Jacob picked up the phone and dialed. After a few rings an operator said, "May I help you, please?"

"Yes, I'd like to place an international call to Lander 2931 in Milwaukee, Wisconsin in the United States…Yes, that's right. Thank you." After an excruciating few minutes Jacob said, "It's ringing." Jacob was nervously tapping his finger on the table when he finally said, "Hello, Mom is that you?…Yes this is me, Mom. You sound like you're a million miles away. You're right, London is a long way from Milwaukee. How are you and Eddie?…Wonderful. You sound great…Yes, I'm just fine…It's good to hear your voice, too." He could tell his mother was crying and asked, "Are you all right, Mom?…Good…Yes, I'm just fine…Yes, I have to stay here for a while. The war with Japan is still not over, and I've got to go back to Berlin for a few days…Yes, I'll be careful. By the way, I saw the Jellineks while I was in Berlin. They said to tell you hello…As far as I know they're OK. I'll check on them when I'm in Berlin…He did…Yes, she's right here. You'll love her mom; she's as wonderful as you are. I'm going to put her on the line so you can talk to her." He handed Janet the phone.

"Hello, Mrs. Halder…I can hardly wait to meet you, also. You have the most wonderful son in the world…I knew you did. I can hardly wait to meet Mr. Halder as well…I'm sure, as soon as they let us. I'm anxious to see Milwaukee. Jacob talks about it all the time…Yes; you have a granddaughter, her name is Caroline…Let me see if she'll say something." Janet put the phone to Caroline's ear and said, "Say hello to Grandmum." Caroline just squirmed, and wouldn't say a word.

"I guess she won't talk when you want her to. When she meets you, she'll probably talk your ears off…Yes, here's Jacob again, Cheery O for now."

"Hello again…OK put him on…Hi Eddie, it's great to hear your voice…I'm just fine. Are you OK?…How's the business?…Is my old job still available when I get home?…Like I told Mom, it's going to be awhile yet…You bet I will. You take good care of yourself, and remember about bold pilots not becoming old pilots." They both laughed at that. "I'll keep in touch. Tell everyone hello for me. Let me say bye to Mom…I've got to hang up now, Mom…I love you too. Take good care of yourself, and I'll be in touch…Bye for now." Jacob hung up the receiver and just stared at it for a few seconds.

"Your mom sounds so nice. It will be wonderful meeting her. You told her you had to go back to Berlin. Is that necessary?"

"I'm afraid so. There's something I have to retrieve."

At 0900 Jacob walked into Colonel Ashburn's office. "Good morning, Colonel. Halder, How's everything at home?" Ashburn asked.

"Everything's just fine. Thanks for helping Janet and Caroline so much while I was gone. Janet said you helped her through some pretty rough times."

"The pleasure was all mine. They're a wonderful pair."

"What's the schedule today?"

"The first thing is to get your measurements for a new uniform. A tailor is waiting for you in the next room."

"And then what?"

"I'm going to pick your brains on how we can best secure German technology before the Russians beat us to it."

"They've got a head start since they were in Berlin first." They spent the rest of the day debriefing Jacob.

The next day Ashburn greeted Jacob. "Good morning, Colonel. You look sharp in your new uniform."

"Thank you. It feels great. Those tailors sure work fast. It's a perfect fit."

"I told you we have the finest tailors in the world. You look presentable enough to meet King George VI. As a matter of fact we have an appointment with him at 0945."

"You've got to be kidding. I'm going to meet the king? What does the king want with me?"

"You'll see." At 0905 they were picked up in a Bentley limousine. When they drove through the gates at Buckingham Palace, Jacob realized that Ashburn wasn't kidding.

"Are we really going to meet the king? What's the occasion?"

"You'll see." They pulled up at an entrance with massive doors. A livery servant opened the limousine door, and Jacob stepped out. They were led into a huge foyer with massive paintings and richly upholstered furniture. They proceeded down a wide hall flanked by statues, and turned into a room that took Jacob's breath away. Never had he seen anything as elegant and imposing.

The king and queen, surrounded by several high-ranking uniformed officers and civilians in formal dress, including Churchill and Eisenhower, looked their way as they entered. Janet and Caroline stood next to the king. Ashburn moved toward them and Jacob followed. Jacob was speechless. The king extended his hand. Jacob didn't know the correct protocol, but he bowed slightly as he shook the king's hand. Janet was smiling radiantly. Jacob glanced at her with a quizzical look on his face. She just kept smiling.

"Welcome, Colonel Halder. I've been informed of your mission and I'm very impressed. I've been chatting with your wife and daughter and they are charming.

"Thank you, Your Majesty. I have the same opinion." Without another word the king removed a medal from a container held by one of the officers and pinned it on his uniform.

"This is the Victoria Cross, Britain's highest award for valor. I take great pleasure in presenting this to you from a grateful nation. May it forever be a reminder of our heartfelt gratitude."

"Thank you again, Your Majesty. I'm overwhelmed"

"After hearing about your mission, I'm the one that is overwhelmed."

The others in the room gathered around him shaking his hand and congratulating him. Eisenhower stepped forward, his famous grin almost in Jacob's face, and grasped his hand with both of his. "Welcome home, Colonel It's good to finally meet you face to face."

"Thank you, sir. It's an honor to meet you, sir." Churchill approached and his chubby hand clasped Jacob's.

"My boy there are no words that can adequately express my gratitude for what you have accomplished."

"Thank you, Mr. Prime Minister."

When Janet was able to get close to Jacob, she gave him a hug and buzz on the cheek. Jacob seemed embarrassed by all the attention.

"How long have you known about this? How did you get here?"

"Long enough. Colonel Ashburn had me picked up."

"Can you believe this? The King of England. My golly."

He picked up Caroline and gave her a squeeze. All seemed right with the world. After all the congratulations were exhausted, they were escorted into another room where tea was served. Jacob said to Ashburn, "How long have you known about this? Why didn't you give me a heads-up? I've never been so scared in my life."

"We thought it was better you didn't know in advance. You would have been nervous for days."

"You're right about that. My legs feel like jelly. Did I act like a fool?"

"You were just wonderful darling," Janet said.

CHAPTER 55

▼

"Eisenhower has returned to Germany. Everything is in turmoil over there right now. We leave for Berlin the day after tomorrow. We've got to retrieve your transmitter. We can't let that technology fall into Russian hands. We'll be working with Eisenhower and his staff to overcome whatever advantage the Russians may have gained," Ashburn commented.

"We'll be OK in the districts we control, but in those areas under Russian control we'll have to do it by stealth."

"Exactly. That's why you're going back."

"What if the Müller's have returned to their home? I can't just walk in on them in an American uniform and say, Hi, I'm Jacob, and I've been pretending to be your son Karl for the past three years."

"Why not? You can tell them the whole story. Tell them their precious Karl is safe and will be coming home soon."

"I can't do that. This is much more complicated than you realize. It's so complicated I can't even figure it out. There are a lot of things I don't know, and I'm not sure I want to know."

"Such as?"

"The questions that keep popping up ever since you discovered me in that officer's pub in London."

"And what are those questions?"

"How come Karl Müller and I look so much alike? And are we twins?"

"Can I give you a little fatherly advice?"

"Of course."

"Just let sleeping dogs lie."

"It's interesting you saying that. That's the same advice I gave myself some time ago."

"Quite."

The DC 3 descended smoothly into Tempelhof Airport at 1120 hours. The memory of his escape from this same location flooded Jacob's mind, and his brain was overwhelmed as he tried to cram the experiences of three years of his life in Germany in the few minutes it took them to land. It was like a dream.

To say the city was devastated would be a colossal understatement. It was virtually obliterated. Eisenhower set up his headquarters in the I. G. Farben offices in Frankfurt. Eisenhower's hatred of the *Nazis* was boiling over. He had been a front row witness to the death and destruction caused by Germany's aggression. He saw first hand the consequences of their evil acts against the Jews when he visited the death camps at *Auschwitz, Dachau, Treblinka* and a dozen others where millions of Jews had been murdered. He ordered busloads of local German citizens taken to these sites and forced them to witness for themselves the atrocities for which Germany was responsible. He did not want future generations to claim such things never happened.

The Joint Chiefs of Staff issued and sent to Eisenhower an order prohibiting the fraternization of occupying forces and German citizens, and a denazification policy that called for the arrest of Germans who had taken part in various Nazi organizations. No *Nazi* was to be permitted to hold a position of importance in public or private enterprise.

These orders were difficult if not impossible to enforce. Who could tell who was a *Nazi* and who was not? Virtually everyone said they were not a *Nazi* nor had they ever been one, or they claimed they were just carrying out orders. Many of the skilled municipal employees were presumed to be *Nazis*. It was difficult to get the city running again without them.

If a soldier gave a child a candy bar, or even a stick of chewing gum, he was technically in violation of the non-fraternization order. In time these orders were eventually relaxed or ignored.

The Russians were the first to enter Berlin, and Stalin, obsessed with finding Hitler if he was alive or his body if he was dead, set up a special unit for this purpose. After an intensive search, the charred remains believed to be those of Adolph Hitler and Eva Braun were discovered just outside Hitler's bunker. Stalin failed to inform the Allies of this find and later implied that Hitler and Eva had escaped Berlin and fled to Spain or South America. Even the Russians were not fully convinced that this was Hitler's body. Whether Hitler was dead or alive remained a mystery.

An army Jeep met Ashburn and Jacob at the airport. The driver was a corporal from the 71st Infantry Division. He didn't look to be more than twenty years old. Jacob gave him Karl's address in Charlottenburg. The driver didn't even know where Charlottenburg was, let alone the street address.

"I'll just give you the directions as we drive," he told the driver. It took a little over an hour to reach their destination. Jacob ordered the corporal to pull up just outside the gate. They had decided that Ashburn would approach the house alone in case the Müller's were home. Ashburn got out of the car and walked up the driveway to the front door. The glass was broken out of one side of the double doors. He stepped through and looked around. It was a mess. As he walked through the house he called out, "Is anyone home?" No one answered. Satisfied no one was there he went back and got Jacob. As Jacob entered the house his heart sank. It was even in worse condition than the *Gestapo* had left it weeks ago. Obviously vandals had gutted it. After a full inspection Jacob realized everything was stolen.

"What a shame" Jacob commented. "It was a lovely home when I lived here. A real gem."

"It's pretty spooky actually seeing the place, instead of just imagining what it was like when you were living here," Ashburn commented.

"The Müllers will be devastated when they see what's happened. I wonder where they are now."

"We'll have a search made for them, but in the meantime let's get your wireless and get out of here." Jacob walked down a hall and into the library, and Ashburn followed. They both stood in front of the infamous left panel.

"See if you can tell which Rosettes to slide," Jacob said.

"Just open it; we don't have time for games." Jacob slid the two key rosettes and rotated the door. Ashburn was fascinated. He tried the light switches, but there was no electricity. Ashburn lit his cigarette lighter and they descended the stairs. The wireless was still on the table. Jacob unplugged it and cut the antenna wire. He placed the wireless in a bag, handed it to Ashburn, and began winding up the antennae wire.

"God save the king!" Ashburn yelled as he held up a bottle of wine, and read the label by the light of his lighter. "Look at this, 1885. Why that's 60 years old. I wonder what it tastes like."

"You'll never know. Put it back."

"Spoils of war, old boy."

"Looting will spoil your career, old boy. Put it back." Ashburn reluctantly laid the bottle back in the rack, looking at it longingly. Jacob wound up the antenna wire as they walked back upstairs. At the landing he climbed the ladder, slid the antennae back through the rubber grommet, and climbed down. They stepped back into the library and Jacob locked the door. "Let's get out of here," Jacob said.

They were billeted in Potsdam, just southwest of Berlin. On the way back, Jacob took Ashburn on a tour of the city and showed him some of the familiar landmarks. They drove by the *Luftwaffe,* and *Abwehr* headquarters where he had spent most of his working days. They found their way to *Charlottenburger Chaussee.* This led directly to the Brandenburg Gate. To the left was the burned and bombed out *Reichtag.* At the Brandenburg Gate they turned right onto Herman Göring *Straße* and drove to the *Reich* Chancellery. Jacob pointed out *Lenne Straße,* the street he used as a runway when he took off in the *Storch.* He noticed all the lanterns were gone.

The people on the streets looked tired and destitute, which they were. Their clothes were ragged and soiled. He wondered how they were feeding themselves. Some were carrying pieces of wood they had gathered to make a fire. The buildings were nothing but rubble. These dreary scenes depressed Jacob.

By the time they reached their quarters they were tired and hungry. A mess hall had been set up and dinner was being served.

"Where to tomorrow?" Jacob asked.

"*Peenemünde.* We want to find Werner von Braun and his rocket teams before the Russians get them.

C H A P T E R   56

▼

The repatriation of German prisoners of war began four weeks after Germany surrendered. Karl was put on a ship with other prisoners, and taken across the English Channel to the port at La Havre, France. He searched the faces in the crowd, hoping to find Franz. As they disembarked, angry Frenchmen shook their fists, and cursed them. They were then put aboard a train, and it headed east. They rattled through Belgium and entered Germany at Duisburg. They passed through Cologne, Dusseldorf, Dortmund, and Osnabruck, enroute to Berlin. The devastation Karl saw as he gazed out the window enraged him. He was excited about returning to Germany but was burning with anger that Germany had been defeated.

"How could this happen?" Karl said to no one in particular.

The person seated next to him replied, "It looks pretty bad. I wonder what Berlin is like?"

"Probably the same. Our guards loved telling us about the air strikes on Berlin."

"I guess I can't blame them. Look at what we did to London."

"I wish we had bombed London off the map." Karl was seething with anger. He had dreamed of walking through London as a conquering hero, but was instead going back to a devastated Berlin like a whipped dog with his tail between his legs.

As they pulled into Berlin, in what was left of the marshalling yards, it was 16 August 1945, at 1400 hours. Karl was stunned by what he saw. He left this city at the height of its rebirth from World War 1, and returned to a city that existed only by its location. It was no longer a city; it was a pile of rubble. He was devastated by what he saw and so depressed he could hardly move. The train stopped and he just sat there. The others were up and moving toward the door.

Someone said, "Were home Karl, let's get off." Karl looked up hoping to see Franz, but it was a man he knew from the prison camp in Perth.

He finally struggled to his feet, stretched, and walked toward the door. As he stepped off the train two American MP's took him by the arms and said, "Come with us." They put him in a military automobile and drove off.

"Where are you taking me?" Karl asked.

"You'll see when we get there." The MP replied.

"What is this all about?"

"I have no idea," said one of them. "We were just told to pick you up." They drove to a building on *Berilchingen Straße*. They took him inside and sat him down in a chair opposite a large desk.

"Just sit here. Someone will be with you in a few minutes." Karl looked around, wondering what was going to happen to him.

He sat in this room for a long time. Finally the door opened and Karl turned around. Standing in front of him was an American officer. Karl gasped. His mouth opened, but he could not form a word. He just stared. Jacob looked down at him and was as tongue-tied as Karl. Jacob moved around him and sat behind the desk. They just stared at one another. Finally Karl said, "Am I looking in a mirror?"

"We do look very much alike, don't we?" Jacob said.

"Yes we do. Who are you?"

"I'm Colonel Jacob Halder of the United States Army Air Forces. Welcome back to Germany."

"Why do we look so much alike? We could be twins," Karl said.

"It seems like I've heard that statement before," Jacob chuckled.

"What do you mean?" Karl asked.

"Never mind. I just wanted to meet you before you go home and offer you some friendly advice."

"What kind of advice?"

"Suggestions that may help you adjust to civilian life more quickly."

"And what advice is that?"

"You have a wonderful father and mother. When you go home they will be quite confused. So will you. Take the time to really see what happened in Germany under Hitler. Open your eyes to the truth, and open your mind to reality. You seem to have a lot of pent-up hate inside you. It's as poisonous to your soul as a rattlesnake's venom would be to your body. Purge it from your system and your life will return to normal much more quickly. The next few days will not be easy for you. If you have inherited a fraction of the character of your parents, you will be all right. Good luck to you. You will be taken home tomorrow."

"How do you know so much about me, and how do you know my parents?" Karl asked. Jacob just smiled.

Jacob took his uniform off and put on his German uniform. Karl's mother and father had been found and taken home. Before the Müllers arrived home, Jacob and Ashburn had the house cleaned and food stocked on the pantry shelves. A piece of plywood was nailed over the entry door where the glass was missing. Silverware, cooking pots, pans and dishes were requisitioned. Army issue bedding was provided. A supply of wood had been stacked by the fireplace. It certainly didn't look like the lavishly furnished home it once was, but it was livable.

Jacob entered the house and yelled, "Is anyone home?"

Friedrich called out, "In here Karl! We're in the kitchen." Friedrich met him in the hall and threw his arms around him. Freya pushed the swinging door partly open with her good hand and was crying with joy. Martha even gave him a hug.

"Well, it looks like the family is together again at last. When did you get home?" Jacob asked, as if he didn't know.

"Just two days ago. When did you get home?"

"I've been home for over a week," Jacob replied. "The place was a mess. I was sick to see so many things stolen. At least we are together and the war is over." Freya, smiling broadly, nodded her head.

"Where did all these supplies come from?" Friedrich asked.

"The Americans and British have been very generous. I provided them with some information and they were most appreciative. *This was a truth the Müller's would never understand.* "Also I gave a British officer a bottle of wine from the cellar. I hope that was all right. He was the one that made all this possible." Jacob had finally let Ashburn take the wine. He felt the Müllers would approve of this gesture.

"We got the better of that deal," Friedrich said.

"That English officer doesn't think so," Jacob replied.

They spent the rest of the afternoon and evening talking about their experiences since they had last seen one another. Friedrich related what happened after they left with *Sturmbannführer* Hans Steiner as they made their way toward the American and English lines.

"We were stopped several times, and Hans handled everything beautifully. At one check point the guard wanted to verify our story and got on the telephone. Hans rolled up the window and sped right through the barrier. We could hear the bullets hitting the back of the car and rear window, but not one came through. Wilhelm was right. That Mercedes is bullet proof. Tell us what happened to you, Karl."

"Nothing that exciting. I just high-jacked a plane and flew to England." They all began to laugh uproariously.

Finally, Friedrich was able to get control of himself, and through tears said, "You always did have an overactive imagination, Karl. I hope you gave your regards to the king while you were there. I'd hate to think your manners were lacking."

"As a matter of fact, I did." They all laughed again, including Jacob.

CHAPTER 57

▼

Jacob left the house very early the next morning. He took one last look around and walked out the front door. His emotions were very near the surface. His eyes moistened. It was hard to just walk away. His relationship with the Müllers had ended. Just like that, it was over. He walked out to the street and got into the waiting automobile.

"Are you all right?" Ashburn asked as Jacob got in the car.

Jacob just sat there before answering. Finally he took a deep breath and said, "I'll be OK." They rode in silence, each with his own thoughts as the car wove its way back to their headquarters.

Jacob took off his German uniform and put on his American uniform. His German uniform was delivered to Karl and he was told to put it on.

"Where did this come from," he asked.

"Never mind. Just get dressed; you're going home." That was good news to Karl. It would feel good to be in a German uniform again, and he was excited about going home.

Karl got out of the automobile just outside the gate. As it drove away he walked up to the house. He was shocked by its appearance. He walked up the stairs, opened the door, and walked in. He was even more shocked when he saw inside. His father was just coming down the stairs. Upon seeing Karl, he said, "*Guten Morgen,* Karl. I didn't expect you back so soon."

"YOU DIDN'T EXPECT ME BACK SO SOON? I've been gone for three years and you say something as ridiculous as that! Where's *Mutter?* Is she all right?" Friedrich stopped dead in his tracks, a stunned look on his face.

"Are you all right, Karl? You're sounding very strange."

"*I'M SOUNDING STRANGE!*" Karl shouted. "I've been gone for three years, and you asked me why I'm back so soon! Something's strange, but it's not me!"

Friedrich tried to remain calm. "I believe Martha has breakfast ready. Let's join your *Mutter*."

Martha was busy at the stove and Freya was sitting quietly at the table. They turned to look at Karl as he entered the kitchen. Upon seeing his mother in a wheelchair Karl blurted out, "What's wrong with you, *Mutter?* Why are you in a wheelchair?" Freya looked at Friedrich with confusion on her face.

"You know why your *Mutter's* in a wheelchair, Karl. The stroke you know," Friedrich said.

"No, I don't know," Karl snapped, his voice rising. "Has everyone gone mad? I must be losing my mind." His parents thought he had, but Martha understood. Friedrich tried to calm Karl by humoring him. He suspected he might have suffered a nervous breakdown.

"While you were away, your *Mutter* had a stroke. She's just starting to use her limbs again, and to talk a little. It's been slow, but she's improving."

"I'm glad to hear you're getting better, *Mutter*. When did this happen?"

"Shortly after you were shot down," Friedrich replied.

"What happened to the house? Why is all the furniture missing? The place looks like it's been hit by a tornado. What happened?"

"We abandoned the house and fled west to avoid the Russians. It was ransacked while we were gone. Don't you remember? You arranged it all."

"I arranged it! How could I arrange it? I wasn't even here!"

"Now listen, Karl. You're upsetting your *Mutter*. After you escaped from that prison in England and returned home, you were transferred to the *Abwehr* and worked for your uncle Wilhelm after the *Luftwaffe* grounded you? Maybe the strain has been too great and your mind is playing tricks on you."

"There's nothing wrong with *my* mind, but I believe you have all lost yours. I've been in prison in Scotland and London since I was shot down over three years ago. I just returned, and you all act like I've been here all along."

"But...you...have...dear," Freya stammered.

"This is ridiculous. I have not been here these last three years! An American officer, who could have been my twin he looked so much like me, interviewed me just this morning and had me dropped off in front of the house a few minutes ago." Friedrich and Freya looked at one another, confused. Suddenly, a dawning expression came across Karl's face.

"Ah hah. Now I'm beginning to understand. You have all been duped. Someone has taken my place while I was in prison. You say he, or you think I, worked at the *Abwehr?*"

"Yes, your uncle Wilhelm arranged a transfer when you were grounded. You were very professional and very effective in performing your duties there."

"I bet I was. I've got to hand it to the British. It was a pretty ingenious plan. They substituted a look-alike and you all fell for it." Karl began to laugh almost hysterically. Friedrich and Freya glanced at one another. They didn't know what to make of it. Martha just stared at Karl. She knew he was telling the truth. She realized the real Karl was back in their lives, and she was not amused.

When they were alone Freya asked, "What's…wrong…with…Karl?"

"I really don't know. He seems to believe what he's saying, even though we know it's not true. Maybe the stress has been too much for him. For the time being I suggest we go along with whatever he says as if it was true. I'll invite *Doktor* Grundewald over for dinner so he can observe Karl. I'll tell him the whole story. Maybe he can make some sense out of all this."

"Won't…Karl…be…upset…having…a…psychiatrist…here?" Freya stammered.

"*Doktor* Grundwald is an old university colleague. We've had him here before. I'll invite some of our other friends and it will appear we are getting together like old times." Freya just nodded.

After the last dinner guests had gone and Friedrich was alone with his old university friend, he anxiously asked, "Well, what do you think Hellmuth?"

"It's an interesting case. You're right; he's very convincing. He cites dates, names, circumstances, and it all sounds plausible. In his own mind he really believes he has not been here, but has been a prisoner of war for three years. It's a classic case of schizophrenia in my opinion."

"Oh…dear, is…is…it…serious?" Freya asked.

"I wouldn't worry too much. It's not life-threatening, or anything like that, but he should receive counseling and be medicated as well."

"How can we convince him to get treatment? You don't know Karl as well as we do. He can be very stubborn. I wish we had the other Karl back." Martha also wished the other Karl was back. She knew there *was* another Karl. She realized with a shudder that the real Karl had returned and was as nasty as ever.

CHAPTER 58

▼

"What's for dinner tonight, Cooky?"

"Vegetable rice soup with a little beef in it, Harry. Tastes pretty good, if I do say so."

"I can't believe we feed him so good. Do you know what they fed us at *Stalag* 18 for four years?"

"No, what?"

"Thin cabbage or turnip soup, and when we did find a little meat in it we suspected it was dog or rat, but we were so hungry we ate it like it was filet mignon."

"You speak German, don't you Harry?"

"Aye, you pick it up after four years."

"Who do you think he is, Harry?"

"I haven't the slightest idea, but I'd sure like to know."

"Better get that soup down to him before it gets cold."

"If it were up to me, I'd serve it ice cold."

The prisoner was a mystery to his guards at the Tower of London. Their instructions were to have no conversation with him. They were not even supposed to look at him, and they were to completely ignore anything he said and discuss him with no one. Any deviation from those rules would result in immediate dismissal.

Harry carried the tray down the long flight of stairs. When he reached the cell door he opened the slot to slide in the tray. He looked around and then took a peek inside. A small light bulb hanging from the ceiling lighted the cell dimly. He could just barely make out a man dressed in black. He had a full beard that covered his features. He was stooped and looked very frail. His left arm hung awkwardly at his side. His eyes were sunken and lifeless, and his shoulders slumped. Seeing the guard peering at him, he cried out like a wounded animal. "Let me out! I demand you let me out straight away. Don't you know who I am? I'm Adolph Hitler!"

"Yeah, sure you are mate, and I'm Napoleon Bonaparte."

978-0-595-34905-0
0-595-34905-6